Resurrecting Cyb

MW01714403

Jenifer Mohammed

Published by Jenifer Mohammed Publishing

Available from Amazon.com, CreateSpace.com, and other retail outlets

Cover Design by Melody Simmons of eBookindiecovers

Chapter 1

The stench of fear permeated the sulphurous air around her. She gasped for breath, inhaling life-giving oxygen. Perspiration dripped from her face. She quickly wiped it away with the back of her hand. She could glimpse a faint light at the end of the corridor. Bile rose in her throat. Was that the sound of merciless laughter? No. She had not come so far only to be defeated now. She would not go down without a struggle. She was the Goddess incarnate. Scheherazade. She would challenge the Fates and create her own meaning.

No. Wait. That's how the story ended. It had begun quite differently. I'd better try again.

Perhaps it was fitting that the month that began with the Day of Fools, ended with the Day of her Birth, for while Cybele Moondragon was no fool, she was no Tiresias, either.

Hmm. Perhaps, I have gone too far back in time. It's always so hard to determine beginnings. Endings are so much simpler.

Maybe I should open a little less melodramatically. Just the facts. Leave guilt and blame for the reader to decide.

All right. Once more, with a little less feeling.

Cybele Moondragon sat upon her as-yet-not-fully-paid-for bright purple leather sofa. Disgustedly, she opened her mail. From what she saw on the exterior of the envelopes, she already knew they were all bills. Visa. MasterCard. American Express. Zellers card. Sears card. Student Loan. Oh, wonderful. A letter from the University of Manitoba. It was time to meet with her advisor and go over her progress report for the year or –in her case- lack of progress. She just couldn't seem to get motivated to writing her Masters' thesis on Canadian poetry. Veiled Sexuality and the Romantic Excesses of Isabella Valancy Crawford. It sounded a lot more exciting than it actually was. She sighed heavily. Work just seemed so uninspiring and lacklustre, compared to everything else she wanted to do in her life, beginning with – having a life.

She reached over for the remote and turned towards her television. As always, just the sight of her television made her smile. Not too many people get a free television. Luckily for her, after first having charged her credit card for three televisions, although she had only purchased one, Sears then proceeded to refund her the price of all the televisions. She would have called to inform them of their accounting error, but they had given her such a hard time about whether or not she had really bought the three televisions, her only thought upon discovering their accounting error was: Good, the gods don't like when you screw with people or their credit.

Let's see what wonderful things are happening in the world. She turned the television on to FAUX. Nice. Blood and broken rubble. I wonder which side is dropping the bombs or shooting the missiles today. No matter. Tomorrow the other side will strike back – the death and destruction will be the same – only the bodies will be different. Life's such a never-ending cycle of blood and violence. Why can't people just get along? Oh, too clichéd. Now, I'm quoting Rodney King. Poor sap. Took a licking and kept on ticking. She yawned. Gods, I hope dinner will be ready soon. I'm starving. Where the hell is Janus? Why can't he ever be on time?

There was a knock on her apartment door. She yelled, "It's not locked," and got off the couch to greet her guest. "How did you get in without buzzing?"

Janus strolled in and hugged her hello: "It helps when you have an honest face. No one can fathom the depths of depravity that lurk beneath the mask of civility."

"True. That's why all those idiots who live beside serial killers are always interviewed on television saying: 'But, he was such a nice, quiet neighbour. Never made any noise at all.' Meanwhile, Mr. Gentility is in the basement hack-sawing hitchhikers and torturing the neighbourhood pets."

"You're in a good mood tonight. Maybe I should have bought over a bigger bottle of wine."

Cybele leaned towards him and sniffed affectedly. "Maybe you should have brought over some of that beer I smell on your breath. What did you do, stop off for some drinks with the guys and forget we were having dinner?"

"*Mea culpa*. I just wanted to be sociable – celebrate TGIF. Just making connections – wanting to get ahead at the Loaves and Fishes."

"Ok, I'm sorry. I didn't mean to be snide. It's just these damn bills. I keep thinking there must be a better way to make a living than as a professional student."

"Well, you could always do what I did. Inherit money. Then you could spend as long as you like working on your thesis. I know I am."

Janus raised one eyebrow archly. "Of course, your parents would have to die first."

Cybele grabbed the bottle of wine from him and walked into the kitchen. "Very funny." She turned and winked back at him. "Unlike you, I actually get along with my parents."

"Touché." He walked over to the slow cooker bubbling away on the countertop. "Mmmm. Something smells good. Looks like beef stew."

"Yep. It is." She looked pointedly at her watch. "It's been ready for a while." She handed him a glass of wine. "Let's just sit down and eat. I'll dish it out." She gently pushed him towards the living room. "You get the movie set up. May as well start the previews while we're not paying attention."

They began to watch *Star Wars.*

Janus reached over the coffee table to refill their glasses with wine. "God. I can't believe how many times we've seen this movie." He shook his head ruefully. "We must be the ultimate *Star Wars'* geeks." He looked over at Cybele and laughed. "How pathetic are we that we can recite all the characters' lines before they even say them?"

Cybele raised her glass in a mocking toast. "Touché." She laughed. "But how would we ever make sense of the abyss that is our lives, without George Lucas' bible? He makes life seem so simple." She took another sip of wine and absentmindedly patted Janus's hand. "Good and bad are so absolutely absolute in the *Star Wars'* universe."

straight moral codes

"Well, maybe, until you start to get into the *Empire Strikes Back* and *Return of the Jedi*. Then things start to become less clear –

Beware that this Bible is CAPITALIST – Capitalist & accessible morality becomes a lot more ambiguous." He began to pop his knuckles. "Hell. We even find out that Yoda lies."

Cybele stood up and began to pace back and forth. "I know. But." She stopped to take a gulp of wine. "That makes perfect sense. There are no eternal truths. Morality and Truth are just a matter of perspective. Just big staffs used by those in power to control the masses – the sheep." She looked down at Janus and snorted. "I'd rather be the shepherd than the sheep. Wouldn't you?"

"Well, duh." He gestured up at her with his fork. "No big surprise that religion is the opiate of the masses. As for me, I'd rather be the drug pusher than the drug user."

Cybele sat down and grabbed an uneaten carrot off her plate. "Speaking of religion, do you know that in the last Canadian census, according to FAUX, many Canadians listed their religion as Jedi?"

"You're shitting me." Janus refilled his glass of wine. "Well, if FAUX says it, then it must be true." He snorted derisively. "I mean, it's not like they're a laughably, transparent instrument of propaganda for the Conservative Movement."

Cybele laughed and sang out a little unsteadily, "J-I-N-G-O-And Jingo was his name, oh." She reached over and patted Janus on his hand. "But, you're missing my point."

"You actually have a point?" Janus took a long sip of wine. "I thought you were just talking to hear the sound of your own voice." He looked over to see if she was even listening to him.

Cybele glared back at him. "Bastard." He's a fine one to talk. Narcissus to a tee. Of course, I guess that pretty well describes me too. Birds of a feather flock together. She relented and laughed. "My point is that people are unsatisfied with mainstream religion. But, they still need to organize their lives around stories and mythology to make sense of their lives and their fears of living and of dying." She thumped her glass dramatically on the table, startling Janus who had been drifting off to sleep. "That's why the Force is so seductive. It's because of the idea that everything is connected to everything else. Nothing ever dies. Death is just a transformation of energy."

Janus yawned and began to crack his knuckles again. "So, what are you suggesting? Should we dress up as Jedi Knights and run around quoting lines from *Star Wars*?" He winked. "That does have a certain appeal. But there are conventions and asylums for that sort of thing."

"No." Cybele rolled her eyes disgustedly. "As Quark would say: 'where's the profit in that?' If we joined someone else's religion, we would be the sheep, and they would be our masters. However, if we pulled a L. Ron Hubbard and started our own religion, we would be the ones in control." Cybele paused for dramatic effect. "And ultimately, WE, would be the ones making all the money."

Janus fought off another yawn. "What did L. Ron Hubbard...?"

Gods. Cybele groaned inwardly. Sometimes, it's like talking to a child. She forced herself to sound patient. "Hubbard founded Scientology. And look how many people believe in that crap. John Travolta does – that's why he made *Battlefield Earth*."

"That's right. I'd forgotten." He laughed. "So, Obi-wan, what kind of religion do you want to start?"

Jackass. I'm trying to be serious and he's cracking jokes. Cybele took a deep breath and slowly let it out. Must remain calm. She took another gulp of wine. "Well, obviously, it would have to be something that would fulfill people's deepest desires and have no unpleasant rules." She waved her now-empty glass in the air. "No one likes being told what not to do. And doesn't it suck that all the funnest things in life always turn out to be sins. Sex, drugs, rock and roll." She sighed deeply. "You get the picture."

Wow. She's really on a roll tonight. She's like one of those toys you just wind-up and watch them go. Janus leaned over and refilled both their glasses with the last dregs of wine. "So, you want to create a religion without rules? Interesting approach."

Cybele shook her head. Dumbass. "That wouldn't work because people are basically stupid. They need rules and structure in their life." She stood up a little unsteadily and began to pace. "The trick is to make people enjoy following your rules. Bread and circuses – religion for the masses."

God. Stop circling the airport and bring the plane in for a landing, Cybele. Janus yawned and stood up to stretch. "Well, what did you have in mind? Frolicking around nude, performing pagan rites, and smoking pot to get in the mood?"

Aargh! I'm a giant in a land of midgets. Cybele took a quick sip of wine. "Yeah, I don't think that would go over well in Winnipeg's climate. Although, I guess the pot and the spirits would help dull the pain of the frostbite and the resulting amputations." She stood up unsteadily. "Actually, I was thinking of something a little Wiccan but with our own spin."

"Our spin?"

"Of course." Cybele closed both eyes in a drunken attempt at a wink. "You can't seriously think I would start a cult without my best friend as my partner."

"I'm touched."

"In the head, which is why you'd be perfect as my ritual partner." She leaned towards him. "Come on – be Attis to my Cybele."

"So, you're thinking of a fertility cult – mmmm...orgies."

"Trust me, I'd be the perfect reincarnation of Cybele – I could definitely get used to being worshipped by a bunch of Galli."

Janus looked puzzled. "Who the hell are Galli?"

Gods. Doesn't he ever remember anything I say? "The Galli were her priests." Cybele giggled. "Although, they were eunuchs and I'm not sure that would go over well - at least in the beginning - with our first members."

Janus laughed incredulously. "You're kidding, right. Someone would have to be a real dingdong to castrate himself for the sake of religion."

"No, they would have to lose their dingdongs." She sang off-key, "Ding Dong the witch is dead. The evil witch is dead."

I can't believe she wants to be a god. I wonder if it's just the wine talking. Janus shook his head. "I think you might be losing your always tenuous grip on reality."

She doesn't intend to be worshipped as a God.

"By the gods, Janus, of course, I'm kidding. In fact, the last thing in the world I would want is to start a cult which inspires that kind of religious fervour. I don't want to end up as the Canadian poster child for David Koresh or Jim Jones." She sang off-key again, "Mamas, don't let your babies grow up to be Cybele Moondragon."

"No Kool-Aid parties then." Janus looked sadly at his empty glass

Bread and wine ritual

of wine. If she's going to keep talking, I'm definitely going to need something else to drink.

"I'm serious." She waved her hand wildly in the air. "The premise of my cult." She paused to take a deep breath and then exploded into speech. "Which I have decided to name The Mysteries of Cybele and her Lesser Consort Attis, will offer peace and salvation to the masses, interspersed with some less than sparing use of hallucinogenic herbs and alcohol." She sighed regretfully. "As much fun as marijuana is, it should probably have no prominently significant place within our rituals of worship because we don't want to get busted for illegal drugs. We don't want to do anything that will draw the eye of the establishment too closely to us." *** Tell me about it!

Cybele began to pace a bit unsteadily and gestured wildly with her wine glass. Wine spilt upon the mauve carpet. "Oops. Where was I?"

"No establishment." Janus stood up and stumbled over to the kitchen cupboards to look for snacks. what kind of good ??

"Right. Our cult will be a force for moral good." Cybele took another sip of wine. "We will be a matriarchal cult and I will be in charge." She gestured towards herself. "After all, I certainly have the figure to play the role of a fertility goddess."

Criticism against catholicism but what about it occurring outside, the church?

"Well, not quite." Janus carefully looked her over. "If you were a true reincarnation of a fertility goddess, you'd probably not be able to walk without falling flat on your face. Top-heavy and all that." He ripped open a bag of chips and walked over towards Cybele. "However, I always imagined Mother Goddesses with flowing black hair and dark brown eyes. You look like that. Well, except your hair has purple streaks."

Cybele gave an exasperated huff. "If I may continue." She grabbed a chip and began to munch. "We will have no sexual abuse of our flock. No pedophilia." She paused thoughtfully. "In fact, only adults will be eligible to join. We will have no doomsday ending. We will simply be a group of free-spirited people who want to have fun, reconnect with Mother Nature, and throw off the chains of patriarchal prosecution."

"Persecution?"

"That's what I said. No patriarchy…And that's not all. We will start a website to advertise our new religion and sell trinkets, amulets, potions, etc. They'll all be certified as blessed by the Goddess Cybele under the light of the full moon." She nodded seriously. "You know, there's a very big market for new age religious artefacts. We'll be doing a public service."

"And making money."

"It's the American way."

"Yeah, but we're Canadian."

"We'll pay lots of taxes." Cybele yawned. "In fact, to avoid religious prosecution, we should probably not register as a religion but as an entertainment business. The CRA won't bother us if we pay taxes. The bastards." She yawned again. "Gods. I'm feeling a bit tired. Must be all the fresh air I got this morning."

Or maybe all the wine you just drank. Janus tried to stop himself from yawning as well but couldn't. Well, the wine we drank. "Me too. I spent a lot of time in the sun today."

Yeah. It couldn't be the beers you had before you came over. She smiled inwardly. Guess you didn't follow the Golden Rule today, eh Janus? Never mix your poisons. You'll pay for that tomorrow. She weaved her way towards the kitchen. "Hey, I've got some instant cappuccino mix in the fridge. The caffeine should wake us right up. Why don't you open the window? Get us some more of that fresh air."

They laughed. Janus opened the windows. Cybele returned with the cappuccino. They curled up on opposite sides of the couch.

Janus picked up the bills still lying on the coffee table, now spotted with beef stew and wine stains. "Seriously, Cyb, if you need money, I've got lots. I could give it to you or you could work for me. I could always use some help with my thesis. You know how much I hate reading all those boring articles on outdated psych theories. You could help me sort through the crap."

"Separate the wheat from the chaff, eh?" Cybele looked over at him mockingly. "I guess your thesis is coming along as well as mine."

Janus glared half-heartedly at her. "You, at least, don't have to fight continually with the Human Ethics Committee about whether or not your tactics might traumatize those poor, helpless street kids, who while not panhandling or squeegeeing your cars, are casing you out for the next home invasion."

Cybele groaned. "Tell me you didn't say that to the Committee."

"Duh. I'm not an idiot." He laughed cynically. "I know how to survive." He shook his head. "I just pretend I'm deeply concerned about the possible ramifications of my interactions with the little darlings."

Cybele bit the bottom of her lip worriedly. "Janus." She sighed. "Just because your parents were psychologists, doesn't mean you have to be one."

Great. I'm getting advice from a would-be fertility goddess. He shrugged. "I might as well. That's where the big bucks are, you know."

"I'm just saying you don't have to follow someone else's blueprint for your life." She leaned over and patted his hand half-mockingly. "Remember, there's no Fate but what we make for ourselves."

"That's deep." Bullshit. "Words of wisdom from *Terminator II: Judgement Day*?"

"What's wrong with the Gospel of James Cameron?"

"Well, James Cameron is the King of the World. I guess that makes him a god. Hey, a Canadian, ex-truck-driver god. Who'd a thunk it?"

Cybele grabbed a potato chip and slowly began to lick off the salt. "Try to focus, Janus. Wouldn't you like to do something that is pure fun and pure profit?"

Yuck. I wish she'd just eat the damn thing. Janus forced himself to look as if he was paying attention. Must focus. He blinked his eyes several times to keep awake.

Cybele put the uneaten chip down beside her on the table and reached for another one. "You know, Janus, there's a lot of money to be made in religion especially, if you're in it from the beginning." She jumped up and restlessly began to pace back and forth. "We would be the top of the pyramid. We would be an awesome cult. We wouldn't abuse our power. We would just give people salvation who would want to turn that down?"

Janus began to massage his forehead. Whoa. Energizer bunny, slow down. You're making me nauseous. "I had no idea you were so power hungry maybe you can be Canadian god number two."

Cybele stopped and sniffed. "That would be James T. Kirk also known as William Shatner. And anyway, it's not about having NEGATIVE power, Janus. It's about having POSITIVE power."

God. I wish her voice wasn't so shrill. He forced himself to follow her reasoning. "You'd be a benevolent deity, of course."

Cybele thumped the television with her hand. "Wouldn't our lives be morally simpler if we lived in a *Star Wars* universe? Or a *Star Trek* one where people lived in peace and harmony with their friends and environment?

What the hell has she been smoking? Janus looked at her oddly. "What series are you talking about? Didn't Captain Kirk go around shooting people and blowing up a lot of things?"

Aargh! Why do I have to always explain everything in one syllable words? "All right, a *Next Generation/Voyager/Deep Space Nine/Enterprise* universe. I'm not saying they always did the right thing but they usually tried to. That's what I want to create – an environment where people try to do the right thing. How could anything go wrong with that?"

Janus looked dubiously at her. "It seemed to go wrong an awful lot in the series."

Cybele sighed tiredly. "That's because that was fiction and this is real life."

"You're serious about this, aren't you?"

No. Dumbass. I'm talking just to hear the sound of my own voice. "Look. I really think this would be a good idea. As long as we keep it legal, don't break any drug laws or contribute to the delinquency of minors, I think this could be a great business opportunity. We just can't give the authorities any excuse to impose their misguided sense of morality upon us. We just pay our taxes, get the proper business licenses etc., and we'll be home free. We can just sit back and count our money."

Janus considered the idea carefully for a second and then admitted, "Properly handled, we could make piles of money. It really is impossible to have too much money, now, isn't it?"

"Yep." Cybele reached for another chip and began to lick off the salt. "And you're forgetting the best part. We get to dress up like goddesses and gods, play loud music, burn incense, and drink spirits – enhanced with certain special herbs, of course. We get to make up our own religious rituals – heck, we can put them together in a Book of Shadows and sell them on our website too. And people will flock to us as if we were manna from heaven."

"Didn't manna have an expiry date?"

"Yes, but properly manna-ged, we don't have to." She shrugged nonchalantly. "Or if we get tired of playing gods, which is hard to imagine, we can always sell the business – maybe open franchises around the world. We could be bigger than Scientology. Eat our dust, L. Ron Hubbard."

Janus staggered off in the general direction of the bathroom. "Speaking of making tracks, I think I better drain the lizard and then hit the road. It's getting very late."

Cybele groaned. "I don't know what Achates sees in you. I hope he's not at your house waiting up for you." She moved closer to the bathroom door which was slightly ajar and yelled, "Don't forget to flush. I don't need to see your lizard's excretions the next time I go in. And wash your hands." She giggled. "Don't forget. Cleanliness is next to godliness."

Janus came out of the bathroom. "Achates won't be waiting up for me. He's supposedly on a business trip in Toronto."

"Why, supposedly?"

Janus looked annoyed. "I don't know. He's been a little distant lately, but he says he's just tired from working hard." He shook his head dismissively. "I'm sure it's nothing."

"O-kaaay. Whatever." Cybele looked closely at him. "But are you sure you don't want to talk about it?"

"Hey, I may be gay but I'm still a guy."

"Funny." Jerk. "Everyone knows that men are the worst gossips of all. Hey, seriously, we've had a lot to drink tonight. Are you sure you don't want to sack out on the couch?"

"No. I don't want to wake up thinking I've been swallowed up by Barney, the Dinosaur." Then, he sung, in perfect pitch, "I love you. You love me. We're a twisted family." He stopped singing and grimaced. "Besides, I'm as sober as a judge."

"Or a Canadian politician in the Land of the Lotus-Eaters?"

"Only if I'm from one of the provinces or territories."

"In vino veritas."

"God Save the Queen."

They laughed together a bit unsteadily and hugged goodbye. Janus walked down the stairs with the greatest of delicacy in a precision that came from extreme drunkenness. Cybele shut the door after him, cleaned up the mess they made, and then headed off for bed where she immediately passed out.

Chapter 2

Cybele awoke the next morning with a painful groan. The sharp rays of the sunlight pierced through her eyelids and created a beautiful prismatic effect that, had she not been so hung-over, she would have enjoyed. As it was, all she felt was nausea and a deep irritation that she had forgotten to close her blinds the night before. She groaned, drew the blanket over her head, and fell back asleep for the rest of the morning. *In vino veritas*, my ass.

She awoke to a giant crash. Oh no, Cassie must be up, cooking in the kitchen. I should probably drag myself out of bed and go talk to her. Humming "Onward pagan soldier," she got out of bed, dressed, and went off to talk to her roommate.

Cassie looked at Cybele's face and shook her head in mock commiseration. "Wow, Cyb, you look like something the cat had too many standards to drag in."

"I'll have you know that I feel much worse than I look," groaned Cybele. "I'm just waiting for these seven little men with pickaxes to stop mining in my head. Heigh-ho, Heigh-ho, to the aspirin I go."

Cassie handed Cybele four aspirin and a glass of water. "You and Janus must have had fun last night. Sorry I had to work late and miss the party."

"You missed quite an event." Cybele leaned against the kitchen counter and swallowed the aspirin. "I heard some MAJOR gossip last night."

"Really?" Cassie looked intrigued. "What?"

"Janus thinks Achates might be sleeping around when he goes on all those." Cybele paused and made quotation marks in the air with her fingers. "BUSINESS TRIPS."

Cassie took a sip of coffee and shook her head. "I find that hard to believe. Achates doesn't seem like the type to cheat. He just seems too uptight and conservative."

Cybele snorted. "Please. The most conservative ones are always the biggest sinners." Gods. Doesn't she ever watch the news? "But, it's just kind of ironic that Janus is afraid of Achates cheating when..." Cybele stopped and gave Cassie a half-guilty look.

"Oh my gods. Spill those beans, Cyb."

At first, Cybele felt torn, but the urge to gossip quickly overcame her desire to keep Janus's secrets. She leaned towards Cassie confidingly. "Well, it's just that, Janus goes barhopping when Achates is out of town, and sometimes I wonder if Janus always ends up in bed alone." She looked knowingly towards Cassie. "Janus seems to have such a desperate need to be loved and accepted that I think he looks for it wherever he can. And it's not like Achates is the most openly affectionate mate I've ever seen. I just don't think Janus has been completely faithful, which is why it's so funny that..."

"That he's afraid Achates is the unfaithful one." Cassie shook her head. "You know, I'm actually not surprised to find out Janus might be a bed-hopper. With that brown hair and hazel eyes, he's always reminded me a little of the guy who played Daniel Jackson on *Stargate* – the *SG1* series, not the motion picture. Pretty cute in an

It is just fooling around
No family involved

intellectual kind of way. Although James Spader's no dog either. What's his name?"

"Oh, I think you mean Michael Shanks. He does look like him. Strange. I never noticed it before. What's funny is that I always thought you looked a little like Teryl Rothery. Remember her? Dr. Janet Fraiser on *Stargate-SG1*?" Cybele paused to scrutinize Cassie. "That's probably because you both have dark brown hair, cut in a short pixie style with bangs, and dark brown eyes, and you're both kind of buttoned-up on the outside. Private but hiding deep emotions. Of course, you're much chubbier than she is but," she looked over at Cassie, whose mouth now hung open in disbelief, "but I digress. What were you saying?"

Cassie carefully closed her mouth. That's textbook Cybele. Open mouth and insert foot. "Anyways. Have you ever thought about telling Achates what Janus might be up to? He deserves to know, if even just for health reasons. You can't tell me that Janus always wears condoms?" → People want to feel real sex

"I've thought about it." Cybele looked guilty. "I really like Achates but...Janus and I have known each other since Kindergarten. We became best friends from the moment we made the discovery that we both loved grape Kool-Aid and peanut butter cookies. How can I stab him in the back by telling Achates that Janus might be fooling around? I don't think Janus would ever forgive that kind of betrayal."

Crap. It's too early in the morning to debate morality. Cassie slowly rubbed the back of her neck. "Don't you think he would realize you were only trying to do the right thing and forgive you for it?"

L NEVER

→ Always my topic

"Oh, of course." Idiot. Cybele shrugged. "I mean if you were cheating on some guy, and I told him, and you found out –why, you'd forgive me in a heartbeat, right?"

"Touché." Cassie took a quick gulp of coffee. Gods. I really need the caffeine right now. "I'd think you were a meddling trouble-maker and we'd have to stop being roommates."

"I know. So, you can't talk about this to either Achates or Janus. We shouldn't try and run other people's lives. Only egomaniacs think their lives are so perfect that they can tell others what to do." She held the cold glass against her forehead and sighed. Gods. My head is killing me. She shrugged. "Everyone else knows enough just to leave well enough alone. Partly self-preservation maybe, and partly because we can't look into the future and know what's going to happen."

"You're so deep," Cassie mocked gently.

"At least six feet under. Just to be on the safe side. Anyways, enough about Janus and Achates' soap opera. Back to the important stuff – me and my life."

"Ah, humility. You fairly reek of it."

"That's the carpet. I spilled some of the wine last night." Cybele chuckled and immediately regretted it as the inside of her head exploded in pain. Damnit. Must have been something off with the wine last night. She forced herself to focus on what she was saying. "Anyway, are you going to mock me or listen to how I discovered the meaning of my life?"

"Meaning of life stuff? Way cool. Okaaay. What life-changing decision did you make? Have you switched your primary allegiance from *Deep Space Nine* to *Stargate*? Will we be spending Saturday afternoons watching the adventures of Captain Sisko or the misadventures of Colonel O'Neill?"

"You know, I do have an existence outside of television." Cybele looked momentarily offended as she took an annoyed sip of her water. Then she relaxed and laughed. "And, just for the record, that kind of switch would happen only when Hell froze over."

"So, that would be Winnipeg in the winter?"

"Funny." Enough of this damn water. Best hangover remedy, my ass. Cybele reached past Cassie and poured herself a cup of coffee. Ahh. The nectar of the gods. She carefully took a sip. Blissful.

Cassie rolled her eyes. Gods. Maybe when she's done having an orgasmic moment with her coffee, she'll get back to her point.

Cybele bit the bottom of her lip and watched the steam rise from her cup. She carefully avoided looking at Cassie as she spoke. "Actually, I've decided that I don't want to do a thesis anymore." She raised her cup in a mocking toast. "Goodbye Master's. Hello Life."

Cassie half-spit out her own mouthful of coffee. She grabbed a napkin and began to dab at her mouth. "You're joking. You've spent so much time and effort on it. How could you quit now?"

Cybele shrugged. Well. She took that well. Klutz. "I want to do something different – something fun and exciting. You know, take a road less travelled."

"Which is?"

Cybele waved her cup in a grand gesture. "Listen and learn, my young Jedi apprentice. I have decided to start a web business." She took a quick sip of coffee and watched Cassie's face to gauge her level of acceptance. "You know, set up a pagan website that sells magical amulets, charms, potions, and other assorted trinkets to those in need of spiritual enlightenment." Damn. Cassie looks a bit unsure about the whole thing. Aargh! Why are geniuses so unappreciated by their friends? Cybele sighed. Guess I'll have to reassure her. She patted Cassie on her hand. "It'll be only pure, light stuff, no dark magic."

Cassie began to look intrigued. "That's actually an interesting idea. You do have an extensive background in herbs and the gods know, you have dabbled in a lot of the new age religions, especially Wicca." She began to rub the back of her neck. Gods. Cyb wants to start a magic business. Yeah. Like that's not insane. Why me? She shook her head. "But are you sure there's really enough support there for you to make enough of a profit?"

Cybele looked slightly defiant. Now comes the harder part. Trying to convince her that starting a cult is a good idea. Must sound rational not emotional. She calmly took a sip of coffee. "Well, there's the rub. To make a really good profit, I need to have a base of worshippers established. I don't want to horn in on someone else's religious interpretations. They would be too much competition for me. Plus, I'd probably have to follow their rules." She took a deep breath. Must speak slowly and sound completely logical. "So, I have decided the only solution is to start my own religion. You know, peddle a little spirituality. Make a lot of money."

Cassie choked on her toast. "You're not going to go all whacko Waco or Ruby Ridge on me, are you?" She carefully brushed the wet crumbs off her top.

Wow. I guess Cassie may not be quite the swallower her last boyfriend told Janus. Cybele giggled guiltily. "Well, I do have a little bit of lumbago, but I promise not to go all Wounded Knee on you either."

Cassie looked up in surprise. "You're really not kidding, are you?"

"Why does everyone ask me that? What's so irrational about wanting to start a cult?" Cybele began to pace back and forth. "You know, someone has to – these things don't just come out of nowhere, you know." She put her cup down with a heavy thump. "And, I'll have you know that led ALL of the major religions in the world started out as cults." She began to tap her fingers on the rim of her cup. "Perhaps, in two thousand years, my cult will be the dominant religion in the world. A force for good – for tolerance in a world far from the Federation so envisioned by Gene Roddenberry."

I really hope she's not serious about this. Cassie rolled her eyes. Better humour her. She's probably still a little drunk. "Well, it would be nice to live in a *Star Trek* universe. Holosuites and replicators would be cool to have."

"Not to mention space travel and transporters."

"Absolutely." Cassie munched thoughtfully on her toast. Better humour her. I'm not up for more speeches this early in the morning. "You've convinced me. So, tell me all about this cult that you want to start."

Cybele took a sip of her coffee. "Well, I would be the Alpha and Omega of it, of course."

Cassie calmly took a sip of her coffee. "Yep. Seems logical to me."

"It is." Cybele nodded happily. Finally. She's beginning to come over to my side. "And it would be matriarchal and not exploitative or manipulative of its followers at all." She shook her head emphatically. "There would be none of that bad stuff that caused the downfall of other cults, which, of course, were all patriarchal, anyway."

Cassie snickered. "But, of course, yours would be a bright Manitoba crocus surrounded by the excrement of those which came before you."

Why can't she be serious? Doesn't she know how important this is to me? Cybele looked over at Cassie and shook her head. Must not react. Must behave like the sober adult that I am. She forced herself to speak calmly and deliberately. "A more apt comparison than you could know, Cassie. I have decided to base my cult on the mystery rites of Cybele."

Cassie began to rub her eyes. It's too early in the morning for this level of pomposity. "Which you'll make up, of course?"

"Sort of. There was a real Cybele, you know. She was a Mother Goddess figure of Phrygia, in ancient Asia Minor. Nobody knows much about her rites. Well, except that they were pretty orgiastic – full of cymbals, drums, horns." Cybele grabbed a slice of bacon off Cassie's plate and casually waved it in the air as she continued. "Sometimes even self-mutilations – although my rites won't go that far of course."

"I hope not." Cassie tried hard not to laugh out loud. She is entertaining. I'll give her that. "I'm pretty sure lawsuits would become an unpleasant reality, if your cultists started mutilating themselves, probably while under the influence of hallucinogenics."

"Yep." Cybele began to eat her bacon. "We'll definitely stay away from anything that could bring the authorities down on us."

Cassie bit the inside of her cheek and tried hard to sound sincere. "Was that the royal we, or have you convinced Janus to join up with you?"

"I tried but it's hard to know if Janus will go for it. He's a riddle, wrapped in a mystery, jammed into an enigma. A tough nut to crack."

Cassie nodded thoughtfully. "What role do you want him to play? Besides provide the start-up money?"

"Well, money would be a definite help, but Cybele does have a consort, Attis. Janus could have a lot of fun playing his role."

"What does Attis do?"

Cybele laughed. "Well, it's kind of a twisted story. You see, Cybele was born from the earth as a bisexual god. However, her penis fell off and an almond tree grew where it landed. Then a flower from the tree somehow managed to impregnate Nana, the daughter of a river god and she gave birth to Attis."

You've got to be kidding me. Cassie poured herself another cup of coffee. "So far, it sounds absolutely charming."

Cybele frowned slightly. She doesn't have to sound so snarky. No. I won't rise to the bait. I'll just ignore her. "Anyways, Nana didn't want

Attis so she left him outside to die, but he was raised by a billy-goat. When Attis grew up, Cybele fell in love with him and…"

"Nothing like a little incest to spice things up."

Cybele determinedly ignored the interruption. "Anyways, Attis fell in love with a mortal woman, which pissed off Cybele. She drives him mad and he ends up castrating himself. "Violets." She looked sharply at Cassie. "Not, unfortunately, your beloved Manitoba croci, blossomed from his blood, and Cybele repented and resurrected him. So, all's well that ends well."

Cassie started laughing. "Are you aware of how much castration there is in that little story of yours? Freud would have a field day with you on his couch."

"Not necessarily." Cybele winked forgivingly at Cassie. "Sometimes a castration is just a castration. Besides Freud was a patriarch and I'm a matriarch. A matriarch would interpret the story as Cybele being born with an extraneous part, a useless appendage of a less evolved time, like why we still have tailbones for vestigial tails. She simply shed it and moved up the great evolutionary chain of being."

Cassie decided to enter in the spirit of fun. "And you think Janus would be happy playing Attis to your Cybele, Major Kira to your Captain Sisko?

"Absolutely. Why wouldn't he? Performing religious rituals would be a blast and I'm sure that I can convince Janus to play along. If not, well Cybele is a great goddess. She can have many consorts – all beneath her, if you know what I mean."

They laughed.

Cassie sobered up. "Your idea is very interesting," she said, "but I think, no matter how good your intentions may be, starting a cult might be a little more dangerous and unpredictable than you bargained for."

Cybele shook her head dismissively. "It'll be fine. I'll offer people an opportunity to break loose of social conventions and participate in a spontaneously, structured environment. What could go wrong?" She saw the dubious look on Cassie's face and inwardly groaned. Please don't answer that. It was a rhetorical question. She began to rub her forehead. "Gods. My head is killing me. How about we stop talking for now and instead do some major league imitations of couch potatoes."

"Good idea." I certainly can't think about anything after that cult bombshell. "What did you have in mind?"

Cybele walked into the living room. "Well, Space Channel is running the 8 hour *Dune* mini-series right now. How about we crash on the couch for the rest of the day and watch it?"

"8 hours? Sure you won't overdose on patriarchal mythology?"

Cybele started to sing, "I will survive for I will have," but Cassie cut her off. "You have a bucket of ice water," she said in a voice that Cybele thought was slightly condescending.

"Funny." Cybele plopped herself down on the couch. "Say, how about we order Chinese food in a couple of hours when I start to fei wiel human again?"

"Good idea, O Mother Goddess."

Cassie sat down and they spent the rest of the day watching *Dune*.

Waking up the next morning to the piercing peal of church bells, Cybele cursed softly and groaned. "Morning has broken like the first damn morning. Who the hell thinks it is a good idea to get up before Helios is at least half-way across the sky?" She struggled out of bed and went to her window to look out at all the people walking in the parking lot of the neighbouring church. There you are, all dressed up in your best, eagerly waiting for your weekly dose of salvation. Wonder if my dear old ex is down there? She peered more closely into the crowd. Nope. I don't see any signs of sulphur and brimstone. Must be pulling a Homer Simpson, although the gods know that he's not the Ned Flanders he pretends to be. She snorted. Go ahead mindless minions. Participate in the charade that you actually believe what you hear as if you practiced those tenets the rest of the week. Hypocrites. For most of you, the Ten Commandments are just a stick you can use to beat others over the head with. Wonder how these Hatfields and McCoys would react if they knew they were under pagan surveillance? Guess I'd be lucky not to be burnt at the stake.

She moved slowly away from the window. Another time. Another place perhaps. Right now it's time to do a little shopping and then go tackle Janus at the Loaves and Fishes. Get him to be the Robin to my Batman.

Gods, Portage Place is so deserted on Sundays. I should come downtown to do my shopping more often. Then again, maybe not, she thought as she saw two very dishevelled young men approach her outside the Salisbury House on Portage. When they neared Cybele, she was unsurprised to discover they were two very pungent panhandlers. She spoke firmly to them. "Sorry. I don't have any money to give you. Actually, I'm quite broke myself. But, if you truly want to get help, go to the Loaves and Fishes. It's a soup kitchen and youth shelter. For the price of listening to one of their sermons, they'll help you out."

The two politely declined her offer and Cybele continued on her way. Wonderful, now I feel slightly guilty. I did, after all, just buy a purple leather jacket. Granted, it was deeply discounted, but maybe it would have been the charitably pagan thing to do to give them something. Well, I offered to take them somewhere they could receive food and shelter. I think that fulfilled my moral responsibility to them as fellow members of the human race.

Cybele walked down Main Street towards the Loaves and Fishes. She smiled as the murals on the shelter's walls came into her view. She may not have been the most artistic of painters, but she had enjoyed donating her time that summer to help paint the sides of the building with the other volunteers. She was not a big fan of organized religions as she always felt they were more interested in rules and bureaucracies than in truly helping people, but Matthew Cain, the director of the shelter was definitely one of the good guys. It was always a miracle to see someone who practiced what he preached.

She walked into the foyer of the shelter and looked around for Janus. Matthew noticed her.

"Cybele, good to see you. Are you here to help us make dinner for the evening crowd?"

"Not today, Matthew. I'm looking for Janus. Have you seen him?"

"I think he's in the rec room talking to some of our residents."

"Thanks. I'll see if I can catch him." As she turned to leave, she pulled a ten dollar bill out of her wallet and gave it to him. "For the food bank," she said and went off in search of Janus. Good. Now, I've made up for not giving money to those two panhandlers.

She walked into the rec room and stopped as she noticed a very nicely shaped butt backing down off a wobbling stepladder. She rushed over to stabilize the ladder.

"Thanks. It was a bit awkward coming down with this pesky broken light bulb..." With an expression of surprise on his face, the man trailed off as he turned fully to look at her. "Are you a new resident?"

Oh good gods. Do I look like someone who lives on the street? I knew I should have stopped to brush my hair when I passed the bathroom. "No. I'm a visitor. I'm here to meet a friend for dinner. Not here of course. Not that there's anything wrong with the dinners here. But I just don't need to eat at a soup kitchen. Not that I think there's wrong with people who have to. I'm sorry. I'm babbling. It's a bad habit I have and sometimes the only way to stop is..." She quickly placed both hands firmly over her mouth. "Help."

She smiled up at him. Boy. He is definitely yummy. Tall. Wiry. Beautiful, deep green eyes. Reddish brown hair. Looks just like James Spader when he played Daniel Jackson in the *Stargate* movie.

Mmmm. Even the freckles look adorable. Gods. I'm staring. He probably thinks I'm a maniac who's wandered in off the street.

He laughed. She is definitely cute. A splash of colour and life in an otherwise dreary room. A bit of a Chatty Cathy but nothing wrong with that. "Who are you?" he asked, shaking his head in bemusement.

"I'm Cybele Moondragon," she said as she deliberately dropped her head slightly and then looked up at him from under her eyelashes. Gods, I would have to pick today to be dressed so conservatively. Nothing low-cut or high-cut on me today. Damn. Oh well, probably a good thing. He might be a little conservative too.

"Cybele. Isn't that the name of a Greek goddess?"

"Sort of." Cybele hesitated. She knew she had a tendency to overwhelm people with too much information and the last thing she wanted was to see him start to edge away. "She's actually a Phrygian goddess from Asia Minor." She beamed up at him. "But, unlike you, most people have never even heard of her."

They stood there looking at each other and smiling. Cybele wound her finger around one of the curls in her hair, pulling it out and letting it spring back.

"This is where you're supposed to give me your name."

"Ahhh. Of course. My name is Gabriel Anderson but my friends call me Gabe."

"Gabe. After the archangel." She moved a step closer to him. "Say, did you ever see the movie *The Prophecy* starring your namesake? It's all about the angels fighting the war that began in heaven with the fall of Lucifer, only this time the fighting has come down to earth."

"I did. It's one of my favourite movies. Christopher Walken does a great job playing me."

"Funny." She arched her back ever so slightly. "It's actually one of my favourite movies too. I love the way biblical mythology becomes such a literal presence in contemporary human society." Oh yeah. He's definitely interested. Think I've almost hooked him. "I thought the special effects were great – although seeing the battlefields in heaven were deeply disturbing."

"Me too." Gabriel moved a step closer towards Cybele. "It actually reminded me of *Paradise Lost* when Milton describes the inventions of war that the good and bad angels came up with during their war in heaven."

"Wow. I love *Paradise Lost* too."

"Oh, I think the sequel is called *Paradise Regained*."

Laughing, Cybele said, "I know. I meant..."

"I know. I was just playing with you," he laughed back.

Okay. Time to close the deal. Look available but not needy. "So, Gabe, what do you do here?"

"I work as one of the support staff. I'm actually trying to gain experience in this area before I go back to school this fall to get a degree in Recreational Studies. And what do you do?"

Oh shit. I set myself up for that one all right. He might be scared off if I mention the cult. I'll just gloss over it. "Oh, I'm in-between jobs right now, but I definitely see myself starting a small business soon and then who knows?" Her voice trailed off as she saw Janus approaching.

"Cybele, what are you doing here?"

Okay. Act innocent. He'll forget we didn't have plans. "Oh, I thought we were supposed to have dinner together tonight. Didn't we decide that Friday?"

"Oh. I guess I forgot. Let's go then." He turned and nodded firmly to Gabe. "Gabriel."

Gabe nodded back equally as firmly, "Janus." Then he turned to Cybele, "It was nice meeting you. Perhaps I'll see you the next time you come in."

"That would be nice." Cybele regretfully turned away and walked off with Janus. Damn. So close and yet so far. Oh well, the flirtation was off to a very promising start. Too bad Janus seemed to have such a stick up his ass around Gabriel.

Cybele sniffed exasperatedly at Janus. "So, what's up with you? Why the cold shoulder to Gabe? He seemed nice enough."

"Well, he's not." Janus stopped in his tracks and frowned at her. "He's definitely someone who doesn't know his place. He's always hanging around the soup kitchen and always asking the street kids questions. I don't like him snooping. He's after something."

Yeah. Cybele rolled her eyes. Clearly, he's after the Crown Jewels so cleverly concealed in a homeless shelter. "He says he's planning on going into recreational studies. He's probably just doing research."

"That's not his job," Janus said flatly. "You didn't tell him anything about me, did you?"

"No, O Supreme Overlord. Hard as it may be to imagine, your name did not come up in our conversation."

God. Doesn't she take anything seriously? "Cybele," Janus whispered angrily, "I shouldn't have to remind you that I don't advertise the fact that I'm gay here. I don't want to be tarred with the same brush as all those damn perverted priests and counsellors who molest children. You know, those pedophiles are usually mislabelled gay by the media and the other jackasses of the world."

Cybele reached out and touched his hand, "Hey, chill. I know that child molesters are not gays. They're pedophiles."

"YOU know that but most people don't bother to make the distinction." He began to walk away. "I just don't want trouble here."

Cybele scurried behind him to catch up. "You can't possibly think that Gabe is spying on you because he's trying to out you and get you fired?"

"Maybe." Janus slowed his steps to match hers. "Just watch what you say around him, okay."

"Okay." Cybele gently bumped against him. "I won't do anything that might hurt you. You know that." She clapped her hands together. "Now to more immediately pressing concerns. If I'm going to make you dinner, we'll probably have to go grocery shopping. Superstore's the closest, so tin man, into the lion's den, we shall go."

STIGMA

No boundaries

Just like I hid my homo sexuality in eng

You hurt me

You don't hurt people
Unless you're in a war
or a war is against you

Chapter 3

"Let's make this as quick as possible," said Cybele.

"A straight in and out," said Janus with a smirk.

Cybele groaned, "Does that line work for you when you're picking up dates?"

Janus smirked. "You'd be surprised."

"Lecher."

Forty-five minutes later as they walked into Janus's house, Cybele was still fuming. "Can you believe that lady who held up the whole line while she dithered around trying to decide what chocolate bar to buy? Gods. Just pick one and move along. It's all chocolate. Aargh! I'm never going to Superstore again on a Sunday."

Janus looked pseudo-solemnly at her. "That might be wise. I thought you were going to come to blows. For future reference, the next time you mutter under your breath that 'a Rom by any other form is still a Rom,' you might want to be a little quieter just in case the person you're insulting is a *Deep Space Nine* fan and knows you're calling her an idiot."

"Point taken. Now, pour me some wine and let's get dinner started."

"Your will be done."

"And don't you forget it."

They chopped up vegetables to make a stir-fry and boiled a pot of rice. They sat down to eat dinner in front of the television and began to watch a TNN marathon of *Deep Space Nine*.

"Oh, wonderful," said Cybele. "This is one of my favourite episodes. It's the one where Major Kira goes through the Orb of Time to find out whether her mother really died in a labour camp or was Gul Dukat's mistress and a collaborator. She ends up having to decide whether to forgive her mother for her betrayal or to kill her."

Janus snorted. "Great. Nothing like learning from TV about how to live my life." He bowed mockingly towards the screen. "Tell me, oh glowing box of mysterious lights and shadows, should I forgive Achates for sleeping around or cut him from my life?"

Cybele waved her fork at him admonishingly. "Gods, you can't still be thinking that Achates was ever unfaithful. He's as loyal to you as Spock is to Kirk or Robin is to Batman." She calmly swallowed another forkful of food. "Not that they were ever having an affair – but, you know what I mean."

"I don't think so." Janus leaned back and continued eating. "He keeps finding excuses not to spend the night and when we're together he never says anything." Janus put down his fork and slowly pushed the plate away. "I think he's found someone else and he just doesn't have the guts to tell me."

"Maybe." Cybele passed him a napkin and indicated that he should wipe a spot on his face. "Have you thought that: maybe…?"

"What?" Janus asked warily.

Cybele looked away from him a little guiltily. "Maybe he thinks that you're the one having the affair."

Janus balled up his napkin and threw it down on the table. "You didn't tell him about that time I was drunk and…?"

"No." Cybele shook her head vehemently. "Of course not." She gnawed her lower lip. I'm sure I never let anything slip. Gossip just gets around. This is Winnipeg not Toronto. There are no secrets here. Yep. "But he's not an idiot. He might be sensing it or someone else might have seen you at Ganymede's, buying drinks for other guys, and told him."

"Maybe." Janus frowned. She's not looking me in the face. She better not have...Damn. She's such a gossip.

"Look." Cybele looked up from contemplating her plate and started slightly when she realized how intently Janus was staring at her. Damnit. I didn't let anything slip. Why does no one ever believe me? She coolly continued. "Why don't you just talk to him and find out what's going on. If it's over, put a period to the relationship, and move on."

"Thanks, Judge Judy." God. She's lucky she's my best friend or I might really be pissed at her.

"And next time, practice monogamy." Cybele winked. "It's really not a dirty word."

"Yes, mother." Yep. She's damn lucky I don't hold grudges.

"Not to change the subject, Janus," Cybele said hesitantly, "but, have you given any more thought to the web business and cult?"

"Were you really serious about that? I thought you were just blowing smoke."

"Nope. Just burning incense." She pushed her plate away and began to dab at her face with a napkin. "But I am serious about getting into the magic and religion business. It's a growing market."

She stood up and began to pace in front of the television. “You see, people want spirituality, but they don’t want the bureaucracy that comes with most organized religions. So starting a cult that doesn’t require members to follow any strict rules or give up anything they don’t want to, is just a brilliant idea.” She thumped her hand on the television. “We’ll seduce them with the thrill of freedom.”

Janus cracked his knuckles. “No Lent, eh. Everything would be just one big Carnival.”

Cybele put her hands on her hips. “Well, which one would you rather be a part of?”

“Touché.” He leaned forward and began to listen more intently. This crazy idea actually seems to have some possibility. “So, how would this business of yours work?”

Good. I think I might have hooked him. He’s starting to take me seriously. “Look. You already have a sideline business growing herbs in your greenhouse and selling them to Winnipeg restaurants, right? Well, all you have to do is expand that and start growing things like damiana, coltsfoot, and angelica. We can use them in amulets, sachets, poppets, and as ingredients for our ritual fires.”

“I do have a lot of experience,” he said thoughtfully. “I’ve helped Achates design websites for his business in my spare time. And we could always order other herbs we might need over the net until we can start growing them in sufficient quantities.” He began to drum his fingers on the table. “You know, this really could work.”

Cybele plopped down in front of him. “Yes. It will work.” She leaned forward eagerly. “We both understand how people tick. How hard could it be to create rituals that satisfy their innermost wants and desires?"

Wow. I can't believe Cybele is making this insane idea actually sound sane. Janus placed his hands behind his head and lounged back against the couch. "This could be a lot of fun. You know, I've always wanted to be God."

"Hey." Cybele slapped him gently on the knee. "Don't forget this is a partnership. Gods, PLURAL." She paused. "I'm thinking in terms of a *hieros gamos*, never consummated for the obvious reasons."

"Yeah, the gay thing. There's always the option of bi." He laughed. "But I would have to be drunker than I've ever been and probably a little high too."

Like that's a lifestyle stretch for you. She smirked. "Although I'm clearly flattered at the thought of how drunk you'd have to be, I don't think so. Let's just say that you've dipped your wick into too many places for my tastes."

They sang together to the tune of Frère Jacques. "Wear a condom. Wear a condom. It protects. It protects. Johnny didn't wear one. Now he's got a sore one. Ding Dang Dong. Ding Dang Dong."

"Gods, Janus, I can't believe we still remember that. Everything seemed so much simpler in elementary school."

"I know." He stood up and began to crack his back.

Gods. Cybele shuddered. I hate when he does that. It's such a revolting sound.

Janus looked down affectionately at her. "Look, your idea really does sound great. I just need some time to think about it. Selling magical charms and potions on the internet is not such a big deal – with the mark-up, we could make a killing. But, being associated with a cult could damage my professional reputation if I ever finish my Master's. And then there's Achates. You know how strait-laced he is. He might not be too happy about it. He already thinks you're a bad influence on me."

"What! You're kidding." Cybele jumped up. "Why does he think that?"

"He thinks I spend too much time with you, that I value your opinion more than his. And he thinks you're a bit of a whacko." Janus paused for effect. "I believe his exact words were 'damn tree-hugging hippie.'"

Cybele snorted incredulously. "That bastard. How dare he quote *South Park* and Cartman against me?" She began to tap her foot angrily. "I AM Cartman. You know, the regular evil one. Not the goody two-shoes who comes through from the alternative universe with the facial hair. You know." She gestured towards Janus. "In the episode that's a parody of the *Star Trek* one where we meet the evil Spock and Kirk."

"Yep. I remember." Janus nodded solemnly. She's such a firecracker. "You definitely want to be the evil Cartman without the facial hair. Or the evil Kira that Major Kira meets when she and Dr. Bashir have that wormhole accident." He sighed pseudo-wistfully. "She was seriously hot in that bathtub scene."

"Funny. You're gay remember." Cybele grimaced. "I'm seriously pissed now and F.Y.I., I'm not a hippie either, I'm a pagan. There's a huge difference."

"Really." Janus shook his head in mocking encouragement. "Do tell."

Cybele looked sharply at him. "Hippies." She paused deliberately. "Believe in peace and love." She took a deep breath and expelled it in a furious rush of air. "Flower power and all that crap. Probably because THAT movement sprouted in California. Land of the Eternal Childhood. But PAGANS understand that everything comes with a price." She looked over at Janus to see if he was still paying attention. He seemed to be focussed on cracking his knuckles again, but she continued anyway. "If you want power, you take it." She shook her finger warningly at him. "Just don't be a whiner when it comes to paying the piper."

Janus looked up once he heard her stop talking. "No tree-hugging, eh?"

"Oh, I've hugged my share of trees." Remembering the experience calmed her down and she smiled. "It was actually a very restorative experience. There is a certain sense of freedom and peace that comes with wrapping your arms around the trunk of a tree and just pressing your body against it as hard as you can."

Janus's head shot up and he began to pay attention to what she was saying. "Wow, Cyb, sounds pretty sexual to me. Getting all hot and bothered by a tree, were we?"

Jackass. Cybele pointedly ignored him and continued on with her reminiscing. "A blissful melding of two into one." Then she returned back to the present with a vengeance. "But hippies always forget that old Gaea can be one heartless bitch. Spend a little time wandering lost in the woods as she attacks you and tries to reduce you to fertilizer." She snorted. "You won't be singing kumbayas very long." She paused to make sure Janus would get the point. "In this world, Gaea's the predator and we're the prey."

Janus looked puzzled. "I thought we were the ones destroying nature. Sort of makes Gaea our bitch then, doesn't it."

Aargh! It's like talking to a brick wall. "No!" she shouted. "If we're stupid enough to destroy what gives us life, we're only killing ourselves. She can go on without us – we can't go on without her."

Janus walked over and patted her on the shoulder. "Wow. That's really deep."

"Knee-deep in bullshit, eh?"

"Oh, we're definitely talking over our heads." He began to walk towards the kitchen. "In fact, I think we'll need some fruit of the vine to wash it down."

Cybele followed him. "Just as long as it wasn't strained through your fruit of the loom."

"Funny." Janus poured out two glasses of wine and handed her one.

Cybele took a long sip. "Ah. The nectar of the gods." She ran her finger aimlessly over the rim of her glass. "Seriously though, I'm a little upset that Achates has such a low opinion of me. I guess I'm not as good a judge of character as I thought."

Janus raised his glass in a toast to her. "It doesn't matter what he thinks. I like you and I would choose you over him any day. That's probably why he never made me choose."

She gently tapped her glass against his. "That's sweet but maybe that's why you're having problems."

Janus took another long sip. "Oh, it will work out. He'll come to his senses."

"Yep. Everything happens for the best, in this, the best of all possible worlds."

"Comedian. Hey, it's getting late. We better call it a night."

"Yeah." Cybele tossed back the rest of her wine. "I should probably get up bright and early tomorrow and not work on my thesis."

Janus put his glass down. "Come on," he said, "I'll drive you home."

"Great." Cybele yawned. "Time to put the genie back into her bottle."

Gabe Anderson looked carefully around the foyer of the Loaves and Fishes. Good. It was completely deserted. Everyone must have gone over to the residential area in the back. Lights out would begin in five minutes, at eleven p.m. Maybe he should wait until then just to be on the safe side. He stood in the shadows watching the minutes pass on the clock on the wall. It was so quiet he could hear the sound of his own heavy breathing. He smiled wryly to himself. What could he possibly be afraid of? Employees had better things to do with their life than come to work this late on a Monday evening.

Yes. It was exactly eleven p.m. Time to begin. He moved down the dark hallway, carefully moving his little penlight. Don't want to attract the attention of the police or anyone in the residential house. Have them think I'm a burglar. He chuckled softly. Especially, since I am about to do a little break and entering. Thank God for the talents that come from a misspent youth. He paused. I wonder if that Cybele Moondragon had a misspent youth. She looked like quite the character. Cute. Smart. Funny. Purple hair. Someone he definitely wanted to get to know better. Too bad she was a friend of Janus's. Doesn't know how to pick her friends, I guess. Ahh. Here we are.

Gabe stopped in front of the locked door to Janus's office where he held his counselling sessions for the street kids. He held the penlight using his lips as he bent over the door with two metal skewers he had slipped in his pocket earlier when he was in the kitchen. He placed the skewers in the lock and started to jiggle them. Let's see if I still got the touch. Slowly, he felt a little give. Yes. Still got the magic touch. He pushed the door open and removed the skewers from the lock. He slipped them in his pocket as he carefully walked into the office. Good. The streetlight from outside shone brightly enough that he didn't have to worry about stumbling into anything.

Let's find out if you're as aboveboard as you seem, Janus. He walked over to the file cabinet and tried it. It slid open easily. Forgot to lock it, did you? He sat down on the floor and began to flip through a stack of files that had been held together with a rubber band. Hmmm. Tan Talus' file. That's strange. Janus doesn't seem to keep his files in alphabetical order. Wonder why? Gabe skimmed the comments: *braggart, very easy to manipulate for a twenty-two year old, quite stupid – probably lost too many brain cells sniffing glue and smoking dope*. Gabe shook his head. Aaah. The compassionate counsellor. Next, we have Ardiaeus Peters. *Nineteen years old*. Nice. *An easily manipulated bully who likes to play with matches.* Ixion Smith, come on down. *Twenty-one years old*. Hmmm. *Most definitely a mindless follower who will do whatever he is told.* Wow. Janus, the caring healer, an oxymoron. Why do you even come here to offer your services? Your contempt for these kids fairly jumps off the page. What's driving you? You're a man who walks around like he's hiding something big. Something illegal, maybe? He looked down at the next file in his hand: Ajax Lister. *Twenty years old. Whiner. Completely malleable. Will always go to the winning…*

Gabe's head snapped up. What's that? It sounds like someone is coming into the building. Damn.

He quickly gathered up the files and jammed them back into the filing cabinet. He slipped the penlight into his pocket and made it to the door just as the hallway light switch went on and framed him inside the doorway.

"What the hell are you doing in my office?" demanded Janus and headed straight for Gabe.

Gabe's mind raced as he tried to think of a plausible excuse. Calmly, he replied, "Chill, Janus. I'm just doing my job and making sure everything is secured before I leave the building."

"Really? And that includes breaking into my office." Janus deliberately moved to block Gabriel from leaving the room. "If you were looking for drugs, I'm not that kind of doctor."

Annoyed, Gabriel deliberately spoke to Janus as if he was an idiot. "It's actually quite simple, Janus. I was working late when I thought I heard a noise. I thought some of the kids had snuck back in." He paused. "I wanted to CATCH them so I came down the hallway without turning on the light. I couldn't see anyone, but as I was about to leave, I noticed your door wasn't completely closed."

Janus shook his head dismissively. "I always shut it before I leave."

"Well, I guess this time you didn't. I was just double checking your office hadn't been broken into when I heard a noise and came out to find you here."

Janus rocked back and forth on his heels. "And I'm supposed to believe that?"

Gabriel moved closer to Janus and stood directly in front of him. "I really don't give a damn whether you believe me or not. It's the truth. Something, even you, in your clearly PARANOID state should understand. Maybe NEXT time you should double check that you've shut your door before you leave. So, I don't have to do your job for you."

Janus snarled. "Who the hell do you think you are, talking to me like that?"

"Look. I've been up since 6 a.m. working here and I'm too tired to put up with the third degree. Take a pill or get laid. Just leave me the hell alone. That's the last time I'll do you a favour." Gabe moved closer towards Janus who reluctantly moved out of the way to let him pass.

Janus stalked into his office and flipped on the light switch. He quickly looked around but could not find anything that seemed out of place. He walked over to the filing cabinet and tried it. Damn. I must have left it unlocked unless. He turned his head toward the doorway. Could Gabriel have broken into his office hoping to find something to out him? Was he trying to threaten him with the comment about getting laid? Not that Matthew would fire him if he found out but things would change. He might have more trouble getting the kids to trust him. Too many incidents with priests and altar boys had poisoned the environment. Damn pedophiles. Put them in jail and throw away the key. They were the one group that never seemed to benefit from therapy. Habitual offenders. Bastards.

God. Was he being paranoid? Had he not shut his door tightly enough when he left? Damn that Gabriel. Always snooping around. What was he up to?

Damn. Gabe closed the front door firmly and leaned up against it. He couldn't believe he had been caught by Janus. Why the hell had he come back anyway? Just his luck. Now getting the inside shit on what might be going on at the shelter would be much harder to find. Matthew Cain couldn't possibly be as perfect as he seemed. Not in this day and age. Not if he hired someone as cold hearted as Janus to be a counsellor. No. He just had to keep digging. The public had a right to know how and where their tax money was going.

"Janus, is everything okay? I thought I saw a light on in here. You're working very late tonight."

Janus looked up, startled. "Matthew, I didn't hear you come in. I guess I was just thinking about something else."

Matthew leaned against the doorway. "Anything I can help you with? You're not having problems with one of the kids, are you?"

"Oh, no. They're fine." Janus pushed himself up from the filing cabinet and walked towards his desk. "It's just that when I came back to get my wallet, which I had forgotten in my desk drawer, all the lights were out, and I saw Gabriel coming out of my office."

Matthew moved further into the room. "Oh. That's kind of strange. What did he say?"

Janus began to drum his fingers on his desk. "He claimed he had heard a noise and was just trying to sneak up on whoever was making it."

Matthew frowned. "That's a pretty reckless thing to do – to try and surprise a potential burglar."

"He said he thought it was just kids messing around."

"Well, don't you always lock your door when you leave?"

Janus shrugged. "I thought I had but Gabriel said the lock hadn't caught and the door was ajar."

"Is anything missing?"

"No. It's just that I didn't like Gabriel's attitude when I asked him what he was doing. He seemed a little too defensive and hostile."

Matthew sighed. "Well, I'll speak to him about the proper procedures he should follow if he thinks there might be intruders in the building. And I'll speak to him about his attitude. You had every right to be concerned when you saw him in your office. But, Janus, try to cut him some slack. He's new here but he's a hard worker. He just doesn't know all the rules yet."

Janus stood up. "You're right. It's been a long day and I guess I'm just a little tired."

Matthew flipped him a quick salute. "Go home counsellor and get some sleep. I'm sure we'll see you soon enough tomorrow."

"Good idea." Janus took one last look around the office, grabbed his wallet, and followed Matthew out the door.

Chapter 4

"You know, maybe Achates had a SMALL point when he said we spend too much time together," Cybele said as she found herself once again chopping up vegetables up for another dinner with Janus.

Janus tried to hide the concern in his voice. "What do you mean? Would you rather be doing something else?" God. Is she hanging out with me because she thinks Achates is about to dump me? Have I become her pity friend?

Gods. What's up with Janus tonight? He looks like he's about to jump out of his skin. Patiently, she explained. "Well, it's Tuesday evening and instead of going out on a date, I'm here having dinner with you."

Janus took a quick gulp of his wine. "Well, your last boyfriend was such an idiot, you're better off here with me anyway. I can't believe you dated someone with such a pathetic sense of humour." He snorted. "And, it's not like Achates is here for me to spend time with. He's still in Toronto."

Cybele raised her glass in acknowledgement. "Good point." She took a quick sip of wine. "Besides, I'm still mad at him about the hippie comment."

Janus tossed a tomato at her. "But, it's not like you're holding a grudge or anything."

Cybele caught it and neatly chopped it into eighths. "No, of course not." She popped a piece in her mouth. "If I was holding a grudge, I'd probably say something like, Achates is so cheap, he'd pry Christ off the cross to get the nails. But since I'm not holding a grudge, I won't say that."

Janus laughed. "Vanderhaeghe, right?"

"Yep."

Janus reached over and grabbed a piece of tomato from her. "Achates doesn't have much of a sense of humour either, so don't say that in front of him." He squirted the tomato at her.

Cybele bobbed away and then threw a kitchen towel at him. "I know. That's why it is so funny."

Janus ducked and the towel fell on the floor.

Cybele placed her elbows on the counter and leaned forward. "So, Janus, are you going to tell me what's bothering you or are we just going to pretend nothing's wrong?"

Nonchalantly, Janus picked up the towel and tossed it into the sink. "What makes you think something's bothering me?"

"Besides the fact that you've pulverized the hell out of the chicken that you're supposed to be cutting into cubes, oh nothing."

Janus looked down at the flattened chicken breasts. "Oops." He paused and took a sip of wine. "I think Gabriel might have broken into my office and searched it yesterday evening."

Gabriel? Gods. I thought he was still obsessing over Achates. "Okay." Mr. Paranoid. "What makes you think that?"

Janus moved away from Cybele and began to wash the chicken off his hands. "Well, I went back to my office to get my wallet and saw him coming out of it. He had no right to be in there."

Cybele straightened up and crossed her arms. "What did he say when you confronted him about it?"

"Oh, some nonsense about hearing a noise, coming down the hallway, and seeing my door open. He said he was just checking there was no one inside."

"Well, was anything missing?"

Janus looked around for a clean towel to dry his hands. "No."

Cybele pulled open the drawer full of towels and tossed one to him. "Then couldn't he have been telling the truth? Maybe the door just hadn't shut properly. He could have been just playing the Good Samaritan. He doesn't have to be the villain of this piece." She slammed the drawer shut. "Or he could just be a snoop. Remember on *Seinfeld* when Jerry searched his date's medicine cabinet and found that antibiotic cream that was for some kind of weird rash?"

Janus laughed. "Oh, yeah. He was so freaked out he ran away before he could sleep with her."

"And then later he finds out it was for her cat only now she's too pissed off to sleep with him."

"Yep. Poor Jerry. He should have made sure what pussy it was for before he confronted her."

"Stop!" Cybele giggled. "Those jokes only work if you're a brassy haired Mrs. Slocum and we're in *Are You Being Served?*"

"God. I love the British." Janus took another sip of wine. "But back to Gabriel, the wolf in sheep's clothing. I don't trust him and I want to know what he's up to."

"Okay." Cybele began to tap her finger on the rim of her glass. "Say he did search your office. So what? What could he possibly have expected to find? Love letters? A male blow-up doll? A Gay Pride button?"

"Very funny."

She took a quick sip from her glass. "Look. I'm not saying you shouldn't be upset he was in your office but what's the worst that can happen? He'll find out you're gay and blab it to everyone? So what." She gestured at him with her glass. "You've worked at the Loaves and Fishes for five years, first as a youth volunteer, then as a counsellor. You think Matthew doesn't suspect you might be gay?" She shook her head pityingly at him. "Do you really think he would care?"

Easy for you to say. You have no professional reputation to lose. Janus began to drum his fingers on the counter. "I just don't want to be gossiped about."

"Duh. No one does." She took another sip of wine. "Remember Hermia."

"Vaguely. Wasn't she that girl in your department who was such a terrible gossip and snoop?"

"Oh, yeah." She gossiped about everybody and what she didn't know, she made up."

"Charming individual." Janus picked up the chicken and threw it into the wok.

"A true joy to be around." Cybele took another sip of wine. "But, actually, she was just a very insecure person who used gossip as a weapon to gain power and prestige over others."

"Whatever happened to her?"

Cybele casually leaned across him and tossed some basil in the wok. "Oh, it took several months, but she pretty much alienated everyone. No one could trust that she wouldn't be gossiping about them too. So, they basically shut her out. She was too dangerous to know. A viper always ready to strike."

"Sounds like she'd be fun at parties."

"Actually, she was QUITE the party animal." Cybele took another sip of wine. "Hermia would drink like a fish and then tell everyone what she really thought of them."

Janus tossed in the vegetables and quickly flipped them. "That actually sounds quite funny."

"It was a hoot." Cybele sat down with a tired sigh. "What was even funnier is that despite being such a gossip herself, she was absolutely paranoid that everyone was gossiping about her. She clearly never watched the *Buffy the Vampire Slayer* episode where Jonathan is in the school tower with a rifle about to kill himself."

"I remember." Janus turned to face Cybele. "He's upset because no one wants to be friends with him. And Buffy tells him that people aren't deliberately snubbing him. They're just too consumed with their own pain to notice his."

"Right. People are really too obsessed with their own lives to care about the lives of others." She got up to refill her wine glass. "So, while it's never pleasant to be gossiped about, people know the real you. Your true friends won't believe what they hear and what do you care what strangers think?"

He smiled back at her. “I guess I’ll just have to let my reputation do my talking for me.”

“Plus, you really don’t know for sure that Gabe is like Hermia. He might not be a gossip. Be on your guard but don’t make a pre-emptive strike against him. That’s what I think. Gotta give him a chance to prove himself.”

“It is the Canadian way.” Janus held out his glass for Cybele to top it off.

“Yep.” Cybele sat back down. “We’re the Federation of the twenty-first century.”

“Then who’s the Dominion?”

“Oh. Too easy.” Cybele snickered. “Our neighbours to the south. The ones who live in perpetual fear that someone smaller and less powerful than them will attack them. Talk about paranoia.”

Janus turned off the stove and began to dish out the stir-fry. “Strange, how in all those apocalyptic movies, when their society breaks down into lawlessness and anarchy, Canada is always the haven of safety, the place people want to escape to.”

“I know.” Cybele got up to grab a plate. “Remember *Barb Wire* and *Red Dawn*.” She shook her head in disbelief. “Yep, they’re odd ducks. Love’em or leave’em, I guess.”

They sat down and began to eat.

Janus waved his fork at her. “So, have you convinced any others to join your coalition of the willing?”

“Oh, you mean the blind leading the blind?” She paused. “Well, as a matter of fact, Cassie HAS agreed to support me in my crusade to bring a new religion to the world that will usher in a new era of peace and salvation." She sighed dramatically. "Although, you know her…"

"Yep. Always the voice prophesying gloom and doom. Too bad no one ever listens to her."

"I know." Cybele rolled her eyes. "Especially as she has this uncanny ability of always being right." She shook her head. "Well, she's got to be wrong sometimes and that time is now."

Janus put down his fork and turned towards her. "You know, Cyb, I've been thinking."

Cybele winked. "Be careful you don't pull a muscle."

"Funny." Janus stood up and began to stretch. "You know, I really think we could make a good business out of selling magical stuff on the net. As long as we make it clear, they're only for entertainment, don't guarantee results, and don't sell to minors, we should be able to make a profit and avoid getting sued."

"Well, that's great." Cybele pushed her plate away and gently patted her stomach. Good stuff. She stood up. "We definitely don't want to be like poor Madame Rio who ran that psychic hotline on television and ended up getting indicted for fraud. So unfair. She always ran that disclaimer about it being entertainment, but I guess she screwed herself by always insisting she was a real psychic."

"Yeah." Janus turned towards her. "Speaking of indictments, I'm still not sure about starting the whole religion thing. Despite L. Ron Hubbard's success, I'm still a little dubious. I think I need to run that one by Achates before I commit to anything."

Cybele ran her fingers in little circles anxiously over her stomach. "But, you're okay with the web business, right?"

"Oh yeah, I'm in for the magic show. It should be a wild ride." Just hope that Achates doesn't throw a fit about it. Oh, screw him, if he doesn't. That unfaithful bastard. I'll show him that I can get by just fine without him. He took another gulp of wine. "We can do it fifty-fifty. We'll pool our resources and come up with the money for that."

Cybele jumped up and down. "Yippee! I knew you'd agree. It's going to be such a blast."

Janus smiled wryly. "Hopefully, not literally," he said.

Cybele gave him a fast hug. "Oh, don't be such a party pooper."

Janus hugged her back and then exaggeratedly wiggled his finger at her. "Just don't let it get around that I'm associated with something as off-the-wall as this. I don't really want to be linked with something this pagan." He moved slightly away from her. "I'm not quite the free spirit that you are."

Cybele grabbed his finger and lightly shook it. "That's okay. We'll take baby steps. I have faith in you. One day, you'll be able to express the inner pagan that your ego keeps suppressing."

"That will be a good day." Even if hell might have to freeze over first.

"Hey, isn't that what Colonel O'Neill says after SG-1 has made an alliance with the Tok'ra, and the Tok'ra leader says one day, by working together, they will be able to defeat the Goa'uld?"

"You're right." He raised his glass. "We need to toast the new alliance we've just formed."

distress at having been humiliated

Cybele clinked her glass against his. "To the chagrin of fundamentalists of every stripe."

He solemnly looked over at her. "A new day has come."

"Oh my God!" Cybele swatted his head. "Don't start quoting Celine Dion now."

"My heart will go on..."

Cybele clapped her hand over his mouth. "That's my cue to leave. You can sing the show-tunes without me." She walked towards the door and paused. "I'm glad you're going to be part of my adventure. It wouldn't be the same without you."

Janus blew her a kiss and watched her through the window until she drove away.

Janus shook his head in frustration. God. Why does everyone try to duck out of work early on Friday afternoons? We all get stuck in the same traffic jam. And now I have to watch this stupid train keep moving backwards and forwards, one centimetre at a time. We definitely need an overpass here. Hurry up. I need to get home to get Achates' welcome-back dinner ready. Let's see. Candles. Wine. Anything else from the grocery? No. Good. It's finally moving. Crossing rails are coming up. The car ahead of me is starting to move. Yes. We're going. Now I just need to get home and everything will be fine.

Janus took a last look around. Okay. The table was set. Everything was in its place. The wine was chilling in the fridge. Perfect. He heard a knock on the door. Strange. Why didn't Achates just use his key?

Janus walked to the door and opened it. Achates stood there looking slightly uncomfortable.

"Hey, why didn't you use your key?"

"Guess I wasn't thinking. It's been a long week and I'm pretty tired."

"Well, I'm glad you're back. I missed you." Janus leaned towards Achates to kiss him. Achates stiffened ever-so-slightly and moved his head back so that Janus ended up kissing him on the cheeks instead of the lips.

Janus pulled back and looked questioningly at Achates. What the hell is going on? Am I some stranger to get a damn kiss on the cheek? Curtly, he said, "Why don't you come in? We may as well have dinner before it gets cold."

Achates pretended nothing was wrong. "Great. I'm starving." He brushed past Janus and walked inside. "So, what have you been up to while I've been gone?"

Janus followed behind him. "Working hard. Trying to get my thesis proposal to meet all those ethical hoops the Committee is making me jump through." He reached for his glass of wine. "But hey, it's always darkest before the dawn. Can't drag on much longer, right?"

Achates pointedly reached for the bottle and filled his own glass. "So, that's all you've been doing, slaving away on your thesis?"

"Well, I did see Cyb a few times this week, of course."

"Of course." Achates crossed his arms and leaned against the table. "So, what's the hapless adventurer up to now?"

Janus leaned against the counter and took another sip of wine. "She actually has a wonderful business idea that she wants me to go in on."

"Which is?"

Janus shrugged defiantly. "To set up an internet business that sells pagan supplies. You know - potions, oils, incense, and poppets. The usual."

Achates sneered. "How charming. But why stop there? Why not brooms and cauldrons, pointy noses and warts?"

"Don't be ridiculous." Janus straightened up. "Listen, we could actually make a good profit in pagan sales. It's a rapidly expanding market."

"Of course it is. The world is full of lunatics like your friend Cybele." Achates sniffed angrily. "I go away for a few days and you lose your mind. I can't believe you would ever consider going into business with her."

"Oh. My. God." Janus slammed his hand down on the counter. "This is not about Cybele. It's about trusting me and my judgement of what a good business investment this would be."

Achates growled. "Of course, it's about her. She has way too much influence over you."

Damnit. I can't believe he's picking a fight after everything I've done for him today. How ungrateful can one man be? Janus took a deep breath. "I know what I'm doing," he said coldly.

"Right." Achates began to pace back and forth angrily. "She's flighty, and when you're around her, you're flighty too. This week it's

changing minds erratic or irresponsible

a magic shop. Next week she could decide to join the French Foreign Legion." He paused. "Oh wait. She doesn't like getting up early so that's out. How about joining Greenpeace so she can throw herself in front of French fishing boats and get sunk by the French navy." He took a gulp of wine. "Or even better, why doesn't she join Save Our Seas and ram Spanish trawlers that overfish in Canadian waters?"

"That's enough." Janus threw his hands up in the air. "Stop talking about her like that. What's your problem? I spend a lot of time and effort to make a nice meal for you and all you can do is criticize my best friend."

"Maybe." Achates paused for emphasis. "That's the problem in a nutshell."

"What the hell is that supposed to mean?"

"Maybe I'm tired of always feeling like the third wheel." Achates gestured into the air with his glass. "You clearly care more about her feelings than mine."

"That's ridiculous. Look, let's not fight. We've both had a long day. Let's just have a nice dinner and go to bed. We can talk about this in the morning."

Achates put his glass down and turned away from Janus. "I think we should talk about it now."

"Fine," Janus said flatly. "Talk."

"Damnit! I should be your best friend not her. Cybele should be the one feeling like a third wheel. Not me."

Janus put his glass down and walked towards Achates. "So, what do you want me to do?"

Achates turned back towards Janus. “Stop spending so much time with her. Start spending more time with me and my friends.”

Janus stopped and sighed. “When? You’re always out of town on business. Do you think I should stay home waiting for you to come back and for my life to begin again?”

“Hey, I didn’t inherit money from my parents. I actually have to work for a living.”

Janus slammed his open hand against the wall. “And I’m just some shithead who doesn’t? Is that what you’re trying to say?”

Achates stamped his foot down hard. “You just refuse to see my point, don’t you?” He turned furiously away.

Prick. Janus forced himself to calm down. “You haven’t made a point. All you’ve done is complain that I don’t spend time with you and your friends.” Janus turned reproachfully away from Achates and reached again for his glass of wine.

Achates roughly pulled out the kitchen chair and straddled it. “You spend more time with her than with me.”

“That’s not true.” Janus gulped down his wine. He mechanically swirled the wine in his glass in an attempt to avoid making eye contact with Achates.

Drunk. Achates looked questioningly at Janus. “When was the last time we went out with my friends?”

Janus gestured aimlessly in the air with his glass. “Your friends are boring. All they do is talk about their work. They have no sense of adventure. No sense of embracing the unexpected.”

Thankfully I'm no longer one of those people

I don't have to win

Achates rocked his chair back and forth. “You’ve got to be shitting me. Have you lost your mind? Grow up, Janus. Lunacy is charming only in the very young.”

“What the hell is that supposed to mean?”

“You lose your mind when you’re around her. Jesus, Janus, it’s like she brainwashes you.”

Janus spit out some of his wine in surprise. “What the hell do you mean – she brainwashes me? Do you think I’m some kind of moron?”

“Not a moron.” Achates shook his head angrily. “You become a jackass. You act irreverently towards all the things which make our society work. You act like one of those damn anarchists who have no respect for anything or anyone.” He paused. “You EMBARASS me.”

“I EMBARASS you?” Janus slammed down his glass. “Why do you care so much about what people think of you? Don’t you know that people are far more concerned with their own lives to concern themselves with yours? People live their lives so full of pain and self-doubt, they don’t have time to be anything other than self-centred. Remember the *Buffy the Vampire Slayer* episode when…”

“Damnit. Can’t you see?” Achates banged his head frustratedly against the table. “This is exactly what I’m talking about. Life is not a damn television show. That’s fantasy and this is reality. You act like you can’t tell the difference.”

“You’re so wrong.” Janus sank into a chair beside Achates. “Don’t delude yourself. Life is as much of a constructed reality as anything shown on TV.” He picked up the bottle of wine on the table and took a gulp. Yep. The shit’s finally going to hit the fan tonight. He sighed glumly. "Whether we are men dreaming we are butterflies or butterflies dreaming we are men, the one truth is that all life is an illusion. We are all wandering shades." He patted Achates on the back and offered him the bottle.

Achates pushed it away without looking up.

Janus shrugged and took another swig. "I've just broken my shackles and left the cave and you're still inside - shocked and awed by the smoke and shadows."

Achates rubbed his forehead. Ow. That hurt. He waved Janus away. "I can't talk to you when you get like this, Janus. It's like talking to a child."

Janus carefully put the bottle back on the table. "This has nothing to do with Cyb. You've been using her as a scapegoat. You've had a bug up your ass ever since you walked through the door. Why don't you tell me what's really going on?"

Achates sighed heavily and ran his hand through his hair. "I didn't want to get into this tonight but maybe it's for the best. I've been thinking that I would like to run for political office one day and I need a partner I can count on not to do anything that would embarrass me or draw me into a scandal. As long as you're hanging around Cybele, that's not you."

"What does that mean? If I stop seeing her, all will be well in the world again?" Janus reached for Achates and then pulled back. "Just be honest. Damnit. You're having an affair."

Achates stood up. "No. I'm not. But I just think our relationship has run its natural course. If you're honest with yourself, you'll know it's true."

"Bullshit." Janus jumped up and kicked his chair across the floor. "You're having a goddamn affair. Someone you met on one of your so-called business trips."

"It's over. For God's sake, don't make this harder than it has to be. Let's just say our good-byes and walk away. We're both adults." Achates turned his back on Janus and walked towards the door.

"Wait. Don't leave me," Janus said desperately.

Achates paused with his hand on the door knob. His body stiffened and then relaxed. He turned the handle and walked out.

Janus walked up behind him and closed the door very softly. He walked back into the kitchen and sat down. He looked at the once-perfectly set table full of food. He filled his plate and very coolly began to eat his dinner. He drank his glass of wine and then finished off Achates' glass. He stood up and blew out the candle centerpiece. He carried the dishes to the sink and scraped the uneaten food into the garbage. He threw the rest of the food into the garbage and put all the dishes into the dishwasher. He grabbed a bottle of beer from the fridge, opened it, and walked out the sliding doors onto his deck. He sat down in the utter darkness of the evening and began to drink his beer.

He raised his beer bottle in a toast. Thank-you God. Who says you don't have a sense of humour? You have Achates break up with me. With me. He shook his head. And you put my best friend – the one

Did this ever happened to you mohammed?

person I trust and care for most in the world, in the body of a woman. Cheers. He sighed. I did love Achates. I just couldn't be the person he wanted me to be. Bastard.

He looked up at the starry sky and laughed. Twinkle, twinkle, dying star. How I wonder... what? Do you know your light is just a shadow of the giant you once were? Do you know that by the time we see your light, you are already dead? How's that for the meaning of life? We only become visible in death. Life's a bitch and then we die. Oh God. Now, I'm thinking in clichés. *Nolite te bastardes carborundorum*. Time to go back inside and get very drunk. Why am I always left behind? Why couldn't he love me no matter what?

God has a sense of humour

Chapter 5

Those damn bells. Gods. I hate Sundays. Why doesn't everyone else understand the importance of sleeping in? Cybele dragged herself out of bed and got dressed. As she walked into the kitchen to make breakfast, her buzzer went off. Without first asking who it was, she pressed the button to let the visitor in. *Wonder if it's for me or someone else? Could be a Jehovah's Witness. Other cities go by robins or bluebirds, but Winnipeg's first sign of summer is when we first start seeing Witnesses sprouting everywhere. Oh well. At least the* Watchtower *is something to read when I have a few minutes to kill. Better a watchtower than a clock or bell tower in a public square, I guess. Less semi-automatic fire.* She laughed. *Amazing how no one bothers me when I read religious propaganda on the bus. Maybe the next time someone wants to chat when I'm busy, I'll just pick a religion and start proselytizing. Could be fun.*

There was a loud knock on the door.

Damn. They're at my door. Now listen, Cybele, she said firmly to herself. *You can talk politely to them at the door, but whatever you do, don't let them cross the threshold or you'll never get rid of them. Remember what happened the last time.* She shuddered as memories of her last proselytizing experience washed over her. Reluctantly, she went to open the door.

Cybele jumped back in surprise. "Janus? What are you doing here? It's not quite noon yet."

Janus forced himself to fake a breezy nonchalance. "Oh, I couldn't sleep very well, so I thought I'd come over bright and early to see what you were up to." He waved a cup enticingly in front of her. "I brought you a mochaccino from The Second Cup."

"Normally," she spoke through a yawn. "I'd say, beware Greeks bearing gifts, or is it gifts bearing Greeks? But I would love that mochaccino, so come right in."

Janus came inside and immediately slumped down on her living room sofa. Immersed in inhaling the fragrance of the gods, Cybele remained oblivious of his true feelings. She followed him slowly into her living room and perched on the opposite end of her sofa.

Cybele saluted Janus with her cup. "So, what's up, doc?

Janus cracked his knuckles. "Well, good news, actually."

"Great!"

"Yep." Janus leaned forward and looked off into space. "I've decided that there's nothing more in the world I'd rather do than start a cult with you." He sighed half-heartedly. "You know, play Attis to your Cybele."

"That's." Cybele paused uncertainly. "Wonderful." Gods. He looks like someone shot his dog. Or would look if he had a dog. She looked dubiously at Janus. "But what about Achates?"

Janus stood up and cracked his back. "Oh, I don't think he would want to be your Attis. He really doesn't like you, remember?"

"That's not what I..." she stopped suddenly. "Okay, did you and Achates have a fight?"

"Not quite." Janus shook his head scornfully. "We did break up but it was all scripted by Achates. I was there just as a member of the audience. I don't really want to talk about it now though, okay."

"Okay." Better let him stew awhile.

"That bastard." Janus jumped up. "Do you know what he said to me?"

"Not yet." Cybele sighed. But I guess I'm going to find out. "No."

Janus stood up and paced tensely back and forth across the room. "He says that I don't know the difference between television and reality. He says that I embarrass him in front of all his big-shot friends because I continually see the world in terms of *Star Trek*." He stopped and fell back onto the couch. "Guess I should be more like him. Some humourless sour-face, severely lacking in *joie de vie*."

Cybele slid across the couch and put her arm around Janus. "Don't listen to him. The man's an idiot. Don't you remember what Tyr Anasazi once said on *Andromeda* to Dylan about that very thing?"

"No." Janus sunk his head into his hands. "What?"

Cybele patted him on the back. "He said that when you wake up one morning and the universe has gone totally insane, you can either accept the madness as your new reality, or you can exert your will upon the universe and remake it into the image you want. All you're doing is reinterpreting the world to make sense to you."

Janus massaged the back of his neck thoughtfully. "I'm just Socrates leaving the cave and Achates is the Athenian government trying to pull me back in."

"Right." Cybele jumped up and grabbed her coffee. "And the last thing you want is to let him because you can't survive in there. He'll make you drink hemlock." She raised her cup and toasted him.

Janus jumped up. "Damn good point."

"Yep. I'm just a fount of wisdom after drinking this much caffeine and chocolate so early in the morning."

"Just don't turn into a geyser. Remember the time I cracked you up in the car and when you started laughing, the Orange Crush you were drinking came out of your nose?"

"Shhh. That was never supposed to be mentioned again. All those damn bubbles actually hurt. How embarrassing." She stretched her arms over her head and yawned. "Hey, as long as you're here, why don't we start working on a pseudo Bible for our cult's beliefs?"

"Sure. Not like I have anything better to do today." He sat down cross-legged on the floor. "So, Yoda, what should we have to believe in to belong to our little cult?"

Cybele looked slightly disconcerted as she tapped her coffee cup. Oops. Cardboard. Not too environmentally friendly. "Hmmm. Definitely a do-no-harm philosophy towards nature." She took a sip of coffee. "This won't mean not interacting with the environment but just not doing damage to it."

Janus looked up teasingly at her. "So, starting ritual fires will be okay..."

Cybele swatted him on the head. "Right, but burning down the forest will not be."

The Flush
↳ No puritan ideals, just how we are
→ But what about Human Rights?

"Okay. But what about the great divide – carnivore or herbivore?" He stood up and thumped his chest. "Me-Tarzan. Me eat meat."

Cybele gave him a reproving look. "We can eat meat or we can choose not to. No rules – remember?" She pinched him. "This won't be a peace and love hippie cult. Remember, Cybele was an embodiment of Nature and we all know that Nature can be one scary bitch."

Living up to our standards! Harmony? X

Janus threw his hands up in the air. "I surrender. No more hippie versus pagan diatribes, okay?" He nudged her. "Too bad we're not going to be hippies. It would have been fun to have Casper the Friendly Ghost in our rituals."

"No." Cybele pinched Janus a little harder than before. "Think Aeneas filling a pit with blood so he can talk to the ghosts from the Underworld."

"Gotcha." She's so easy to manipulate.

Cybele took another sip of coffee and leaned back against her television. "I was also thinking about using some of what Yoda says to Luke on Dagobah in *Empire Strikes Back*."

Hmmm. Interesting. "You mean about how the Force is around us everywhere and it's only how we use it that determines whether we stay in the light or go over to the dark side." This could work.

"Yep. If we substitute "energy" for "The Force," I think it would be more relevant and meaningful to our followers, don't you think?"

Janus drummed his fingers on top of the television. "Okay. But what about *Star Trek*?"

→ To think that how we behave and our life is in our will is the (neo-liberal) argument. It neglects context and factors such as poverty and constraining situation like dysfunctional family

Cybele walked towards the window and looked out. She shook her head at the sight of the church. "Well, I was definitely thinking about using some of *Star Trek*'s beliefs about the principle of non-interference."

Janus walked towards her. "Good point. The last thing we want is a cult full of self-righteous meddlers. Then we'd be like most organized religions in the world already."

"It's not just that." She took a quick sip of her coffee. "Although I do hate meddlers." She turned her back to the window. "But the last thing we want is for some of our followers to commit illegal acts in our name and then have the authorities come after us legally. We'll try to weed the whackos out. But you never know with people."

Janus smirked. "Well, I guess we'll know our cult's made it when we start splintering off in different factions and each one goes off to start a new interpretation of our basic message."

Cybele rolled her eyes. "Yep. That will be a good day. My ultimate spiritual progenitor will have achieved immortality again."

Janus yawned. "What about *Stargate*? Any ideas from that?"

Cybele sat down on the couch and leaned back with a sigh. "I'm not sure. *Stargate* relies pretty heavily on Egyptian mythology."

Janus curled up beside her. "Well, *Stargate Sg-1* uses Norse Mythology. It has the Asgard who turn out to be the Roswell aliens. They're the good guys."

"I know, but the only message the more advanced aliens seem to give is that knowledge is dangerous if it is given to a species that is not

-Knowledge can be used in the hands of the wrong people.

yet advanced enough to use it wisely. It's basically the Prime Directive rewritten."

"Yep." Janus grabbed a cushion and shoved it behind his back. "*Stargate Sg-1* is more a work in progress. A blueprint of where we are as a human race and our attempts to advance." He stretched out with a contented sigh. "We need a model for Shangri-La."

Becoming more interested in what he was saying, Cybele crossed her legs and leaned forward. "I WAS impressed with the episode when Apophis is badly injured and they capture him and they give him medical treatment instead of just torturing him for information and killing him."

No exceptions

Janus arched his eyebrow. "Colonel O'Neill wanted to."

Cybele poked Janus in the ribs. "But General Hammond said no. He said that Apophis had to be treated with all the rights of any other prisoner of war."

"True." He hugged himself and rocked slightly back and forth. "I guess if they had written that episode now, they would have declared him an unlawful combatant and done God knows what to him. And no one would have said a thing in protest. Cowed by American tactics of shock and awe. The genocide of political conscience."

Cybele crossed her arms and shook her head. "Kind of sad to think that within such a short time we've already regressed from that small ray of hope *Stargate SG-1* offered."

Janus groaned. "Great. Now I'm feeling depressed again. Got any strong coffee."

"Yeah." She stood up. "I'll go make some instant cappuccino."

Good scenery

They are trying to come up with a bible for their cult

Cybele made coffee and they sat on the couch drinking it.

Janus broke the silence. “So, what else have you come up with?”

“Well, I was thinking about the *Batman* movies. But with the exception of Poison Ivy, the personification of Nature’s Wrath, I couldn’t find any really strong matriarchal messages.”

“Hey, what about Catwoman?” Janus gave an exaggerated leer. “She sure looked hot in that black leather.”

Cybele kicked him. “Well, she was an example of female empowerment, but a little too much on the dark side, don’t you think?” - YES

Janus sighed. “You’re right. *Batman* really is just a patriarchal reinterpretation of Judaeo-Christian mythology.”

Slightly exasperated, Cybele tapped the rim of her cup. “I know. The Penguin being put into a cradle and floating into the sewers – clearly meant to represent Moses. And the kidnapping of all the first-born sons of Gotham. Puh-lease. I’m surprised they didn’t have a literal Angel walking around Gotham. And Poison Ivy was also a rip-off of Lilith – the hard-assed feminist who MUST be cast out of the ironic Eden that is Gotham.”

Janus leaned forward. “You know Catwoman also makes a neat Jezebel figure.”

Cybele rolled her eyes. “Most sexually powerful women who are also cast as villains could probably be interpreted that way.” She rolled her cup between her palms. “But that’s not helpful to us because I want a matriarchy where strong women are not villains.”

Why am I not comfortable with the idea of a villain?

Janus patted her knee comfortingly. "Good point. No villains, male or female, in our cult."

"Yeah." Cybele bit her lip. "We really don't want another Heaven's Gate or whatever the name was of that weird cult where they all committed suicide because they wanted to go off somewhere in a spaceship."

"You're right." Janus squeezed the bridge of his nose thoughtfully. "Although purely intellectually, I do wonder about how all the players interacted to produce the kind of atmosphere where that idea seemed reasonable."

"I know." Cybele tapped her fingers broodingly. "I guess they just gave up their sense of individuality and became absorbed into something larger than themselves. You know, like what Jung believes." She leaned forward. "Or like on *Deep Space Nine* when Dukat took over the cult of the Pah Wraiths and then started sleeping with that Bajoran woman who had a Cardassian baby."

The idea of collectivity or being a herd

"Yeah." Janus took a slow sip of his wine. "At first... he said it was a miracle of the Prophets and then when it looked like she might tell the truth to her husband, Dukat tried to kill her."

"Exactly." Cybele jumped up and began to pace back and forth. "And to prevent the truth coming out, Dukat tried to convince the whole cult to commit suicide."

"Yep." Janus began to pop his knuckles. "But Kira stopped them before they could." Interesting possibilities though. Definitely something to consider.

"I know." Cybele tapped her foot worriedly. "But they were ready to die. And that Vedek took the poison and died anyway." She rubbed the back of her neck reflectively. "That's why it is so important not to have those kinds of elements in our cult. I don't want those kinds of deaths on my conscience. This is all about fun and profit. Not death."

Janus saluted her mockingly with his cup. "Just eat, drink, and be merry, eh?"

"Hey." Cybele tossed a cushion at him. "Doesn't that end, for tomorrow we die?"

Janus ducked and picked the cushion off the floor. "But that's tomorrow." He threw the cushion back at her. "The future is always in flux."

Cybele tossed the cushion back on the couch. "Don't forget. We never step in the same pile of shit twice."

They laughed. Cassie's bedroom door opened and she walked yawning into the room.

"What's going on in here? You two are making enough racket to wake the dead."

"And behold, Persephone enters in all her glory," said Cybele.

Cassie stuck out her tongue. "The Queen of the Underworld, I'm SO flattered."

"Well, I'm pretty sure your last boyfriend Brahma said you were a swallower," Cybele replied. "Or maybe it was wallower?"

"Funny." Cassie walked tiredly into the kitchen. "You clearly have had too much caffeine this morning."

"Hey, we're sorry if we woke you up," interjected Janus. "We should have been quieter."

"It's okay." Cassie leaned up against the wall and stretched. "I had to work late at the shop last night decorating a wedding cake for one of those Bridezillas. You know. One of those, 'I want the icing to be in off-white but that's not the right shade of off-white, it has to be the perfect off-white.' Gods. Everyone knows colours look different in artificial lighting than in natural light. Good thing the figurine of the groom has a ring through his nose. He'll be wearing it for the rest of his life."

"Well, as long as you're not bitter, right?" gently mocked Cybele.

"Never." Cassie started to rummage in the fridge. "Hey, you guys want some food. I'm feeling in a cooking mood."

Cybele patted her stomach. "Well, I'm hungry and you know Janus never turns down a hot meal."

"Never." Janus walked towards the kitchen. "I'm always ready for food."

Cybele smirked. Or anything else if the rumours about Ganymede's are true.

"So, what else have you guys been up to?" asked Cassie as she began to prepare brunch.

Cybele beamed. "Oh, great news! Janus has agreed to be a full partner in my cult." Her voice suddenly trailed off. "Oh, and Janus and Achates have broken up."

"Yep." Janus took a long sip of coffee. "Guess he's off to fertilize greener pastures."

The exploitation of a cow

"Hey, do you remember that pasture party we all went to near Starbuck?" asked Cybele.

"Yeah. In high school. We all got completely wasted and were introduced to the fine art of cow tipping," replied Cassie.

"Never again," answered Janus. "I felt like a complete monster when I saw that cow fall over and heard her confused moo."

Cybele agreed. "Oh, me too. Good thing those PETA Nazis weren't around that night."

Cassie shook her head fondly. "Yeah, you two really ran away from that cow pretty fast."

"Hey, cows are big and scary." Janus laughed. "I much prefer them on my plate than in the flesh."

Cybele smirked. "So speaks Tarzan – the carnivore."

Janus glared at her over his cup. "Good one." He paused. "We, who are about to eat death, salute you." He casually flipped her the finger.

Cybele opened her mouth to reply, but Cassie broke in.

"Playtime is over kids. Brunch is ready. Eggs, toast." She winked at Janus and Cybele. "But, since we're out of cow, you'll have to settle for bacon."

Cassie sat down at the table and started to eat. "So, have you guys actually decided where you are going to hold your cult meetings?"

Cybele looked over at Janus. "Janus has that little guest house on his property. I was thinking it would be a good cult house." She used her teeth to tear off a piece of her bacon and carefully chewed.

Meals are important

The Character's personalities displaying

"Maybe we could use the grounds to perform our outdoor rituals. We'd have complete privacy."

Janus sat down beside Cassie. "Yeah. We can use it as the office for our web business too. That way I don't have a lot of strangers in my actual house and I get to keep my privacy."

Cassie, in spite of herself, chimed in. "And if the police ever decide to raid your property, they'll need warrants for both houses before they can search them." — The realistic

Cybele softly kicked Cassie's knee under the table. "Ah, Cassie. Always the optimist."

"I try." Cassie kicked Cybele's knee back a little harder. "So, how are you planning to decorate this little cult house of yours?"

Oblivious to the *sub rosa* exchange, Janus replied, "Well, we definitely need a ritual meeting room – and the unfinished basement might be the best place for that."

Grimacing subtly, Cybele rubbed her knee. "We should probably paint the walls in strong, powerful colours, like red and black."

"Maybe use Pompeian red like in all those wall paintings in the houses they excavated in Pompeii," suggested Cassie.

"That a girl." Cybele threw her a forgiving smile. "Use that degree in Classics for good not evil." With a twinge of guilt for her flippancy, Cybele continued. "It's too bad you can't recreate some of those wall paintings like those in the Villa of the Mysteries."

"That's more than we can afford right now, but once our cult takes off, we'll see," said Janus.

Cybele began to run her finger around the rim of her cup. "We need to find a way to make the room really hot – maybe by using space heaters. Our goal is to put people into a receptive frame of mind. A hypnotic state," she said in a confiding voice.

Janus began to tap his fork against his cup. "We should also use rhythmic noises, like chanting and drums, to help relax people."

Cassie snorted. "Don't forget the alcohol."

Cybele rolled her eyes. "Duh." She leaned forward. "You know, with our experience in pagan rites, Cassie and I can create some brew, using herbs like wormwood to help induce a state of intoxication."

Cassie nodded in agreement. "And don't forget about incense. Scents are very important in relaxing people."

Cybele stood up and stretched. "But, since I will be the incarnation of a Nature goddess, we have to have outdoor rituals too."

Cassie began to look more worried. "Which means using fire and water."

Cybele began to rock the back of her chair excitedly. "Hey, we can re-enact famous mythological scenes like when Aeneas contacts the ghosts of the Underworld. It'll be such a hoot."

"Well," Janus broke in, "as long as we have a good fire extinguisher that sounds like a good plan." Note to self. Review fire insurance policies before Cybele burns my house down.

"Are you guys going to have robes and stuff like that?"

Janus threw his hands up. "Whoa! I'm not dressing up like Merlin."

Gods. What is it with men and dresses? Cybele forced herself to sound patient and not condescending. "They don't have to be

- Profit
- Helping induce an state of intoxication
- Creating an illusion
- Avoiding getting into legal trouble

stereotypical magician robes, Janus, but we SHOULD make an effort to create an otherworldly atmosphere. It will add to the illusion we want to create."

"Cyb's right, Janus. You will need to wear something other than street clothing, but we can find something you'd be comfortable with." She patted him reassuringly. "Don't forget that religious rituals always use smoke and mirrors. If you break the illusion, you break the spell."

Cybele broke in animatedly. "Don't you remember how angry we were when we saw the *Buffy the Vampire* episode where Buffy is catatonic in the psych ward of a hospital and all her adventures turn out to be just mad delusions?" She thumped her fork against her plate splattering food on the table. "None of the characters we have followed over the last few years turn out to be real people."

Cassie agreed. She quickly grabbed a paper towel to clean up the mess Cybele had made. "It was such a betrayal. We need Buffy and the Scooby gang to be real, to save the world from monsters. Even if we know it's just television, they still have to be real on television. By turning them into delusions, Josh Whedon just killed them."

"That bastard," Janus said vehemently.

Oblivious to Cassie's cleaning efforts, and now on a roll, Cybele felt compelled to reminisce further. "And remember how disappointed we were with how they wrapped up *Voyager*? How the hell could they have had Seven of Nine end up with Chakotay, when clearly EVERYONE knows that she should have ended up with the Doctor?" She shook her head in disbelief. "They were the ones who had built up a relationship over the years and now we're supposed to believe that Seven and Chakotay are right for each other. Puh-leeze."

Damnit. Janus sighed resignedly. "Both of you are right. If I don't throw myself into the game, it won't work. I won't be the Whedon who breaks the spell."

"Don't be such a grump," admonished Cybele. "Just remember that life is supposed to be fun. Enjoy the thrill of becoming someone else. Think of it as a mask you wear. It will help you avoid being self-conscious."

Cassie leaned back in her chair. "Not to be the cold voice of reason, but have you thought about the start-up costs for this business? How are you going to pay for them?"

Cybele's eyes widened. "Good question." She turned to look at Janus. "Janus, you're the businessman. Do you have any ideas?"

He squeezed the bridge of his nose thoughtfully. "Nothing springs to mind immediately. We should first make an estimate of the sort of things we will need to begin and then figure out costs."

Cassie, as usual, was unable to resist getting in a subtle dig, and interrupted. "I don't think they give small business loans for people who want to start cults."

"No," chided Janus. "But if we do some brainstorming, I'm sure we can find some inventive ways to pay for the initial costs. Then when the internet magic business takes off, we'll be rolling in the dough."

Beginning to become a little bored with the whole discussion, Cassie stood up. "Well, why don't we crunch some numbers, think about some moneymaking ideas, and then meet back up again, and

Great and accurate description of movie theatre.

compare plans." She rolled her eyes at her own business-bullshit. Too much time around that bitch Marie Antoinette. "Meanwhile, I feel like a little entertainment. Why don't we see if there are any good movies playing at Cinema City Eight?" ✓ Winnipeg.

Feeling a little overwhelmed by the financial aspects of starting her own cult, Cybele took immediate advantage of Cassie's desire for a break. "Good plan. I'm in the mood for outrageously overpriced popcorn with rancid butter and maybe one or two oversized chocolate bars." She turned to Janus. "Did you buy a paper when you went for coffee?"

"No." He jumped up. "But there are always one or two good matinees on Sundays. Let's just go and see."

Cybele gestured grandly in the direction of the door. "Then once more into the fro, dear friends."

Just remember that life is supposed to be fun. Enjoy the thrill of becoming someone else

Think of it as a mask you wear. It will help you avoid being self-conscious.

- The money-making purpose is clear

Chapter 6

Gabe got out of his car and walked towards Shangri-La. God. I hate Mondays. Just another reminder that the weekend is over and the daily grind begins again. Hmm. He sniffed the air. Something smells good. They're supposed to have a really good lunch special here. Hope it lives up to its billing. He walked through the front doors and looked around for his employer, Iris Pontus.

There she is at the corner table, reading the menu and talking into her cell phone. God. What on earth is she wearing today? A bright red t-shirt and orange pants? She looks like she's on fire. And what's up with those green streaks in her greyish-black hair? Is she trying to look like a Christmas tree? Doesn't she look in the mirror before she goes out in public? I'm surprised they let her in.

Gabe walked up to Iris' table and sat down. She immediately waved him to silence as she finished yelling at whomever was on the other line. Then she put her phone away and smiled over at Gabe. "So, got anything interesting for me?"

"Well, the information I'm getting from these street kids on what it's like to be a member of the despised underclass is fascinating. Many of them aren't really kids. They're in their early and mid-twenties." He glanced over at Iris to gauge the effect of his report on her. She didn't look as if she was daydreaming, so he kept going. "In fact, a lot of them come from respectable middle class families and this is just their way of rebelling during the day and going back to a warm bed and hot food at night." He paused to take a sip of water.

"But, there are also a lot of others, the runaways and dropouts, who really do live on the street and need our help."

"Good." Iris leaned back and began to read the menu. "Sounds like you have enough information to do a series of articles, A Day in the Life of a Street Kid, etc." She looked up. "So, what's the hold-up?"

To give himself a moment to find the right words to convince her, Gabe pretended to flip through the menu. "I just think there might be a bigger story here than just that." He tossed his menu back on the table. "Do you know there's a rumour going around that Matthew Cain, the director, was in prison for involuntary manslaughter?"

They fell silent as the waitress came up to take their orders. They both ordered the lunch special – a B.L.T. with fries on the side. Once the waitress left, they returned to their conversation.

"Really," she said with a smirk. "Well, if it's a rumour, it must be true." She leaned forward. "According to your unverified sources, who'd he kill?"

"His twin brother, Abe." Gabe tapped his fingers on the table. "The details are sketchy. Apparently, they got into a fight over money. Abe accused Matthew of stealing from him. And when the dust cleared, Abe was dead."

"Wow." Iris' eyes widened in surprise. "Juicy. But, even if it's true, then," she said dryly, "other than him clearly NOT being his brother's keeper, so what? He's served his time. In fact, it looks like he's turned his life around and is making a difference to his community."

"Well," Gabe said uneasily, "I really don't think it's a good idea for someone who committed murder after he was accused of stealing to be in charge of disbursing public and governmental donations. It's like letting the inmates run the asylum."

Iris looked closely at Gabe. "Do you have any real evidence or is it all conjecture?" She leaned forward to take a sip from her water.

"I just need more time." Gabe looked up hopefully. "I need to investigate some of the employees too. One of them, Janus Styx, gives off really bad vibes." He began to tap his knife against the table. "He's clearly hiding something."

"Really? Why?" Iris sounded more intrigued. "Do you think he's working with Cain?"

"I don't know for sure." Gabe began to look a little more uncomfortable. "I searched Janus's office last Monday evening and I found some files he had on some of the kids." He began to trace ever-widening circles on the tablecloth with his knife. "His comments were pretty condescending." Gabe put his knife down with a thump. "He clearly thinks he's better than everyone else."

They fell silent again as the waitress came with their food. They quickly started eating.

"Mmmm. This is delicious." Iris waved her sandwich at Gabe. "Look, last time I checked, being elitist is not a crime. Do you have anything more tangible?"

"No." Gabe clucked in annoyance. "Unfortunately, he came in before I was done searching. I pretended I had seen his office door open and was just closing it."

"Did he buy it?" Iris scowled as some of her bacon flew out of her sandwich and onto the table. Damn. What a waste.

– Gut Feeling
– Benefit of the doubt

"Not quite. But what could he say? Nothing had been taken." Gabe frowned. "Although I did get a lecture from Matthew the next morning about proper procedures to follow if I think there's been a break-in."

"Are you sure there's really something there?" Iris dabbed at her mouth with her napkin. "Janus could be perfectly innocent, you know. Maybe you and he are just two dogs pissing in the same territory." Unconsciously, she picked up pieces of the bacon that had fallen on the table and popped them into her mouth.

Gabe flinched slightly at the sight. "No," he disagreed, "my gut tells me there's something big that's going on."

"You haven't been a reporter long enough to have a gut, Gabriel." Iris looked mockingly down at his stomach. "A bit of a beer belly, maybe."

Gabe patted his flat stomach and snorted. "I don't have a beer belly." He thumped his hand on the table. "I'm sure there's a bigger story here than just street kids. Give me time and I'll find it."

The passion of the young. Iris nibbled on the remnants of her fries as she smiled fondly over at him. "Gabriel, I've known you since you were in diapers. Your mother was my best friend. After she died, well… She would have wanted me to look out for you." She swirled a fry aimlessly in her ketchup. "That's why I'm going to give you some more time to search for a bigger story. But it's got to be based on facts. We're not the mainstream media. We can't print wild speculations as truth and then hope everyone forgets we were wrong the next day."

– wild speculations
– Just trying to find something to publish

The need to publish lies in Academia

"I appreciate that, Iris," Gabe said sincerely, "and I don't want truth to become the first casualty of my story. And I'm not trying to take advantage of..."

Iris cut him off. "I know that, Gabriel. But while you're doing this extra investigating, I still want you to be writing up those articles on the daily lives of Winnipeg's street kids. *Mixed Berries* is coming out in a few weeks and we need articles for it. You got me?"

"Gotcha." He paused. "Aren't you afraid no one will understand the title and you'll end up in the Cooking and Gardens sections of bookstores?"

"God. I hope not." Full now. Iris lightly licked the tip of her finger and began dabbing at the loose crystals of salt on her plate. "We'll do lots of publicity to prevent that– television, radio, print – the works." She leaned forward excitedly. "And we'll have billboards with big bowls of raspberries, strawberries, and blackberries, and they'll say, '*Mixed Berries*, the more varied the berries, the sweeter the juice.' Our audience will get the message and even if others buy it by mistake, once they read it, they'll keep on reading."

Gabe forced himself to focus on her words and not on her quest to find every last speck of salt that had been left behind on her plate. "Still, you're taking a big chance with this magazine. They're always a risky investment."

She smiled as she wiped the grease off her hands with her napkin. "My baby stores are being franchised all over Canada." She crumpled up her napkin and pushed away her plate. "I took a big risk when I opened my first It Takes a Village but I knew that people would flock

Taking big risks

to a store that offered products from all over the world, and that donated a share of its profits back to the women in the Third World who made them and used them in their own cultures."

"I guess life's a gamble." Gabe spoke under his breath. He pushed his plate away from him as well. "Sometimes, you just have to go with your heart."

"Yeah, you do." Iris swatted his hand playfully. "And this magazine comes from my heart. It will provide a voice for people who are tired of mainstream messages. It's something I would have liked to read when I was trying to discover my place in the world."

"Me too." He wiped off his mouth roughly with his napkin. "That's why I'm so glad you asked me to write for it. I want to make you proud of me."

"I am." She swatted his hand a little harder than before. "But I want more progress on the story. Be a little more forceful in your investigation. See if there are any other ways or people to get information. Look at family and friends. Check police sources and find out if they're doing any investigations into the Loaves and Fishes. Because pretty soon, it'll be time to piss, shit, or get off the pot. You got me?"

"Gotcha." He paused. "Matthew seems to spend all of his time at the shelter. He doesn't seem to have a life. But, I think Janus might have a girl friend or at least a good female friend who might be worth investigating." He rubbed the back of his neck. "I think you'd like her. She dresses a bit like a hippie. Lots of colour. She also seems pretty talkative. I should be able to pump her for information without much effort."

Iris narrowed her eyes. "She sounds pretty cute."

Gabe nodded pseudo-innocently. "Purely coincidental, I assure you."

Iris groaned. "Just make sure that information is the only thing you pump her for."

"Iris," Gabe gasped, laughing.

"I mean it. Do your thinking for this story with the head on your shoulders not the one below your waist." She chuckled. "You know, my poor grandmother once told me that the way to a man's heart was through his stomach. Life has taught me that it's actually a few inches lower. Now get out there and get me a good story."

Gabe stood up, leaned over, and kissed her on her cheek. "It'll be well worth the wait." He leaned down to pick up the bill.

Iris waved him off. "I'll take care of it. You have a hippie to start pumping."

Gabe laughed and walked out to his car. He leaned up against it and looked for his keys. Piss, shit, or get off the pot. Strange. Why would I piss while sitting on a pot? Unless it was for a bet like trying to write my name in the snow while sitting down. Pretty awkward and messy though. Must be a woman thing. He got into his car and drove off.

Janus rolled off the couch and fell laughing onto the floor. "*Puppets Who Kill* is one sick show." He pulled himself into a sitting position and tried to remain straight-faced.

Cassie thumped the armrest of the couch for emphasis. "It's absolutely brilliant. I just can't believe Dan gives Buttons a rabbit to teach him how to love and then Dan kills the rabbit to make rabbit stew on Valentine's Day for everyone. He's one sick bastard."

Janus smirked. "Yeah. And he's the counsellor at the half-way house. The murderous puppets are the ones he's supposed to be trying to rehabilitate."

"All of them are sick. This is one subversive show."

Janus nodded. "That's why I love it. One of my favourite episodes is the one when Buttons is dating a flower child Wiccan and by the end of the episode, she's an evil Satanist. It's hilarious."

There was a loud fumbling at the door and then Cybele burst through, scattering the stack of newspapers left by the door for recycling.

"Eureka! Come my friends, dance with me the Dance of Joy." Cybele began dancing wildly, slapping her knees in the air, and then slapping her heels behind her back.

Janus leaned over to Cassie and stage-whispered, "Dance of Joy?"

"From *Perfect Strangers*," Cassie stage-whispered back, "remember Bronson Pinchot's series that he got after his bit part on Eddie Murphy's *Beverly Hills Cop*."

"Janus, Cassie, aren't you glad it's Wednesday? The day is almost done and that means the week is almost over. Weekend, here we come."

"Whoa Cyb. How much caffeine have you had today?" asked Janus.

"Only a couple cups of mochaccino. But enough questions now. Dance, puppets, dance."

Cassie began to dance the Dance of Joy opposite Cybele. Janus shrugged, got up, and began to dance his version of the Chicken Dance.

Cassie collapsed on the floor. "So, are you going to explain what that was all about, or do we get to guess?"

"Give me a minute." Cybele looked over at Janus and winked. "I've got to go and drain the lizard."

Janus threw himself on the sofa panting. "I hate to break it to you but you don't have a lizard."

Cybele laughed and began pirouetting towards the bathroom. "You're so wrong," she shouted back. "I'm the Incarnation of Cybele before the final apotheosis which rid her of all unneeded appendages." With a final twirl, she hip-slammed the bathroom door closed.

"Don't forget to wash your hands," Janus yelled at her.

"Wow. Someone's a little high on life today," said Cassie. She walked over to the newspapers and restacked them into a neat heap, a bit farther away from the doorway than before.

Janus rolled over and grabbed a cushion. "I think you mean on caffeine. Did you see how dilated her pupils were?" He hugged the cushion against his chest and curled his legs under him. "Maybe we should slip an Ativan into her next cup of coffee to calm her down."

Cassie took a quick look at the bathroom door. "Shhh. She's coming back."

"So, Cyb, what's up?" asked Janus.

"What's not?" She threw her hands exuberantly up in the air. "Sitting at the Second Cup this afternoon, while drinking the ambrosia of the gods…" Cybele slammed her hand down against the top of the television. "A lightning bolt came out of the sky and struck me with inspiration."

"Strange. I don't recall any lightning today." Janus turned to Cassie. "What about you?"

"Maybe it was a metaphorical bolt." Cassie nudged him over to make room for herself on the couch. "You know, like what Constantine saw on the Milvian Bridge."

"Aaah. A portent from the gods. Sunspots and ice crystals? Makes sense. It is summertime in Winnipeg. So," Janus said as he turned towards Cybele, "in what sign shall we conquer?"

Cybele playfully swiped his cushion. "The sign of the times – spiritual counselling," she replied. She threw the cushion lightly back at him.

Janus reached up, caught it, and hugged it possessively to him. "Cyb, my over-caffeinated chum, what the hell are you talking about?" he asked.

Cybele shuddered dramatically. "First of all, never call me chum. It reminds me of *Jaws* and how they were always chumming the waters to attract the sharks. I like to think I'm higher on the scale of being than rotten fish guts fishermen use for bait."

"Just above," joked Cassie. She nudged Janus. They high-fived each other.

Cybele determinedly ignored their teasing. "Second of all," she continued smoothly, "it's about what we can do to make money to help pay for the start-up costs for our little cult."

"Spiritual counselling?" asked Janus. He looked up interestedly. This could have real potential.

"For you. If you want to," said Cybele in a surprised voice. "Meditative counselling for me." Cybele looked beseechingly at Cassie. "And Cassie, if she wants to have a little fun with me."

Janus pulled uneasily at the stitching on his cushion. "But you and Cassie aren't really counsellors," he said hesitantly.

"Silly." Cybele brushed aside his qualms with an air of unconcern. "Anyone can call herself a counsellor. It's perfectly legal. She just can't pretend she has degrees in counselling if she doesn't because that would be fraud."

Becoming more fascinated by the prospect, Cassie leaned towards her. "Okay, but what exactly would we do?"

"It came to me today while I was watching television at the Second Cup. Yogi Bear and Booboo were stealing picnic baskets in Jellystone and I made the connection." Cybele clapped her hands together gleefully. "Yogi and yoga." like I used to.

Perplexed, Cassie looked at her. "You want us to dress up like Yogi and Booboo and teach yoga?"

The purpose of the cult is clear: MONEY

Not aware

"Could you imagine the reaction if we did?" Cybele slapped her hand against her forehead. "But no, that would be a trademark infringement. I'm sure we'd get sued. Besides, that would hardly help us spread the message of our cult which is a cult of Cybele and NOT a cult of Yogi Bear."

"Then what?" asked Janus. Damnit. Bring the plane in for the landing, Cyb.

These people are childish

Cybele fell gracefully onto the floor in a cross-legged position. "Cassie and I have both taken yoga for years. So, we start a class which basically steals some simple yoga moves, change them slightly, and rename them something like..." Cybele paused as she thought. "Hmmm. Like Cybelean Contemplative Motion. We can then attract a wide range of students who want to learn a new meditative, body and mind, technique, and charge them for the lessons."

"That's a really good idea," said Cassie in a slightly surprised voice. "And if we hold them in the cult house, then we'd have a very low overhead."

Cybele decided to ignore the surprise she had heard in Cassie's voice and continued unabated. "Especially, since they'd have to bring their own towels, mats, water bottles, etc."

"I like it. But what if they say something? What if they know its yoga?" asked Cassie fretfully.

Gods. Do I have to come up with everything? Doesn't anyone else have an iota of imagination? Or at least a LITTLE ability to bullshit. Cybele forced herself not to sound condescending. "We simply explain that all physical movements meant to connect human beings to their

Cybele has ideas and is motivated

spiritual selves are pretty similar since human body parts can only move in so many directions. That should shut up any troublemakers and if we incorporate some incense into our classes that should make them interesting and keep people coming back," replied Cybele. "You just have to have faith in my powers of persuasion."

"Powers of bullshit more like," Janus said mockingly.

"Hey, a rose by any other name," retorted Cybele.

Cassie brought their conversation back to the work that had to be done. "But, what about Janus? He doesn't know anything about yoga."

Cybele enthusiastically rocked back and forth. "He doesn't have to. He has real counselling experience. He can do religious counselling. You know - persuade people that the answer to their problems lies in reconnecting their spiritual and physical halves."

Janus tried to consider his position as he spoke. "I guess, I could sell our cult's philosophy in a slightly, but not overly underhanded way, through therapy sessions. And I don't have to mention our cult specifically because …"

"If you hold the counselling sessions in the cult house, then they'll automatically be exposed to our message," said Cassie, becoming swept up in a wave of enthusiasm.

"Exactly," said Janus.

Cybele shook her head uncomfortably. "But we have to make sure that people who come to you for this religious counselling know exactly what kind of religious counsellor you are. We don't want to mislead or manipulate people who might be expecting something else and feel betrayed when they arrive and realize what we are." She sighed. Damnit. Life would be so much easier if I was just a little more unscrupulous. "The best way to do that is put our cult's name on any and every flyer or advertisement we put out, so people know ahead of time what to expect."

"I agree," Cassie interjected. "I guess Mom was right. Honesty is the best policy."

"Yep," said Cybele. "Making money is fine but not doing harm is more important."

Janus shook his head in bemusement. "Boy, for a bunch of anti-establishment pagans, you two are sure fond of ego and superego imposed ethics. Whatever happened to free will, sex, drugs, and rock and roll?"

Cybele looked at him in disbelief. "I can't believe that you still don't understand what I've been trying to tell you about paganism."

Janus winced. Damnit. I tried to yank her chain and now she's going to subject me to another lecture. Life sucks.

Unaware of his inner turmoil, Cybele continued on with her lecture as she began to pace back and forth across the floor. "Actions have consequences. If you abuse power, that abuse will come back to haunt you. My motive for starting this cult might come out of a desire for profit but I'm not going to get it at the expense of others. I don't need to. In exchange for their money, I intend to give them back a sense of spirituality that they may not have in their lives already."

"*Mea culpa*," said Janus. Thank God. She hadn't gone on for too long this time. Note to self. Don't yank Cybele's chain when she's in an over-caffeinated state.

Cybele smiled forgivingly. "It's all right. You'll get paganism eventually."

With a mental jerk, Cassie brought herself back to the present. Ahh. Cybele's stopped pacing. The lecture must be over. "Speaking of getting members," Cassie said, although they had not, in fact, just been, "Where do you think we should advertise for them?"

Janus replied, "Definitely put up flyers at the U of M and the U of W. Then put up flyers around Portage Avenue. There are always lots of people around there."

Cassie patted Janus's shoulder. "Why don't you see if you can get some of the street kids you work with to help distribute the flyers? And as long as they're over eighteen, they can come to the meditative sessions as well."

"Good idea," agreed Cybele earnestly. "They could benefit from a little reconnective therapy. They always seem far too angry and alienated from the natural environment and their spiritual selves."

Janus stood up and stretched. "You know all these ideas are good but we might need to make more money to pay for our start-up costs - more than these ideas will earn."

As she began to come down from her caffeine high, Cybele sighed tiredly. "Gods. How do other cults pay for their expenses and still manage to make a profit?"

"Do you have any specific ideas in mind, Janus?" asked Cassie.

He began to crack his knuckles. "I'm thinking of something related to telemarketing but I haven't thought of anything specific yet."

"That's a good area to explore," said Cassie, "after all Winnipeg is the telemarketing capital of North America." She shook her head distractedly. "I'm sure I saw that on a billboard somewhere. Maybe religious counselling through a 1-800 number?"

"Just make sure it's not a psychic network. I don't want to end up indicted like poor Madame Rio," Cybele chimed in.

"I might need to do some research on how other religions raise money. I'll crunch some numbers and get back to you guys," Janus replied.

Cybele yawned. "Well, we'll leave that research in your capable hands. I'm beginning to crash from all this caffeine. How about we call it an evening?"

Wanting to get started on his research without any further interference from Cybele, Janus agreed. "Sounds like a plan. I'll see you guys later."

When he left, Cybele turned to go to bed, but Cassie gently caught her by the arm and stopped her.

Cybele gave her a puzzled look. "What's up, Cassie?" Wow. She looks like she has a bad case of indigestion.

Cassie bit her lower lip. "Cyb, I don't want you to take this the wrong way, but I think I got a little carried away tonight. Your excitement was so contagious that I was swept up in it."

She's very excited

Cybele blinked her eyes as she tried to focus on what Cassie was saying. "Okay. And now that the glow has faded, and reality has set in..."

Worried about hurting Cybele's feelings, Cassie blurted her words out as fast as she could. "I'll still help you with the initial yoga sessions but I don't really want to be intimately connected with this cult. My job at A Taste of Indulgence is a full-time commitment and I just don't have time to be a partner with you and Janus."

Cybele winced as her head began to explode. Memo to self. Drink less coffee tomorrow. She waved Cassie's words off a bit patronizingly. "It's okay, Cassie. Don't worry. I had a feeling you might start to get cold feet. You're not the kind of person who would be comfortable running a cult for profit." She rubbed her forehead. Gods. I'm beginning to see spots. "I would never ask you to compromise your beliefs." Wow. If it wasn't for the pain, this could be quite a psychedelic experience. She forced herself to continue speaking. "You know, it's not the pagan way."

Cassie sighed. "I have faith in you." Her eyes narrowed as she peered into Cybele's eyes. Although you do seem a little out of it, right now. "I'm just worried that not everyone may be as enlightened as you are and you could get hurt."

Cybele yawned. "Don't worry about me, Cassie. I'm the ultimate survivor. I'm a gambler." Singing under her breath, she walked away. "You gotta know when to run, when trouble, your way, comes..."

Cassie looked at her, sighed again, and then went off to bed herself.

Chapter 7

Cybele reached over the table and snagged another slice of bacon. "Thanks for inviting me over for brunch today, Janus. It's such a blessing not to spend my entire Sunday hearing Church bells."

"I guess it can get pretty irritating after a while. The musical equivalent of living beside a flashing neon light."

Cybele shuddered. "The horror. The horror." She took a bite out of her bacon. "It's just like on *Seinfeld* when that Kenny Rogers' fried chicken restaurant opens up outside their apartment and Kramer's room is always filled with that bright red light."

"Yeah. That was pretty funny. Especially when he became addicted to the chicken and couldn't stop eating it." Janus placed his fork protectively over his last slice of ham. "But, good as it is, I actually didn't invite you over to talk about fried chicken, believe it or not."

Cybele waved her bacon tauntingly at him. "Hey Ripley, aren't we breaking the stereotype here? I'm supposed to be the one who loves fried chicken. You're supposed to love olives and ouzo."

"You're the one who loves olives." Janus picked up his last slice of ham and casually waved it at her. She's such a salt addict. "Give me watermelon any day."

"Well, watermelon filled with ouzo is pretty good," said Cybele refusing to respond to his bait.

"Ah, well, since I'm only half Greek that must explain why I only like the ouzo."

Cybele rolled her eyes. "Oh yeah, that must be the logical explanation."

She's such a card. Janus laughed. "Okay, once watermelon comes into season, we can have a watermelon and ouzo party. I'll bring the Chicken Delight, you bring the kalamatas." He cleared his throat nervously and blurted out his words all at once. "Um. To get back to what I was saying before being so wilfully distracted. I. um." He scratched his face. "I've been doing some thinking, and I've come up with a great telemarketing idea."

"Which is?" asked Cybele impatiently. Gods. Get to the point.

Janus forced himself to look at Cybele. Note to self. Show no fear. Or she'll go for the jugular. "Well, we need something that will make a lot of money and still somehow be faithful to our message of empowerment and freedom from patriarchal constraints, right?"

Cybele looks at him warily. "Right. So, what issue are we dancing around, Janus?"

Janus walked over to his living room coffee table and returned with a piece of paper. He silently handed it to her.

Cybele read it over. Her mouth dropped open in disbelief. "Good gods. Tell me, you haven't already distributed this flyer around the city or put this advertisement in any of the papers."

"Well, as a matter of fact," replied Janus huffily, "I have. I think it's a great idea and it will definitely allow us just to sit back and rake in the money."

Cybele pushed her chair away from the table and stood up. "Oh, it's definitely a money-making idea all right. I'm just curious about what, handing out a flyer?

whether or not you've lost your mind." She threw up her arms in disbelief. "I don't think this idea is even legal much less completely moral and you know that the most important requirement for starting our cult was that we weren't going to break any laws."

Janus put his hands on his hips and glared at her. "As long as we get the proper licenses, it's completely legal, so I really don't know what your problem is. Instead of overreacting, think about this with a logical, less bourgeois attitude."

"How?" She waved the flyer under his nose. "Where did you get the inspiration for this brilliant gem?"

Annoyed, Janus grabbed the flyer out of her hands. "From you, actually."

"From me?" Cybele laughed disbelievingly. "I NEVER suggested we do this. It NEVER even occurred to me."

Janus looked at her pseudo-patiently. "Don't you remember when you were talking about Madame Rio and her psychic hotline? It made me think about late night television and the kinds of people who stay up to watch all those infomercials."

"I see." Cybele took a deep breath and slowly let it out. Note to self. Remain calm. Do not jump up and down in anger. Despite her best efforts, she spoke scornfully. "You thought of all those stupid *Girls Gone Wild* videos and those ridiculous shows with surgically ballooned women frolicking on beaches and begging lonely, horny guys to call their 1-800 numbers. Yep. Clearly, I gave you this idea when I told you we should not do a psychic hotline for fear of being indicted. All my idea."

Janus began to get angry. That's gratitude for you. "There's no need to be sarcastic. This is much better than YOUR idea of having me do religious counselling..." He crumpled up the flyer in his hand. "Whatever the hell that was supposed to be." He threw the crumpled ball across the room. "With the money we can make from this, you wouldn't even have to do those yoga rip-off classes."

Her feelings hurt, Cybele sank down in her chair. "Those yoga classes...by whatever name I called them...will give people a chance to achieve balance and harmony in their lives. They're meant to help people, not just make money for me."

Beginning to feel he had gone too far, Janus sat down beside her. "Well, my business will help people too."

"Really, do tell," said Cybele sarcastically.

Janus forced himself not to rise to her bait. I just need to speak her language to convince her I'm right. "All the callers will be able to achieve sexual ecstasy, which is a very important part of achieving balance and harmony in one's life, you know. In fact, the purpose of those orgiastic rituals, which the original Cybele worshippers held, was designed to do the same thing. You've told me a million times about the role of enthusiasm and ecstasy in pagan rites."

Cybele nodded her head slowly. "Yes. Ecstasy originally meant to go outside your body and enthusiasm meant to have the god come inside your body." She sighed. "No pun intended, of course. You couldn't have one without the other. But a phone sex operation, Janus? I'm just not sure it's a good idea."

"Why not?" Yes. I'm getting through to her. "Think about it. Religion and sex have always gone together."

Seeing Cybele's reluctant nod of agreement, Janus continued. "One is the repression of primal urges and the other is its expression. It's really no wonder ministers are always being caught with prostitutes or having affairs. It's just the natural order of things reasserting itself."

"The superego and ego battling the id, eh? A classic struggle throughout the aeons." She looked over at him and shook her head. "I see the point you're making but you should have consulted me before you started advertising this business. We're in this together as equal partners, remember?'

"You're right," said Janus apologetically. "I just got so excited about this idea that I couldn't wait to run it past you. Plus, I knew you would see its potential once we talked about it."

"Well, I definitely see its potential, but I'm still uncomfortable having our cult associated with it. I wanted to create a ritual that brought people back into touch with the natural world, not perpetuate alienation for people through an increasingly heavy reliance on technology."

Janus patted her on the shoulder. "Don't be such a Luddite, Cyb. Think of all the people we can reach through this business. We can advertise as an encounter session in which callers can explore their religious and sexual fantasies with amateur but open-minded counsellors of sexual healing in a safe and accepting environment.

How can encouraging openness and allowing people to get in touch with their innermost feelings be a bad thing?"

Cybele rolled her eyes. "I guess it's true," she said mischievously, "the devil can quote Scripture for his own ends."

"Ouch. Come on. You know you're totally against censorship. We'd be encouraging free speech and the open exchange of..."

"Bodily fluids," said Cybele, unable to resist another jab. "Okay. You've made your point. It's a great idea. But you know, this is something probably only men will do, so we'll need to hire female operators to answer the phones."

"Don't be so sexist. I'm sure there are lots of women wanting to explore their sexual fantasies."

"Oh. I didn't say there weren't," said Cybele sardonically. "But, the essential difference between men and women is that women don't like to throw away their hard earned money for something they can get for free. That's why women usually don't pay for prostitution. They can get sex by walking into any bar pretty much anytime they want."

"Good point. I hadn't thought of that."

Cybele smirked. "Well, let's hope that's the last thing you haven't thought of concerning this business idea."

"Meow," said Janus playfully, hoping to tease her out of her bad mood.

Cybele glared at him and then relented and laughed. "So, have you received any responses to these ads yet?"

"Not yet." Janus walked across the room and picked up the crumpled flyer. "But I only put them in yesterday." He began to smooth out the wrinkles.

"Well, when you do, I want to be part of the interviewing process." She rubbed her chin thoughtfully. "Have you thought about creating a bible of sexual fantasies – a template for our operators to follow, in case they don't have an overactive imagination?"

Janus flashed a triumphant smile. "We don't have to. I managed to get a copy of one from a friend of mine – you know Falstaff - who did his thesis on escort agencies in Vancouver. He lifted it from one of the escorts. It's pretty interesting, a wealth of information."

"Okay. Great." She reached up to grab the flyer from his hands and re-read it. "Why don't you make copies and give me one to read, so I can see what the first official bible of our cult will be." She stood up. "I have a million errands to run today so I'd better get going. See you later." She walked to the front door, and then deliberately turned to wave the flyer in front of him. "Keep me informed of ANYTHING new that comes up."

"Of course." Janus closed the door behind her and walked back into the kitchen. God. You think she would have been a little more appreciative of all the time and effort I spent trying to turn this brilliant idea into reality. She's too damn bloody conservative for someone who's supposed to be a free-spirited pagan. Hypocrite. He cracked his knuckles. But I knew I could convince her that I was right. I just have to speak her language.

Chapter 8

Cybele walked into A Taste of Indulgence where Cassie was waiting on a customer. Cybele moved over to the display case and began lightly running her ring finger in an aimless circle around and around the decal of a little bride and groom on top of a wedding cake. Ah. Pygmalion. Why did you have to keep trying to change me? She started as Cassie came up and touched her on her hand.

"Hey. What's up? I know how you feel about the sexist customs in most traditional weddings but that's no reason to try and rub out the bride and groom. Plus, I'm the one Marie Antoinette is going to make clean off those fingerprints."

Cybele shook her head and smiled wanly. "Sorry. Where is the Wicked Witch of the Gateway to the West, anyway?"

"She's out delivering some cakes. For some reason, everybody wants to be a June bride."

"Yeah." Cybele groaned. "Go figure. Fifty percent of marriages end in divorce and yet people still feel this compulsion to go out in the world two by two. And they think nothing of going into huge debt to pay for something that's really nothing more than a big party." She lightly punched the decal of the groom, focussing on his head. "Maybe they should spend some of that money on therapy to make sure they're ready to spend the rest of their lives stuck sharing bathroom space with some person who'll probably never leave the seat down, leave little hairs all over the sink, and somehow never seem to manage to refill the toilet paper roll."

Cybele looked up at Cassie and shrugged. "Sorry. I didn't mean to go on a rant. Just had a bit of a bad morning. Felt the urge for an emotional purging. Thought of you. She giggled. "Of course."

Laughingly, Cassie shook her head. "Of course. And I'm truly flattered that the thought of purging yourself made you think of me. So, what's put you in such a mood?"

Cybele rolled her eyes. "Well, I just came from brunch with Janus, and I found out what his big plan is for us to make money."

Wow. Cyb looks like she just sucked a lemon. This ought to be good. "And you don't think it's a good idea?" asked Cassie in a pseudo-innocent voice.

Cybele nervously tapped the top of the display case. "Oh, I think it will make money but I definitely don't think it's a good idea."

Trying not to laugh, Cassie asked, "Well, are you going to make me guess?"

With a sigh of resignation, Cybele gave up the information. "Religious sexual fantasy telephone counsellor."

Cassie grabbed her stomach and bent over with laughter. "Did you say 'Religious sexual fantasy telephone counsellor '?"

"Oh yeah." Cybele began to smile. "Apparently, I'm moving up in the world. From graduate student to cult leader to telephone pimp."

"What made him decide on phone sex?" asked Cassie as tears began to fall from her eyes.

"Apparently, I gave him the idea when I brought up the psychic hotline."

"Well," Cassie said, as she wiped away her tears, "I've always said the quiet ones are the most repressed."

Cybele shook her head as she saw Cassie trying to stop laughing. "I'm pretty sure I'm the one who's always said that."

"Then clearly, you're psychic because I'm always thinking it. Hmmm." Cassie bit down on her thumb to force herself to focus. "Is it even legal to set up that kind of business in Manitoba?"

"I'm not sure." Cybele became more interested as they started to explore the potential of Janus's idea. "But look at all those chat lines. They always give local numbers. I'm sure sex comes up in those conversations."

"True. And don't forget that Janus knows all the tricks of running a business and getting licenses. He'll find a way to get this religious sexual fantasy telephone counsellor thing up and running," said Cassie reassuringly.

Cassie waited expectantly for Cybele to continue their banter but Cybele seemed oblivious to the opening Cassie had given her.

Cassie shook her head in disbelief. "Poor Cybele, when you pass up the chance to make sexual innuendoes, I know you're upset." Cassie walked behind the display case and returned with a plate of cookies. "Some Imperials will make you feel better. They're hot out of the oven."

Cybele leaned up against the wall and began to munch on one. With her first bite, she began to feel better. "You know, it's not that I'm against the idea of phone sex. I just never imagined myself operating that kind of business. I feel like I'm exploiting the women who work there and the men who call in."

"You're not." Cassie waved her cookie to emphasize the point she was making. "The men who call in are no more being exploited than if they bought a Playboy or rented a porno movie. They're just looking for a quick fix."

Cybele took another bite and let the warm cookie dissolve in her mouth. Mmmm. Sugar and butter. What a combination. "Well, what about the women?"

Cassie popped the last piece of cookie in her mouth. "You're giving them jobs. Allowing them to make a living just by talking. How hard a life is that?"

Cybele sighed. "I know that, in theory, but reality is always different."

Cassie smiled at her affectionately. "Do you know what your real problem is?"

"Why do I think I'm about to find out?" Cybele said as she wiped the crumbs off her mouth.

"You are the most wildly romantic person I know. Idealism seeps through every pore of your body."

(Caring. It does matter because of identity)

Cybele's head snapped up in surprise. "I think you must be smelling the garlic sausage that I ate this morning."

Cassie shook her head knowingly. "Laughter is a defensive mechanism."

Cybele rubbed the back of her neck. "Thank you, Freud. Shouldn't you be salivating over a cigar right now?"

Cassie wagged her finger at her. "You've just proven my point, Cyb."

"Touché. Okay." Cybele looked curiously at Cassie. 'What makes you think I'm such a hopeless, helpless romantic?"

"You believe in the best of people. You want them to live up to their potential within. Cassie looked carefully at Cybele to gauge her level of acceptance. "How many times have I heard you quote Yoda when he says, 'luminous beings are we, not this crude matter'?"

Oh. Damn. I think Cassie might be right. How the hell could she see what I couldn't? Cybele bit the bottom of her lip. "Probably a million times. But I'm really cynical about people, Cassie. I'm not a romantic."

Cassie took another cookie off the plate and began to munch on it. Mmmm. So good. She looked over at Cybele. "Beneath the heart of a cynic, lies the pain of a frustrated idealist. Humanity has disappointed you so many times that now you don't even want to admit your hope that it will transcend pettiness and become what you believe it was meant to be."

Surprised, Cybele looked over at her. "I've never heard you speak like that before, Cassie." She reached over and grabbed a cookie for herself.

Cassie laughed. "That's because normally, I don't have to cheer you up. You're usually like a firecracker that's just gone off."

Cybele raised an eyebrow. "Well, I've always been fond of big bangs and dramatic climaxes."

"Aha. A sexual joke. You're feeling better."

She smirked. "I yam what I yam. As Sally Fields would say, 'You like me, you really like me.'" She began pacing around the shop. "You know what really bothers me about this whole religious sexual fantasy telephone counsellor thing is that Janus did it behind my back. He started advertising for workers without even telling me first. He had to know it was something I would have a problem with." She stopped and stamped her foot. "Damn it. We should have talked about it first."

"Did you talk to him about that?"

"Yeah. He said he thought he was doing me a favour by getting everything set up and presenting it as a *fait accompli*."

"Well," said Cassie as she tried to think of a way to resolve the problem, "then chalk it up to a miscommunication and just keep a closer eye on him to ensure it doesn't happen again."

"Oh," Cybele said quite firmly, "I will." She hesitated for a moment. "It's just that..."

"What?" What else could be bothering her? Is there something she's not telling me?

Cybele reached over and casually grabbed a third cookie. I need this fix. "Well, part of me feels like such a hypocrite."

Cassie looked puzzled. "Why?"

Cybele groaned as she licked jam and icing off her finger. "Because here I am this big defender of free speech and advocate of sexual freedom and I act like such a bourgeoisie about the idea of phone sex."

Cassie chuckled incredulously. "Cyb, you weren't bothered by the idea of phone sex." Even I know better than that. She handed Cybele a napkin and indicated that she should wipe the corner of her mouth. "You were worried at the thought that you might become an exploiter, a collaborator within the system of oppression you want to overthrow."

"Yes." Cybele's face lit up. "Like what Kira had to do when Bajor signed that Treaty of Non-Aggression with the Dominion and she had to work with the Cardassians." Cybele dabbed the napkin haphazardly over her mouth. "Kira became one of the people she had despised while fighting in the Bajoran resistance against the Cardassian Occupation of Bajor."

Yes. She's made the connection. Cassie smirked. Funny how she can see the truths in TV but not about herself. Okay. I know where to go from here. Cassie grabbed Cybele's crumpled napkin and tossed it into the nearby garbage. "Right. Eventually, she had trouble looking at herself in the mirror and had to become part of the Resistance again."

"Well, I guess I have to make sure it never comes to that point for me." Cybele shook her head. "I just hate being hoisted on my own petard. Here I am, this free-spirited pagan who goes around pontificating on the insanity of our vice laws and I still haven't broken completely free of patriarchal control. I've internalized it."

Cassie smiled reassuringly. "Hey, you're a pagan, not an anarchist, and like all of us, you're a work in progress."

"I know." Cybele thumped her hand on the display case. "I still believe that it's ridiculous for women to be able to walk into any bar they want, have sex with as many people as they want, but it's illegal if they want to charge for the use of their body."

Not that women particularly enjoy sex

"I agree," said Cassie, who was trying not to laugh at Cybele's earnestness. "It's just another example of women being underpaid for their work in a patriarchal society."

"Yep. I guess the difference is that it's one thing to believe that women should have control over their own bodies and sell themselves if they want to, and another to be the one running a business that takes a percentage of the profits from their work." Cybele began to poke the groom decal harder and harder with her index finger.

Cassie winced. Gods. Get over Pygmalion, already. She pushed Cybele gently away from the display case. "It's different because if women are the entrepreneurs, then you don't really believe they're being exploited. They're the ones in control. But if they're working for you, then you're the one in control, and you then become a potential exploiter."

"Maybe," said Cybele thoughtfully, "I'm just afraid of power." She began to gnaw on her bottom lip.

"Don't be." Cassie winked at her. "Just remember that with great power comes great responsibility."

"I will, Spiderm'am." Hmmm. This could work. Cassie's deeper than I thought.

Cassie looked at her watch and groaned. "Damn. It's getting late. I should probably get some work done now before Her Royal Highness gets back."

"I'd better get going too. Do some window-shopping while the stores are still open." Cybele walked to the door and stopped. She turned and gave Cassie a quick wave of thanks. "Maybe I should rename you Petra. Have you become the rock upon which I will build my cult."

Cassie watched as Cybele left. She shook her head and then went back to decorating wedding cakes. She sighed. May you live in interesting times. Mercedes Lackey had it right. It was the greatest curse of all.

Janus sat working in his office at the Loaves and Fishes. What a wonderful way to spend a Saturday morning. God. I hate this job. I need to get a more exciting life. He laughed bitterly. I need to get a life.

There was a hesitant knock at the door. He sighed. More problems on two feet no doubt. "Come in."

Janus looked up to see four of the residents walk in looking angry. Janus motioned for them to take the seats in front of his desk. He carefully shut down his laptop and then turned to them.

"Tan Talus, Ardiaeus Peters, Ixion Smith, and Ajax Lister, the Fab Four. So, what can I do for you, young men?"

Tan spoke up first. "It's Matthew, man. All he does is boss us around and give us a hard time."

Ixion broke in. "Yeah. Just because we were smoking in the back parking lot and drinking some beer, he had to hassle us."

Ardiaeus snapped. "Like, where does he get off. It's not like we were smoking pot or shooting up. Like, give us a break."

Janus turned to Ajax who was squirming in his chair. "And what's your version, Ajax?"

In his usual irritating way, Ajax immediately began to complain. "He's always picking on us. Always trying to make us do stuff around here."

"This is a shelter not a hotel," said Janus exasperatedly. "If you want to live here, you have to follow the rules. You know that Matthew doesn't want you smoking and drinking on the premises, so don't. If you want to do those sorts of things, just make sure you're out of his sight."

"Man, why can't Matthew be cool like you?" said Tan as he tapped his foot in frustration.

Janus smirked. "That's because Matthew cares about you, thinks you have the potential to change your life around." He reached into his desk drawer and pulled out several chocolate bars. He tossed them to the boys. "On the other hand, I don't really know. That's why I don't hassle you. I say, live and be free. What's the point of life if you can't have fun?"

Unaware that Janus was serious, the boys laughed and began to rip open the bars.

"So, what's your punishment?" asked Janus as he stood up and began to stretch his back.

Tan sniggered. "Talking to you and we have to help wash dishes in the kitchen and help serve the meals today."

"And we have to clean the bathrooms tonight." Ajax continued to whine as he delivered the rest of his complaints. "Living here is like living in a prison. With all these rules, it's worse than living at home."

"Don't do the crime, if you can't do the time." Janus paused. Guess this is as good a time as any. "Say how'd you like to do a little work for me?"

"Anything would be better than washing dishes and cleaning toilets," said Ixion, interested.

Janus shook his head. "No. You'd still have to do your punishment chores. That is if you still want to continue living here. Matthew's house, Matthew's rules. I was thinking of some extra work that I would pay you for."

"Like putting up more flyers, man?" asked Talus.

"Eventually." Janus nodded. "But right now a friend of mine is starting up her own business and needs some help fixing up the place. It's twenty-five dollars a day and I'll provide the pizza and drinks."

"Beer?" asked Ixion, hopefully.

Janus sat back down and looked at them sternly. "Pop. I don't want you getting drunk on the job." He paused thoughtfully. "On the other hand, I don't take care if you go outside to take smoke breaks as long as you get your work done."

"Sounds like a plan," said Tan. "We're in."

"What kind of business are we talking about?" asked Ajax, slightly more cautiously.

Janus shrugged his shoulders nonchalantly. "Some new age, alternative, spiritual movement. I don't really know all the details. I'm just helping her out a little."

Tan decided to reassert his leadership role within the group. "Sounds cool. We're in." He glared over at Ajax who reluctantly shut up.

"Great," said Janus. Now I need to ensure that they won't blab everything the minute they leave. As he spoke, Janus looked directly at Tan. "Might be better not to advertise that you're working for my friend. Some of the others might try to cut you out for the jobs. And Matthew might not be too thrilled that you're working for a pagan."

Ardiaeus grimaced. "Yeah, like he might try harder to save us."

"That would suck big time," agreed Ixion.

Ignoring them, Janus wrote down the address on a piece of paper and handed it to Tan. "I want you all there tomorrow at 10 a.m. Don't let me down."

Tan carefully folded the paper and put it into his pocket. "We won't." He walked to the door, stopped, and turned around. "Hey, Janus, this pagan friend of yours, is she like a Satanist?"

Ardiaeus broke in. "Man, that would be so cool. Black masses and ritual sacrifices. My parents would be so pissed if I became a Satanist."

Ajax chuckled at the idea. "My parents would probably spend all their time in church praying for my soul."

"Trust me," said Janus. "She's the furthest thing from a Satanist you'll ever meet. And if you have any sense, you won't bring that topic up when you meet her."

"Why?" Ixion asked curiously. "Will she put a hex on us?"

"Is she a witch like from *The Wizard of Oz?* Like the one the house fell on who had the red shoes or is she like the good witch who helped Dorothy?" asked Ajax.

God. I'm surrounded by fools. Janus forced himself to answer patiently. "She's not a witch and she won't put a hex on you. But she will sit you down and talk *ad nauseam* about the difference between paganism and Satanism until your ears start bleeding and you want to fake a heart attack to get her to stop. And if she's had a couple of mochaccinos then, like the Energizer bunny, she just won't quit. You'll begin to wish she was a Satanist because then at least she'd eventually kill you."

Tan shook his head in disbelief. "She sounds like some of the teachers I had in high school before I dropped out. They would never shut up either. That's why I finally stopped going. Had better things to do with my life."

"Just think, if you hadn't made that decision, you wouldn't be lucky enough to live your life like this. Complete freedom and no stupid teachers telling you how to live your life," said Janus, knowing they wouldn't see the irony of what he was saying.

"You got that right," Tan said.

"Right." Janus stood up. Time to get some peace and quiet. "Now, you have some chores to do. You don't want to give Matthew a reason to give you more for tomorrow."

The boys left the room and Janus carefully closed the door behind them. He sat down behind his desk and began to review the faxed resumes he had received at his home office. So many applicants for positions as phone sex operators. Who would have thought there would be this kind of interest? I should start setting up interviews soon. Don't want Cybele to have a cow again so I'd better call her to let her know. Mindless peons. I am so much better than this life. I just need a chance to prove it. By the time I'm done, this cult will be bigger than anything else. We'll be making money hand over fist. Scientology will be nothing but a long forgotten memory compared to mine. Achates will be sorry he said I was a loser.

Chapter 9

Another day, another dollar. One more day to Wednesday and then the week is almost half over. Cybele slowly walked up the driveway to Janus's guesthouse. She sighed. I don't want to go in and have to start interviewing applicants for this damn phone sex operation. Maybe I should just make some excuse and leave. This is Janus's baby. He should be the one to change the dirty diapers. No. This cult has my name on it. I am responsible. I must do my duty.

She stopped right before the doorway. I wonder if it's too late to give up this whole idea. Go back to not writing my thesis. She shook her head. No. I have to take this chance. Make a change in my life. Properly managed, this cult could be a force for spiritual good in the world. I just have to keep believing that. That will be the light at the end of this tunnel. She sighed again. I wonder if L. Ron Hubbard ever felt this way. Well, no one ever said starting a religion is easy. She laughed. Actually, come to think of it, I can't think of anyone who ever started a religion who had it easy. Makes sense. It's hard enough to get people to change their brand of coffee or favourite beer, much less their brand of religion.

She walked through the door and towards the little bedroom that had been turned into her office. Time to see if anyone else has faxed in any more resumes for these jobs.

Janus walked out of the bedroom on the opposite side of the hallway that served as his office. "Cybele, you're in early this morning."

Cybele turned towards Janus. "Just came in to do some paperwork and then get ready for the applicants coming in this afternoon."

Janus hesitated. "So, you're sure you want to sit in on the interviews?"

"I feel that I should. We are in this together."

"Right." He paused. "Look. I know you're uncomfortable with this idea. Why don't you just leave it up to me?" He patted her on the shoulder. "You can trust me to do the right thing."

"I do trust you," said Cybele, "but I need to do this." She rolled her eyes. "After all, if I'm going to star in my own cult, I should be able to hire phone sex operators. So, when are the first applicants coming in?"

Janus glanced through the front window as he spoke. "Actually, I've scheduled some to begin in half an hour. They should be here soon."

"Good." Cybele rubbed the back of her neck as she looked around. "So, where do you think we should do the interviews?"

"Hmm. Why don't we have them wait in the dining room and then do the actual interviews in my office since it's bigger than yours?" suggested Janus.

"Great idea." Cybele walked into the kitchen. "I'll just make some coffee while we're waiting."

Janus followed her inside. "Sounds like a plan."

"You know." Cybele paused as she looked for where Janus had hidden the sugar. Aha. Found it. "One thing we must really make clear to our applicants is that this is strictly religious sexual fantasy telephone counselling. They can't be making appointments over the phone for private meetings between customers and clients. The last thing we need is to be accused of running a brothel."

"No Mustang Ranch, eh?"

Cybele swatted him on the head. "Absolutely not. And I'm pretty sure that Mustang Ranch went out of business. I think they didn't pay their taxes and the IRS got them."

"Tax evasion." Janus smirked. "Wasn't that how they brought down Capone?"

"I'm not sure." Cybele handed him a cup of coffee. "But the important lesson to learn is always pay your taxes. Never give the government an excuse to shut you down."

"Don't worry." Janus patted her reassuringly on the shoulder. "I've got the proper licenses for everything and I'll make sure all our taxes are paid."

"Good." Cybele took a sip and screwed up her face. Gods. How old were Janus's beans. She gasped. "No tax revolters here."

Janus gave her a strange look. What the hell's wrong with her now? "Just tax revulsers."

Cybele laughed and began to lighten up. "I can't believe we're actually starting a cult."

"I know. It's so cool. Something very few people in the world have done successfully." He took a sip of his coffee and tried not to spit it out. Yuck. What the hell had happened to the beans? He gamely swallowed. "We're going to be so awesome at it." I can't wait for the games to really begin.

"You're right." Cybele raised her cup and was about to take another sip when she stopped. Gods. Have I lost my mind? I can't drink this crap but Janus is so damn touchy about his beans. I don't want to upset him now that we've made up. She faked a swallow and then looked over at Janus. "We're not doing anything illegal or immoral. Let's have some fun with these interviews and with the whole phone sex business."

Janus looked over at her and smiled. I can't believe she's drinking this crap. So much for her taste in coffee. "You're on."

They both turned as they saw shadows moving across the dining room window. The doorbell rang.

Cybele took a deep breath and slowly let it out. "One small step for Woman, one giant leap for Humankind.

Janus laughed and went to answer the door. Three very different women walked in looking both excited and nervous at the same time.

"You're here to apply for the job to be a telephone solicitor?" asked Cybele as she gave them a reassuring smile.

They nodded.

Janus closed the door and came back towards them. "Would you like some coffee before we begin the interview process?" Oh. Wait. The coffee. Damnit.

Cybele's eyes widened. Oh. Damn. Say no. They'll think we're trying to poison them.

"Oh, I'm too excited to drink anything," said the one who looked like a red-headed Tinker Bell.

"Me too," said the second dark-haired woman, who looked like Hathor from *Stargate SG-1*.

"Actually, would it be all right if we were interviewed together?" said the third women, a dead ringer for Julianne Moore in her role as Clarice Starling from *Hannibal*.

Janus looked perplexed. "Why do you want to be interviewed together? Are you friends?"

"Actually, we're sisters," said the Hathor look-alike.

"Oh," Cybele said, "that's certainly not what we expected."

Tinker Bell spoke up decisively. "I'm Thalia Vervain." She pointed to the Julianne Moore look-alike. "That's Euphrosyne Benzoin."

"And I'm Aglaia Plumeria," said the dark-haired woman.

"Well, interviewing you together shouldn't be a problem. By the way, I'm Cybele Moondragon and this is Janus Styx. We're the owners of this business."

Janus gestured towards his office. "Why don't we all go into my office and get started."

Janus sat down behind his desk. Cybele sat in a chair beside him. Thalia, Euphrosyne, and Aglaia sat in chairs in front of them.

"So, what kind of business place is this?" asked Aglaia curiously. "The brass sign on the door said 'The Mysteries of Cybele.'"

Cybele looked over at Janus before answering. "It's actually a multi-faceted business. Part spiritual, part mundane."

Janus nodded his head in agreement. Better be her faithful little echo. "Your participation, if you are hired, will be in the more mundane, but nevertheless, highly important aspect of our organization."

"You see," said Cybele as her face began to light up with enthusiasm, "we are in the business of re-introducing a new spiritual belief system to the world. It goes back to prehistorical times, but it died out when matriarchal governance was subjugated by patriarchal rule."

Janus chimed in as he saw the bewilderment on the faces of the sisters. Better dumb it down for the proles. "It's based on the Mystery religion of Cybele which is slowly becoming more prevalent in the world today."

"So, we'll be working for a religious organization?" asked Thalia doubtfully.

"I'm sorry. That wasn't the impression we got from reading your flyer," said Aglaia raising an eyebrow.

"No," giggled Euphrosyne. "We thought we were answering an ad for a business that needed phone sex operators."

Cybele laughed a bit uncomfortably. "Well, actually, we prefer the term religious sexual fantasy telephone counsellor."

Janus glared over at Cybele. Damnit. Just keep things at a level they can relate to. "Well, in essence that is what you'll be. But since you will be part of a subsidiary business of The Mysteries of Cybele, we like to couch what we are doing in more religious terms."

"That's okay. We like euphemisms too," said Thalia confidingly.

"Yes," agreed Aglaia, "it's always fun to reshape the reality of our jobs by redefining our job descriptions."

Euphrosyne broke out in a fit of giggles. "In fact, all of us used to be escorts for Around the World With Eighty Ladies."

"Well, escort is a euphemism, of course, for what we actually did," said Thalia.

"That's great," said Cybele hesitantly. Oh dear. "But, here with us, we would expect your contact with callers to be strictly over the phone. No giving out personal information or arranging private, hands-on sessions."

Aglaia nodded serenely. "Oh, that's no problem. We're out of the escort business. We got married and our husbands didn't want us to see other men."

"Well, other than them," said Thalia with a knowing wink. "They were actually escorts whom we married. Like Julia Roberts in *Pretty Woman*."

Euphrosyne laughed a little snootily. "Well, except Julia Roberts played a street prostitute and we were definitely a cut above that."

"Well, that's wonderful." Unsure where to take the conversation, Cybele tried to sound properly motivating. "You clearly have lots of valuable experience and would be an asset to our organization." Either that or I'll be arrested for pandering.

Janus looked over at Aglaia, Thalia, and Euphrosyne. "Why don't we talk some more about what the requirements for this job are?"

Cybele began to regain her equilibrium at interviewing such enthusiastic experts. "Yes. That's a good idea, Janus."

"We have a bible of sexual fantasies that we have put together that you are expected to be familiar with. If there are any fantasies which you do not wish to talk about, we will need to know before we set you up with a caller," Janus said.

"Yes." Cybele leaned forward to examine the sisters' reactions closely. "You MUST be comfortable improvising, because not everything will be covered in the bible."

Aglaia gave Cybele a knowing look. "Oh, that's no problem, dear. We're quite used to mirroring back the words our clients use, in order to heighten their fantasy."

"Actually, you might find this even easier than creating fantasies in a more purely physical environment," said Janus.

"Exactly," said Cybele as she became more confident in her role as interviewer. Her natural enthusiasm began to take over. "For instance, since the caller cannot see you, you can pretend to be whomever he wants. The best way to do that is if he asks you what you look like, don't tell him right away. Instead, ask what he thinks you look like and play off that image."

Not bad, Cyb. Janus nodded approvingly. "Just be off slightly enough so that he thinks you really look like the description you're giving," he said.

"That makes sense." Thalia tilted her head back and thought of an example. "If he thinks I'm 5'8'', I'll just pretend to be 5'7'', but wearing heels."

This one's no fool. Janus smiled. "Perfect."

Euphrosyne cheerily rocked back and forth in her chair. "I guess it helps that we're not exactly amateurs in this type of business."

"Absolutely," said Janus. What enthusiasm! She's a natural.

Aglaia looked over once more at Cybele. "So, how exactly would this business operate?"

Janus immediately broke in to detail the specifics. "If you are hired, we would have the call system so that all initial calls come here first. We take the caller's credit card number and find out what kind of sexual fantasy he wishes to confess and explore in greater detail. Then we forward the call to your own home on a separate line. You take care of the fantasy and then we charge them for however long you spend with them."

"And how much will we be making per caller?" asked Thalia.

Cybele looked over at her to judge her reaction. "You will be making a percentage of what the caller is charged."

Janus chimed in. "Twenty percent. So, if a caller spends 5 minutes with you on the phone, you will receive four dollars. That's not bad for five minutes work."

"Plus," said Cybele, "you will be working in the convenience and privacy of your own home. No one will have to know what you are doing and you never have to leave your home."

Janus looked over at the sisters. "So, is that something you would be comfortable doing?"

"Sounds pretty good," said Thalia. "We're just looking for a part-time job, something to keep us busy while our husbands are away."

"Yeah." Aglaia winked conspiratorially. "You know, rocking the cradle of civilization and keeping the world safe for private enterprise. And we just couldn't get excited about selling cookware or cosmetics."

"No," Euphrosyne said sassily, "We'd thought we'd go with our strengths."

Cybele couldn't help but chuckle at the sisters' effervescence. "Well, that's great." She paused warningly. "There will be a six month probationary period but I have a good feeling about all of you."

Janus looked over at the sisters. "We have to do some more interviewing today and tomorrow, but we'll get back to you with more specifics, signs to form etc. We just won't be making formal job offers until the interview period is officially over."

Everyone stood up. Cybele escorted the sisters to the door, while Janus remained behind in the office.

Cybele ran back to Janus and gave him a quick hug. "Gods. You were so right, Janus. This is going to be a great money-maker. Those sisters are perfect."

"Not feeling so guilty now, eh?" Janus forced himself not to sound smug. "No more qualms about being the great exploiter."

Cybele playfully swatted him on the shoulder. "No." She paused. "You know, I think you have everything in hand. I'll leave the rest of the interviewing to you while I get started working on the information that we can put on our web site."

Janus gave her a gentle push towards the door. "Good plan. May as well divide and conquer."

Cybele blew him a kiss and left for home.

Janus walked over to close the door. Yep. I knew this was a brilliant idea. I can't wait to see what happens next. So many opportunities, so little time. With a complacent smile, he started preparing for the next round of interviews.

Cybele walked through her apartment door four hours later and did a truncated version of the Dance of Joy. Yippee! Everything's starting to fall together. The phone sex business looks like it really might work and all those flyers promoting Cybelean Contemplative Motion should attract lots of people to my cult. She walked over to the kitchen and packed away the groceries she had bought. Probably should put the pizza in now to cook so it's ready when Cassie gets home.

She slid the pizza into the oven and then walked over to her laptop sitting on the coffee table. She sighed. I should probably get started on writing the copy for the web site. She flipped on the television to the Space Channel and began to work on her promotional materials for the web store.

There was a slight noise outside the door and Cassie walked in.

"Hey, Cassie. How was your day?"

"Oh, pretty good. No difficult customers. Always a plus. So, how did your first set of phone sex interviews go?"

Half-embarrassed at how well the interviews had gone, Cybele tried to avoid showing too much glee. "Our first set of interviews for religious sexual fantasy telephone counsellors went great, thank you very much."

"Oh really?" said Cassie as she dropped her bag by the door and walked into the kitchen.

Cybele followed her. "Yes. Actually, it was kind of fun," said Cybele as she reached into the fridge for two cans of diet Coke. "I only stayed for a little while but it was clear that Janus had everything under control." She tossed one of the cans at Cassie.

Cassie caught it and pressed the cold can against the back of her neck. "Ahh. That feels good. It was so hot outside." She opened it and took a gulp. "So, have you kissed and made up?"

"Yes." Cybele took a sip of her Coke. "His idea was a good one. It just took some getting used to it. But I think it might be very profitable."

"So, does that mean no more yoga classes?"

"No." Cybele leaned against the counter and took another sip. "I'm really looking forward to teaching a class on contemplative motion. I don't just want to make money. I also want to give something back to the community."

"Just out of curiosity, how does phone sex do that?" said Cassie as she looked inquiringly at Cybele. "Other than underwriting the costs of running the cult."

Cybele replied defensively. "Well, I think we should donate a portion of the profits from both the phone sex business and the web site business to good causes. Plus, if we make a point of saying that on the web site, people might be more likely to buy something. You know, make a donation while buying something you want anyway."

"It's always nice to see altruism and profit go hand-in-hand," said Cassie smoothly. "So, what else are you up to?"

Cybele exhaled frustratedly. "Trying to come up with some ideas for a mission statement for the web site. I want to include something about environmental awareness on it."

"Why?" Cassie looked puzzled. She took a long gulp of her diet Coke. Ohh. Ice cream head. With an effort, she forced herself to continue. "Isn't the web store going to be just, like, for magic herbs and potions, stuff like that?"

"Well, to a point," said Cybele. "But I also want it to serve as an ad for the cult itself. So, I definitely need to have a warning on the site reminding people that if they want to use magic to harm or manipulate people, this is not the site for them."

"That's a good plan," said Cassie relieved that Cybele was making some attempt to screen out kooks and weirdoes. "But don't forget to have a disclaimer that everything sold on the site is for entertainment purposes only. You don't want to end up like poor Madame Rio."

"Good point." Cybele paused thoughtfully. "But I also want to make the connection that how we interact with our physical environment is an important part of our spiritual awakening process."

"You're not going to get involved with the environmentalists, are you?" asked a dumbfounded Cassie. She began to burp. Damnit. That always happens when I drink too fast. "You know..." She spoke to Cybele between ever-increasing burps. "A lot of them are pretty radical and that could definitely cause you problems in the long run."

Cybele looked defiant but resolute. Gods. Take a deep breath or chug some water. "I know. That's one of the problems with reaching out to the more reactionary segments of society." She struck a dramatic pose and spoke as if reciting from one of Janus's psych textbooks. "They are a mob whose passions can be easily aroused but not easily controlled once their rampaging starts. A lesson learned well from the excesses of the French Revolution."

Cassie ignored Cybele's dramatics as she quickly drank down a glass of water. "So, then..." She paused to see if she would start burping again. Nothing happened. "It's BETTER just to stay away from them." Why borrow trouble?

"Not necessarily." Cybele looked slightly patronizing as she unconsciously continued to quote from another article she'd recently read. "Righteous anger and passionate intensity only becomes dangerous when coupled with a sense of anger and alienation."

Aargh! It's like trying to convince a child not to play with fire. "Personally," said Cassie as she tried to convince Cybele of the folly of associating with them, "they've always scared me. They're anarchists. And I just can't understand what they have against McDonalds." She chuckled. "I mean, sure their food is full of saturated fat, but a Big Mac and a chocolate milkshake are a pretty unbeatable combination."

Cybele laughed as she momentarily dropped her guise of preacher. "I agree. But McDonalds is just the most pervasive symbol of globalization they can find." She pounded the counter excitedly. "Their problem is that they're fighting an almost hopeless cause."

Gods. Calm down. Definitely too much sugar. "McDonalds isn't necessarily going to be around forever," said Cassie dismissively. "People will eventually find healthier, fast food alternatives like Subway and Tim Horton's. Well, not the donuts, of course, but their lunch baguettes."

Aargh! She's so literal. Can't she ever see beneath the surface? "I'm not talking about food but about the problem of language." She began to pace back and forth, enthusiastic as always at being able to talk about her favourite subject: the language of propaganda. "You see, the anti-globalization youth allow their struggle to be tied to the pro-globalization's definitions for discourse."

"You've already lost me, Cyb," said Cassie as she leaned back against the counter, hoping it wouldn't be a long speech. Gods. I am definitely getting a headache.

Cybele paused and then tried to use more concrete terms. "Pro-Business people always talk about expansion in terms of being competitive because it's hard to argue that a company shouldn't be competitive."

"Okay," said Cassie as she took a gulp of her Coke. "Makes sense. If you're not competitive, you'll go out of business." Business 101.

"Right. But," said Cybele as she paused for emphasis, "if you change the word competitive to the word profitable, you can blow that argument away."

Cassie thought for a moment. This is almost making sense. She slowly took another sip of her drink. "Because you can argue that a company is greedy if it exploits its workers just to make as much money as it can – way more than it needs to be successful."

Cybele clapped her hands excitedly. "Yes." She winked. "Profits, like shit, should roll downhill. See, that's why the anti-globalization kids are fighting a lost cause." She thumped her hand on the counter again. "NEVER allow the enemy to define your terms. If you want to win a war of propaganda, you must be able to manipulate language to expose the truth." She took a long sip of Coke. Gods. My throat feels a bit hoarse. She put her can down with a thud. "Destroy the potential of language to express different ideas and you cause the extinction of critical thinking."

Gods. I can actually understand the point Cybele is making. Who would've thunk it? Cassie nodded thoughtfully. "That's what happens in *1984*. The whole point of Newspeak was to reduce language down to one word."

Yes. Cybele looked over at Cassie approvingly. She does remember what I tell her. "And with that one word, you will be able to say everything and nothing at the same time. A wet dream for every would-be tyrant. Control language and you control the world." Exhausted from her spiel, she sank down on the couch. "People can be such sheep."

"So," said Cassie as she curled up on the opposite end of the couch, "does that mean you're going to try and reach out to these disaffected youth? Teach them to be the shepherds and not the sheep?"

"Better sheep than wolves." Calmer now, Cybele began to consider Cassie's point of view. "I'll try to reach out subtly but, you're right, some of them are pretty radical in their beliefs and actions. Spiking trees...Burning down ski lodges. Those kinds of people are too fanatical to be members of my cult." Cybele took another sip of Coke, unaware of the humour in her words.

"Hey, I'm all for respecting the environment," said Cassie, "but eco-terrorism definitely does more harm than good."

"Yep," Cybele agreed, "Violence is really the worst way to make a point. But it still might be a good idea to try and reach out to them with the whole peaceful stewards of the earth idea."

"Nice," said Cassie. "The change through evolution not revolution shtick. Well, you may as well promote positive things."

"I know." Cybele gestured with her can. "Peace. Love. Goodwill to All. You think those ideas would be self-evident." She shook her head. "But all you have to do is look around and see they haven't quite germinated yet."

"Well, maybe your religion can be the one that will change the world," said Cassie trying to cheer her up.

"I'm not trying to change the world in one big bang," said Cybele lethargically as her caffeine high began to wear off. "However, maybe if people feel less alienated from the natural world, they will be more inclined to take the steps necessary to protect it." Cybele sighed gloomily. "I live in hope."

"Better than in fear," said Cassie, ignoring her subdued tone. "So, any other ideas for the cult?" She grabbed a cushion from the couch and propped it behind her back. Better get comfortable while the genius pontificates.

"Well," said Cybele, sitting up a bit straighter. "I need to do some more work on creating religious rituals for our members to follow once the actual cult gets up and running." She began to perk up again.

"Such as?" Yep. I knew that was only the calm before the storm.

Cybele leaned towards Cassie. "Well, I definitely want to use stuff from modern Wiccan fertility rituals but also get stuff from historical ceremonies too." She began to look more energized. "You know, create a cult of many colours."

"Sounds like fun."

As she thought about the fun she could have, Cybele jumped up in excitement. "It could be such a blast." She began to pace back and forth, gesturing in the air as she spoke. "Pageantry and drama, who could resist? Plus, I have some great ideas for different herbal mixes I can use to create the incenses and aromatic oils for the rituals. I can't wait to get started on that."

"Well, if you need some help, just ask." Cassie paused thoughtfully. "You know, if the web site takes off, you could also expand into candle making and soaps. People are willing to pay a lot for homemade products."

"Especially," said Cybele as she paused for emphasis, "if we put them into a nice basket."

Unable to resist, Cassie chimed in. "Tie a ribbon around it and the sky's the limit."

Cybele shook her finger mockingly at Cassie. "Well, you know the connection between cult members and basket weaving."

She's such a lunatic. "Well, you seem to have everything under control," she said. At least, for now.

"Don't sound so surprised," replied Cybele mock-defensively. "Planning is everything."

"Right. The gods are in the details." Cassie paused and sniffed the air. "Oh..."

The smoke detector went off shrilly.

"The pizza!" Cassie ran to the oven and turned it off.

Cybele opened the living room window to let the smoke out. She then grabbed a towel and began to fan the smoke detector.

Cassie poked her head out from the kitchen. "Your pizza's ready...for the garbage." She collapsed into laughter.

Cybele stopped fanning. "Once the damn alarm stops, let's just go out for dinner."

The damn alarm stopped. Cassie looked at Cybele. They grabbed their purses and left before anything else could go wrong.

Chapter 10

Monday morning. Gabe shook his head in disgust. Two weeks of skulking around here, doing background checks on Janus and Matthew, and nothing. Damn it. I know something is going on around here. Well, look who's here bright and early, loafing around at the Loaves and Fishes. Tan, Ardiaeus, Ixion, and Ajax. They've been making themselves scarce for the last few days. Yes. All my spidey senses are tingling. Wonderful. Now, I'm Peter Parker, cub reporter. The Caped Crusader. No, wait, that's Batman. No. That doesn't quite work. The players don't fit. Hmmm. I guess it would work if I was Robin Hood. This could be Sherwood Forest. Matthew could be Friar Tuck. Janus would be the Sheriff of Nottingham and those kids could be his henchman. I could see Cybele in one of those cone shaped, pointed Maid Marian hats. God. I have to stop reinterpreting my life through my favourite cartoons. He turned his head sharply. Hmmm. There's Janus. Wonder what he's up to now?

Janus strode in and walked past his Fab Four, Tan, Ardiaeus, Ixion, and Ajax, who were standing in the corner gossiping. He nodded hello, unlocked the door to his office and entered. The door closed behind him.

Gabe quickly walked past Janus's office. He unlocked the door of the adjacent janitorial closet and entered as quietly as possible. He relocked the door from the inside and crouched down by the small hole he had drilled into the wall a few days earlier. Hope this works or I'm going to have to find a spy shop that sells surveillance equipment.

He placed his ear against the hole and listened. Sounds like singing. Johnny Cash?

Janus sat at his desk and began go over his spreadsheets that had profit projections for the phone sex operation based on its first two weeks of operation. Subconsciously, he sang softly, under his breath. "And you can't take it all, my empire of gold..."

There was a knock at the door and it opened. Tan, Ardiaeus, Ixion, and Ajax swaggered in. Janus looked up at them. He smiled and motioned for them to take seats in front of his desk. Janus reached down into his desk drawer, pulled out some chocolate bars, and tossed them to the young men.

"I am very pleased with the job you've been doing for my friend Cybele and her business. You've worked hard and been very discreet."

Tan smiled in appreciation. "Thanks, man." He ripped off the wrapping and began to devour his bar.

The others chimed in their thanks through mouths full of chocolate.

That's disgusting. Even wild animals chew with their mouths closed. Janus choked back his contempt and forced himself to sound friendly and sincere. "How would you like to keep working for this business? At a management level of course. You would have others working for you."

"That would be awesome," said Ardiaeus excitedly.

"Yeah." Tan replied more calmly. "But, what kind of work would we have to do?"

"More of what you've been doing. But I'd also like you to feel out some of your friends, see if they'd be interested in coming to work for Cybele, and if they can also be discreet as well," said Janus.

"Why the big secret, man? We're not doing anything illegal, are we?" asked Ajax.

Janus was quick to reassure the boys. "No... Of course not. It's just...YOU know how uptight everyone is around here. No sense rocking the boat as long as you have to live here."

"Makes sense, man," said Ixion knowingly. "Matthew would shit himself if he knew we were working for a pagan business."

"Yeah," Tan agreed. "He'd probably think we were Satanists and bore us to death with prayer."

"Right." Janus looked closely at them to gauge their reaction. "Most people here might think you were joining a cult or something, just because you worked for a pagan who sold magical artefacts and held pagan rites and rituals."

"A cult," said Ardiaeus, unable to contain his excitement at the prospect, "that would really freak people out."

What idiots. "I know," said Janus smoothly. "People get upset when they hear the word cult, but it's just a different word for religion." He leaned forward. How did Cybele put it? "Pagan cults just tend to be more attractive than other religions because pagans understand the importance of having fun and don't complicate their lives with a lot of commandments."

"That is so cool," said Tan.

"Yeah," Janus scrutinized them closely. "And a lot of what you guys will be doing for the business will be fun, like helping to mix incenses and potions." I need them on board so I'd better appeal to their baser motives. "And, as more people are hired, you guys will be the ones in charge of making sure they do their jobs well." Yep. Power is the ultimate seducer. "That's why you need to start recruiting some of your friends. But..." He shook his finger warningly at them. "No hardcore druggies, ok? We need people who can work hard and think straight."

"That's no problem. We can find some people for you," said Tan. He looked meaningfully at his friends. You damn well better not let me down. We could make a killing in this.

"Good." Janus stood up and looked down at them. "We need to get started on making this stuff right away because I expect a lot of orders within the next few weeks." He paused to make sure they were paying attention.

They were fixated on him, tongues slightly protruding from their mouth as a sign of their intense concentration.

Good. Janus continued. "I also want you to start posting flyers advertising this new business and the upcoming seminars. Post them all over wherever you see people your own age, plus around the universities."

"What about high schools?" asked Tan. High school girls and drugs. That would be sweet.

"No," said Janus regretfully at the thought of the lost opportunities for profit. "Because alcohol will be served during these rituals, only adults can attend. We don't want to draw the attention of the authorities."

Ixion began to rock back and forth in his chair excitedly. "Well, what about us? Can we come to the parties?" he asked.

"Sure." Janus shrugged nonchalantly. "You're all over eighteen and any of your friends over eighteen can come. I'm sure we can give you an employee discount or if you actually work during the rituals, you can attend free of charge."

"Cool," said Ardiaeus. He reached out and forcefully stopped Ixion's rocking. Damn fool's embarrassing us.

"But first things first," said Janus. "Start recruiting. We need workers. As part of my inner circle, I'm trusting you to make sure you pick people who will work hard and not cause trouble."

"You can count on us, man," said Tan. He glared over at Ixion and Ardiaeus. They'd better knock it off before I knock some damn sense into them.

"I know I can." Janus said. He determinedly ignored the interplay between Tan, Ardiaeus, and Ixion. "Now take these flyers and get out of here. Get to work."

The young men left the room. Janus leaned back in his chair, flushed. This is much more fun than having to jump through hoops for some tight-assed committee. Running a cult is far more fun and profitable than working on a thesis. Dance, puppets, dance.

Gabe straightened up inside the supply cupboard. Well, I feel like I've been playing Telephone. That was definitely no therapy session. Thought I heard them say something about Satanists and cults. I definitely need a better listening device. Something's up. Maybe I should try following some of the guys. He stretched his arms above his head and sighed in pleasurable anticipation. Yep. Life's definitely starting to get interesting around here.

Cybele stood up on her tiptoes and stretched her arms above her head. She sighed in pleasure as her painful muscles slowly tightened and then relaxed. Gods. I'm sore. Who would have thought that so many writers could make pagan religions sound so mind-numbingly boring? All those historical footnotes. Maybe for dramatic effect I should pick up some of these books and throw them against the wall. She picked up one book and threw it. It bounced off Cassie's stereo and knocked several CDs to the ground. Damn. She walked over and picked them up. I guess dramatic effects work better with an audience.

She yawned. I'm tired. I think I've done enough work for a Monday. I need a quick pick- me- up. Time for the opiate of the masses. She walked over to the kitchen for a cup of coffee. She returned back to the living room and stretched out on the couch. Ahh. Wonder what's on television now. She looked up as Cassie walked through the door.

Wow. She looks pretty wiped out. "Hey, Cyb. Given birth to the new world order, yet?" asked Cassie.

"Still suffering labour pains." Cybele sighed. She held up her coffee cup and the remote control. "But the epidural should help."

Cassie sat down at the end of the couch and leaned forward sympathetically. “Still having trouble deciding what rituals to use?”

Cybele pulled herself up into a sitting position. “More like trying to figure out how to incorporate them safely. I definitely want fire to be involved in the outdoor ones. I’m just concerned about accidents.”

“Yeah.” Cassie continued worriedly. “Combining alcohol and outdoor fires is not the smartest thing to do.”

“Not to mention the judicious use of hallucinogenics,” said Cybele. “For medicinal use only, of course.”

“Of course.” Cassie continued dryly. “I’m sure they’ll be on the shady side of barely legal.”

Cybele snorted. “Of course. I’m not an idiot. The last thing I want is to give the police an excuse to raid us. You know how paranoid conformists get around alternative religions.”

Cassie decided to wash her hands of any minor infractions of the law Cybele might commit and returned to the problem of the outdoor rituals. “Why don’t you have a couple of fire extinguishers standing by, just in case?” She paused thoughtfully. “You could always decorate them like fertility maypoles and have them as part of the display.”

“Great idea. Nice combination of form and function.” Cybele leaned forward in surprise. “Got any more gems?”

Cassie yawned. “I’m definitely empty. Feel the need for a little inspiration.” She looked over at the television. “Anything good on?”

"No. The American channels are all showing news," said Cybele annoyedly. "The Leader of the Free World." She raised an eyebrow archly. "Is giving a speech *ad nauseam*. Wrecking perfectly good regular scheduled programming with the newest instalment of reality TV." She took a sip of her cold coffee and groaned. *"Survivor U.S.A."*

"What about the Canadian channels?" asked Cassie.

Cybele stood up and slowly stretched. Still got some kinks to get out. "Oh, they're following the U.S.'s lead. Except for the CBC. It's showing a *Red Green* marathon."

"Those Canuckistan subversives," said Cassie mockingly.

"Yep. The television is definitely falling down on its job to illuminate and entertain our lives tonight. Must be cursed."

Cassie wagged her finger at the TV. "Bad television. How will we get through the night without you?"

Cybele straightened up excitedly and looked at Cassie. "We'll just have to perform an exorcism." She pointed dramatically at Cassie. "Get a tape."

"Oh. I don't think duct tape will save us tonight," said Cassie. Gods. She's winding herself up again. She is so the Energizer bunny.

Cybele threw a cushion at her. "A movie tape." Dumbass. Get in the spirit. "We can watch *Lord of the Rings*. Have a morality lesson and voyeuristic adventure at the same time."

"Morality lesson?" said Cassie as she placed a cushion behind her and leaned back with a resigned sigh. More talking. All I want to do is sleep.

"The dangers of unbridled power." Cybele paused for dramatic effect and then solemnly began to speak. "One Ring to bring them all, and in the darkness bind them."

Cassie threw the cushion back at her. "You're so deep." In six feet of shit.

"Hey, I'm just the humble prophet, The Word of Tolkien." Cybele stood up and bowed. "His humble vessel."

Cassie waved her finger at Cybele. "Aren't you supposed to be starting a matriarchy? You don't want to get too embedded with the patriarchy and lose all sense of objectivity," she said in mock-warning.

"Gods." Cybele slapped her forehead. "You're right. The brainwashing is just so insidious. The tape must come out. Must exorcise the evil spirits on television using a more matriarchal approach. Get thee behind me, Tolkien." She removed the tape and gave it a reassuring caress. "At least for the moment. We won't forsake you forever."

Cybele turned off the television. "Time for a little spiritual cleansing." She turned to Cassie. "Why don't you get a soup bowl and a box of salt?"

Cybele walked over to the end table and pulled out a box full of incense bottles.

Cassie pulled herself off the couch with an audible groan. I may as well. She's not going to let this one go. She walked over to the kitchen and filled a soup bowl half-full with salt. With a half-hearted flourish, she handed the bowl to Cybele.

Cybele placed the bowl on the ground absent-mindedly as she continued to rummage through her box of supplies. "Let's see. We'll do a simple spell, just to contact the Goddess, and ask to be filled with divine inspiration." She took out two sticks of myrrh and three sticks of frankincense. "Now we just need some cinnamon oil." She stuck the ends of the incense in the bowl of salt and sprinkled the sticks with cinnamon oil. "Perfect."

Cassie grabbed a pack of matches from the end table and carefully lit the tops of the incense sticks. She waited until the ends were completely engulfed in flame before she blew them out. They began to smoulder. Cassie then placed the bowl on top of the television. She and Cybele moved the coffee table to the side of the room. When Cybele returned, she knelt down in front of the television.

She looked up expectantly. "Come on, Cassie. If you want to be part of the ritual, you have to kneel down too."

With an amused sigh, Cassie knelt down besides Cybele. Oh well. This does beat the regularly scheduled programming.

Cybele raised her hands in supplication and spoke passionately. "O Great Far-Seeing Goddess. You whose wisdom shapes our minds and our destiny. We beseech you. Cleanse our souls of the propaganda spawn from those who abuse your greatness. O Mighty Sibyl of the Twentieth Century..."

Cassie nudged her and whispered, "Twenty-first."

Cybele continued unfazed, with the necessary modification. "Twenty-first Century. We desire to experience the ecstasy of leaving our bodies and being filled by your essence. We are nothing without you. Empty vessels. Mindless sheep. Save us for we are lost without you."

Unable to resist herself, Cassie interjected. "Lost without your regularly scheduled programming."

Cybele placed her hands upon the TV screen. "Yes. You are the bread and circuses of our existence. Come back to us. Do not forsake us."

Needing to piss badly, Cassie brought the prayer to an end. "Return us now to the program already in progress."

"Yes," said Cybele, "I feel the Spirit within me again." She touched her stomach in sudden discomfort. Or maybe just gas from not having eaten in several hours.

"Me too." Cassie stood up. "I am filled with a sudden surge of enthusiasm and an inexplicable desire to have dinner." And piss like there's no tomorrow.

"Great. Janus is coming by with Chinese take-out." Cybele stood up and stretched. "He wants to go over some business stuff with me."

"Whatever will we do in the meantime?" asked Cassie as she began to walk away.

"Why don't we watch *The Long Kiss Goodnight*? See Geena Davis kick some ass." Cybele patted her stomach gingerly. Might need some of the pink stuff. Don't want to spoil dinner with an epidemic of farting.

"Great," Cassie yelled from inside the bathroom.

The apartment buzzer went off and Cybele bounded off to let Janus in.

Janus strutted into the apartment carrying bags of food. “Eat, drink, be merry my friends. We are sitting on the mother of all lodes. Sex and religion. An astronomically winning combination.” He looked at the bowl of incense on the television. “Damn. Did I miss a ritual? Nothing with drugs, I hope.”

Cybele handed him a glass of wine. “Only succulent grapes from the vine of life will be on the menu tonight.”

Cassie walked into the living room. “Sounds like business is going pretty good, Janus.”

“It’s the MOAB,” he replied.

Cybele spit out some of her wine. “The MOAB?”

I knew she’d like that. “The Mother of All Businesses.” Janus smirked. “In fact, we’re doing so well we need to hire more phone sex operators.”

“You mean religious sexual fantasy counsellors,” said Cybele wiping off her face with a paper napkin.

“Absolutely.” Janus took another sip of his wine. “I’ve already set up some more interviews.” He looked over inquiringly. “Do you want to be there for them?”

Cybele paused thoughtfully and then shook her head. “No. I’m pretty swamped planning these rituals. And Cybelean Contemplative Motion is really beginning to pick up momentum.”

Great. No Cybelean interference. “Ok. Once you’ve finished working out the planning, you should start the ritual sessions as soon as possible. Just make sure you give me enough of a heads-up on what we have to do to prepare the grounds for the rites" said Janus warningly.

Time to stir the pot a little. Feeling a bit left out, Cassie chimed in mischievously. "Well, have YOU already started interviewing your minions? They're the ones who are going to be doing the manual labour for the rituals, eh Janus?"

"Oh yeah," said Janus, oblivious to her teasing. "The world is full of street kids ready to work for under-the-table money. Thank God no one cares about screwing the government."

Cybele looked worriedly at him. "We can't have kids working for us, Janus. And I really don't think we should cheat the government. That's how they got Capone, remember?"

"Relax," said Janus soothingly. "They're not really kids. They're appropriately rebellious young adults."

Cassie interjected curiously. "What about the taxes?"

"Fine. Once we start holding official rituals, I'll make sure they're all on the payroll. Happy now?" said Janus exasperatedly.

"Ecstatic." Cybele giggled. "See the rituals really do work."

"Of course," said Cassie light-heartedly. "I'm a true believer." Not.

"You know." Janus paused to look carefully at Cybele's reaction to his horning in on her territory. "These guys are really excited about participating in some of the rituals too."

"Of course," said Cybele, "As long as they're legal, they'll be welcome."

"Yep." Cassie poked Janus in the ribs. "Don't want to get charged with corrupting minors."

"Perish the thought," said Janus as he rubbed his side. Damn. Cassie's stronger than she looks. At least Cyb seems fine with the Fab Four being part of her ceremonies.

Cybele patted her stomach. "I'm starved. Let's eat." Better soak up all this gas with solid food.

They ripped open the bags of food and sat down on the couch with plates piled high. Cybele started *The Long Kiss Goodnight* and they watched half-entranced and half-asleep from the food.

When the movie finished, Cybele began to look for the remote. She pulled it from under a cushion with a triumphant hoot that turned into a yawn. As the tape rewound, she stood up and turned to Janus and Cassie. "Don't you love how convoluted government conspiracies are?"

Janus stood up stiffly and began to crack his back. "Remember, kids, the moral of the story is don't trust anyone who can make money playing off your fears and prejudices."

Cassie forced herself up from the couch. Wow. That food really hit the spot. She shook her head tiredly. "Too deep for me. I just watched it for the scene where they machine gunned the frozen lake and then jumped through the window and into the ice cold water."

Cybele nodded quasi-solemnly. "I loved that part too. But, remember." She yawned again. "What you saw on the frozen surface did not accurately reflect the situation below."

Cassie reached down for a cushion and threw it towards Cybele. "You two. Everything doesn't have to be analyzed for hidden meanings. Sometimes a cigar is just a cigar."

Janus gasped exaggeratedly. "Bite your tongue. Conspiracies are all around us. The Truth is out there to find but we have to look hard for it."

Cassie picked up another cushion and threw it at Janus. He caught the cushion and threw it playfully back at her.

Cybele took a last sip of her wine. "Life is one big X-File."

Cassie groaned. "I must have drunk too much wine because you're starting to make sense."

Cybele and Janus yelled out together, "*In vino veritas*."

"Gods," said Cybele. "I can't stop yawning. It's definitely time for bed." She pushed Janus in the general direction of the door. "You'd better get going now, Janus."

Janus looked over at Cassie. "Ahh. The gracious hostess. Notorious in her subtleness." Not.

Cassie walked him out. Then she and Cybele cleaned up the mess they had made.

With a yawn goodnight, Cybele walked towards her bedroom carrying the bowl of incense. She paused at the threshold, leaned her body slightly to one side, and farted. Aaaah. Sweet relief. She looked guiltily at the kitchen. Hope Cassie didn't hear. Cybele carefully placed the incense on her bedroom table so that she could catch the last fumes of inspiration while she slept.

Cassie put the leftovers into the fridge. She cracked open the last fortune cookie to learn her fate. *If we all did the things we are capable of doing, we would literally astound ourselves.* She smiled. I didn't know Thomas Edison wrote fortune cookies. She shook her head and went off to bed. Nobody can ever live up to their potential. That's a fool's dream. Or Cyb's.

Chapter 11

Ostensibly eating his lunch, Gabe sat under a tree that overlooked the back parking lot of the Loaves and Fishes. Why do they always serve tuna on Tuesdays? At least they could use real mayo instead of the fake stuff. Yuck. He heard the sound of animated conversation nearby and looked up. Very interesting. Tweedle Dee and Tweedle Dumber seem to be in a real hurry to leave today. I wonder if where they're going has anything to do with the flyers they've been handing out to all those street kids. He tore into his sandwich annoyedly. I need to get a closer look at them but those damn kids keep hiding them every time they see me nearby. He stood up and watched as Tan and Ixion hurried to their car and quickly got in. They drove off. Gabe quickly rushed to his car and followed them. Hmm. I wonder how many car lengths I should stay back from them so that they don't spot me. He laughed. I keep forgetting this is real life not television. Nobody expects to be tailed as they drive through downtown Winnipeg. I certainly don't have to worry about losing track of a rusty, lime green Toyota Tercel that probably is too broken down even to go the speed limit.

Interesting. They seem to be heading away from the downtown area and towards Kenaston. I don't think it's a coincidence that's the area where Janus lives. Let's see if they turn left on Acheron and then right on Cocytus. Yes. He pumped his arm up in the air. I'm the man! They're heading to Janus's. Gabe slowed down. He watched them turn onto Charon Shore and pull up a winding driveway. They quickly got out of their car and hurried to a little house several metres away from a larger house. Gabe made a u-turn and returned to Cocytus. He parked and then walked back over to Charon Shore. He took a deep breath. Satanists and Black Masses, here I come.

He walked up the long driveway and towards the little house. He stopped and looked at the little brass sign on the front door. The Mysteries of Cybele. Cybele? She didn't strike me as the sort of person who would be involved with Satanism. She seemed so full of colour and life. He shook his head. Not the type to walk around dressed in black, with powdered white faces, and long black fingernails. Or are those Goths? He raised his finger to ring the doorbell and then paused. He lowered his hand and instead tried the handle of the door. It turned. He opened the door and stepped inside.

He sniffed the air. Smells like sandalwood. Nice. He looked around. The house seemed empty but he could hear a woman's voice talking from a nearby room. He called out hello and quickly walked towards the voice. He walked to the doorway of the room and looked inside. Cybele was sitting behind a desk strewn with paper. She was talking animatedly on the phone and typing something on her laptop. Her eyes widened in surprise as she saw Gabe enter. She smiled and gestured for him to come inside.

Gabe entered and looked around the room. It was clearly a home office. He smiled. If office décor was a physical manifestation of a person's inner mind, then clearly Cybele had a very unique mind. A framed poster of Dali's *Ecumenical Council* lay beside what looked like a Renaissance woman weaving a tapestry on her loom. He wandered closer to read the wording at the bottom of the poster. *The Return of Odysseus* by Pintoricchio (Bernardo Betti, 1454-1513). He wandered over to the bookshelf under the window sill and picked up an apparently genderless white figurine playing what looked like a harmonica. He ran his hands over its smooth, clean lines. Beautiful. He carefully placed it back down and picked up the reddish coloured female figurine beside it. Terracotta? A fertility icon? He slowly became aware that the room had become silent and turned to see Cybele's gaze fixed upon him.

She stood up and walked towards him. "It's a steatopygic figurine."

"Steatopygic?" asked Gabe.

"A fertility goddess from the Stone Age. With enlarged breasts and hips. A surviving remnant of a once powerful matriarchal religion." Cybele picked up the white figurine and caressingly ran her finger down its side. "This is a reproduction of a Cycladic figurine. The Flute Player. The real ones are made of white marble and are translucent. They're thousands of years old and yet they look so modern in their simplicity and design. Beautiful, aren't they?"

"Very." With one last caress, Gabe gently placed the fertility goddess back on the bookshelf. "You don't seem surprised or upset to see me here."

Cybele smiled mysteriously. "Should I be?"

Gabe smiled back at her. "Aren't you even curious about what I'm doing here?"

Cybele serenely patted him on his arm. "All things unfold in the proper time." She teasingly ran her fingers down his hand before stepping slightly away from him. "I'm sure you'll soon tell me now that you're done exploring my office."

Gabe unconsciously flexed the hand she had caressed. "Please tell me you're not a Satanist."

Cybele arched her eyebrows. "To be a Satanist, I'd have to be a Christian and I'm a pagan." She moved a step further away from him.

Gabe shook his head in confusion as he took a step closer towards her. "Satanists aren't Christian."

Cybele crossed her arms across her chest and, unable to help herself, began to lecture him. "Of course, they are. They're working within the context of Christian mythology. They just happen to have taken the role of the Antagonist as their religious guide." She paused to catch her breath. "Sort of like on *Deep Space Nine* where you have two sects in the Bajoran religion."

She's cute when she's worked up. Gabe forced himself to pay attention. Good thing I speak *Star Trek*. He nodded knowingly. "Like the Prophets who live in the Celestial Temple and the Pah-Wraiths who had been banished from the Temple and forced to live in the Fire Caves of Bajor."

Cybele winked up at him. Cute and smart. "You're right. It's the War in Heaven all over again. Those who worship the Pah-Wraiths are the Bajoran equivalent of Satanists."

"But you're a pagan not a Satanist?" asked Gabe.

Cybele sighed. "Yes." Why can't people bother to learn the difference? "Pagans tend to be pantheistic. We don't worship one spirit but many."

"Doesn't that get confusing?"

Cybele rolled her eyes. "Why?" She laughed. "Because monotheistic religions which purport to worship one god must be simpler. Even though that one god is accompanied by a cast of saints, angels, and devils."

Gabe laughed back. "Touché. I never quite looked at it like that before."

Cybele nodded solemnly. "Most people don't. Cultural indoctrination can be very pervasive and persuasive."

She's so cute when she's profound. Gabe forced himself to think of a question to keep her gaze focussed on him. "So, pagans worship nature?"

"Well, sort of." Cybele looked a bit taken aback. Odd. Most people start walking away at this point. Too much information. She continued warily. "Paganism comes in as many varieties as any other religion. I don't consider myself so much as a worshipper of nature as much as someone who tries to respect nature and be a steward of her, not a mindless consumer."

This is kind of interesting. There could be a good story here. Gabe leaned his hip against her desk and continued to question her. "Do you give offerings to nature? Make sacrifices?"

"Not in the sense of animal sacrifice if that's what you're thinking. Although some do." She leaned against her desk as well, consciously mirroring Gabe's positioning. She met his gaze and then dropped her own as if shy. "However, since I eat meat myself, I'm not going to be hypocritical and condemn them for such practices." She looked him straight in the eyes as she ran her hands down the hips of her lavender suede skirt. "And I'm quite fond of wearing leather as well."

Gabe took a deep breath and then slowly released it. "You should be. It looks quite good on you."

Cybele dropped her gaze again but then slowly looked back up at him from under her eyelashes. "Thank you. But as I was saying..." She smiled. "Sometimes, in order to put myself in harmony with the forces of nature, I'll use incense and chanting and other rituals to achieve a state of communion with the forces of life outside me."

"It sounds a little strange to me." She's such a flirt. Gabe thrust his lower body slightly closer to hers.

Nice. He's definitely interested. Cybele forced herself to remain still as if unaware of Gabe's signals. "Many religions use incense and chanting during rituals of prayer. Pagans are no different."

Gabe looked confused. Damn. She hasn't moved closer. "So, the Mysteries of Cybele is a pagan cult?"

Cybele shrugged nonchalantly. "Well, I don't like using the word cult, since it has such negative connotations in today's world." She shrugged more exaggeratedly a second time. He's definitely looking but he's pretending not to. Sweet. "I would rather be considered an alternative form of spiritual worship, but I suppose cult is a good a description as any."

Don't look down. Focus on her eyes. Gabe slowly unclenched his hands. "Why the Mysteries of Cybele?" He took a deep breath. "Do you want to be worshipped as a goddess?"

"Well, if not as the goddess, then maybe her avatar." Cybele laughed. "I'm kidding." Sort of. "I certainly don't see myself as a reincarnation of an ancient Phrygian goddess." She ran her hands sensuously over her hips again. "Of course, that doesn't mean I'm not. After all, you know the old saying about paranoid schizophrenics..."

Gabe shook his head and forced himself to laugh. Focus on her mouth. Think of hockey. "That just because they always think there's someone hiding in the bushes outside who's trying to kill them, doesn't mean they're always wrong."

"Right." Cybele swatted his arm playfully. "I mean. I could have just as easily called my religion the Mysteries of Gaea, but that would be silly, since my name is Cybele." She casually picked some invisible fluff off the front of her V-neck blouse. "May as well go with what the gods gave me."

She's killing me. Gabe roughly wiped sweat off his forehead. "Do you really believe there is a real goddess of nature?"

"Not in an anthropomorphic sense." Cybele took a step closer to Gabe. "But I do believe there are powerful spiritual forces in the world." She angled her body teasingly to mirror the position of his lower body. "I just try to remember that I'm a part of the natural world and not somehow above it."

Damn. Gabe turned quickly away from Cybele as he shifted noticeably in his pants. He spoke with a forced nonchalance as he pretended to look out the door of her office. "So, what exactly does this religion of yours do?"

Cybele's mouth twitched knowingly. Still got it. She took pity on Gabe and pretended to look through some papers on her desk. "Well, several things. We have classes based on yoga called Cybelean Contemplative Motion and soon we will be starting to have religious rituals based on the idea of tent revivals that are so popular in the southern United States."

Think of hockey. Lots of ice. Gabe managed to get himself under control enough to turn back and face her. He smirked. "Not snake handling, I hope."

"Well, there are some kinds of snakes, I just don't want to handle." She couldn't resist a quick look down at Gabe to check his reaction to her words. "Besides, I'm always a little nervous when people interpret written texts that literally. That kind of fervour is a little unsettling."

Gabe laughed nervously. "Besides, I'm sure there are probably pretty strict regulations governing wild animal acts in Winnipeg."

"Yeah. And the last thing I want is to attract the attention of those animal rights nuts who always want to picket the Shrine Circus." Cybele walked around her desk and typed on her laptop. She spun it around to face Gabe. "But I'm most proud of this."

Gabe walked towards the desk to look. Keep thinking of hockey. "The Mysteries of Cybele. A web site."

"Yes." Cybele began to speak more excitedly. "It's actually not just to advertise our religious rituals but also to sell magical items like herbs, incenses, oils, potions, poppets etc." She tapped her screen for emphasis. "A whole range of things. For those who want to dabble in paganism and need a handy source of supplies."

Gabe bent down and began to scroll through the site. "Magical items?"

"Well, we have a disclaimer saying everything is for entertainment purposes only." Cybele looked at him regretfully. "But, you sound as if you don't believe in magic?"

"Well, to be honest, I don't." Oops. Hope that doesn't torpedo my chances with her.

Cybele playfully tapped him on his arm. "Magic isn't just mumbo jumbo, you know. It's a way of getting in touch with nature and with our own spiritual power. You know the old saying, mind over matter. That's all magic is. The power of belief is impressive."

"So, are people really buying this stuff from your site?"

"Oh yeah." Cybele pointed to a stack of papers in a file folder on her desk. "These are the orders that I have come in so far. I have to process them and then give our employees working in the greenhouse the specifics on what they need to fill the order. Then they bring the order back to me. I double check it against the original order. Then right before I send it out with a printed invoice, I charge their credit card for the purchase."

Gabe straightened up and regarded her thoughtfully. "That sounds like a lot of work."

"It is." Cybele groaned. "I think I'm going to have to hire an office assistant to help me keep up. With all the paperwork for this business, plus running the Contemplative Motion classes, and then starting the religious rituals, I think I might have taken on more than even I can swallow."

Perfect. Gabe lightly touched her shoulder. "You know, I'm looking for another job. I would love to work in an interesting business like this with such pleasant company."

"Really? What about your job at the Loaves and Fishes?"

Gabe pointed to her website. "This looks like far more fun and it would give me a good opportunity to stretch my horizons. Plus." He shrugged. "It's not as if I would be leaving Matthew in the lurch. There are a lot of people who would love to do that job. "

Cybele shook her head doubtfully. "The job wouldn't pay that much. It probably wouldn't be full time hours either. And until the business really took off, I couldn't afford to pay you more than a dollar above minimum wage."

"That would be fine." Gabe thumped the stack of papers on her desk. "When should I begin?"

"Well, I'll show you around today and you can start as soon as you've told Matthew that you've quit. I'll wait until he's found someone else to replace you."

"That shouldn't take more than a day or two," promised Gabe.

"Good." Cybele forced herself to sound professional in order to avoid sounding too excited. Oh, the possibilities. "Why don't I show you how the paperwork works, then take you on a quick tour of the house, and then the greenhouse where we fill the orders?"

"It's a deal." Gabe came rapidly around the desk to look at the files. His sandaled foot caught on the wheel of the chair. He stumbled and fell hard against the desk. "Ow."

Cybele reached forward to grab his hand. "Are you okay?"

Gabe winced. "Yeah. I think I just broke my foot...and my pride."

Cybele stroked his hand before releasing it. "Oh, I think both will recover." She gently pushed him down into the chair. She bent down to look at his foot. "Wiggle your toes and tell me if it hurts."

Slightly embarrassed, Gabe wiggled his toes. "No, it doesn't hurt."

Cybele gently patted the top of his foot. "Then it's not broken, just a little bruised." Like your ego must be. "The most you'll have to worry about is limping around on a swollen foot for a while." She looked up. "If you put some ice on it, there probably won't even be that much swelling." She chuckled. "If you were Janus, I'd probably make a joke about how your feet would have some swelling up to do before they matched the size of your head. But..."

Gabe broke in. "But, I'm not Janus."

Cybele shook her head. "No. You're not Janus."

Gabe looked firmly at her. "Are you and Janus dating?"

Cybele shook her head firmly back at him. "No. We're not. We're just good friends."

"Good."

Cybele stood up and tilted her head slightly to the side. "Good. Why don't we get started with the paperwork tomorrow? Give you time to quit your job with Matthew and put some ice on that foot. Don't want you to be crippled even before you start working for me."

Gabe stood up and limped slightly towards the door. He turned to wave good-bye. "I'll see you tomorrow then."

Cybele walked him to the front door. "Tomorrow then." She watched him leave and closed the door behind him. She began to sing off-key, "Tomorrow will come soon, my beautiful tomorrow..."

She leaned back against the door and smiled. Then she frowned. Hmmm. I wonder if hiring Gabe was the smartest thing to do. Lust before logic. Janus is already afraid Gabe is spying on him. He might be upset that I've hired Gabe. Probably should keep that under my hat for a while. But, if Janus gives me any trouble, I'll just remind him of the old adage: keep your friends close and your enemies even closer. Gabe is pretty cute though. If he's willing to work for a cult, he can't be as conservative as I feared. She frowned. Although he might be a little unstable if he's willing to work for a cult. Don't want to date a member of any club that would have me. Have to think about that more. Don't want to become involved with a nut. Not that it would be a good idea to become involved with someone I worked with. Hmm. Now I'm rambling to myself. Must stop that. She sighed. All things happen for the best, in this, the worst of all possible worlds. Better get back to work.

Gabe slowly limped back towards his car. Damn. She must think I'm a complete klutz. He shook his head. At least Iris will be pleased with me today. I'm finally getting somewhere in this investigation. They may not be Satanists but starting your own cult is still a little kooky. Cybele seems genuine enough. If there's anything illegal going on, I'm sure she has no idea. Janus is the one to be involved with that. He and his Fab Four. Matthew could still be involved. Maybe he helps recruit the street kids. Working there will give me a good chance to find out what's really going on. He sighed. Cybele sure smelled yummy. Like vanilla and cinnamon. Maybe I should stop by Just Desserts on my way home and get some apple pie for dessert tonight.

Chapter 12

Janus nervously checked his reflection in the glass pillar of the Narcissus Building. Okay. My hair looks good. He leaned closer to the pillar. No blemishes on the face. No noon shadow. Conservative suit. Dark blue is definitely my colour. He looked down at his pants. Fly is up. Maybe I should pull it down. Lead with my most distinguished feature. He looked back up and smiled. I look damn good. No way can Achates resist me. Janus tightened his grip on his bouquet of red roses and confidently strode towards the security desk in front of the elevators.

The bored security guard was more interested in reading his horoscope for that Wednesday than talking. He merely waved Janus into the elevators and then returned to the paper.

Janus smiled. Good. Achates can't be too mad at me or he would have had the security guards ban me from the building. Arachne Web Designs, here I come. He walked out of the elevator and towards Achates' office.

"Janus." Achates' secretary, Maera Chi, rushed to intercept him before he could enter Achates' office. "How nice to see you again. Achates is …is with a client but I'm sure if you just wait a minute, he'll be done and I'll let him know you're here."

Janus nodded yes and sat down on the sofa in the waiting room. He gently placed the flowers down beside him. He nervously wiped the palms of his hands on his knees. He picked up a magazine and pretended to read.

The door opened and a well-dressed middle-aged man stepped out. He nodded pleasantly to Maera and calmly walked towards the elevators.

Janus smirked uncomfortably. Could he have been any fuller of himself? Who did that jerk think he was? Some Immortal walking straight off the pages of *The Thousand and One Nights*, not condescending to acknowledge mere mortals?

"Janus."

His head snapped up and he looked over at Maera.

She smiled uneasily. "Achates will see you now."

Janus stood up, grabbed the roses, and took a deep breath. He nodded once more to Maera and then strode into Achates' office.

Achates looked up from behind his desk where he was busily shuffling some papers. "What an interesting surprise. What can I do for you, Janus?"

Janus awkwardly placed the bouquet on Achates' desk. "I was hoping we could have lunch and talk about us. You know, see what went wrong and how we can put it back together."

Achates sighed dramatically. "I'm really quite busy today. You should have called for an appointment."

"An appointment?" Janus laughed angrily. "To make up with my boyfriend." He shook his head. "God, Achates, don't be so anal. You're the only person I know who schedules moments of spontaneity in your daily agenda."

"For the record, we broke up," snapped Achates. "So, you're no longer my boyfriend and can no longer drop in whenever you please. I'm very busy and can't stop everything I'm doing just because you've finally come to your senses." Achates stood up and pushed his chair forcibly out of his way. "And if I'm so anal, why would you want to get back with me?" Achates crossed his arms against his chest. "Why don't you go out and try to find a male version of Cybele? How is she by the way? Been locked up in an insane asylum, yet?"

"Oh, my God. Get off Cybele. This has nothing to do with her." Janus rolled his eyes contemptuously. "It's about you and me."

"Give me a break." Achates threw his hands up in the air. "It's a little crowded to have a relationship with three people in it. She's the Camilla Parker Bowles, the Yoko Ono, of Winnipeg."

"You're delusional." Janus groaned incredulously. "I can't believe you're jealous of her. How insecure can someone be? I'm here in your office, trying to get back together with you." He glared. "What more evidence of my feelings for you, do you want?"

Achates uncrossed his arms and shoved his hands into his pant's pockets. "It's over between us, Janus. I want someone who puts me first all the time. Someone I can trust not to go off on flights of fancy. Not to get himself arrested or show up on the front pages of the papers protesting some hippie cause like the legalization of pot or some damn peace march."

"What about if it was for some damn pro-war march?" Janus smirked angrily. "If I washed my hands in the blood of innocents, would your religion make me clean?"

"Stop making a joke about everything." Achates started pacing back and forth. "Life is serious business. Adults live in the real world. Children live in the world of fantasy where everything can be settled with flower power. Get a grip on reality."

Janus took a calming breath and walked towards Achates. "I'm willing to make some changes. We were good together. Why don't you lighten up and give us another chance?"

Janus extended his hand to Achates who roughly pushed it away. "It's not that simple, Janus. Even if I could trust you not to embarrass me in the future, it's still too late for us."

"It can't be too late. I mean it's not like you could be already seeing some..." Janus growled. "You bastard, you're seeing someone else."

"Don't overreact, Janus." Achates flushed guiltily. "Life goes on without you, you know."

"Who is he?" Janus started pacing back and forth.

"You don't know him." Achates turned away from Janus. "His name is Jagganath Nod. He's a lawyer."

"How long have you been seeing him?" Janus slammed his hand on Achates' desk. "Were you cheating on me before we broke up?"

"Of course not." Achates waved dismissively at Janus. "We met on one of my business trips to Toronto. Jagg and I were just good friends until you and I broke up." Or close enough anyway.

"I'm supposed to believe that." Janus practically drenched the carpet with his angry spit. "You were faithful to me on all those long, lonely nights away. Bullshit." He clenched his hands into fists.

"The best defence is a good offence, eh Janus." Achates snarled back at him. "You're the best bullshitter I've ever met."

"What's that supposed to mean?"

"Like you didn't spend all those long, lonely nights, trolling at bars, buying drinks for all your new best friends at Ganymede's," said Achates sarcastically.

Janus threw his hands up in protest. "I was completely faithful to you. Those guys meant nothing to me. I just bought them drinks but that was it." He paused for emphasis. "I swear on my parents' grave."

"Well, with your great love for your parents, that must be true, eh?" Achates sighed. "Look, break-ups are never easy. But the truth is that I was as faithful to you as you were to me. Happy now?"

Janus yanked so hard on his tie, he nearly strangled himself. "Ecstatic."

"Good. I don't want to hurt you but we're not going to get back together again. It's over." Achates looked over sadly at Janus. "The truth is that Jagganath and I really have something special."

Janus shook his head in disbelief. "Damn it. Why does that name sound so familiar? Who the hell is this guy?"

"You might have read about him in the papers." Achates beamed a bit smugly. "He's quite a famous lawyer. Queen's Counsel, you know."

"How nice for him." Janus rolled his eyes. "And how nice for you that you don't have to worry about him embarrassing you in front of your smarmy sycophants."

"Stop being such a jackass, Janus. Can't you be an adult about the fact that I'm living with another man."

"You're living together?" Janus shook his head in disgust, "Of course. Why pass up any opportunity of flaunting a Q.C. on your arm, whenever you go out in public?" He smirked. "Lawyers don't have exactly the best reputation in the world. You know the old joke. What do you call it when a bus full of lawyers drives over a cliff sending them to a painful and fiery death and there are three empty seats?" Janus laughed bitterly. "A missed opportunity."

"Typical. Jagg spends his life making the world a safer place for businesspeople and all you can do is mock him."

Janus snorted. "What a noble endeavour that must be, helping all those poor disenfranchised industrialists." He shook his head in contempt. "Jagganath Nod. I knew that name sounded familiar. Isn't he suing those Friends of Gaea eco-nuts for defamation and acts of vandalism committed against his client, Circean Dreams?" He laughed again. "You're dating a lawyer for a pig farmer? Now, that's coming up in the world."

"Circean Dreams is one of the largest farms in Canada and Jagg's retainer is close to half a million dollars a year," said Achates indignantly.

"I'm SO impressed. Better hope Circean Dreams doesn't turn out to be a *Soylent Green* nightmare. Maybe Jagganath can convince them to expand up towards Churchill. Provide the polar bears with a live buffet like that last idiot pig farmer did."

"I don't know why I bother talking to you. Just leave and don't come back." Achates reached down on his desk and grabbed the bouquet of roses. He threw them at Janus. "We're through. If you try to come around again, I'll have security throw you out on your ass."

Janus clenched the bouquet tightly in his hand. The thorns broke through the plastic wrapping and punctured his palm. "Fine by me. Anyone who could date a pig farmer's lawyer is far beneath my standards."

"Pond scum has higher standards than you have, Janus."

"Considering whom I last dated, that must be true." Janus threw the mangled flowers back at Achates. They bounced off his chest and fell to the floor. Janus stormed out, slamming the door behind him. Blood dripped from his hand as he strode towards the elevators. Inside the elevator, he painfully yanked three thorns from his palm. He threw them on the floor. Drops of blood fell on the floor as he exited the elevator.

"Mr Styx."

Janus turned to glare at the no-longer indifferent security guard gripping his walkie-talkie.

"Achates Marshall from Arachne Web Designs wants me to make it clear to you that you are now *persona non grata* in this building. If you attempt to come here again, you will not be allowed back in his business and the authorities will be called. Do you understand?"

"Perfectly," Janus grunted as he slammed the door behind him. Damn Achates. I'll make him pay for humiliating me. Dumping me for a pig farmer's lawyer. Siccing a stupid security guard on me. Bastards. Janus stopped walking. That client who came out of his office. That was Jagganath Nod. Stunned, he brought his palm up to his mouth and began to suck at his wound. Stings like the devil. Don't want this to become infected. They have a first aid kit at the Loaves and Fishes. Better walk over there and get this fixed up. Retribution can wait. He smiled. Revenge is a dish best served cold.

Gabe lugged a heavy box of supplies up the driveway to The Mysteries of Cybele's business office. He grunted. God. I can't believe Cybele needs all this crap for her first Friday evening ritual. It better be worth the hernia I'm going to get. He sighed. At least it'll be something exciting to put in my story. I just hope everything goes well tonight. He stopped and looked inside Cybele's office. Wow. Cybele looks pretty wired. I bet she's already had two mochaccinos and it's only ten o'clock in the morning.

Cybele jumped up frantically. "Gabe, thank the gods, you're finally here." She grabbed the box from his arms and nearly dropped it. "Oomph. Help."

Gabe laughed and grabbed the slipping box from her arms. "Where do you want me to put it?"

A flustered Cybele looked up at him and forced herself to maintain her calm. "Put it on the floor in front of my desk. We have a lot of work to do and we need these supplies."

Gabe peered inquiringly inside. "So, what could be possibly be in this box that we don't already have?"

“Certain types of herbs and incenses that we need to create the potions and sacred fires for the special effects portion of tonight’s special spiritual services. We couldn’t special order them in enough quantities for tonight.” She bent down and hurriedly started to unpack the supplies. “Well, we might have been able to but with all the security at the border, it was too chancy to risk a border delay, when The Magic Box already has most of them in stock. And several of the new hires have picked today to goof off and not come in at their scheduled time.” She growled in frustration. “I’m definitely going to have words with Janus about that because he promised me they’d be reliable.”

“Whoa.” Gabe patted her on her back. “I think you’re buzzed from too much caffeine. Take a deep breath and relax. I’m here and I’m ready, willing, and able to help.”

Cybele laughed and took a deep breath. “Ready, Willing, Able, and Gabe, eh? Good to know you’re the equivalent of four people in one. I feel much better already.”

Gabe shook his head. “You’re such a nut sometimes.” He got down on the floor beside her and started to help unload the box. He said more softly, “It’s one of your most endearing qualities.”

Cybele blushed slightly but continued to check that all the supplies she needed were in the box. Focus on the job, Cyb. Fun and games later. “Okay. I think we have everything we need for tonight’s special mixtures. I need you to help me mix them together for both the indoor and outdoor rituals.”

"Just give me the orders, O Great Goddess, and your will be done," Gabe joked.

"Smartass," Cybele said affectionately. She pulled her Book of Shadows off her desk. "The first recipe we need to make is the Fire of Azrael. Watch closely because this is part of your job as well."

Gabe nodded and handed her one of the wooden bowls half-filled with salt that Cybele had laid out at the side of her desk.

"Add one pinch of sandalwood, one pinch of cedar, and one pinch of juniper to the bowl." She demonstrated the procedure quickly for him. "Like this, see."

"Got it." Gabe proceeded to copy her instructions and make his own bowl of Fire of Azrael. "So, what's this stuff used for?" he asked curiously.

Cybele answered offhandedly. "Oh. It's meant to induce images and apparitions. We'll make up some extra bags of it and use them on the outdoor rituals as well."

Gabe looked perplexed. "We'll burn them as part of the fire?"

"No." Cybele continued to fill her ritual bowls without pause. "After the fire has been quenched, we'll throw them on the coals. It'll be quite a sight." She poked him in his side. "Trust me."

Gabe leaned back on his heels. This is actually a lot of fun. "What's next?"

"An apparition incense for the basement rituals, to get people into the right state of mind. I need one pinch of angelica, one pinch of kava kava, one pinch of star anise, and one pinch of ..." Cybele paused uncomfortably with a quick sideways glance at Gabe. "One pinch of parsley."

Gabe scrutinized their assortment of bottles and vials. He turned back to Cybele. "I can't find the bottle of parsley."

Cybele looked as if he had poked her with a pin. "Oh, that's okay. I have some in my purse." She reached into her purse and pulled out a little baggie full of herbs. "Just put a little pinch in it like this." She started to return the baggie to her purse when Gabe gently caught her hand and took the baggie in his.

"You know, that parsley looks a little like pot."

She smiled but was unable to meet his gaze. "But pot is illegal and parsley is not. Therefore the pot just looks like parsley." She gently gnawed her bottom lip. "I mean the reverse of what I just said." She sighed. "Look Gabe. It's just a tiny bit of a herb that will add immeasurably to people's experiences. It's no big deal."

"I agree, it's no big deal for people who know that they're doing it. But what about those who don't know and have a drug test or something Monday morning." He challenged her gently. "Is it fair to them if they fail it because trace amounts of pot show up and they didn't even knowingly take it."

"Oh gods. I never even thought about that." Cybele looked up at him with startled eyes. "Most pagans use a little pot in their rituals to heighten the divinatory experiences. But we don't usually have the kinds of jobs where we get tested for drugs. I certainly don't want to cause harm to someone else." She wrung her hands. "It's not the pagan way." She sighed regretfully. "I guess I just have trouble understanding why a mood altering drug like pot is illegal and alcohol isn't." She nodded forcefully. "But, you're absolutely right." She picked up the bowl and tossed the contents out the window. She then proceeded to empty her baggie out the window as well. She walked over to a little box behind her desk and pulled out a bottle. "This is star anise. It won't have the same effect as the hemp would have had, but with a little alcohol, it should still help induce visions." They proceeded to make new bowls of incense containing the star anise.

Cybele looked up to see if Gabe was still watching closely. "Now, Gabe, this final incense is for the outdoor ritual fires. It is called Moonfire Incense and you have to be super careful when making it. I make only enough for the ritual and never leave any in storage." She pulled a large metal bowl from off her desk. "Take one pinch rose, one pinch orris, one pinch bay, two pinches juniper, one pinch dragon's blood..."

"Dragon's blood?"

"It's a poetic name. I can't pronounce its real name in Latin. Something like *daemonorops draco*." She paused for emphasis. "The ingredient you have to be very careful when using is the last one. Take only half a pinch of potassium nitrate and add it to the mix."

Gabe pulled back confusedly. "Isn't that an explosive?" What the hell?

"Only in large quantities," Cybele said dismissively.

"Isn't it illegal?" Please don't let it be illegal.

"No. Ironically, while pot is illegal, potassium nitrate isn't. Go figure, eh?"

Gabe still looked dubious. “So, we’re not making explosive incense?”

“No.” Cybele laughed. “That’s why I’m so careful when I make this. We just put enough potassium nitrate in to create a mild sparkling and glowing effect. The incense has far less than you would find in those sparklers people put on birthday cakes. It’s perfectly safe. But I still take the precaution of never keeping this incense mix in storage and I never keep too much potassium nitrate on hand either.” She looked over at Gabe. “I also don’t advertise that I use potassium nitrate or that I keep some in storage. That’s one of the reasons my own personal Book of Shadows is always locked away in my desk drawer. For security reasons.” She said regretfully under her breath, “Herbs should not be abused. People just don’t realize how deadly they can be.”

With an effort, Cybele shook off her suddenly pensive mood and stood up and stretched. “Good. We’ve done the grunt work for the incenses. Now we need to prepare the herbal mixture for the warmed wine we will be serving as part of the indoor ritual. We have to go to the kitchen to get the supplies for that.”

They walked over to the kitchen. Cybele grabbed some cheesecloth and laid it out on the counter. “Take 40 cardamom seeds, 50 whole cloves, and 8 cinnamon sticks. Wrap them up in the cheesecloth. Toss it into the slow cooker.”

Gabe inhaled deeply. “Mmm. Smells good.” Like Cyb.

“Oh, it’ll taste pretty good too.” Cybele went to the refrigerator and pulled out orange juice, lemon juice, and two bottles of red wine. "Gabe, can you get me some white sugar from our coffee supplies?"

"Sure." Gabe brought over a small bowl of sugar. "Now what?"

"Put in all the red wine, 2 cups of the orange juice, 1 cup of lemon juice, and I cup of sugar."

Gabe added all the ingredients and stirred them together. Cybele then pulled a small bottle out of her sweater pocket.

"This is wormwood. Add one teaspoon to the entire mixture. Then take the slow cooker downstairs and plug it in. We will be drinking this mixture as part of our indoor rituals. We will be drinking non-alcoholic wine without wormwood for the outdoor rituals."

"Why? What does wormwood do?" asked Gabe. It sounds so familiar.

Cybele giggled. Wormwood virgin. "Oh, it enhances the narcotic effect of alcohol which is why I used such a tiny amount. That's also why the non-alcoholic wine will be used for the later rituals. I don't want people to become too intoxicated and then have to drive themselves home."

"That's good thinking." She does care about her members. It's not only about profit for her.

Cybele nodded thoughtfully. "Well, it's partially out of concern for their welfare as well as a desire to avoid getting sued if, the gods forbid, they get into an accident on their way home."

Gabe laughed. Oh well. "Well, either way, the end will be the same. No drunks on the road."

"Well, at least not as a result of attending my rituals." She poked him gently. "Enough chit chat. Let's get our work done. Our first guests are coming soon."

Chapter 13

Four hours later, Gabe walked down the basement stairs and drew his breath in amazement. My God. The place had been transformed. The concrete walls painted in red and dark purple swirls seemed almost psychedelic under the dimly lit ceiling lights which were flickering on and off in a deliberate pattern. The room itself seemed several degrees hotter than the upstairs of the house. He looked around and saw two small space heaters set at opposite ends of the basement. They were blowing fiercely. The slow cooker filled with wine bubbled merrily away in the corner like some modern-day cauldron. The bowls of incense burning away in strategic places throughout the basement permeated the air with an intoxicating aroma. A subliminal chanting filled his ears courtesy of Surround Sound. His senses overwhelmed, he smiled in bemusement, and walked over to Cybele.

"This décor is amazing. I'm already intoxicated and I haven't had anything to drink yet."

Cybele looked up from the floor where she was meditating and smiled proudly. "That was the plan. I deliberately tried to appeal to people's senses, to overwhelm them with stimuli, in order to give them as pleasurable experience as possible."

"Well, it worked. I feel like I'm in a dream and you look like you've stepped off the pages of *Arabian Nights*."

Cybele looked down at her outfit. A narrow, diaphanous golden scarf that fell from a gold circlet around her head. A short sleeved dark purple bolero jacket. A translucent gold undershirt. Dark purple gossamer harem pants. Serpentine gold bracelets on each wrist and gold anklets with a tiny bell attached to each one. "Thank you. It's a leftover costume from when I took belly dancing classes. I always knew I'd get a chance to wear it in real life." She laughed. "Well, if a ritual ceremony for a cult can be considered real life." She looked over at Gabe. He was wearing a black turtleneck and black corduroys. "You look nice, if a trifle subdued."

"Well, I'm not the star of the show, only her humble priest."

She tugged gently on the hem of his pants. "Just be sure that you don't throw yourself too literally in the role. No ritual castrations, if you please."

Gabe leaned down and lightly caressed the scarf hanging down the back of her head. "I'll do my best to control my religious fervour. Besides, I can think of far more enjoyable ways to express my devotion to you than with castration."

Cybele stood up and stretched languorously. "So can I." She looked up into his face and smiled flirtatiously. "So, other than making promises which you don't have time to keep, did you have another reason for coming down to see me?"

Gabe coughed and ran his finger along the top of his turtleneck. "Why is it so hot in here?"

Cybele leaned forward more closely to him and whispered. "The heat is meant to lower people's inhibitions, make them more receptive to the ecstatic experience in store for them. Do you think it's working?"

Gabe swallowed and said hoarsely. "Most definitely. I can't wait for the ecstasy to begin."

"Good." Cybele gently pressed her body against his. "Did you want to meditate with me before the rituals begin? It will enhance the quality of your ultimate mind-body connection."

Gabe cleared his throat. "Nothing would give me greater pleasure..."

Cybele winked flirtatiously. "Oh, there are a few things that could..."

Gabe reached down and lightly stroked her cheek. Later. "But I came down to tell you that all our guests are signed in and waiting to be brought down for the rituals to begin."

Cybele took a small step away from him. Back to business. "Have you made sure that they've all paid? Run all their credit card numbers to make sure they're all valid?"

"Yes." Gabe smiled. "Everyone's paid in full. Should I bring them down now?"

"Yes." She looked intently at him. "And remember to call me *Bruja*. I don't want them to think I'm some nut who thinks she's the reincarnation of a Phrygian goddess."

"Got it." Gabe stroked her cheek again. "You're a *Bruja*, not a nut."

Cybele gently caught hold of his hand. "Just wait until later." She intertwined her fingers and his. "I'll get you, my pretty."

Gabe reluctantly pulled his hand away. "I live in hope." He then ran up the stairs to collect the participants while Cybele made a quick check of the room to ensure that everything was in place.

Good. If this doesn't turn out to be an event full of pageantry and drama, I'll give them their money back. She smiled ruefully. Well, no, I won't. But that doesn't matter. With the amount of hallucinogenics in these herbs, they'd have to be hardcore stoners not to get a little high. The noise of people nervously chattering as they walked down the stairs made her look up. Good. They all look young. They should have open minds and be easier to manipulate than more older cynics. She walked over to the centre of the room, clenched in her stomach muscles, to give her voice greater power and resonance, and spoke.

"Be welcome, dear ones." She dramatically gestured towards the centre of the room. "Come sit down on these places which have been prepared for you." She sighed as she saw the anticipation and uncertainty on the participants' faces. They were already feeling the effects of the herbs, heat, and ritual chanting. Come my little lambs to the slaughter. Hmm. She softly shook her head. Not to the slaughter but the place of enlightenment.

"I am a *Bruja* of Cybele. It is my privilege and honour to initiate you into Her Mysteries." She focused on the excited faces in front of her. This is going to be like shooting fish in a barrel. Which I've never understood, because wouldn't the gun fill the barrel with holes, then the water would drain out, and you'd be left with a lot of rotting fish, most of which you wouldn't use because who wants to eat a barrel of fish. Gods. Focus Cybele. Don't let the hallucinogenics cause you to get too high to function.

Gabe coughed softly. "*Bruja*..."

Cybele snapped back to attention and gave Gabe an appreciative nod.

She looked down at her coalition of the willing. "Before you can obtain oneness with the Goddess, you must first cast off the shackles of your mortal coils, the body which imprisons your soul. I will be your mentor, your guide through this amazing journey of self-discovery and initiation so few are privileged enough to make." She crossed her arms against her chest with a dramatic thud. Slowly, she unfolded her arms and gracefully sank down to the floor in front of the group. Sitting cross-legged on the floor, she gave her followers a beatific smile.

"The most important thing that you must learn to do is to find your centre. When you are within your centre, you are invulnerable to the slings and arrows of others. You will be in complete balance and harmony with the earth beneath you." She lay down on her back and placed her feet firmly on the floor. "Please try to copy this position. If you experience any difficulty in following my actions, raise your hand, and I or *Brujo* Gabe will assist you."

The participants eagerly followed her example, some a bit woozily, clearly beginning to feel the effects of the drug induced incenses.

Cybele continued. "Now, I wish you to begin some deep, rhythmic breathing. Try to do it to the beat of the chanting. Inhale deeply through your mouth and exhale loudly through your nose." She looked over and nodded in approval. "Very good, dear ones." She lay back down again. "Now, I want you to hum as evenly as possible on your exhale. Each time you exhale, try to hum more loudly and hold it for a longer period of time."

Cybele stood up and began to circulate quietly around the participants. "Very good, dear ones. Keep humming on those exhales. You might begin to feel a little light-headed. Enjoy the experience. You are being filled with the presence of the Goddess, a religious state of enthusiasm."

She lay back down at the front of her acolytes. "Now, imagine you are melting into the earth, becoming one with Gaea. Envision the luminous being beneath your flesh being pulled down from the soles of your feet and into the earth, into the centre of She who is the Mother of us all. Release all fears and doubts and allow your spirit to become one with the ephemeral world. Be at peace for the Goddess is Love and She fills you with Herself unselfishly."

She smiled to herself. Good. With all that deep breathing and lack of oxygen, they will be in a very susceptible state. "Now when you inhale, see yourself drawing up the power of the earth into your physical body. You are an empty vessel. Fill yourself with the energy of the entire world around you."

She took a deep breath, smiling as she felt herself filled with the intoxicating power of the hallucinogenic herbs. Can't enjoy the experience of inspiration too much. Must focus on the paying customers. "Now, slowly sit up."

The coalition of the willing drew themselves up, awkwardly attempting to mimic their new leader. They were clearly in a lethargic state, dazedly looking around with glassy smiles on their contented faces.

"Very good, dear ones. Now, I want you to pick up the purple rose lying in front of you." She frowned unconsciously. Hope the spray paint has dried. Oh well. She shrugged and continued. "Slowly stand up and turn towards your fellow brother or sister. If you peer closely at each other, you should see an aura of purple light encircling each other. Do you see this light?"

The participants slowly nodded as the flickering lights combined with the hallucinogenics in the air produced a haze within their minds.

"Good. Using the rose, lightly brush its soft petals over your partner's aura. With each caress, imagine you are cleansing their aura of all negative energy. Hum deeply as you stroke their aura from head to toe."

Obediently, the followers began to hum. They began to brush their roses over their partners' auras with gentle strokes in a fervent attempt to cleanse their auras of darkness.

My flock of the willing. Cybele smiled deeply as she looked over her first followers. "Now, imagine yourself surrounded by a pure purple light. Feel yourself be penetrated by the power of the Goddess. She loves you. Feel Her power that she shares with you so willingly."

Cybele stood up and walked a little unsteadily to the slow cooker full of warmed ceremonial wine. She slowly reached for the ladle and with the greatest of precision and delicacy began to fill the cups arrayed in a concentric pattern on the table. She turned to see the upturned eyes of her flock fixed dreamily upon her.

She gestured tenderly with her arm towards them. "Come, my children. Time to partake of the wine, the blood of our Goddess. She who gives of Herself so that we may achieve greater spiritual enlightenment. This wine was consecrated under the light of the full moon, blessed with the powers of Goddess. We must be blessed with Her love before we go out into the darkness to perform our ceremony of gratitude and giving."

Clumsily, the participants began to line up in front of Cybele. With a pleased smile upon her face at the sight of such rapture, Cybele waved her hand over each cup to bless it. She gently handed them to the waiting followers, who eagerly drained their cups to the dregs. They then passed to the left of Cybele, carefully placing their cups on the back of the table as directed by Gabe. After they were all done, Gabe carefully led them up the stairs and to their final outdoor ritual.

Cybele took one final, pleased glance around the basement. She nodded her head in acknowledgement of her own brilliance in executing such a splendidly executed performance and danced up the stairs towards her waiting flock.

The participants stood outside in the cool night air, gazing upwards at the sparkling stars. Their heads clumsily turned towards her as they slowly became aware they were once again in her presence.

Cybele raised her arms upwards in supplication to the unseen Goddess. Her jewellery glittered fiercely in the light of the bonfire. The incense placed strategically around the fire gave off an intoxicating aroma that only dissipated slightly in the still of the night.

"Come, my children, gather close. For now, we must offer our thanks to the Goddess who has filled us with such ecstasy."

The flock slowly gathered around the fire with Cybele as the focal point of their gaze. They awkwardly raised their arms up in imitation of her invocation.

"Praise be to the Goddess, for filling us with Her love and very essence of being."

Cybele looked up at the night sky and inhaled deeply. "As I look out at the night's starred face, I see the magic hand of the Goddess move upon these never-ending symbols of high romance." She paused and looked steadily towards her acolytes. "I have no fears, because although I stand on the threshold of a new existence, I am not alone. The Goddess is with me." She paused for emphasis. "She will lead me through to a new realm of being and seeing."

Her flock faithfully repeated her invocation as they too stared transfixed at the stars.

"Cybele's moonlit sea was once at its full and round earth's shore." Cybele sighed dramatically. "And then, the earth wailed in melancholy, as Her reach pulled back, under the pre-emptive attack of the sun, to slumber in the vast dreamlands and naked breadths of the world."

Cybele extended her arms towards her followers, being careful not to get too close to the flames. “Thanks the Goddess we have found Her again. For this world which seems to lie before us like a land of dreams is, in reality, a land of nightmares. For dear ones, while we are here together on this sunless plain, far away, ignorant armies will clash at the break of day.” She took a deep breath and then slowly released it. “We must hold firm to the Goddess, for it is through our communion with Her that we will achieve everlasting peace and salvation.” She paused. “In the Goddess and our union with Her, must we trust.”

The acolytes obediently repeated. “In the Goddess, must we trust.”

“Bless those who have lost their way, for though they are not with us, it would be too arrogant and foolish to assume that they are against us. We must hope they will one day be as enlightened by the Goddess as we have been. For all is good, if it comes from the Goddess.”

Her flock obediently bleated. “All is good, if it comes from the Goddess.”

Cybele turned towards Gabe who stood watching in the flickering shadows cast by the fire. She held out her hands and he carefully handed her a dagger. Cybele raised the dagger above her head. “Behold the Sword of the Goddess, sanctified by blood…” She then lowered the blade into the flames. “And sanctified by fire.” She moved away from the fire a metre to the right. She knelt on the ground.

Her flock moved closer towards her and knelt beside her also.

By the flickering of the fire, she carefully sawed away a small circle in the earth. She lifted away a piece of the earth with her hands and tossed it into the fire. She carefully handed the dagger back to Gabe.

In return, he gave her an earthenware pitcher.

Cybele stood up and held the pitcher up over her head.

Her acolytes quickly stood up to follow her lead.

"Blessed Goddess, we thank you for this land of milk and honey which you have bestowed upon us. Please accept our gratitude with our libation of love." She lowered the pitcher and began to pour the mixture of seeds, milk, and honey into the circle of earth. "As you have blessed us, now let us bless you."

She passed the pitcher to each member of her flock and indicated that they should pour a little of the libation into the circle. When the last had finished, Cybele handed Gabe the empty pitcher and received another full one from him. She turned to her followers. "Hold out your hands and receive the Goddess' final blessing for tonight."

She began to pour a mixture of honeyed, non-alcoholic wine in their cupped hands. "As you lap this sweet potage of the Goddess from your palms, know that you are Her beloved children." She handed Gabe the now-empty pitcher and turned back to her flock.

"Now, my dear children, the rituals of worship for this evening have reached their climax. You may stay here and bask in the glow of the Goddess for as long as you wish. Only when you feel capable of movement once again, may you leave to return back to your homes, never again alone, for the Goddess will now be with you wherever you go."

Cybele walked away from the fires and towards Gabe standing solitary in the darkness. They stood and watched as the followers began to move down the long, winding driveway. When the last one had left, Cybele turned to Gabe.

"Make sure the bonfire is completely out. I'm going back to the basement to make sure that the incense has burned away and everything else has been put away." She turned to walk away.

Gabe gently caught hold of her sleeve.

She paused and turned back around. "Gabe?"

"Cybele." He paused not knowing quite what to say. "That was quite a performance that you put on tonight."

She spoke softly, "It was meant to be. They deserved to get their money's worth."

"You had them in the palm of your hands," said Gabe in wonder. "Doesn't that bother you, that you have such power over them?"

"A little, but that was the whole point, Gabe." Cybele beamed at him. "In order for them truly to achieve ecstasy, they had to give themselves over to another. Be filled by something from outside themselves. I was just the latest incarnation of the Holy Spirit, whispering sweet nothings in their ears. I did this to help them..." She gently took hold of Gabe's hand. "On their quest to gain spiritual enlightenment. I would never use my powers of persuasion to hurt them in any way. You must believe me."

Gabe lightly touched the back of her head. "I believe you. I just wasn't aware of how enthralling you could be. A veritable Siren." He shook his head in disbelief. "I guess I'm just astonished at how susceptible they were to your words. Worried that some less scrupulous people could manipulate them to do the bidding of evil."

Cybele moved closer to Gabe and clasped him gently just above his elbows. "The sad truth is that most people are only too willing to give up their sense of self and blindly follow the dictates of any would-be tyrant. All I can do is try to ensure that those who follow me gain more from me than I take from them. I can't change human nature, but I will try to care for those under my protection."

Gabe slowly bent his head closer to hers. Cybele took an unsteady breath and angled her head closer to his. Just as their lips were about to meet, Cybele pulled smoothly away.

"It's been a very long day and I'm exhausted." She smiled serenely. "We both have miles to go before we sleep. We should get our work done before Helios comes up and brings Eos with him." She moved away from him and walked towards the house.

Gabe stood and watched her until she passed through the doorway. Then, with a frustrated sigh, he forcefully extinguished the bonfire, using the fire extinguishers Cybele had so lovingly adorned with flowers.

Chapter 14

Gods. I hate Sundays. There should be a law that makes it illegal to have to get out of bed before Helios is at least midway across the sky. Cybele sipped her mochaccino and sighed tiredly. She began to go through the internet orders for magical accessories that were in a frighteningly high pile on her desk. She looked over at the picture of Penelope so industriously working at her loom. Ah, Penelope. Did you ever get tired of being the one responsible for weaving the threads of your own destiny? She sighed. I wonder if you were really happy to see Odysseus. Weren't you even a little pissed that he had taken so long to get back to you? You must have heard stories of his infidelities. I wonder if everything really ended happily ever after or if you managed to pull a Clytemnestra, just more subtly than she did, poor dear.

Cybele stood up and began to stretch tiredly. Gods. I think I must have been a little too pumped these last few days. Nothing like playing Goddess to give one an adrenaline rush. Of course, all that wine and incense probably didn't hurt either. I definitely feel like I'm crashing today. Everything went so perfectly Friday. Hiring Gabe was the best business decision I could have made. He was a great Attis to my Cybele. Not like Janus who didn't even bother to show up. He's about as dependable as some of those street kids of his who also blew off the rituals. At least, I can fire them.

She looked up as Janus walked through her office door and slumped into a chair in front of her desk.

"Well, speak of the devil. Janus, what the hell happened to you this weekend? You look like you've been on a bender." Cybele wrinkled her nose in disgust. "Did you swim in beer? You know, Janus, your maharishi, Marie Antoinette took baths in milk not in beer."

Janus looked up at her and glared. "Oh, go dunk a donut in that swill you call coffee."

Cybele laughed. "I prefer brioche." She sat down in her chair and leaned forward over her desk. "So, tell me, what has reduced you to such desperate straits. Let me make everything better."

Janus grunted. "Achates."

Cybele sighed. "You went to see Achates." Idiot.

"Yes. I was hoping we could try and patch things up. I even bought him the most expensive roses I could find..."

Cybele looked at him expectantly. "But?"

"He's already living with someone else." Janus snorted disgustedly. "Some bastard pig farmer's lawyer."

"Oh." I see. Cybele leaned back in her chair.

"Jagganath Nod." Janus seethed contempt. "One of the chosen few. Someone who can help Achates realize his political and social ambitions."

Cybele rolled her eyes exasperatedly. "So, Achates rejected you and you thought you would get even with him by getting drunk?"

"I was drowning my sorrows." Janus smirked. "It just took a lot of beer to get the job done."

Cybele groaned. "You're such a drama queen."

Janus snickered. "Well, it takes one to know one."

Cybele reached out and patted Janus on his arm. "I am sorry that you and Achates weren't able to reconcile."

"Don't be." Janus shook his head dismissively. "Everything always works out for the best, in this, the worst of all possible worlds, remember?"

Cybele nodded approvingly. "Well, now that you've done your wallowing, are you ready to rejoin the world of the living?"

Janus grabbed her cup playfully away from her. "I might be able to, if you share your coffee with me."

Cybele grabbed it back. "Not a chance. That breath of yours could kill from six feet away. But, I could be persuaded to make a cup of coffee for you, if you ask me nicely."

Janus groaned. "Please O Great and Merciful Goddess, take pity on this poor sinner and share with me the sweet ambrosia of the gods, a cup of caffeine."

Cybele laughed. She and Janus got up and headed towards the kitchen.

Janus looked at her apologetically. "I'm sorry that I missed your first religious revival. How did it go?"

Cybele glowed. "Better than I could have ever expected. I was on a natural high all evening." She chuckled. "Well, part of it was a little herb induced, but still all-natural." She frowned slightly as she remembered she still had a bone to pick with him. "Although a few of the street kids you hired to help with the set-up were no-shows. You told me that they were reliable."

Janus closed his eyes and held his head in an attempt to stop the room from spinning. “Which ones?”

“Oh, those mindless minions known as your Fab Four.”

Cybele nudged him to open his eyes and accept a cup of coffee from her.

Janus took it from her gratefully. “Oh. I’ll speak to them about it. I’ll make sure it doesn’t happen again.”

“It better not.” Cybele frowned. “Otherwise they certainly won’t be working for me again. I need people I can depend on.”

“Don’t worry.” Janus saluted her with his cup. “Be Happy.”

She snorted back. “Thank you, Bobby McFerrin.”

They laughed. Janus’s laugh cut off abruptly as Gabe walked through the front door.

Janus slammed his cup down on the kitchen counter. “What the hell are you doing here?”

Gabe looked carefully over at Cybele before he answered. “I work here.”

Janus’s eyes glazed over furiously. “Like hell you do.”

Cybele broke in calmly. “Yes. Like hell he does.”

Janus angrily turned to face her. “What do you mean he works here?”

Cybele continued to speak in a reasonable tone, determined not to get into a verbal free-for-all with Janus. “I mean that I hired him as an office assistant to help me run The Mysteries of Cybele. I need someone I can depend on and that has proven to be Gabe.”

Janus thumped the kitchen counter with his hand, nearly overturning his entire cup of coffee. "You have to get rid of him."

"No. I don't." Cybele calmly wiped up the drops that had overflowed the rim of his cup and then lightly tossed the sponge in the sink. She turned back to face Janus. "I don't tell you who should work for you and you don't tell me who should work for me."

Janus grabbed Cybele by her elbow and roughly pulled her into his office. He slammed the door. "How could you hire him? You know I think he's spying on me."

"I know you think that but that doesn't make it true."

"Really. Then how did he even find out about this business?" Janus nodded meaningfully at her. His gesture lost some dramatic impact as he immediately had to grab his head to stop the room from spinning again.

"That's a good question. I'll ask him." She shrugged. "But even if he is a snoop, so what? It's not like we're doing anything illegal here. And isn't it better to have him close where we can keep an eye on him than far away where we can't see what he's doing?"

Janus grunted angrily. "I don't like him and I don't trust him."

"Fine." Goddess. Men are such babies. "But I do like him and I trust him to do his job. So, he stays until he stops doing his job well." Or until he stops looking so yummy.

Janus turned away angrily. "Just keep him away from the phone sex business."

No worries there. Cybele snapped back. "That's your baby, Janus, not mine...Why don't you get your Fab Four to help you with that and Gabe can help me with mine?"

Janus leaned against his desk for support. "Fine. Just keep him out of my sight." He forced himself to swallow down his rising bile. I am not going to throw up with that bastard in the hallway.

"Fine. But you better keep your eyes closed if you come into my office." Cybele turned to leave and then paused. She marched back to Janus. "Do you remember how in elementary school we would play defend the castle on the snow hills on the playground?"

"Yes." Odd time to reminisce. Janus straightened up to look down at her. "We would take turns attacking and defending the castle during recess."

"That's right." With the greatest precision and speed, Cybele raised her foot and slammed it sideways into the back of Janus's kneecap.

Janus's leg crumpled beneath him and he half-fell to the floor. "Fuck. What the hell did you do that for?"

"You're too big now to throw over a hill but that doesn't mean I can't still take you down." She smiled grimly. "Don't ever grab me by the arm and drag me anywhere again. I'm a pagan not a pacifist." She walked through the doorway and turned. "If I were you, I'd get an ice pack for that knee. It's going to swell up like a balloon if you don't." She threw him a quick salute. "Happy trails, *kemo sabe*. Look me up when you're ready to apologize. Forgiveness is just one heart-felt 'I'm sorry' away."

Janus limped to the door and slammed it behind her. He doubled over. Bitch. He smiled despite the pain. For a pacifist, she sure has a wicked temper. He sighed. I'll apologize later. I think right now I need two ice packs, one for my head and one for my knee. Maybe a bucket too. Just in case. He sunk down into his chair. What the hell is Gabe up to? I'm definitely going to have to keep a closer eye on him.

Cybele casually strolled towards the kitchen where Gabe stood anxiously drumming his fingers on the countertop.

She placed her hand over his fingers to stop the drumming. "Sorry you had to see that. Janus and I have known each other forever. Our fights can get pretty fierce."

"Are you okay?" Gabe lightly caressed her fingers. "I was concerned about you."

She smiled and shook her head. "Oh, I can take care of myself. Janus is all bark, no bite."

"I didn't like to see him grab you like that."

"Neither did I, which is why Janus will be limping for the next few days." She leaned closer and whispered. "Pretend not to notice."

Gabe whispered back. "Okay."

Cybele straightened up. Enough foreplay. Back to business. "We have a lot of work to do this morning. Grab a cup of coffee and let's get started." She sauntered off to her office. Gabe got his coffee and followed her.

As they began to sort through their paperwork, Janus's door opened. They heard the sound of muttered cursing as Janus heavily limped down the hall and slammed the front door behind him.

Cybele chuckled silently. Good Night, Sweet Prince. That'll teach you to take out your bad mood on me. She looked up to see Gabe watching her intently. How DID Gabe know about this business? He never did say. She smiled back at Gabe but said nothing. We have a lot of work to get done. Good things come to those who wait.

Gabe sighed silently. I am getting way too attached to her. Iris was right. I better make sure the only thing I pump her for is information. Damn it. Riddle me this. Riddle me that. Why did she pull away when I tried to kiss her?

Later that Sunday evening, Janus sat on his deck and raised his bottle of beer in mocking homage to the stars. Fucking points of light in a sea of darkness. The world is in one long spiral of death and despair. Hope is the final casualty of life. He sighed heavily. Revenge is the rough beast whose hour come round at last frogmarches towards Bethlehem to be born. He drained his bottle to the dregs and then threw it against the back bench encircling his deck. The bottle smashed. Shards of glass and droplets of beer flew everywhere. So it goes. He stood up to get another beer. God. I need a soma.

"Hey, man, you don't want to waste good beer."

Janus turned to see Tan approaching from around the corner of his house. Ardiaeus, Ixion, and Ajax were close behind him.

Janus forced himself to smile light-heartedly. “So, what the hell happened to you guys Friday? Take a wrong turn and drop off the face of the earth, eh?”

Tan cleared his throat nervously. “Yeah, sorry about that, man, but we got held up at this really awesome house party in Steinbach.”

Ixion chimed in, eager to explain. “Yeah, a this guy I know was house-sitting for his parents and decided to throw a kegger. You know, have a little fun before the chickens come home to roost.”

Ardiaeus elbowed Ixion roughly in the ribs. “Yeah. We got totally wasted.”

Ixion winced as he rubbed his side. He shot a hurt look at Ardiaeus but said nothing.

Ajax smirked. “We totally tore up the house. He is SO busted when his parents get back home.”

Tan laughed. “That’ll teach them to leave a behemoth like Golly in charge.”

Ixion began to smile again as he remembered everything they had done. “God.” He giggled. “Those jello shooters were a kick. Slid down my throat so easily, I didn’t even have to swallow.”

Janus grunted. Idiots. “I’m thrilled for all of you. Good to know that you take your jobs so seriously, that you don’t even bother to call to say you’re not coming in.”

Tan grimaced. Damn. Hoped he wouldn’t bring that part up. “We’re sorry. We thought you would be cool with it. We had done everything you asked us to do, but that Cybele was bossing us around worse than Matthew."

Ajax scowled. "Yeah. She was giving us orders like we were her slaves or something. So we thought it would be funny if we blew her off and she had to do everything herself."

Janus wrapped his fingers hard around the neck of his bottle. He began to fantasize he was slowly strangling the life out of them. "Well, you pissed her off so much that she wants me to fire you and hire more reliable workers."

Tan winced. "Shit." He began to whine. "Man, you can't fire us for blowing off one day and going to a party."

Janus took a quick swig of his beer. "Well, how do I know that you won't blow me off when I need you?"

Ixion broke in immediately. "Because you're our friend, man. We'll be there for when you need us."

Ardiaeus looked longingly at Janus's beer. A cold one would be nice right now. "Yeah, you can count on us."

Janus smiled inwardly at his own prowess. Right where I want them. "I don't want to fire you, but Cybele is pretty mad." He began to pace back and forth dramatically while they watched him anxiously. "Okay. Here's the deal. I'll convince her not to fire you this time but you can't blow off any more shifts. If you do, I won't be able to stop her next time."

Tan nodded. "Thanks." The others nodded their thanks as well.

Janus shrugged. First the stick and now the carrot. "I don't really blame you for cutting out. Cybele can be pretty bossy." He paused for emphasis. "Tell you what. I'm about to start taking more of an active interest in the business, so how about you start working more for me, and less for her."

Tan perked up. "That sounds great."

"Yeah," the others agreed.

"So, what would we have to do for you?" asked Tan eagerly.

"Well, why don't we talk about it over a couple of beers?" Janus suggested. He pointed to Ardiaeus and Ixion. "Go and get the beers I have in my fridge and bring them out here. There are also some snacks on the table."

They went to get the beer and snacks while Janus, Tan, and Ajax sat down on the deck. Ardiaeus and Ixion returned and passed out the beer and chips. Tan pulled out some joints and passed them round. Everyone including Janus began to smoke them.

Janus inhaled deeply. "That's some good shit, Tan. Thanks."

Tan laughed appreciatively. "You're the best counsellor we've ever had, Janus. You never give us any of that bullshit about drugs being bad and how we have to avoid them because they'll rot our brains."

Janus took another gulp of his beer. "Just Say No is complete bullshit. The only reason pot is illegal is because drug companies haven't figured out a way to make a profit from selling it. If they could patent it, they'd be pushing pot on us for everything from bad hair days to curing the cancer caused by the cigarettes that are deadly but legal."

Ardiaeus nodded solemnly. "Yeah. Life's a bitch and then you die. Can't believe they want you to go through it clean and sober."

Ajax cut in eager to one-up Ardiaeus. "No. Cybele's a bitch. Maybe if she smoked a little pot, she'd loosen up."

Janus glared warningly. "Hey. Cybele's not a bitch and I'd better not hear you call her that again. She's still my friend and your boss, got it?"

Tan broke in and glared at Ajax. "He didn't mean anything by it, Janus. We would never call her a bitch to her face."

"Good." Janus sighed, "I didn't mean to snap at you guys. It's just..." he deliberately broke off. Come to the minnow, little fishes.

"Just what?" asked Tan.

Janus smirked inwardly. "Just that it turns out we have a few snakes in this paradise of ours that we are creating."

Tan looked down quickly at the ground. "Snakes?" The others looked around bewildered.

"Yeah. Seems good old Gabe has decided that working for Cybele is more spiritually rewarding than working for Matthew." Janus looked hard at Tan. "Has Gabriel asked you guys any questions about me or my involvement with this business?"

Eager to contribute to the conversation, Ardiaeus broke in. "He did ask us what made us want to come work here, but nothing really about you."

Tan waved dismissively at Ardiaeus and continued to focus on Janus. "We didn't really talk to him. He's just too nosy. Always trying to ask us about how we feel about our lives and what we're doing. Fucking perv. Like anything about us is any of his business."

Ajax interjected rapidly in an attempt to score points with Janus. "Acts like he's some kind of shrink like you."

Janus nodded. "Yeah. I don't know what made Cybele decide to hire him. He's just acts too fucking superior to everyone else." And he's not. He sighed regretfully. "Well, we're stuck with him until Cybele comes to her senses and fires him. In the meantime, just stay away from him and if he asks you any questions, just play dumb." He smirked. "I know it's a stretch, but I have complete and utter faith in your abilities to do the job."

They all laughed unaware he was mocking them.

Janus inhaled deeply and then looked over at them. "I hope you know how pleased I am with how hard you are working for me. I knew that I could count on you not to let me down."

Tan and the others eagerly nodded their thanks.

Janus shook his head. God. They're like little puppies just waiting for me to pat them on the head and throw them a stick. Wonder if I could get them to roll over and play dead for me. He smiled at that image. "I am giving you each a fifty dollar bonus to show you how much your service to me is appreciated. But don't tell Cybele, since she would probably be pissed that not only am I not firing you for blowing her off Friday, but I'm giving you a bonus."

Tan quickly shook his head. "Hey. Don't worry, man. We'll play as dumb with Cybele as we do with Gabe. She'll never hear anything from us."

Janus looked warningly at them. "Good. I don't need to hear a lecture from her about rewarding the workers she likes, and not the ones I like." He continued. "You are such good, faithful workers. I hope you know that I consider you to be my friends and not just my employees."

They all puffed up with pride.

Janus sighed. "In this world of easy betrayals, where everyone you know is a Judas, just waiting for an opportunity to stab you in the back, it's so refreshing to see people as loyal as you. You're nothing like..." He shook his head dramatically. "No. He doesn't deserve any of my attention even if he's the biggest traitor I have ever met."

Ardiaeus looked puzzled. "Who?"

Janus shook his head again. "No. Let's not waste our time talking of traitors." He drained his bottle dry. "Say, who wants more beer and snacks?" He smiled at the eager chorus of yeses. He went inside and brought back more beer with a few more bags of snacks. He passed them around and everyone hungrily dug in.

Janus looked over them and smiled. Puppets. Manitoba gumbo. Just waiting to be shaped and moulded into my instruments of vengeance. Come into my parlour, said the spider to the flies. Be careful, Janus. The last thing you want is to be accused of inciting others to do your bidding. Must make it be their own idea.

Janus looked up at the stars. "What a beautiful night. It's so nice to be able to inhale the night air without gagging on it."

The others looked confused but nodded in agreement anyway.

Janus continued. "Not like in Lindenwoods, where you can smell the disgusting odour of sugar beets everywhere. Damn factories. Taking all that is good and beautiful from the earth and corrupting it through technology." He took a long, slow swallow of his beer. "Of course, any fool knows better than to drive through St. Boniface with his car window down in the summertime. Not unless he wants to be overwhelmed with the smell of manure from all those damn mushroom farms."

Uncertain what Janus was talking about, Tan focussed on the only idea he thought was important. "Do they grow magic mushrooms there because that would be cool? We might be able to liberate some of them if they did." He took a long drag and then smiled stupidly. "You know, use them for a higher purpose."

Janus grimaced. What an idiot. "No. Just regular mushrooms. You know society never allows people to grow anything for free that would give them pleasure. That's why people who truly want to be free must live outside society's narrow judgement values." He took another swallow of beer. "Why is it that the people most opposed to recreational drugs are the ones who corrupt our world with pollution? Hypocrites. Anything to make money. Don't they have consciences?"

Ardiaeus nodded knowingly. "Yeah. My parents both drive SUVs and they say recycling is just a pain in the ass, so they never do it." He growled. "Hypocrites. They drink and drive all the time but I get caught with a little weed and they ground me. Bastards."

Janus looked over at him approvingly. "Precisely my point. People are hypocrites. They come down hard on us but they get away with far worse crimes than just smoking pot or dropping a little acid."

Ajax nodded sadly. "But we can't do anything. It's us against the system and the house always wins."

Janus clenched his hand. Time to tighten the web. "Sometimes, don't you ever wish you could win?" He shadow-boxed. "Strike a blow for all of us who are ground down by the machine and spit out by all those hypocrites in power." *Soylent Green*, anyone?

Tan shrugged his shoulders. "But how?"

Janus laughed. "Oh, I don't know. I guess every man has to decide for himself how to take revenge for the wrongs that have been done him. I think Shakespeare had it right when he said, 'first thing, let's kill all the lawyers.'" He looked over at his willing minions. Better cover my ass. "Not that I'm saying we should kill those who betray us. No sense in going to jail just to get a little personal justice. But sometimes humiliating one's enemies can be far more enjoyable and satisfying than killing them."

Tan's face lit up in understanding. "Yeah. Like when you got into fights on the playground. Knowing you made someone eat dirt was better than just beating him up."

Janus smiled grimly. "Precisely." He continued. "The best revenge is one that targets your enemy's weakness. If you have someone who is pompous and self-righteous, the best way to hurt him is to make him look stupid." He smirked. "For instance, you know those pig farmers who run Circean Dreams?"

Tan laughed. "Yeah. They have all those cool commercials with the singing strips of bacon dancing with the sunny-side up eggs."

Janus nodded. "They try to pretend they're all healthy and friendly, but they're not." He leaned forward. "Actually, they're the worst polluters in all of Canada. They're destroying our environment just to make more money."

Ajax looked puzzled. "But why doesn't someone stop them?"

Janus forced himself to look sad. "Because they're rich and have good lawyers. With a good lawyer, you can get away with anything." He put down his beer with a thud. "Someone tried to stop them, but now the Circean Dreams' lawyer is trying to make an example out of them so everyone else will be too afraid to fight them ever again."

Ardiaeus grimaced. "That really bites."

Ixion nodded. "Reality bites."

Janus rolled his eyes. "It's sad that in this world there are so few warriors left to fight against injustice." He picked up his bottle and took another gulp. "Our only heroes are those found in comic books."

Ajax nodded in understanding. "Like the X-Men."

Enlightenment dawns. "Yeah. I wonder what the X-Men would do to teach those polluters a lesson," said Janus. "Hmm...They would probably go after the lawyer since he's the one who makes it possible for those bad guys to keep breaking the law." He shook his head. "But it's hard to say what they would do."

Tan rubbed his chin thoughtfully as he started to understand the game they were playing. "Maybe they would try to show the lawyer that what he was doing was wrong and give him a chance to stop."

Finally. "Yes. And if the lawyer was very proud, they might try to humiliate him just a little, so he would be punished for the evil he was doing," said Janus.

Tan began to laugh. "That would be justice. Shaming him. Like when they make people stand up in court and admit to all the bad things they did to the judge, and then they have to say they're sorry and won't do it again."

Janus nodded. "The X-Men would probably do something very simple but make his punishment fit his crime. For instance, since the evildoer makes his living defending the right of pig farmers to pollute the environment with seas of pig shit, the evildoer's punishment could be having the pig shit literally brought home to him."

"Like how?" asked Tan.

Janus leaned closer to Tan. "Well, some modern-day X-Men, wearing gloves, of course to prevent the evildoers from tracking our heroes down and punishing them, could gather up bags and bags of pig shit and throw it all over the evildoer's law office or the front steps of his house. To make sure the heroes' car wouldn't be dirty, they could boost a car and use it to transport their act of environmental vengeance."

Eager to participate, Ixion broke in. "The X-Men could set the shit on fire, like bags of dog shit are on Halloween when people go Trick or Treating."

Janus shook his head. "Setting big bags on fire might draw more attention to the X-Men than they would want." He paused. "There are other things the X-Men might do to gain justice for all."

"Like what?" asked Ajax.

"Well. The X-Men could boost the evildoer's car and drive it into the lake of shit that emanates from Circean Delights," added Janus.

"That would be cool," agreed Ixion. "I've never seen a car drown in shit."

"It would be," said Janus. "But the best part is to make sure everyone knows what happened to the evildoer and why he is being punished."

Tan smirked. "How would the X-Men do that?"

Janus punched Tan meaningfully on the shoulder. "Oh. The X-Men are pretty smart. I'm sure they would go to the *Free Press* or *Sun's* Office and tape a letter by the front door explaining what was done to the evildoer and why. Of course, they would cut letters out of a newspaper to write the message. They wouldn't write it by hand. And they would never take the gloves off. And they wouldn't lick the back of the envelope but use a little wet sponge to avoid leaving any DNA evidence behind."

Tan looked closely at Janus. "What should the letter say?"

"Oh, just what the X-Men did and why. You know, for environmental justice." Janus shook his head. "Maybe to avenge those poor Friends of Gaea heroes who are being persecuted by the evildoer's employer?"

"How would the X-Men know the evildoer's name and where he lives and works?" asked Tan worriedly.

Janus shrugged. "Well, I think if the X-Men googled 'Jagganath Nod', they would find all the information they need to carry out their mission."

Tan nodded at Janus to show he understood what he was supposed to do. "It would be nice to live in a world full of X-Men," he said wistfully.

Janus took a celebratory sip of beer. "It would be. But it's hard to find that kind of loyalty and courage amongst most people of this world. There are so few heroes left." He looked over at his flock. "And of course, most people aren't able to keep their heroic identities and courageous deeds secret like the X-Men do. Pity. The world could use a few real life X-Men."

Tan leaned forward to meet Janus's gaze. "Maybe there are a few avengers still left in the world."

Janus looked straight back and smiled. "I guess, time will tell." He yawned. "Well, it's getting late. Time to call it a night."

They echoed their goodbyes and Janus stood up and watched them as they slowly walked away from his deck and into the surrounding darkness. He shook his head. Will Achates and Jagganath reap what I have tried so hard to sow? Perhaps I was too subtle. No.

Whatever happens, I must have plausible deniability. He smirked. No. Your Honour. I had no idea they would do anything like that. We were just talking about comic book heroes. That's all. Just comic books. Nothing more. Nothing less. He exaggeratedly wrung his hands. I'll get you my pretty Jag-off.

Chapter 15

Cybele stood up from her office desk. She yawned and stretched. Gods. I am so stiff. My back is killing me. I can't believe it's only Tuesday morning and I'm already swamped with paperwork and praying for the weekend. Wonder what's happening in the world today, outside these four walls. She walked over to her radio and turned it on to hear the noon news report. She sat back at her desk and immersed herself in paperwork once again as she listened.

Hmmm. Interesting. Those Jubilee traffic cameras photographed 100 speeders yesterday. People are such idiots. They know the cameras are there and yet they continue to speed. She shook her head. Well, it was a nice day yesterday. I guess people just didn't think about the fines they're going to have to pay. Talk about a lack of foresight. Her head snapped to attention.

What was that? Jagganath Nod was the victim of a terrorist attack last night? Impossible. I must have misheard. There are no terrorists in Winnipeg. Just the news media blowing things up out of proportion as usual. Feeding on public fears. Catering to people's egos that they are somehow important enough to be a target. It's that damn anthrax scare all over again. She sighed. Still no smoke without fire. Something happened to Achates' new boyfriend last night. I wonder if Janus heard anything more on the news than I did. If it was big enough, it might have made the newspaper.

There was a loud burst of noise from inside Janus's office. Curious, Cybele got up and walked across the hall. She paused outside the closed door, her hand poised to knock. Her mouth dropped open in shock as she heard someone exclaim loudly that it served that bastard Jagganath right and then the sound of raucous male laughter from inside. What was going on? She dropped her hand and instead quietly moved closer to the door. She placed her ear against the door and attempted to overhear what was being said inside. It sounds like Janus is in there with his Fab Four, but I can't tell who's saying what. Something about Jagganath getting what he had coming. Cybele frowned. How could Janus delight in someone else's misfortune, even if he was Achates' new boyfriend? Whatever happened to Jagganath last night had clearly been significant enough to have made the news. Damn. If only they would speak up. She just couldn't hear what they were saying. She pressed her cheek firmly against the door in a futile attempt at eavesdropping.

Janus laughed boisterously. "From the news reports today, it sounds like our real-life X-Men had quite the adventure last night. Really struck a blow against tyranny for those of us who must suffer under the rule of hypocrisy."

Tan laughed back. "Man, you should have been there. It was a thing of beauty."

Janus leaned back in his chair. "Well, then fill me with joy forever. Tell me exactly what the X-Men did."

Ardiaeus smirked. "Well, first we..."

Tan broke in, giving Ardiaeus an evil glare. "First the X-Men boosted the evildoer's car from outside his house. Then they drove the evildoer's car and their own car to the sea of shit right outside

Circean Dreams. They used shovels to fill up the evildoer's trunk with shit..."

Ixion clapped his hands together in glee. "And they also put some bags of shit in the trunk of their own car."

Tan rolled his eyes at Ixion's excitement. "Then the heroes drove their car back to the evildoer's house just to make sure there was no sign of the police. Then the other X-Men drove the evildoer's car back to his house."

Ajax groaned as he remembered what they had done next. "Then we filled up Jagganath's backseat with the bags of shit that we had carried in our car. That was so disgusting. That shit really stunk."

Ardiaeus smirked as he savoured his final part in their caper. "Then the X-Men threw some firecrackers into the evildoer's car and drove away really fast in their own car."

Tan threw Ardiaeus a warning glare. "But then the X-Men stopped speeding because they didn't want to draw the attention of the cops."

Ajax shook his head knowledgeably. "Yeah. That's always how the cops catch you." He whistled through his teeth. "That's how they caught Bundy and the Son of Sam, you know. Speeding tickets."

Janus scratched his head. "Can you get back to the story of what the X-Men then did?"

Ardiaeus looked almost orgasmic as he spoke. "Well, the X-Men hadn't gone too far away when we heard a big explosion. Seems the firecrackers didn't react to well with the manure."

Tan nodded thoughtfully. “And, I guess the gas in the tank of the car.” He turned to Ardiaeus. “The X-Men hadn’t planned to use firecrackers. One of them decided to do that on his own.”

Ardiaeus shrugged. “It made a very nice fire.”

Tan punched Ardiaeus in the arm. “Fire that drew the notice of people who may have noticed the X-Men’s car.”

Janus leaned forward worriedly. “Do you think the X-Men may have been spotted?”

Tan shook his head. “The X-Men all wore balaclavas. And they burnt all their gloves and masks in the fire pit outside a place that they knew.”

Janus relaxed again. “That was good thinking on the part of the X-Men. What else did they do that night?”

Ajax rubbed his hands together. “Well, they went down to a certain radio station’s business office on Pembina Highway and stuck an envelope explaining what they had done and why to the front door.”

Ixion shuddered. “But they had forgotten the tape so someone had to use some leftover pig shit to stick it to the door.”

Tan looked scornfully at Ixion’s squeamishness. He was such a cry-baby about it. “Probably a good thing. Let them know it was really us.”

Janus nodded in agreement. “Good. How did the X-Men sign the note?”

Ardiaeus smirked. “The Friends of Gaea, of course.”

Janus tapped his fingers against his desk. “Very good. Hopefully, the X-Men will wash their car thoroughly and burn everything from the vacuum bag in the same fire pit they used before.” He paused thoughtfully. “Looks like the X-Men did everything right. The news isn’t reporting that anyone was hurt in the incident so although the firecrackers were unexpected, well, no harm, no foul.” He looked over at Tan.

“Are your friend’s parents still out of town?”

Tan nodded. “Yes.”

Janus smiled at his flock. “Well, why don’t you all take a few days off work and go back for another visit. You could do a little more partying. You certainly deserve a break from all your hard work.” He reached into his wallet and handed them out some money. “Think of it as a paid vacation. While you’re there, see if any of your friends are looking for work. The magic shop web business is booming and we could always use more workers.”

Tan laughed happily. “You’re the best, Magneto.”

Janus shook his head adamantly. “Janus. There is no Magneto.”

Outside the office, Cybele shook her head in disgust. The door was just too thick. Damn these old houses and their use of quality materials in their construction. Cybele sighed and gave up attempting to eavesdrop. Clearly Janus already knew something had happened to Jagganath last night. She’d wait until he was alone before asking him what he had heard or read. She moved back to her office. Maybe there would be another news update on what had happened.

Janus opened his door and Tan, Ajax, Ixion, and Ardiaeus left whooping loudly with excitement. Janus looked over at Cybele's open door and frowned. Wonder if she heard us in there. We did get pretty loud at times. He walked over and poked his head inside.

"Well, since my arch-nemesis isn't inside, I guess I don't have to keep my eyes closed. Your favourite employee call in sick today?"

Cybele looked up and frowned slightly. "No. He's out trying to find some herbs for the weekend rituals. Our supplier is out of stock so Gabe volunteered to go to search the pagan shops in Winnipeg to see if he can get substitutes."

Janus kicked the side of the door lightly. "What a guy."

"Dependability is a virtue, Janus." She shook her head dismissively. "Enough sniping. Have you heard what happened to Achates' newest boyfriend last night?"

"No." Janus stepped further into the room. "What?"

Cybele looked surprised. "You haven't heard what happened to Jagganath last night?"

"No." Janus sprawled casually against the side of the wall. "He's not a topic I take any interest in discussing."

"You haven't heard anything on the news today?" asked Cybele uncomfortably.

Janus shook his head contemptuously. "No."

Cybele took a deep breath. "That's too bad. I only heard a teaser on the radio about Jagganath being the victim of a terrorist attack. I was hoping you could fill me in."

Janus looked up defensively. “Why would you think I know anything about terrorists?”

Cybele shook her head puzzledly. “I thought you might have read something in the paper or watched the news this morning.” She paused. “Why would YOU think that I would think YOU know something about terrorists?”

Janus laughed smoothly. “Oh. You misunderstood me. I thought you were asking if I had heard anything on the news about a terrorist attack.”

“Oh.” She tapped her fingers thoughtfully on her desk. “But you didn’t?”

“No.” Janus straightened up. “But I don’t really care if anything did happen. Couldn’t happen to a nicer guy.”

She sighed. “I can’t believe you would say that. Jagganath Nod never did anything against you. Your beef is with Achates not him.”

“Whatever.” Janus waved his hand at her. “I guess I’m just over Achates and don’t really want to waste any more of my life thinking about him or his new boyfriend.” He smiled. “Let’s talk instead about how well the web business is doing.”

“Okay.” Cybele shook her head. “We’re swimming in orders. We might need to hire even more people to work in the greenhouse creating products and doing the shipping.”

“Good. Why don’t we set up some more interviews…?” He jerked his head away from her. “Do you hear someone banging on the door?”

“I do.” Cybele got up and followed him to the front door.

Janus opened the door to reveal two strangers standing outside.

Cybele looked around Janus and frowned slightly. The woman was wearing a dark blue pantsuit with what looked like a coffee stain on her blouse. The man was wearing a badly fitted grey suit that had clearly been bought off the rack. Yet, there was something about them that grated on her. Cybele's eyes widened. Damn it. They had the same self-important air that cops everywhere seemed to be born with. She supposed it came with having the authority of the state to back them up.

Janus spoke up. "Yes. How can I help you?"

The woman replied. "I'm Inspector Scylla." She gestured to the man. "This is Inspector Geryon. We're with the Winnipeg Police Service. Are you Janus Styx and Cybele Moondragon?"

Cybele nodded surprisedly. "Yes. We are."

Inspector Scylla smiled tightly. "You run the cult known as The Mysteries of Cybele?"

Cybele frowned slightly. "It's an alternative religious business that sells pagan paraphernalia. Why?"

Inspector Geryon smiled falsely. "Can we come in and ask you a few questions?"

Janus moved to block their entrance. "It's such a beautiful day, why don't we all talk outside?" He motioned for Cybele to walk through the door. She did. The Inspectors were forced to step back to allow her to pass. Janus followed her and smoothly pulled the door shut behind him.

Inspector Scylla looked a bit annoyed at being out-manoeuvred. She and Inspector Geryon followed Janus as he walked to a patio bench at the front of the house and calmly sat down. Cybele followed them but remained standing.

Janus sprawled casually on the bench and crossed his feet. "What can we do for you, officers?"

Inspector Geryon frowned. "Actually, we're Inspectors."

Janus nodded. "Fine. Do you have any identification?"

They pulled out their badges and handed them to Janus. He looked them over carefully.

Cybele rolled her eyes. What the hell was Janus playing at? Like he was supposed to be able to tell the difference between real and fake badges, please. She sat down and tried to mimic his relaxed attitude.

Janus handed them back the badges. "So, what can we do for you, Inspectors?"

Inspector Scylla looked closely at Janus. "I'm sure you heard about the terrible attack on a prominent Winnipeg lawyer last night."

Janus nodded slightly. "I think I heard something on the news this morning about a terrorist attack but I didn't play too much attention to it."

Inspector Geryon looked deliberately puzzled. He loomed over Janus as he spoke. "You didn't pay much attention to the news of a possible terrorist attack?"

Janus shrugged nonchalantly. "These days, graffiti artists are probably considered urban terrorists. When the media constantly hype that term, most people just tune it out. Can't live in a state of perpetual anxiety forever."

Inspector Scylla looked sharply down at Cybele. "What about you, Miss Moondragon? Tuned out the news of a terrorist attack as well?"

Cybele frowned at the Inspector's tone. "Actually, it's Ms. Moondragon." She continued sarcastically. "And while I was concerned that something bad might have happened to another human being in this world, the media really now uses the word terrorist, to apply to anyone and everything the state disagrees with." She paused for emphasis. "Thus, I did not take it seriously enough to pull out the duct tape and begin sealing myself in my office."

At Cybele's words, Inspector Geryon deliberately moved uncomfortably close to Cybele. "Where were you last night?" he asked aggressively.

Cybele rolled her eyes. "Are you accusing me of being a terrorist? Because I'm a pagan?" She shook her head disgustedly. "Typical."

Inspector Scylla frowned angrily. "No. We just want to know where you were last night. It's a routine question."

Cybele raised her eyebrows in silent disbelief. "Then I was at home all night watching television with my roommate."

"Your roommate's name?" asked Inspector Geryon.

"Cassandra Hunter," said Cybele.

Inspector Scylla leaned over Janus. "And what about you, Mr. Styx, where were you last night?"

Janus shook his head in disgust. Typical police behaviour. Trying to rattle me by crowding my space. Amateurs. "At home, by myself, counting the stars, trying to fall asleep."

Inspector Geryon looked sceptical. "And were you with anyone?"

"No." Janus smirked. "That's why I was counting stars to try and fall asleep."

Inspector Scylla broke in. "So, you have no one to vouch for your whereabouts?"

Janus grunted exasperatedly. "No. Why are you here asking us these questions? Don't you have better ways of doing your job than harassing law abiding, tax paying citizens?"

Inspector Scylla smiled tightly falsely. "Achates Marshall gave us your names. He said you were ex-friends of his and quite involved in the environmental movement..." She paused slightly and then continued with a meaningful look at Cybele. "And that you might be a good source of information about some other counterculture movements."

Cybele stiffened angrily. "Is it a crime now to be an environmentalist?"

Inspector Geryon looked at her scornfully. "No. But it is a crime to blow up a car and put the lives of an entire neighbourhood in jeopardy."

Cybele's head jerked in surprise. "A bomb? Someone puts a bomb in a car and you come asking us questions about it?"

Inspector Scylla leaned forward over Cybele. "Mr. Marshall felt that you knew a wide assortment of people and might be able to give us some help on the kind of person who might do something like this."

Janus broke in to pull their focus from Cybele. "I don't know anyone who would put a bomb in someone's car. But Mr. Nod is a lawyer. He must have lots of enemies. You should interview them."

Inspector Geryon turned back to Cybele. "And, what about you, Miss Moondragon? Do you know anyone who would do something like this?" He paused calculatingly. "Do you know anyone who is a member of the Friends of Gaea?"

Cybele narrowed her eyes angrily and then smiled sweetly. "It's Ms. Moondragon. Maybe you should write it down to help you remember." She gently shook her head. "I'm sorry. But I don't know anyone who is a member of the Friends of Gaea. Maybe you should go ask them about their membership not me." She sighed regretfully. "And the only people I know who burn things down are the RCMP. Maybe you should find out if Mr. Nod was planning to hold any meetings with the Black Panthers in his car."

Inspector Scylla blew her breath out angrily. Hippie freaks. This is worse than useless. She glared at Cybele who looked back at her serenely. She forced herself to sound matter of fact. "Would you mind if we took a look inside your business?"

Janus's head snapped up. "Why?"

Inspector Geryon smiled reassuringly. "Procedure. Just to tell our superiors that we were as thorough as possible in our interview with you."

Janus smiled back through his teeth. "No. If you have a warrant then you can come in and take a look. Otherwise, our procedure says, protect our civil liberties."

Cybele chuckled bitterly. "Yeah. You know, do not go gently into that bad night. Rage, rage against the corruption of the light."

Inspector Scylla smiled grimly. "Thanks for all your help. We'll see you again if we have more questions."

Inspector Geryon nodded warningly "Yes. We'll be back."

They turned and walked away.

Janus looked over at Cybele and forced himself to laugh lightly. "*Hasta la vista*, baby. Who did he think he was, Schwarzenegger?"

Cybele shook her head angrily. "I can't believe Achates would think we were in any way involved with a car bombing. I can't believe there was a car bombing in Winnipeg." She snorted. "I can't believe they think being an environmentalist somehow makes you more likely to be a terrorist."

Janus patted her on the shoulder. "It's nothing personal. Wasn't the Unabomber an environmentalist? A Luddite?"

Cybele pushed his hand away and growled. "And the Friends of Gaea? When have they ever bombed anything? They may vandalize things but they don't do things that can hurt people."

Janus rolled his eyes. “Cyb, don’t worry so much. No one could seriously suspect you of being a bomber.”

“Right. Because now, thanks to Achates, we’ve somehow become persons of interest. But since no one is ever wrongfully accused or convicted, we have nothing to worry about.” Cybele started to stalk away and then she stopped and turned around. “I thought you hadn’t heard anything about what happened to Jagganath on the news.” She folded her arms across her chest. “But you told the police that you had heard something about it.”

Janus shrugged. “I just didn’t want to talk about it *ad nauseam*.” He smiled nonchalantly. “No harm, no foul, right?”

Cybele looked closely at him. “Right.” She turned around and walked back towards the cult house. She entered and then deliberately slammed the door behind her.

Janus winced at the loud bang. He smirked. Things are getting pretty interesting around here. Wonder if I should call Achates, express my condolences for what happened to his new boyfriend? Maybe later. Once I can do it with a straight face. I should probably go home for a little while. Do some gloating in private. Stay away from Cybele until she stops wanting to talk about what I knew and when I knew it. He hugged himself happily and walked past the cult house into his own home. Everything’s coming up roses.

Chapter 16

Cybele walked into A Taste of Indulgence and grunted hello. Only a few hours had passed since the day that had begun with such promise seemed about to end on such a nightmare.

Cassie looked up from behind the counter and waved when she saw Cybele. Cassie shook her head amusedly. “Cyb, you have the luck of the devil. I just this moment put on a fresh pot of coffee, not the swill I’ve been drinking all day.”

Cybele waved back weakly and then walked over. “Don’t I get cookies too? Caffeine is not enough. Today, I think I need a sugar fix.” She sighed deeply. “Did you hear about the car bombing this morning on the news?”

Cassie shook her head in surprise. “Was there another one? I heard about a car that blew up last night, but nothing about one this morning.” She handed Cybele a cup of coffee. “Maybe we’re having a biker war like they get in Montreal every summer. I sure hope that doesn’t become yet another thing we become infamous for. Being the murder, arson, and stolen car capital of Canada is quite enough for our one little city.”

Cybele smiled weakly. “I don’t think the police think it’s the result of a biker war.” She arched her eyebrow. “Didn’t the name of the victim ring a bell?”

“Not really.” Cassie looked a bit puzzled. “The news said he was a prominent Winnipeg lawyer but I don’t really follow the news.

The weather report gives me all the information I need to know to get through my day."

Cybele shook her head. "That's right. Sunday night, I never told you the name of Achates' new boyfriend. Just that Achates was dating again."

Cassie's eyes widened in shock. "Achates' new boyfriend's car just blew up? Wow. Achates needs to pick his friends more carefully."

Cybele grunted. "Oh. My sympathy for Achates is a bit underwhelming this morning."

Cassie looked more closely at Cybele. "That's not something you would usually say. Are you all right? You look a little bit shell-shocked."

Cybele snorted. "That's one way to put it." She leaned back against the front display case and took a deep sip of her coffee. "Have you ever thought about how deceitful words can be? I mean they start out so honestly. They describe reality and then they become part of the illusion. Propaganda."

Gods. Here we go again. Cassie forced herself to sound interested. "I'm not sure I follow you, Cyb."

"Shell-shocked." Cybele looked at Cassie impatiently. "The condition of being shocked because people were dropping shells on you and trying to kill you. But that wasn't good enough. Too real. So shell-shocked became battle fatigue. Tired of fighting. Tired down to the bone and the soul, I guess." She ran her finger in circles over the rim of her cup. "But we couldn't stop there. Still too real. So now we suffer from PTSD. Post-traumatic stress disorder. A name that covers everything and yet tells us nothing at all." She shook her head. "I am...I am..." She took another sip of her coffee. "I am shell-shocked."

Cassie gently pulled Cybele into a nearby chair and sat down beside her. She patted Cybele comfortingly on the hand.

"Cyb, what's wrong?"

Cybele shook her head in disbelief. "The police came by the business this afternoon to interview Janus and I about what happened to Jagganath Nod's car last night. Seems faithless Achates gave our names to the police as people they might be interested in talking to." She snorted. "You know us pagans, always quick with those bombs. Too busy worrying about the environment to care about human beings."

"The police can't seriously think that you had anything to do with bombing someone's car. I mean..." Cassie laughed incredulously. "What possible motive could you have? If anything, Janus would be a FAR more likely suspect, the lover scorned, you know."

"You're right." Cybele gnawed her bottom lip. "It's just that...I got the distinct impression they were focusing on me as a suspect not really Janus. Which is strange because why would I care about whom Achates is now dating?" Now curious, she leaned forward. "I wonder what Achates could have told them about me that would make them ask me for an alibi."

Cassie began to look worried. What have these two been up to? "Did they ask Janus for an alibi as well?"

"You know, I can't remember." She thought hard for a moment. "They must have," she said doubtfully.

"See." Cassie tried to sound positive. "They're not focusing on YOU as a suspect. They're probably just doing routine interviews of everyone connected to Achates and what's his name."

"Jagganath Nod." Cybele still looked concerned. "And I hope you're this blasé when they come a-knocking on your door to verify my alibi. I told them we were together last night watching television."

"Well, we were." Cassie shrugged nonchalantly. "So, I'll just tell them the truth if they come by to check up on you."

Cybele smiled. "Always go with the truth whenever possible. It'll never trip you up." She bit her lip again. "You know, I don't think it was my imagination that the police were especially hostile towards me. They really seemed to think that either I had something directly to do with it or knew someone who had." She paused uncomfortably. "You know, they asked me about counterculture movements..."

Now Cassie snorted. "Oh, you mean Public Enemies Number One. I can't believe the mainstream is still so threatened by people who want to march to their own drummers."

Cybele forced herself to ignore the golden opportunity Cassie had given her to go off on a diatribe about mainstream society. She continued on with her real worry. "You know they asked me about the Friends of Gaea. They wanted to know if I knew anyone who was a member."

"That's strange." Cassie rubbed her forehead in confusion. "Why would they care about those guys?"

"I'm not sure." Cybele spoke adamantly. "The Friends of Gaea are not eco-terrorists. They may do a few acts of nuisance vandalism, but nothing like a car bomb." She paused thoughtfully. "Maybe the police don't think the attack on Jagganath Nod was personally motivated. Maybe the Friends of Gaea are somehow connected to him."

"Well, that's good. That pulls you out of the picture. You certainly have nothing to do with the Friends of Gaea." Cassie looked over at Cybele's guilty face and groaned. "You don't, right?"

"Very, very tangentially." Cybele tried to downplay her growing sense of unease. "The founder of the Friends of Gaea was an old boyfriend of mine in high school. You know him." She poked Cassie's arm. "Remember Hector Troy? He and Janus were like oil and water."

"Vaguely." Cassie tried to picture Hector's face. "Wasn't he always protesting one injustice or another? Didn't he get arrested at Oka for assaulting a police officer?"

Cybele leapt to Hector's defense. "That was blown out of proportion. He was just one of those protesting outside the reserve. His picket sign accidentally slipped and hit a policeman who was trying to drag him away. The cop was just mad because his head started to bleed a little." She shrugged. "But you know how head wounds are."

Cassie rolled her eyes. "Right. So, is that your only connection to Hector?"

"Well, he had no money for bail, so I lent him the money." She frowned suddenly. "Which, come to think of it, he never paid me back for it. I should call him up and ask him for my money back." She shook her head. "Polonius was right. Never a borrower nor a lender be."

Cassie shook her head. Give me strength. "Don't call him now and ask him for money, okay? Just let it go. Were you arrested at Oka too?" She tried hard to remember if Cybele had called her to make bail that time.

"No." Cybele looked regretful. "I had pneumonia and couldn't go." She smacked her hand forcefully down on the arm of the chair. "But they had a just cause, you know. Trying to build a golf course over burial grounds is disgusting."

"Whatever." Cassie sighed. Get to the point, Cyb. "Have you seen Hector since then?"

"On and off." Cybele found it unexpectedly hard to meet Cassie's gaze. She looked away as she continued to speak. "But he became a little too much the radical activist for me, so we ended up going off in different directions."

"Good." Cassie scratched her head thoughtfully. "Then you have no real connection to Friends of Gaea if it turns out they were involved."

Cybele determinedly ignored Cassie's implicit question. "So, the only other person with even the slightest motive is Janus, and he's not stupid enough to be involved with a car bombing. Petty acts of vandalism, maybe, but a car bombing, no way."

Cassie nodded. "I can't see Janus bombing his ex-boyfriend's new boyfriend's car."

Cybele agreed. "No. That's not something Janus would do..."

Hearing the hesitation in Cybele's voice, Cassie looked up. "But..."

Cybele squirmed. "But...Janus lied to me about it. First he said he knew nothing about it, and then he told the police he had heard about it on the news."

Cassie forced herself to put the best spin on this disturbing revelation. "Well, maybe, he's still angry with you about hiring Gabe." She nodded to herself. "Janus might not want to trust you with personal information if he thinks it might get back to Gabe."

"I'm not a gossip. I know how to keep secrets. It's not like I ever told you about the time that I ..." Cybele smiled guiltily. She quickly gulped down her now cold coffee and handed the now-frowning Cassie her mug. "Wow. Look at the time, I'd better get going." Cybele rushed out the door before Cassie could say another word.

Cassie groaned. I never know when she's pulling my leg or not. She paused. What could she have done to me and never told me? Maybe I should do a tarot reading tonight and see if the cards have any answers for me. She smiled. Or I could just get Cybele drunk and see what information she spills. It's not like her middle name is Silence.

Cybele sang under her breath as she skipped up the sidewalk to her apartment building. Someday, we'll find it. The love connection... She laughed. Gods. I can't believe that I suspected for one minute that Janus had any connection whatsoever to a car bombing. Cassie's right. He's still mad at me for hiring Gabe. And I haven't been overly sympathetic to his pain from breaking up with Achates. Not since I found out how much Achates clearly hates me. Sending police to interview me about possible links I might have to counterculture terrorists. Jackass. She stopped in surprise as she saw Gabe pacing inside her apartment foyer.

"What are you doing here?"

Gabe quickly ran his hand through his hair. "I saw your note that you were leaving early and I just wanted to make sure you weren't sick or anything."

"Oh. No." Cybele beamed up at him. "I'm fine."

Gabe looked a little uncomfortable as he tried to pump her for more information. "I thought that you might have been upset by the police coming by."

Cybele looked puzzled. "How did you know that the police...?"

Gabe shrugged. "Some of the workers in the greenhouse said they saw police talking to you and Janus today."

"Oh." Cybele bit her lower lip. "So, I guess the rumour drums are beating pretty fiercely right now."

"Yeah." Gabe moved a step closer to her. "I think they think that you're drug dealers or something. You know, because of the herbs."

Cybele chuckled. "I've never really had the desire to be a drug dealer. And not just because of the draconian possession with intent to sell drug laws we have in this country. It's just never really been an ambition of mine. I think the only drug I deal is spirituality." She winked. “Although YOU certainly know that I’m not opposed to the moderate, recreational use of certain mood altering substances.”

Gabe playfully caressed her cheek. “Well, the police certainly have better things to do with their time than harass the occasional recreational user.”

“Yeah.” Cybele looked up teasingly at him. “It’s not worth the paperwork to them. As long as you only have a tiny amount on you, all they’ll do is make you pour it out and then watch as it blows away. Pot in the wind. They’ll only come after you if you do it large scale.” She pulled slightly away so that his hand fell away. “Or if you rub it in their faces. You know, like that artist who lit up a joint right outside a window that opened into a classroom full of RCMP officers. They laughed themselves silly but they sort of had to arrest him.”

“Provocation.” Gabe captured her hand in his. “So, if not drugs, why were the police at the office today?”

Cybele reluctantly pulled away. “It’s sort of complicated. Why don’t you come up and we can talk about it over coffee?”

Cybele unlocked the entrance to her apartment foyer. She and Gabe went inside and up to her apartment.

Gabe’s eyes widened at his first sight of the interior. “I can’t believe your landlord let you paint the walls purple.”

Cybele reached out and fondly patted the wall beside her front door. “It’s my favourite colour. The colour of Easter. You know chocolate and marshmallow eggs, jelly beans, and the eternal Easter Bunny.” She shrugged. “Our landlord was supposed to repaint before we moved in, but she didn’t have time. So, we made a deal that she could do that repainting after we moved out. And, in the meantime, we get to do our own decorating."

Gabe looked at her questioningly. "We?"

"I have a roommate, Cassie. She's at work right now but should be back soon."

Gabe nodded. He followed Cybele into the kitchen and watched as she made coffee.

"So, the police?" he prompted.

Cybele squirmed. "I'm sure you heard about that car bombing last night."

"Yes." Gabe looked at her puzzledly. "But wasn't it more like an explosion than a bomb?"

Cybele sharply scrutinized him. "An explosion?"

"Yeah. Not a bomb timer. More like firecrackers or something." Gabe began to sound more doubtful. "Plus gasoline and fertilizer, I think, that's what I heard on the news."

Cybele moved into the living room. Gabe followed her. They sat down curled up on opposite ends of the couch.

"Fertilizer." Cybele gnawed worriedly on her bottom lip. "Are you sure?"

"I think so." Gabe looked at her expectantly. "Why?"

Cybele shook her head in confusion. Fertilizer? Maybe the police think an eco-terrorist group used fertilizer as some sort of environmentally friendly, explosive calling card. That could be why they were asking me questions about the Friends of Gaea. But that makes no sense. The Friends of Gaea have never been that violent.

Why would the police want to know if I have a connection to them? Are they after me or Janus or the Friends of Gaea? What piece of the puzzle am I missing?

Cybele looked cautiously at Gabe. "That day I hired you. How did you even know about the business? Where it was? What it was?"

Gabe looked startled at the *non sequitor*. "I…I overheard Tan and Ixion talking about this great business opportunity working for Janus. I was curious about what it was so I decided to tail them to the business, to see what it was all about." He laughed. "I guess I had watched a little too much *Get Smart*. I should just have asked them."

"But you didn't. You spied on them." Cybele looked deeply into his eyes. "You and Janus don't get along. Why would you want anything to do with a business he was running?"

"I didn't want to work for him. I just wanted to know what he was up to."

Cybele frowned. "Did you think he was doing something illegal?"

Gabe forced himself to meet her eyes and not sound too defensive. "I thought maybe he was. I knew he had a small business growing and selling herbs."

Cybele's tone became more aggressive as she started to fear Janus might have been right about Gabe. "And you thought he might be selling drugs?"

"It crossed my mind." Gabe smiled down fondly at her. "But that was before I realized you were involved. I knew you wouldn't do anything that was illegal."

Cybele looked up at him in disbelief. “How? We had just met.”

Gabe tried to project sincerity in his voice as he spoke from his heart. “Partly from the way Matthew spoke of you and partly from the impression you made on me.”

“Right.” Cybele shook her head distrustfully. “Are you a cop? Trying to build a file on a budding, possibly subversive organization? You’ve already got me on possession. What are you planning to do now?” She laughed tensely. “Just so you know, I don’t scare easily and I’m no Judas either.”

“Cybele.” Gabe sighed ruefully. “I’m not a cop. I have no intention of turning you in because I saw you with pot. It’s not like I’ve never used it before.”

Cybele sighed sadly. “Then why are you working for me?”

“For exactly the reason I first told you.” Gabe looked earnestly at her. “It’s more interesting than anything I’ve ever done before. It’s a great job and I think you’re a great boss.” He smiled patiently. “I’m willing to put up with Janus’s temper tantrums if it means I get to see you every day.” He paused to sip his coffee. “If you mistrusted my motives, why did you hire me?”

Cybele looked away from him. “I was curious about your motives and I wanted to learn more about you.”

He moved closer to her. “Keep your friends close, and your enemies closer, eh?”

Cybele looked as if she had just been punctured by a pin. “I never thought of you as an enemy. Just an enigma that I wanted to solve.”

"I'm glad." Gabe smiled down meaningfully at her. "I don't want you to think of me as your enemy. I'd rather be your friend."

"Really?" Cybele laughed as she began to recover her equilibrium. "Because you know...I keep my enemies closer to me than my friends."

Gabe slid even closer to her. "Surely, there must be some friends you keep even closer to you than your enemies. You know, to shield you from the slings and arrows of outrageous fortune."

Cybele's mood became unexpectedly serious as she too spoke from her heart. "Only those I trust completely. And trust is earned through actions not words. Trust takes time. It's fragile and can be shattered with the first betrayal."

Gabe sobered up as well. "The voice of experience?"

"Yes." Cybele looked pensive. "I do believe that people are inherently good. Some just choose to live lives of selfishness and eventually their potential for goodness is diminished. But I trust until I am given reason not to trust."

Gabe winced inwardly. "Once bitten, twice shy, eh?"

Cybele nodded solemnly. "Fool me once, shame on you. Fool me twice, shame on me." She smiled wistfully. "So, I am going to trust you, Gabriel. I'm going to believe you when you say that you're not working as an undercover cop."

"Good. Because I'm not." He paused. "I think you're a good person and I would never betray you."

"Good." Cybele smiled up at him flirtatiously. "Because I think you're a good person too."

"Good. Now that we have agreed that we're both good people, can you tell me why you were so shocked to hear that fertilizer was involved in the car explosion?"

Cybele sighed uncomfortably. "Because I really hadn't been paying attention to the radio when the news was on and I just thought it was a bomb. You know, like a Unabomber bomb. But a car one, not a mail one. And the police didn't tell me what kind of bomb it was. They led me to believe it was a car bomb."

Gabe looked worriedly at her. "Why were the police even questioning you and Janus about it?"

"It's so surreal. I'm not really sure." She stood up and began to pace back and forth in front of her couch. "Janus, yes. His ex-boyfriend, Achates…"

Gabe broke in. "Janus is gay?"

"Yes." Cybele looked warily over at him. "You're not a homophobe, are you?"

"No." Gabe shook his head vigorously. "I think it's great that he's gay. I thought you and he might have once, you know…"

"No." Cybele shook her head. "I told you we were just friends…"

"Good." Gabe forced himself not to grin stupidly at her.

"Good." Cybele paused. "But Janus doesn't like to advertise the fact he's gay. He's afraid of prejudice, you know, gay-bashers and all that crap."

"Don't worry." Gabe waved his hands. "His being gay is not newsworthy. I won't spread it around."

"Okay, then." Cybele continued with her story. "So, Achates' new boyfriend is Jagganath Nod, the owner of the car that blew up."

"So, the police were just making sure the old boyfriend didn't have a motive for blowing up the new boyfriend's car?" asked Gabe trying to obtain all the facts he would need to further his own investigation.

"I guess." Cybele looked indignant. "It's ridiculous. Janus isn't the type of person who goes around blowing up things." She rolled her eyes. "I could see him wrapping toilet paper around Achates' house or something but nothing violent."

"Were the police asking you to alibi him?"

"Not quite." Cybele rubbed her forehead thoughtfully. "The police were asking me for my own alibi."

"That's ridiculous," said Gabe indignantly. "You would never be involved in something like that."

"I know." Cybele beamed approvingly at him. "Unfortunately, Achates doesn't seem to like me very much. I have a feeling he painted me to the police as some wild-eyed nihilist just waiting for an excuse to bomb something. You know, like in the movie *Annie*, when some anarchist comes running into Daddy Warbucks' study and throws a cheery bomb or something? Has no reason other than just wanting to bring down society."

"This Achates sounds like a real jackass, if that's what he thinks of you."

"I agree." Cybele began to feel more worried. "But I think the police might be influenced by him. They seemed to focus their questions to me. And they asked me about several other 'counter-culture' organizations."

Gabe leapt up and hurried over to Cybele. He grabbed her by the arm gently. "What did you tell them?"

Cybele sighed and rubbed her forehead. "Nothing. I don't personally know anyone or any organization that would do something like this. And I'm not going to re-enact the McCarthy era and start blackballing other people to get the focus off me."

Gabe slid his arm down her arm to grasp her hand. "Okay."

Cybele swayed slightly towards him. "I don't believe that using violence is a good way to make a philosophical statement or to try and change the world," she said earnestly. "If I knew of anyone who was capable of blowing something up just to make a point, I would tell the police." She began to gnaw on her lower lip. "But I don't. And I won't speculate on something as serious as this."

Gabe put both his arms around her and hugged her. "Don't worry so much, Cybele. The police would have to be completely brainless to meet you and think that you could have anything to do with a bombing."

Cybele sighed and hugged him back. She muttered into his shoulder. "I have a slight problem dealing with state appointed figures of authority. I think. It might be possible that I antagonized them."

Gabe rolled his eyes. "Tell me you were polite to the police."

"If polite means insulting them, then I was very polite to the police." She groaned. "I just hate feeling like I'm being backed into a corner. It makes me want to come out fighting. It's that damned fight or flight response."

Gabe tightened his arms around her. "If the police come back with more questions, be polite this time. You've done nothing wrong. You have nothing to worry about."

Cybele laughed sarcastically. "Boy. You surely haven't been on the wrong side of a police interrogation before. I don't have quite the same faith in the justice system that you seem to have. There have been way too many wrongfully convicted people set free for me to believe the police…and the crown attorneys always act as they ought to." She shook her head determinedly. "No. If the police come back and start making threats, then I'll definitely get an attorney to make sure my rights are protected."

She sighed and unconsciously snuggled even closer against Gabe's body. Then she stopped and moved slightly back. "What are we doing?"

Gabe smiled comfortingly. "Holding each other even closer than enemies?"

Cybele giggled. She pulled slightly away but still remained pressed against him. "Trust takes time," she warned as she tilted her head slightly up to look at him.

Gabe bent down to kiss her.

Crash.

Cassie burst through the door trying to balance several shopping bags.

"Cyb. Help. The apples and oranges keep trying to escape." She stopped at the sight of Gabe and Cybele. "Oh. I didn't mean to interrupt."

Cybele pulled away from Gabe and gave him a teasing smile. She blew him a kiss and went to help Cassie corral the falling groceries.

Gabe shook his head and mentally groaned. The roommate. The Fates are conspiring against me.

Cybele beckoned. "Gabe, come meet Cassie."

Gabe and Cassie exchanged introductions made slightly awkward by the knowledge of what had been occurring before her entrance.

Cybele gave Cassie a meaningful wink.

Cassie winked knowingly back and went off to her room to give Cybele and Gabe a few moments of privacy.

Cybele's eyes sparkled as she spoke. "I'm really glad you dropped by today, Gabe." Gabe nodded. "So am I." He paused. "Pity that your roommate came home just when she did."

"Oh, I don't know." Cybele reached up and gently stroked the outline of Gabe's ear and down the side of his neck. "Trust takes time and anticipation can be a most enjoyable state of being." She gently took him by the hand and pushed him backwards through the still open door. "See you at work tomorrow."

Cybele closed the door in Gabe's face. He sighed and shook his head. She is such a tease. He groaned and walked down the stairs. Tomorrow. Let the games begin again.

Cassie came out of her room and chuckled. “So, that’s the infamous Gabe. Pretty cute.”

Cybele hugged herself and sighed happily. “Yes. He is.” She sauntered into the kitchen. “Let’s discuss how wonderful he is while we make dinner, shall we?”

Cassie laughed. “We shall.”

And they did.

Chapter 17

Wednesday afternoon Gabe walked into Atlantis discreetly trying to check his watch to see how late he was in meeting Iris for lunch. 1:20 p.m. Damn. He sighed. Oh well, she won't be too mad at me when she hears what I have found out so far. He spotted her and walked over to her table.

Iris looked up and then pointedly looked at her watch.

Gabe immediately began to explain as he leaned over and gave her a friendly kiss on the cheek. "I know I'm late, but I couldn't get away earlier. Cybele had me double checking some of the incenses we had made to make sure the right ones were being sent out." He shrugged. "She's the boss. I had to stay."

Iris snorted. "Well, I hope you have something good to make it worth my while."

The waitress came up and Iris quickly ordered lunch specials for the both of them.

After the waitress had left, Gabe leaned over, and laughingly asked, "What's the lunch special?"

Iris chuckled. "What you'd expect in Atlantis. A platter of fish." She leaned back in her chair. "What have you found out for me about Matthew Cain and his shady past?"

Gabe looked slightly uncomfortable as he spoke. "Actually, that story turned out to be more smoke than fire."

Iris shook her head knowingly but said nothing.

Gabe continued. “Turns out that Matthew was running a homeless shelter in Vancouver called The Garden. Matthew’s twin brother, Abe was a heroin addict there who Matthew was trying to help get clean.”

Iris sighed in remembrance of the struggles her own husband had undergone but failed to overcome. “Poor man. Heroin is an almost impossible habit to kick,” she said sympathetically.

Gabe nodded ruefully as he also thought of Iris’ late husband. “Matthew tried a bit of tough love. Cut his brother off the gravy train. Hoped it would force him to get treatment.”

“But?”

“But one day when Abe apparently really needed a fix, he attacked Matthew, hoping to get some money. Matthew resisted and pushed Abe. Abe fell against a table and apparently hit his head pretty hard on the table’s edge. He refused to go to a doctor and ended up dying of a blood clot on some street corner.”

“That’s horrible.” Iris shook her head. “Is that when the rumours started that Matthew killed his brother?”

“Yes. But there were witnesses to the fight, so although Matthew was investigated, he was never charged.” Gabe shrugged uncomfortably. “But once thrown, mud sticks. After the death of his brother, Matthew couldn’t stay in The Garden, so he decided to go east, but, he ended up staying in Winnipeg, and opening up another shelter here.”

Iris patted him reassuringly on his hand. “Well, it wasn’t a total waste of time. You might be able to use that information to write a human interest story. You know, the humanitarian who can't stop being a Good Samaritan, even after the tragic death of his brother."

Gabe nodded gravely. "I've already started writing a story about it. Make up for listening to rumours instead of just looking at all the good works he was doing." He squirmed. "But I think there might be something strange going on at the Mysteries of Cybele."

They stopped talking as the waitress returned with their food. They resumed their conversation once she had walked out of earshot.

Iris groaned. Here we go again. "Gabriel, my dear boy, please tell me you're not going to become one of those people seeing a conspiracy around every corner."

Gabe laughed uncomfortably. "No. This is a bit different. I really think there's fire behind this smoke."

Iris arched an eyebrow. "So, what do you think your new girlfriend is up to?"

Gabe hurriedly shook his head. "Cybele is not my girlfriend." He paused. Yet. "And whatever wicked goes that way is all focussed on Janus. Cybele is not involved with whatever illegal things he might be doing."

Iris looked over carefully at Gabe. "Are you sure that you and Janus are not just two bison butting horns over the same girl? That might account for the animosity you two seem to feel towards each other."

Gabe shook his head. "No." He looked uncomfortable as he tried to prove to Iris that she was wrong about his motives. "Cybele told me that Janus was gay. But it was in confidence, so I don't want that information to get around, at least not because of me."

Iris rolled her eyes. "Just because Janus is gay doesn't mean that he might not feel possessive of Cybele's attention. Especially, if they've been friends for a long time."

Gabe paused thoughtfully. "That could explain why he's so hostile towards me."

"And why you were so antagonistic towards him?"

No. "It's not just that. There's something about him. He's not what he appears to be."

Iris drummed her fingers on the table. Hmmm..."Do you have anything solid to base your suspicions on? Because extrasensory perceptions don't stand up real well as evidence when we're being sued for defamation of character."

Gabe leaned forward as he spoke forcefully. "How about a possible connection to the explosion of a prominent Winnipeg's lawyer's car Monday evening?"

Iris' eyes widened in surprise. "You're not bullshitting me, are you, Gabriel?"

"Nope," he said smugly.

Iris shook her head wonderingly. "Jagganath Nod. Can you really connect his car bombing to your girlfriend Cybele?"

Gabe put up his hand to halt Iris' dangerous train of thought. "NOT Cybele. Just Janus. Cybele would never be associated with something as violent and illegal as that."

Iris sighed deeply. "Gabriel. I know you're attracted to her, but that doesn't mean she's the person you think she is. You wouldn't be the first man to let his little head do the thinking for his big head. She might be more of a player and less of a pawn than you think she is."

"You're wrong. She's not a pacifist but she's pretty damn close." He shook his head confidently. "If she knew anything concrete about that explosion, she would do something. She wouldn't sit by and let something like that happen again. She wouldn't want people to get hurt."

"So, if she's so noble, why do you think her good friend might be connected?" asked Iris curiously. "Birds of a feather flock together, Gabriel."

Gabe ignored her insinuation and continued with his story. "The police came by to do some 'routine inquiries' of Janus and Cybele at work Tuesday afternoon."

"Really? What drew the police to them?"

Gabe smirked. "Guess who Jagganath Nod's new boyfriend's ex-boyfriend is?"

"Not Janus?"

"Oh, yeah. That sounds pretty promising, don't you think?"

Iris smiled broadly. "What do the police always say? Nine times out of ten the motive for a crime is always domestic?"

"A spurned lover takes revenge on the car of his ex-boyfriend's new lover." Gabe shook his head. "It's the modern-day

Fatal Attraction. If Mercedes-Benz made a Rabbit, it would have been too perfect."

Iris rolled her eyes. Not again. "Life is not an episode from the movies, Gabriel."

Gabe sighed wistfully. "I know." What a pity.

Iris continued pumping Gabe for information. "So, why were the police questioning Cybele? Was she giving Janus an alibi?"

Gabe paused, unable to meet Iris' gaze. "Actually, I don't know if she was able to alibi him or not. She did tell me the police were asking her for her alibi as well."

"What was her alibi?"

Gabe said nothing.

"Gabriel, tell me, you asked her what her alibi was?" Iris shook her head in frustration. "Did you ask her what Janus's alibi was?"

Gabe began to stammer out an explanation. "I forgot...We were talking...She was upset and ..."

"Damn it, Gabriel." Iris pounded the table. "You're supposed to be a reporter. That means you get information from the people you are investigating. You don't sit around holding their hands because they're upset." Iris groaned. "You're becoming too emotionally involved. You've lost your sense of objectivity and detachment."

"No." Gabe leaned forward and met Iris' gaze squarely. "No. I haven't. I couldn't ask her too many questions. It would have been the wrong time for me to do that. She would have pulled away and probably kicked me out of her apartment."

Iris wrinkled her forehead suspiciously. "And you were in her apartment because?"

Gabe subtly relaxed. I'm covered here. "I had gone there to question her about the police visit. But she was suspicious. She even asked me if I was an undercover cop. I had no choice. I had to pull back. That was the right thing to do. She trusts me now more than she trusted me before."

"Why would she think you were an undercover cop?"

Gabe shook his head a bit too dismissively for Iris' liking. "Cybele felt the police might be trying to infiltrate counterculture organizations. Big Brother is everywhere."

"She's perceptive." Iris frowned. "You ARE there undercover and Big Brother IS everywhere."

Gabe rolled his eyes. "She was just upset because she thought the police were focusing their questions to her, but that would have been ridiculous. Janus is the one with the motive not her."

"The one with a motive that you know about. Maybe she helped plan the explosion. People who feel guilty usually have a reason to feel guilty," said Iris musingly. "Maybe the police were focusing on her. Maybe the fact that Janus was the ex-boyfriend was just a coincidence."

Gabe shook his head. No way.

"Gabriel, you need to find out more about what the police are thinking. Use your sources." She thumped him eagerly on the arm. "And find out everything you can about Jagganath Nod. See if he is in any way connected to Cybele. Either personally or through his cases."

"I will, but I know Janus is the key. He would have no compunction about doing something like this." Gabe smiled fondly. "Cybele is more principled. Her connection is only through her friendship with Janus." He drummed his fingers on the table thoughtfully. "I hope the police are also looking at Jagganath's ex-boyfriends as well as any enemies he might have made. He has been a lawyer for a long time."

"If they aren't, you will be." Iris sighed. "Gabriel, be careful. Someone who would blow up a car is someone you need to be careful around. Janus might be involved or even Cybele. Don't be lulled by a pretty face into letting your guard down. Everyone is a suspect until proven innocent."

Gabe nodded.

Iris reached out and patted his hand gently. "This could be a really big story. Don't blow it by losing your objectivity."

"I won't."

"Good." Iris waved him off. "You should get going. Your boss probably won't be too thrilled if you take too long a lunch."

Gabe got up and kissed her good-bye on the cheek.

Iris watched him leave. I hope he's not getting in over his head. Investigating a cult is bad enough but now a car bombing. She shook her head. *Que sera, sera.*

Cybele looked at her watch. Good. Gabe shouldn't be back for at least half an hour. She hurried from the greenhouse back to her empty office. She deliberately closed her door and then walked over to her desk. She reached into the bottom drawer and pulled out a small locked box. She pulled her key chain from her purse and opened the box.

Okay. The bottle of potassium nitrate looks about the same level as the last time I used it. How much should be left? She reached into the drawer for her supplies book. I've used it for 75 incense mixes since I bought it which means there should be about half of it gone. She looked at the bottle. Yes. It looks only half empty. She smiled. I guess I should say half full. Good. That means that none of my supply of potassium nitrate went anywhere it was not supposed to go. Everything I have has been accounted for. So, I have nothing to worry about. Janus couldn't have borrowed my supplies to use in a prank that went wrong. She bit her lip worriedly. He would have had more sense to mix fertilizer, gasoline, and firecrackers anyway. You would have to be unbelievably stupid not to know that would cause an explosion not just a light show and then to throw potassium nitrate into the mix. She sighed. You would have to have a reckless disregard for the safety of others. That's not Janus. Still. I need to find out what he and his favourite employees were talking about before the police came. What did they mean when they said that bastard Jagganath Nod got what he deserved? Were they just talking about the news report or did they know something more than what Janus had said.

She stood up. I guess I'll just have to ask Janus about that myself. She picked up the bottle of potassium nitrate and put it back into the lock box. Then she stopped. She took it back out and put it in her purse. Better be safe than sorry. She relocked the box and put it back in her desk drawer.

Time to beard the lion in his den. Remember be conciliatory not accusatory. You catch more flies with honey than with vinegar. Cybele stopped in front of Janus's door. She took a deep breath and then knocked on the door.

Janus came to the door. "Oh. It's you. Come in."

She looked up at him in forced amusement. "Who were you expecting?"

"It's been a weird few days." He shrugged. "I thought maybe it was the police again." He moved slightly to block her entrance into his office.

Cybele placed her hand on his chest and gently pushed past him. "Yeah. That was really strange. That they thought we would have some knowledge of a car bomb. What's up with that?"

Janus reluctantly followed her back inside his office. "I'm not sure. It seemed pretty strange."

Cybele moved further into his office and looked at him expectantly. "Cassie and I thought that maybe the police were asking us questions because of you."

Janus began to look uncomfortable at the train of Cybele's questions. "Why because of me?"

Cybele looked at Janus strangely. "Because the car that was blown up belonged to Jagganath Nod. Your ex-boyfriend's new boyfriend. They might have thought it was done out of jealousy."

Janus laughed uncomfortably. "I'd have to be pretty violent to blow up someone's car. Do you really think that's something that I would do?"

Cybele pointedly pulled a chair from in front of his desk and angled it sideways so that she could sit and look at him. "No. Of course not. It's just I was worried that maybe you had pulled a prank that had gone horribly wrong."

Janus sat down with his hip half on his desk and looked down patronizingly at her. "I'm a little too old to be pulling pranks. This isn't high school, and we're no longer tipping cows."

Cybele gazed hard into his eyes trying to decide if he was hiding anything from her. "I guess I was just upset because when I asked you about Jagganath Nod and the car bombing, you told me you hadn't heard anything, but you told the police that you had."

"So, you do believe that I had something to do with a terrorist act." He shook his head angrily. "I thought we were friends and you come in here and accuse me of being a terrorist."

Cybele jumped up. "Good gods, Janus. Take a pill. I'm not accusing you of being a terrorist. I just don't like the fact that you lied to me about the news story."

"I didn't want to get into it with you," said Janus exasperatedly. He stood up as well. "You would probably have given me some damn lecture about it being wrong to take joy in someone else's misfortunes. And you know what?" Janus glared at her. "I thought it was the funniest thing I ever heard. Couldn't have happened to a nicer person."

Cybele frowned. "I can't believe you would say something as asinine as that. A car bomb couldn't have happened to a nicer person?" She punched Janus forcefully on his shoulder. "Have you lost your mind?"

Janus began to rub his shoulder unconsciously. "Not just the car bomb, but the fact that the explosion showered Jagganath's house with shit." He smirked. "A fitting metaphor, don't you think?"

Cybele crossed her arms angrily. "I don't think of real-life car bombs as metaphors."

Janus crossed his arms emphatically. "And that's why I didn't want to discuss the news with you...Look, I'm not saying I'm a fan of people going around and blowing up cars. Clearly, that's pretty dangerous. Innocent people could get hurt. I'm just saying that since no one got hurt, I'm able to appreciate the humour in what happened." He laughed angrily. "Achates treated me like shit when I went to see him and now his new boyfriend's yard is full of shit. You should be happy. The karmic circle has proven itself once again."

Cybele rubbed her forehead incredulously. "I'm not happy. And, if I were you, I'd be a little more discreet in my joy since it will just make you look like the prime suspect to the police."

Janus gestured angrily towards the open door. "And are you going to run off and tell the Thought Police? Has it become a crime just to express joy in a situation that may not be politically correct?" Janus began to sing bitterly. "Under the spreading chestnut tree, I sold you and you sold me."

Cybele groaned. “Stop that. If you say you had nothing to do with the explosion, I believe you. I just wish you were a little more horrified about how violent it was. How much damage it could have done.”

“Well, why don’t you run off and commiserate with your new boyfriend. I’m sure he’ll only be too eager to agree with you. The horror. The horror. How can bad things happen to good people?” Janus snorted. “Or, in this case, unfaithful and cruel people.”

Cybele rolled her eyes. “Gabe is not my boyfriend, so get over it. And has it occurred to you, that I’m here talking to you, because I’m concerned about you.”

Janus shook his head condescendingly. “Let me guess. You did a tarot reading and are concerned because the cards say that I’m walking the paths of uncertainty that could lead to darkness and despair if I choose the wrong turning.”

“No. I haven’t done a tarot reading for you.” Cybele looked up at him with a penetrating gaze. “But is that your own subconscious reading of your own situation?”

Janus groaned. “Please don’t warn me to beware looking into the chasm of the abyss.” He bowed mockingly. “for when you look too deeply into the abyss, the abyss also looks deeply into you.”

Anger began to burn deep behind Cybele’s eyes. “All right. How about a little Agatha Christie instead? If you open your heart and mind to evil, evil will enter.” She looked meaningfully at him. “How’s that for profundity?”

"Perfect." Janus began to back away from her. "Maybe that's something you should be more concerned about."

She took a step towards him. "What are you talking about now?" she asked curiously.

Janus took another step away from her. "You lied to the police yesterday," he said smugly.

Cybele looked away guiltily. "I did not."

"The police asked you if you knew anybody who was a member of the Friends of Gaea and you said no."

Cybele looked at him uncomfortably. "I don't know the names of any members."

Liar. Liar. Pants on fire. "Your old boyfriend is the founder."

"That's right. He's the founder." She paused. "Not a member."

"Semantics." Janus smirked. "You lied to the police."

Cybele drew herself up as if she was delivering a familiar speech. "The Friends of Gaea is not a violent organization. It doesn't advocate violence anywhere in its mission statements or through its actions. The police were on a wild goose chase with that line of inquiry." She looked over at Janus to gauge his reaction. "I was doing them a public service by not contributing to speculations and rumours."

Janus laughed. "Yeah. I'm sure the police will be grateful for your thoughtful attempt to save them time in their investigations."

Cybele shuffled her feet as she spoke. "What possible connection could the Friends of Gaea have with Jagganath Nod?"

"Oh nothing." Janus paused for emphasis. "Well, unless you count the fact that he's suing them on behalf of his client, Circean Dreams."

Cybele rubbed her forehead. Damn. "He's the lawyer for Circean Dreams?"

"Yeah. That makes them a pretty big suspect in an explosion that blew up his car and showered his house with manure." He patted her on the shoulder. "Now, do you see the irony in what happened?"

Cybele sighed. "Gods. But that doesn't prove anything. There are plenty of eco-groups out there that are upset with Circean Dreams. Surprisingly, most people don't want to live beside a lake of pig shit, or have it contaminate their ground water. Nobody wants to smell it either, especially on our long, hot summer days." She shook her head. "Not to mention that it must be a breeding ground for flies and mosquitoes. They're probably in bug nirvana."

"You're probably right. But like flies to wanton boys, are we to the police. They torment us for their sport." He smiled derisively. "I'm sure they'll be quite understanding if they find out you have a connection to the Friends of Gaea. When they ask you why you misled them, you can explain it was just a question of semantics."

Cybele groaned. "Very funny."

Janus shrugged. "Look. For what it's worth, I agree with you. There are far more likely suspects of eco-terrorists than the Friends of Gaea. I'm just saying that people in glass houses shouldn't throw stones. I didn't suspect you of being involved, even when I heard you lie to the police. I just wish you trusted me as much as I trust you."

"I'm sorry. I should have trusted you." Cybele moved closer to him. "It's just that ever since Achates broke up with you, you've been so angry. I was just worried that you had played a practical joke that had got out of hand."

"I have been angry. Achates did betray me, but so it goes. I got over it." He shook his head light-heartedly. "Trust me. I have better things to do with my time than fill people's cars with manure and blow them up."

"Okay." Cybele began to smile in relief. "I'm just glad we cleared the air."

"Me too." Janus walked over and hugged her. "Friends forever."

Cybele hugged him back. "Forever friends." Reassured, she left his office and went back to her own.

Janus sat back down in his office chair. Let the Fates play what games they intend. The die has been cast. He sighed. *Et tu*, Cybele?

Chapter 18

What a way to spend a Thursday evening. Janus looked around at his new best friends sitting on his deck and grimaced. I'm surrounded by incompetence disguised as mediocrity. He raised a beer in mocking salute.

"Here's to the wondrous exploits of the X-Men. Long may they continue to baffle the police who search so diligently the ranks of the Friends of Gaea, while the real patriots of the earth remain undetected."

Tan smirked. "The X-Men really fooled everyone with their last marvellous quest. Pity, they don't have any follow-up adventures to perform to show off their superior powers."

Janus shook his head. "No. The X-Men have to lie low for a while until things are no longer so explosive around here."

Ardiaeus laughed. "Pity. Explosions can be fun."

Janus glared at Ardiaeus. "But they draw too much attention to our actions."

Tan nodded as he punched Ardiaeus warningly in the stomach. "Janus is right. The police are still snooping around everywhere looking for eco-terrorists."

Ixion broke in annoyedly. "There are so many undercover police walking around as street people and asking questions that they're taking away a lot of the money we make panhandling."

Ajax nodded bitterly. "And it's not like the police need the money. They're stealing money out of our mouths."

Janus shook his head. “You shouldn’t need to be panhandling anymore. Not with the money I pay you to work for me.”

Tan shrugged. “We don’t need the money now but it’s good to keep in practice. You never know when you might need some extra cash.”

“Whatever.” Janus looked closely at Tan. “What are the police hearing on the streets?”

Tan looked blank. “Nothing. No one knows anything about terrorists.”

“Good.” Janus smiled. “As long as all the X-Men keep their secret identities and their secret adventures secret, the police will have nothing to find out. They’ll eventually write it off as some misguided members of the Friends of Gaea. But since it wasn’t them, the police investigation will stall and eventually die.”

Tan nodded as he looked meaningfully at Janus. “We know better than to talk about what the X-Men have done. There are too many villains out there who would sell the X-Men out for a few bucks.”

Janus smacked Tan approvingly on the shoulder. “Very smart thinking, Tan. Too many people are found out because they couldn’t keep their mouths shut. The police don’t have to do any real work, just wait for their informers to let them know who was bragging about doing what.”

Tan drank deeply from his beer before he spoke. “We know how to keep our mouths shut.”

Ixion chimed in again eager to be part of the conversation. "It's fun though to watch people talk about what happened and who might be behind it. They have no idea it was us."

Janus snorted. "You mean the X-Men, don't you?"

Tan glared back at Ixion. "The X-Men."

Janus shook his head a bit worriedly. "The X-Men did a good job of covering their tracks, but if they start to brag, they might find the police will pay a lot of attention to them."

Tan looked at Janus reassuringly. "Then the X-Men won't brag about what they've done. It's enough that they know they've fooled everybody. They don't have to let everybody know what they've done."

"Good thinking, Tan." Janus smiled. "The X-Men clearly have a capable leader." Janus continued, reluctant to put ideas into their heads but needing to cover all the bases. "But, if the X-Men were pulled in for questioning for any reason, it would be wise for them not to say anything to the police. The smartest thing the X-Men could do would be to ask for a lawyer and say nothing until they got one."

Ixion looked suddenly troubled. "What if the X-Men don't know any lawyers?"

Janus sighed. "There's always Legal Aid lawyers. They have to defend you."

Tan smiled broadly. "Of course, we could always call you and you could get us a good lawyer."

Janus looked startledly at Tan. "Call me?"

Tan nodded. "Sure. Or Matthew. You ARE our counsellor at the Loaves and Fishes. Who better to help us in our time of need?"

Janus nodded thoughtfully. "Yes. I am. It would be very logical for you to call your counsellor for help if you were being interrogated by the police about something you had nothing to do with." He looked more sternly at Tan. "But you should then make it clear to the police that your counsellor is getting you a lawyer and you're not saying anything until your lawyer gets there."

Tan laughed. "Of course. We know our counsellor won't let us down."

"Of course I won't." Janus sighed. God. Looks like these idiots might become more trouble than they're worth. I can just see them turning the police on me like a pack of jackals just to save their own skins. Why did that idiot Ardiaeus have to use firecrackers? This whole thing would have blown over if it hadn't been labelled a terrorist act. I could say that I had nothing to do with it but the police might not believe me. He rubbed his forehead in frustration. I guess I'm going to have to neutralize the threat they pose because I have no intention of going to jail because of these imbeciles.

Janus forced himself to sound light-hearted as he spoke. "Who wants more beer?" He laughed as their eager faces snapped up to look at him. Pavlov's dogs. "Ardiaeus, why don't you grab some bottles from the fridge? Ajax, why don't you grab some more snacks from the counter? We should be celebrating the X-Men's victory over the forces of evil not worrying about their possible counterstrikes."

Everybody laughed and the tension that had crept up amongst them evaporated. Ardiaeus and Ajax quickly returned and passed around the beer and snacks.

Janus looked around him and smirked. Mindless minions. This is almost too easy. "Out of all the people I counselled at the Loaves and Fishes, I knew you were the chosen few. The ones who were so clearly better than their surroundings. Your actions have more than justified my faith in you."

They all smiled and looked proud of what they had done.

Janus continued. "My only fear is that others may not understand the great deeds you are destined to go on and do. Their fear of your greatness may cause them to turn on you. To betray you to the robots in power who will seek to crush you when they realize you cannot be conquered." Janus shook his head gravely. "It is a truth universally forgotten that great spirits have always encountered violent opposition from mediocre minds."

Tan took a long chug of his beer. "That's deep, man." He burped loudly.

"It is, isn't it?" Janus shook his head. Albert Einstein rides to the rescue. Heigh-ho, Tonto. "The truest things are usually pretty deep." In bullshit. Or perhaps pig shit would be more fitting. "The X-Men are the noble heroes who must battle the forces of mediocrity who are trying to control them and change them into pale shadows of their former selves."

Tan pumped his fist in the air. "Go X-Men!"

Ixion, Ardiaeus, and Ajax quickly followed his lead. "Go X-Men!"

Janus laughed and pumped his own fist in the air. "Go X-Men." He continued. "One day when the world has been made over in the image of the X-Men, they can come out of hiding and proudly proclaim their deeds to the worshipping world." He sighed dramatically. "Alas. That day has not yet come. But the deeds of the X-Men will not be forgotten though they must conceal their identity through pawns who do not know how lucky they are to be given credit for the deeds of the X-Men."

Tan burped again. "The Friends of Gaea are lucky. They got the credit for the blow we struck in their name against the evildoers."

Janus took a long sip of his beer before he responded. "They don't know how lucky they are."

Ajax and Ardiaeus nodded thoughtfully. "They are lucky."

Ixion chimed in again. "Yes. It's not fair the X-Men didn't get credit."

Janus groaned silently. Idiot. He turned to look patiently at Ixion. "It is fair, Ixion, because the X-Men don't save the world because they want the credit for it. They save the world because they are noble and courageous warriors and saving the world is just what they do."

Ixion's face lit up. "Right. The X-Men don't need credit for saving the world. It's just what they do."

Parrot. No. That's not fair to parrots. They have bigger brains than Ixion. Janus smiled approvingly. "That's right, Ixion. That's the mantra of the X-Men." He turned to the others. "However, my Fab Four, who are most assuredly not the X-Men, do get rewarded for the good work that they do."

They looked up and smiled eager anticipation. "Really?"

"Really." Janus smiled and pulled four cards out of his pocket. "Each card entitles you to a free ninety minutes of..." He smirked. "Sexual fantasy telephone counselling." He handed each of them a card. "Just give the number on the card when you call in, and the time you spend on the phone will be deducted from the time available on the card. It's my special gift to you." He laughed. "The gift that keeps on giving." Or coming.

Tan smirked. "That's a great gift, Janus, thanks." The others quickly chimed in with their thanks as well.

Janus smiled back. Sex and drugs. The opiate of the masses. "Well, I just happen to believe that the loyalty and discretion you have shown me deserves to be rewarded." He paused. "In fact, I want you all to come as my guests to the rituals Cybele will be holding Friday evening. Just make sure that you get all the prep work done beforehand. That way Cybele won't give you any attitude when you show up as participants later on."

"We will." Tan shook his head. "You're the best boss ever, Janus."

Janus nodded. "Just remember, I will always reward those who are loyal to me." His face grew stern. "But those who are disloyal to me will be cast from the inner circle. I have no patience with traitors." He smiled once again. "But I have no fears that you will betray me. You are my elect. The ones who have seen the Truth and remained unflinching." He looked into their confused faces. "I think you had all better leave now. You have a big day ahead of you tomorrow. You don't want to be late for work."

"Okay." Tan stood up to leave and the others followed him.

Janus chuckled meaningfully. "Don't spend the rest of the night using up all your time on the phone cards. Remember, slow and steady wins the race."

They laughed. They left still looking confused but excited at the reminder of the phone cards they had been given.

Janus sighed. That should make them think twice about betraying me to the cops to save their own skins. He shook his head. But unless the heat dies down soon, I might have to think of a more irrevocable solution. Loose lips, sink ships. Hmmm. I should probably call Achates. See how much of a suspect I might be in the eyes of the police. Bet Achates is no longer as proud of the Q.C. he's bagged. Now that his prize has been showered with shit. Might have taken the bloom off the rose. He laughed a bit unsteadily. Better call it a night before I pass out. Lonely bed, here I come. He got up swaying. He staggered inside and went straight to sleep.

Janus took a deep breath. Time to see if Achates' order to the security guards barring me from entering the Narcissus Building was taken seriously or not. He looked at the steady stream of people entering and leaving the building. Thank God everyone wants to go outside for lunch. Catch a few rays before Friday comes to an end and the weekend begins. He forced himself to relax as he walked through the doors and towards the elevator.

The security guard looked up but his glance passed over Janus with an air of disinterest. Doesn't look like an undesirable. Seems to know where he's going. Probably has legitimate business in the building. Not worth the hassle of finding out where he's going. The security guard returned his attention fully to his magazine.

Janus smiled. Victory. Count on the minimum wage earners to do a minimum wage job. He shook his head. Now, whatever you do, don't gloat about Jagganath's misfortunes. Remember, you're here to offer sympathy and understanding. Find out how much the police consider you to be a probable suspect and then move on.

The elevator doors opened and Janus got out. So far so good. Now to beard the dragon in his den. But first his trusty watchdog. Maera Chi came out from behind her desk to greet him.

"Janus, how good to see you again." She smiled falsely. "Is Achates expecting you?"

"No. But please tell him that I am here and would very much appreciate seeing him." That humble supplicant attitude should please Achates. He always liked playing Lady Bountiful dispensing alms to the poor. And that Maera Chi. Have to find a way to get back on her good side. She's looking at me like I'm something stuck on the bottom of her shoe.

Maera walked back slowly. "Achates only has a few minutes, but he'll fit you in."

Bitch. She liked saying that. Janus smiled falsely. "Thank you." He reached into his book bag and pulled out a heart shaped box of chocolates. "Just a little something to say I'm sorry if I was a little abrupt the last time I saw you."

Maera took the box gingerly and placed it on her desk. "Thanks, Janus." She gestured to the open door. "You can go right in."

Janus sauntered in.

Achates stood by his window overlooking the busy street. He turned slowly. "I'm surprised security let you back into the building. Someone clearly fell down on the job today."

Janus forced himself to smile and shrug off the provocation. He reached into his book bag and pulled out freshly made biscotti from The Second Cup. "Peace, Achates. I'm a Greek bearing gifts. All we need is some of your specially brewed coffee and we can break biscotti together."

Achates laughed unwillingly. "I hope you're not suggesting that we kiss and make up." He shook his head warningly. "Because that boat has sailed, Janus."

"I know. But that doesn't mean we can't be civil to one another." Janus sighed. "I know you've been a trying time lately and I just wanted to offer you my sympathy. I hope Jagganath is doing okay."

Achates walked over and took the biscotti out of Janus's hand. "Chocolate, my favourite." He walked over to the still-open door. "Maera, please bring Janus and me some coffee."

He sat down on the couch beneath his window. Janus sat down beside him. Maera brought them coffee and left, closing the door behind her.

Achates looked over at Janus carefully. “I’m surprised that you care how Jagganath is. You certainly seemed pretty angry at him the last time we spoke.”

Janus nodded guiltily. “I was angry. But Jagganath had nothing to do with the problems between us. I realized that once I had cooled down. We were having problems long before he came onto the scene.”

“We were. I needed you to be someone that you weren’t.”

“Yes.” Janus gritted his teeth, forcing himself to speak calmly. “And I wanted you to be someone you weren’t, which was wrong of me.”

Achates smiled smugly at Janus’s apologetic tone. “And you were too easily influenced by Cybele. You were allowing her rash impulses to overwhelm your sense of good judgement.”

Janus bit the inside of his cheek hard enough to draw blood. “Perhaps you’re right. Cybele might be a bad influence on me.” Idiot. You still fail to see that I influenced Cybele far more than she influenced me. Oh well, whatever gets me the information I need.

Achates sat up straighter and chuckled. “Well. It’s nice to see that you’ve lost your knee-jerk reaction to defend her against any criticism.” He paused for emphasis. “However true it is.”

Janus nodded in chagrin. "I guess I've done a lot of reflecting since you left. Trying to see what I did to drive you into the arms of another."

"That's good." Achates nodded approvingly. "Growing up is hard to do, Janus, but you've put it off for long enough."

Smug bastard. Sitting there so calmly, dipping your biscotti, and pretending that your shit doesn't stink. Janus smiled falsely. "I'm trying to think more of others than of myself." He leaned forward. "That's why I was so shocked when I heard about what had happened to Jagganath." He shook his head dramatically. "A car bomb in Winnipeg. I mean, sure we're the murder and arson capital of Canada, but is nowhere safe?"

Achates looked a bit nonplussed. "I guess not. I was at his house that night, you know. The explosion was so loud. I thought someone had cut into a gas line."

Janus patted Achates comfortingly on his hand. "Well, thank goodness, no one was hurt."

"Yes." Achates slowly pulled his hand away from Janus's touch. "But the police still cordoned off the whole area to look for other bombs."

Angry at Achates' rejection, Janus spoke a bit more mockingly. "I guess you can't be too careful these days."

Achates shook his head proudly. "Not when you're as important as Jagganath is. His firm hired him extra security to make sure nothing like this happens to him again."

"It must have been such a terrifying experience." This time, Janus patted Achates on the shoulder. "Did you actually see pieces of the car still falling when you ran out of the house?" I wonder if you were showered by shit. That's toxic rain, for you.

"Well, no." Achates unconsciously relaxed into Janus's touch. "The car was still burning, of course, so no one went to close. And the smell was horrible. Burnt steel and rubber." He shook his head. "I'm sure you can imagine."

"Oh, I don't think anyone who hasn't been in that situation could imagine it." How delicate of Achates not to mention the pig shit. Guess that image undercuts the drama of his story. "So, do the police have any suspects for this horrible attack?"

Achates smiled and leaned forward confidingly. "Well, they think it might be someone who has a grudge against Jagganath."

Janus managed to avoid rolling his eyes. No shit, Sherlock.

Achates continued. "They think it might be someone Jagganath is suing or has sued."

"Really. That must be a long list."

Achates stiffened slightly. He shifted slightly so that Janus's hand fell away from his shoulder.

Janus quickly elaborated as he forced himself to sound sympathetic. "Considering he's had such a long and distinguished career."

Achates relaxed. "Yes. I think because of the construction of the bomb that they're looking at possible eco-terrorist groups. Jagganath is currently suing Friends of Gaea, so those militants are going under the microscope." He sighed. "But nuts seem to be attracted to other nuts, so I'm sure they have a long list of groups to check into." He looked over at Janus curiously. "I'm surprised the police haven't been to see you. They did ask me and Jagganath about ex-boyfriends we might have who might be looking for a little revenge."

Janus forced himself to look hurt. "You can't possibly think that I would have anything to do with something like a car bomb?"

Achates sighed guiltily. "Not really. Not on your own initiative." He leaned more closely to Janus as he spoke. "But I could see Cybele talking you into doing something like that. Making a political statement and getting a little payback for me dumping you." He shook his head thoughtfully. "I always knew that she hated me." He patted Janus on his shoulder. "She saw me as a threat to her control of you."

Janus forced himself to show no expression as he spoke. "I'm sure Cybele doesn't hate you." He laughed to himself. I don't think Cybele ever thought about you unless you were standing right there in front of her. Talk about paranoid. Like Cybele would ever have the guts to take revenge on anyone the way I did. Yeah, right. Someone who gives mosquitoes three chances to fly away before she swats them is going to plant a car bomb. He looked solemnly over at Achates. "Actually, the police did come to see us on Tuesday. They said it was just routine investigating." He sighed. "Unfortunately, I didn't have an alibi. Ever since you broke up with me, I just haven't wanted to do anything. I just sit home and think about how empty the house is without you in it."

Achates nodded smugly. I knew you would see the light. Too bad, you couldn't see it before I had to leave. "What about Cybele? Did she have an alibi?"

"Yes. She was with Cassie the whole evening."

"Oh," Achates said in obvious disappointment.

Janus shook his head. "Look, Achates. Cybele may be many things, but she's not a violent anarchist." He sighed. I definitely don't want the police thinking Cybele was involved. That brings it back too close to my backyard. He smirked. Literally. "I think the police are on the right track looking for eco-terrorists. Especially, since Circean Farms makes a habit of suing protesters for vandalism. That's probably enough to drive those righteous do-gooders over the edge. Some of them probably thought they would make their point by attacking the lawyer who's making their lives such misery."

Achates nodded thoughtfully. "You're probably right. That's what the police think, I'm sure."

Good. I think I've got all the information I need. Achates doesn't seem suspicious of me, just of Cybele. Janus shook his head scornfully. His blindness never ceases to amaze me. Janus got up and looked down at Achates. "I know you've got other clients waiting and I don't want to overstay my welcome."

Achates stood up too. "Thanks for coming by to express your condolences on what happened. I'm glad we were able to clear the air." He held out his hand for Janus to shake. "No reason we can't be adults about this."

Janus took Achates' hand and pulled him into a quick hug. "I just wanted you to know how glad I was that no one was hurt in that explosion." Achates stiffened and Janus reluctantly released him. He moved annoyedly away from Achates. God. He's so smug. The gracious leader saying good-bye to his underling. Express my condolences, my ass. "Just let me know if I can do anything for you and Jagganath in your time of need." Maybe get you a car alarm for your new car. A shit detector. No. It would go off every time you or Jagganath spoke. Don't react to his provocation. Keep smiling and walk out of the office. You're home free.

Janus stopped at the door and spoke without turning back. "If you need anything, you know my number." He walked past Maera's desk without a word as he continued determinedly to the elevators. Yes. Now as long as those idiots keep their mouths shut, I have nothing to worry about. And even if they do talk, they have no evidence of my involvement. They could have just been trying to do something to impress me. I have no control over what others might do to try and get on my good side. Yes. Life is good. I'm bullet-proof.

Chapter 19

Cybele rubbed her forehead. Gods. I've got such a headache. Where on earth are Tan, Ardiaeus, Ajax, and Ixion? Janus promised me that they had turned over a new leaf and would be in this morning bright and early to prepare for our Friday evening rituals. She checked her watch. It's nearly two o'clock and they still haven't shown up. Well, that's it. Unless they've been in some horrible car accident, they're fired. Janus can have them work for the phone sex business, but I need reliable workers. Why did I give Gabe the afternoon off? He could have helped me handle all this chaos. She groaned. At least he's coming in this evening to help with the rituals since Janus has disappeared again. Why am I surrounded by incompetence?

Janus poked his head in her office door. "Got a minute?"

Cybele shook her head. Speak of the devil and there he is. "Barely, your Fab Four haven't shown up for work today. Guess another weekend of drunkenness and debauchery appealed to them more than a day of honest work."

Janus looked puzzled. "Strange. They seemed excited about participating in tonight's rituals and I told them to make sure they came in to help set up."

"Well, they haven't and I had to move some of my workers in the greenhouse outside to help set up the fire pits and clear away any debris. Fire Safety first, you know." Cybele shook her head angrily. "No more second chances. They're no longer working for me. Not unless they have a really good reason for being so late."

“Where’s your trusted Friday? Surely he can pick up the slack. That IS what an office assistant is for.”

“He’s coming in later today.” Cybele waved her hand dismissively. “He had a podiatrist appointment and wanted the afternoon off. Besides HIS job is not to do the job of the employees YOU hire who fail to show up.”

“Meow.” Janus shook his head laughingly. “I’ll help with the fire pits. Now, do you want to hear the extremely good news I’ve got?”

“Sure.”

“I had coffee with Achates today.”

Cybele looked up in surprise. “I thought he never wanted to see you again.”

“I guess seeing his boyfriend’s car blown up made him a bit more humble. Well, as humble as he’s ever capable of being. Anyway, I pumped him for information about what the police knew about the car bombing.”

“And?”

“And they seem to have focused on eco-terrorist groups as the most likely suspects. It probably had something to do with the manure that was used. The police probably thought it was some kind of signature.”

Cybele looked a little sick as she spoke. “Are they concentrating on any groups in particular?”

Janus smiled smugly. “Unfortunately, I think your ex Hector might be in some very hot water. The Friends of Gaea seem to be a prime suspect." Janus looked over meaningfully at her. "Good thing you haven't seen him in years. Otherwise, you might have drawn us into a very messy criminal investigation."

Cybele pressed both hands firmly against her forehead. "Gods. Why do they think Friends of Gaea was involved?"

Janus shook his head. "I don't think Achates knows. Maybe because Jagganath is suing them on behalf of Circean Dreams. But that's Hector's problem not ours." He looked more sharply at her. "Unless you've been seeing Hector behind my back and the police can somehow connect him back to us." He groaned melodramatically at the sight of her guilty face. Didn't think I knew that you still met occasionally with Hector, did you? There are less than six degrees of separation when you're in Winnipeg. Everybody knows everybody else.

Cybele sighed. "I have had lunch with Hector every few months. Just to keep in touch. He's still out there fighting the good fight. I may not approve of his actions but I admire his passion and dedication in trying to save the environment."

Janus came further into the office as he looked down thoughtfully at her. "The ends justify the means, eh?"

"No." Cybele's eyes narrowed warningly. "They don't. But I don't write off people who were my friends just because they end up taking a different path than I have."

"Well, that's a pity, Cyb, because your misguided actions have placed us in a very compromising position." Janus shook his head in apparent consternation. “If the police find out about those lunches, the word conspiracy might pop into their small minds.”

“What conspiracy?”

“The fact that you have a close, personal connection to the alleged perpetrator, and that I have a close personal relationship to the boyfriend of the victim.” Janus sighed. “It’s a short leap from that information to thinking we colluded together to kill two birds with one stone. Get revenge on the Circean Dreams’ lawyer who also happened to be my ex’s new boyfriend.” Janus sunk down into the chair in front of Cybele’s desk. “Damn it, Cyb, how could you have been so careless?” He dropped his head into his hands and began to rub the sides of his forehead in apparent distress. “You know how much Achates distrusts you. If he finds out you’re connected to the Friends of Gaea, he’ll never believe you’re not connected to the car bombing.”

Cybele reached over and patted his head a bit condescendingly. “I can’t worry about what might be, Janus. I had nothing to do with the bomb. And despite what the police or Achates may think, I doubt the Friends of Gaea did either. Just because someone in power says something doesn’t make it true. It’s just propaganda. The government using fear tactics to crack down on dissent.” She stood up and began to pace. “There’s nothing wrong with associating with dissenters either. I have no intention of denying my friends or blackballing them because I’m afraid that some nebulous black cloud of societal oppression might descend upon me.”

Janus raised his head and clapped mockingly. "Brave words, my friend. But, haven't you already denied knowing any members of the Friends of Gaea?"

Cybele gnawed her lip anxiously. "I was trying to protect them by not giving out members' names. If the government wants to know that information, let them get a warrant and do it the old fashioned, judicial way." She crossed her arms and spoke more belligerently. "If they had asked me specifically if I knew Hector, I would have told the truth. But they didn't, so I didn't share information that I didn't have to."

Janus glared at her. "Well, I just hope your indiscretions don't come back to haunt us, Cybele."

Cybele began to pace again. "Friendships are not indiscretions, Janus." She threw her hands up in the air. "And don't worry, even if I'm interrogated, I'm not going to write any false confessions that implicate any of us in something we had nothing to do with." She sank down in her chair and groaned. "The Thought Police may be prevalent but they're not all-powerful and The Ministry of Love hasn't officially been launched yet in Winnipeg."

"Good." Now it was Janus's turn to pat her condescendingly on her head. "However, to be on the safe side, I've put one of the best defence lawyers in Winnipeg, Ananias Foley, on retainer."

"You've got to be joking." Cybele looked up in protest. "Isn't that overkill?"

"We have to protect our business and employees, Cybele." Janus shook his head at her in mock-consternation. "Your actions have placed us in jeopardy. Meeting with a militant environmentalist who has a grudge against a lawyer whose car ends up being blown up." He shook his head in disbelief. "I don't know what you were thinking."

Cybele glanced sharply at Janus as her mind struggled to put all the pieces together. "But you put the lawyer on retainer before you knew I had been having lunches with Hector, right? So, that couldn't have been the real reason you hired a lawyer."

Janus sighed impatiently. "I hired a lawyer after the police came to ask us those so-called routine questions. When they started focusing on the Friends of Gaea, I knew they might make a connection between you and Hector and between you and me. It just seemed prudent to protect ourselves."

"Right." Cybele drummed her fingers on her desk as she began to speak more sarcastically. "Because the fact that the Friends of Gaea might be a red herring and the police might actually think you had a very good personal motive never crossed your mind."

Janus snapped uncomfortably. "Of course, it..." His cell phone rang and he stopped to answer it.

"What? Tan, where are you? The police have you?" He stopped talking and looked uncomfortably at Cybele still standing there with her mouth slightly open ready to continue their fight.

He mentally shrugged. Damn. She's heard too much already. No sense trying to hide what's happened. "Don't say anything to the police until I get there with your lawyer. Don't worry. Everything will be okay." He hung up and turned back to Cybele. "Well, it looks like the third degree of our employees might have already begun. Apparently, Tan, Ardiaeus, Ixion, and Ajax have been asked to assist the police with their inquiries at the police station. Luckily, they don't know anything about your connection to the Friends of Gaea, but I better get down there anyway. Who knows what they might be entrapped to say?"

Cybele bent down uncertainly to pick up her purse. "I should come down with you."

"NO." Janus softened his voice as he continued. "No. You have too much work to do here for the rituals this evening. I'll go and sort this mess out." He started to walk out the door and then paused. He spoke without turning back. "Don't worry, Cybele. You're right. We had nothing to do with this whole mess, and the sooner the police find that out, the better."

Cybele sighed as she replaced her purse beneath her desk. "Just keep me informed."

"I will." Janus left. He speed-dialled Ananias's number and left a quick message instructing Ananias to meet him at the police station on Pembina and Coventry. Then Janus got into his car and quickly drove away.

Cybele walked to the front door and watched Janus's car drive away. A most unpleasant turn of events. She shook her head gloomily. Things fall apart. The center cannot hold. She sighed. I need safe harbour. I need perspective.

Cybele stood in one place and anxiously began to tap her right foot. Gods. I can't believe that I'm doing this. What am I, stalker boss? Maybe it would be better if he's not home. Maybe I shouldn't even knock on the door. She bent slightly to examine the door knocker more closely. A brass sphinx. Unusual. AAargh! I should just walk away and pretend I was never here. Yes. That's best. She turned away from Gabe's door and began to walk back down his front steps.

"Cybele? Where are you going? I've been standing inside watching you just standing in front of my door for the last few minutes." Gabe laughed nervously. "Is this a house call to make sure I really had a doctor's appointment and wasn't just blowing off work?" Wonder what's wrong. She looks a bit on edge. Better not do anything to make her suspicious at finding me at home.

Cybele turned around and groaned silently. Damn. Caught hook, line, and sinker. Now to avoid sounding like a complete idiot. She forced herself to smile breezily. "Actually, I was just running some errands in the neighbourhood and thought I'd drop in and see if you were home." She wrapped a finger around strands of her hair and played with them as she began to speak more flirtatiously. "Maybe try to entice you to come to work a little earlier than planned as Janus's oh-so-reliable employees have failed, yet again, to come in to work on time."

"You're kidding." He moved a step closer to her. "I thought you didn't want them to work for you after the last time."

"I didn't, but Janus convinced me to give them another chance." She smiled weakly as she focussed once more on the trouble she and Janus were now in. "And, you know me, I love to give people a second chance to prove themselves."

She forced herself to sound more unconcerned as she walked back up the front steps to stand in front of Gabe. "And, they actually have a good reason for their no-show today."

"Really?" He looked doubtfully at her.

"Yes. Really." She looked up at Gabe and winked. "Aren't you going to ask me in for a cup of coffee? That's what I did when you showed up on my doorsteps the last time, you know."

Gabe winked back and gestured for her to enter. "You're right. *Mi casa es su casa*."

Cybele entered. Gabe followed her, closing the door behind him.

Gabe watched silently as Cybele began to wander around his living room.

Cybele paused in front of his small fireplace. She reached up on the mantle and picked up a small carving of a brightly coloured totem pole. Intriguing. She ran her fingers over the outthrusts of wood. A thunderbird. She casually flicked the wings and was surprised to see them move. She turned to look more consideringly at Gabe. The man's got taste. "This is so unusual. Did you get it in British Columbia?"

"Yes. I've always been fascinated by totem poles. There's something so beautiful and compelling about them." He reached over and stroked the carving. "It's not hard to understand why Emily Carr devoted her whole life to painting them."

Cybele nodded in understanding. "I have a collection of postcards of her paintings. I haven't been able actually to use them as postcards because I don't want to give them away." She gave the thunderbird to him and reached for his soapstone carving. "This igloo is so detailed. I love how sensuous soapstone feels when you stroke it." She stroked it sensuously as she looked over consideringly at him. "I have a soapstone polar bear on my bedside table. It's so raw and powerful. Of all my sculptures, it's my favourite." She carefully placed the igloo back on the mantle and began to look over his framed pictures. "You must really like the outdoors. None of your pictures have people in them. They're all nature shots."

"I've always wanted to be another Robert Bateman." He shrugged in apparent nonchalance. "I'm not there yet but maybe someday."

Undeceived, Cybele reached up to caress his cheek. "Never give up on your dreams. If you believe in something strongly enough, you can make it happen."

Gabe reached up to hold her hand against his face as he looked more deeply into her eyes. "Or as Epictetus might say, 'First say to yourself what you would be, and then do what you have to do.'"

Cybele pulled away slowly. She forced herself to speak lightly to break the spell holding them together. "I was trying to spare you my fortune cookie wisdom, but if you insist..." She paused for dramatic effect. "As Thomas Paine might say, 'It is necessary to the happiness of man that he be mentally faithful to himself.'"

Gabe forced himself to laugh. He turned and gently tugged her towards him and the kitchen.

Cybele allowed him to lead her through his house. In the kitchen, she leaned against the counter and watched him carefully. She sighed wistfully. Do I dare to eat a peach? She reached over and deliberately plucked an apple from the bowl of fruit beside the fridge. "Catch."

Gabe looked up in time to catch the apple she had thrown him.

"An apple a day keeps the doctor away." She shoved her hands in her pockets to avoid reaching out to him. "You're the only reliable employee I have. I can't afford to give you more time off."

Gabe laughed. He handed her a cup of coffee. He placed the apple carefully back in the bowl and drank slowly from his own cup. "Don't worry. No more sick days."

Cybele took a quick sip. Yuck. This tastes like sludge. Or what sludge would taste like if I ever actually had to drink it. Just take sips to be polite. When he turns his back, I'll pour it down the kitchen sink. She smiled weakly. "Interesting coffee."

Gabe nodded in amusement. "It's decaf."

Decaf. Gods. Is he trying to kill me? Cybele swallowed audibly. "Tastes like it."

Gabe chuckled. "It's pretty stale. If I knew you were coming by, I would have bought fresh crystals." Hmm. Cybele looks a lot less rattled now than she did when she first came in. Maybe she's had enough decompression time. I should try to find out why she really came by my place today. She could have been suspicious about my fake podiatrist appointment. Good thing I had time to put away all my research on her and Janus when I saw her walking up my front walk.

Gabe cleared his throat as he tried half-heartedly to interrogate her. "You know, Cyb, I'm surprised you're actually going to give a second chance to those slacker employees Janus loves so much. That must be some good reason they gave you for not showing up today."

Cybele closed her eyes and shook her head. "It was and knowing the grapevine at work, I'm sure everybody knows by now what happened."

Gabe forced himself to sound nonchalant as his reporter's instincts began to kick in. "Which was?"

"The police took Tan, Ardiaeus, Ixion, and Ajax in 'to help them with their inquiries.'" She snorted angrily. "I'm sure that means that Janus and I have become those notorious persons of interest so blathered about by the media."

Gabe put his cup down with a thump. "You don't know that for sure. Besides, what information could those four possibly have on you?" He reached over and covered her hand reassuringly. "You had nothing to do with that explosion and the police will soon figure that out. As the ex-boyfriend, Janus is the only one with a possible motive, not you."

"Janus talked to Achates this morning." Cybele bit her lower lip as she half-looked away from Gabe. "He got the impression that the police were focusing on the Friends of Gaea."

"Well, that's good." Gabe paused and looked at her more carefully. "Isn't it?"

Cybele pretended to take a great interest in the contents of her coffee cup as she muttered, "I just don't think the Friends of Gaea would set off an explosion. That could have injured people and that's not their way."

Gabe stroked her comfortingly on the side of her head. "There are always radicals in every group, but at least you can stop worrying now. It's not like the Friends of Gaea are connected to The Mysteries of Cybele, right?"

"Right." Cybele looked up at him but was unable to meet his eyes. "The organizations definitely aren't connected."

"Good." Gabe pulled her in for a hug. "Then the police don't have a motive for you and Janus being co-conspirators with the Friends of Gaea."

Cybele stiffened slightly. "Right." She began to gnaw on her lower lip again.

Gabe pulled slightly back and looked closely down at her guilty face. Is she lying to me? What isn't she telling me? He quickly ran through what she had just said. Something struck me as odd. A weird phrasing. The organizations aren't connected. He sighed unconsciously. The organizations? He shook his head. She does love to play with words. He looked more suspiciously at her. "Cybele, are you or Janus personally connected to the Friends of Gaea?"

Cybele spoke slowly into his chest. "Not with the organization."

Gabe frowned as he carefully analyzed her words. He tried again to pin her down. “But with a person whom the police might perceive, rightly or wrongly, as having some sort of connection, however remote, to the Friends of Gaea?”

Cybele shrugged uncomfortably. “It’s possible that the police might find a connection between me and the founder of Friends of Gaea. Although, I still don’t know why they would question our employees about it. It’s not as if I’m dumb or arrogant enough to plan an explosion and parade around in the open with a potential conspirator.” She rubbed her forehead. “The police should give me some credit.”

Gabe groaned. “You don’t want the police to give you that kind of credit, Cybele.” He shook his head exasperatedly. “And what sort of personal connection do you have to the founder of the Friends of Gaea?”

Cybele walked away from him and peered pensively through his kitchen window. “He was an old boyfriend from high school.” She shook her hand dismissively in the air. “We’ve drifted apart over the last few years, but if the police are looking for a past connection, there’s certainly a paper trail.”

Gabe moved to stand behind her. He placed his hands tentatively on her shoulders. “But you haven’t seen him recently?”

“No. Not in the last few weeks” Cybele slumped down against the counter.” She spoke a bit more defensively. “Winnipeg is a small town. People bump into people all the time. It’s only polite to say hello and have the occasional lunch or dinner with them.”

Gabe's hands tightened slightly. "Polite, right." He forced himself not to sound accusing. "But you had no idea he might be planning something like this?"

"Of course not." Cybele rubbed her forehead thoughtfully. "Plus, I still don't think he did it."

Gabe's hands relaxed. "What about Janus? How close is he to your ex-boyfriend?"

Cybele turned around to face him in surprise. She shook her head. "Janus? He and Hector never got along. They're not close at all."

"Good. Then the police can't possibly connect them together unless it's through you." Gabe looked searchingly at her. "And since you had no knowledge or suspicion that something like this might happen, you and Janus are safe."

"That's right." Cybele looked at her watch. "Wow. It's getting late. I'd better get back to work. Those rituals don't just plan themselves, you know."

Gabe sighed at the thought of all the work ahead for him. "I'll drive back with you. It's almost time for me to have left anyway. I just need to change." He walked out of the kitchen. Can't push her any further right now. She's starting to hedge again. Patience. All things come to those who wait.

Cybele watched him go. She walked back over to the sink and emptied her full cup. Janus and Hector would never have got together to do something like that. The enemy of my enemy is not my friend. Only people who write fairy tales believe that aphorism. Or those short-sighted fools who practice foreign policy for a livelihood. She groaned. Time to get back to work.

Chapter 20

Gods. It's certainly hot enough in here. Now that the weather has finally become warmer maybe I should turn down the space heaters a little more. Well. Maybe not. Heat does make people more susceptible to the ritual's influence and it will definitely intensify the effects of the wine. Cybele took a quick glance around the basement. Everything seems to be in place. Flickering lights. Quasi-subliminal ritual chanting courtesy of the powers of modern technology and a twenty-five dollar CD. Twenty-five dollars. Hmmm. Maybe I should suggest to Janus that we branch out into ritual CDs. Should be easy enough to burn some. The software is readily available. Have to make a note of that. She inhaled deeply. Intoxicating. Those incenses will definitely give my followers their money's worth tonight. She wandered over to the table to check on her slow cookers. Double, double, toil and trouble. Fire burn and cauldrons bubble. The wine should be mixing nicely with that wormwood and honey. Mmmm. Nothing better than homemade absinthe. She yawned. Gods. I'm so tired. Or maybe it's the hallucinogenics in the incense. Oh well. Got to get the show on the road. Give the people their money's worth of spirituality.

Cybele wandered over to the meditation area and sat down on the floor. Should unwind with some Cybelean Contemplative Motion moves. She began to perform some simple stretches to centre herself for the upcoming ritual. She looked up as Gabe came down the stairs towards her.

"Have our guests started to arrive?" she asked.

"Yes. I'll bring them down once they've been checked in and we've made sure their credit cards are good." Gabe reached down and tugged gently on the sheer lavender scarf that fell from a golden beaded circlet around Cybele's head. "You look amazing in this costume. Exactly how many belly dancing outfits do you have?"

Cybele looked up and smiled flirtatiously. "I guess you'll just have to wait and see."

"I look forward to it." Gabe knelt down and kissed Cybele on her lips. "For good luck."

Surprised, Cybele kissed him back deeply and then slowly pulled away. "Time to begin the games again. You should collect our flock and bring them down."

Cybele shook her head as Gabe walked away. Why he insists on wearing black, I don't know. It may be elegant but he needs some more colour. Maybe I'll buy him something in purple. Make him a more fitting Attis to my Cybele.

Cybele stood up and stretched languorously. She watched smiling as her flock began to file down the stairs. Good. They're all repeat members. I don't have to worry about them feeling self-conscious about anything they might be asked to do. Let the enthusiasm and ecstasy begin. She opened her arms in a welcoming gesture. "Enter and be seated in the places which I have sanctified for you." She smiled as she saw the eagerness at which they hastened to do her bidding. This Goddess thing is such a rush.

Cybele sat down in front of them and gently smiled. "As a *Bruja* of Cybele, it is my pleasure and privilege to initiate you into this evening's rites. As always, we will begin with deep rhythmic breathing." She lay down on her back and placed her feet firmly on the floor. "Since all of you are faithful adherents, you know the procedure that is to be followed. However, if any of you feel the need for personal instruction, I or *Brujo* Gabe will be at your service."

The participants fervently began their deep breathing exercises.

Cybele got up and began to wander around the room to check on their progress. Good. The heat and the drug-laced incenses are beginning to do their work. She smiled a bit wickedly. Although I shouldn't underestimate the effect of the innate willingness of human beings to let go of their inhibitions and give themselves up to something larger and external to themselves. "Very good, dear friends. Now please begin to hum deeply on your exhalations. And remember, the light-headedness you are feeling is the presence of the Goddess. She is blessing you with her love and filling you with the joy and peace we all so desperately search for in this fallen world of ours."

Cybele gazed contentedly across the room at Gabe. So yummy. She forced her attention back to her followers. Good. All that deep breathing and lack of oxygen will make them very receptive to the power and suggestion of my voice. She took a deep breath, filling her lungs with the enthralling aroma of offertory incense. "Now, I wish you to sit up slowly. Be careful. The effects of the Goddess will be strong within you."

Her flock slowly sat up. They were clearly in a state of intoxication, looking slightly off-balance, but with smiles on their dazed faces.

Cybele continued. "Very good, dear friends. Now, I wish you to sit with crossed legs."

Her flock obediently crossed their legs.

Cybele nodded as she observed their correct positioning on the floor. "Good. Now place the palms of your hands flat upon the ground beside your knees. Breathe in deeply from the center of your very being. With each deep breath you take, imagine the primal energy from the earth is being drawn through the palms of your hands and up your arms. You are being filled with the power of the Goddess. Enjoy the sensation of being filled with pure light."

Cybele watched closely as her followers attempted to follow her instructions and infuse themselves with the primal life-force of the earth. "Very good. You should now be tingling with the love of the Goddess. Begin to hum now as you inhale and draw up the untamed power of the earth. You are now creatures of the Light." Cybele walked back to her place at the front of her followers. "Luminous beings are we, not this crude matter." She opened her arms wide as if to embrace the room. "Now cup your hands together in front of you. Envision the light. See it stream from your hands and form a glowing ball of purple energy around your hands. If the light is too intense for your corporeal eyes to focus on then close them. See the light through your mind's eye."

Cybele sighed inwardly as she observed how many of her flock had to close their eyes. I am SO good. Thank the gods that I use my powers for good and not for evil.

In another time, another place, I could have been a prophet, a messiah. The world could have definitely benefited from the Mother Goddess religions. She shook her head sadly. Too bad they were replaced by patriarchy. Oh well. At least, through me, the Goddess can once again flourish.

Cybele breathed in deeply as she spoke. "Now take this glowing ball of purple energy and raise it above your head. Feel it expand and pour down over your body like gentle drops of rain. Once you are completely covered by the purple energy, then slowly turn to your partner beside you. Use the power of your mind to expand your own aura towards your partner's aura. Work together to mesh your energy with your partners." She paused to check on how her followers were doing. Good. They are focussed completely on my words. She continued. "There must be balance in the force. Breathe in deeply for the energy you need to fuse your aura with your partner's aura. Hum strongly as you envision yourself becoming one with your partner."

The basement resonated with the sound of deep breathing and humming as the participants struggled to control their auras and meld them with their partner's.

Cybele looked over them fondly for many minutes. Then she walked to her cauldrons full of warming wine. She began to pour the wine into the cups arranged on the table. She turned back to her followers and extended a welcoming arm. "Come, my children. You have done well. The Goddess is pleased with your mortal struggles to accept Her light and ascend to a higher level of being. Time to partake of the blessed wine, the blood of our Goddess. We must be sanctified by Her love before we go out in the darkness to perform our ceremony of gratitude and giving."

Cybele's flock unsteadily got to their feet and line up in front of her to receive the Goddess' blessing. After receiving their blessing and swallowing their cup of wine, they moved past Cybele. Once they were all sanctified, Gabe led them up the stairs for their final ritual outdoors.

Cybele turned off the empty slow cookers and tossed a little salt on the incense pots to hasten their demise. She unplugged the space heaters. There. No fire hazards left unattended. So far, so good. With a tired yet exhilarated sigh, she hurried upstairs to lead the last ritual of the evening.

Cybele walked towards the smoking fire where her flock stood patiently meditating in the darkness. Hmm. That fire is really smoking. I think I'll have to go a little easier on the valerian and rue the next time I prepare the incenses for it. Well. I'll be damned. Looks like Janus managed to get his flock of four released from police custody. Wonder if his lawyer is lurking around somewhere too. She rolled her eyes. How nice that they all felt it important to show up for this ritual without having done any of the work needed to set it up. Oh well. It will give me a chance to pump Janus for information once the ceremony is finished and my faithful have gone home.

Gabe gently reached over and touched her arm. "*Bruja*, I hope everything is set up to your satisfaction."

Cybele sighed softly. "Yes." My faithful *Brujo*. My subtle cue to begin. She raised her arms in supplication to the Goddess. "Come, my beloved children, for it is time to offer our thanks to the Goddess for filling us with Her love and Her life-force. Praise be to the Goddess for the gifts She has blessed us with in this world."

Her flock dutifully raised their arms and offered their thanks to the Goddess.

Cybele looked up at the moonlit sky and inhaled the night air deeply. "As we wander lonely as a cloud through this wide world of ours, we ask the Goddess to be our guiding light. To give us this day our much needed blessing and forgive us our trespasses for we do not always understand the significance of what we do." She looked around at the upturned faces of her followers. "Our spirits may be oftentimes weak. Mortality weighs heavily on us like unwilling sleep. Each imagined pinnacle and steep of godlike hardship tells us that we must surrender and die. Yet, we fear not these mortal coils. For we have the love of the Goddess to resurrect us. In the Goddess and our union with Her, must we trust."

Her acolytes obediently repeated. "In the Goddess and our union with Her, must we trust."

Cybele continued solemnly. "We do not question the will of the Goddess. We recognize that She moves in mysterious ways. We simply are thankful that She chooses to bless us with Her love. For all is good, if it comes from the Goddess."

Her flock nodded in unison. "All is good, if it comes from the Goddess."

Cybele lowered her arms but held them out as if to embrace them all. "What we give out in this world is what we get back from it. That is the balance of life. The natural order of the universe. There are those who seek to upset this natural balance. Do not hate them for they know not what they do. Their actions will have consequences for them. The balance will be maintained. But it is for the Goddess to redress these wrongs and not for us." Cybele shook her head sorrowfully. "Do not act in anger or hate towards those who corrupt the natural good of the people or the earth around us. These stained ones will have to face the Goddess' reckoning but, so will you, if you take your righteous rage out upon them. Release your negative emotions. They will only bind you to the evildoers. Fill yourself with the love of the Goddess and She will set you free. For all is good, if it comes from the Goddess."

Her acolytes chanted dutifully. "All is good, if it comes from the Goddess."

Cybele turned towards Gabe. He carefully placed a dagger in her outstretched hands.

She raised the dagger dramatically above her head. "Behold the Sword of the Goddess, sanctified by blood." She lowered the dagger into the flames. "And sanctified by fire." She moved slightly away from the fire and began to dig a small hole in the earth. She gave the dagger back to Gabe and he handed her a clay pitcher.

Cybele stood and slowly raised the heavy pitcher above her head. Damn. It's heavy. Maybe I should get something plastic instead. "Blessed Goddess, please accept this libation of love as a symbol of our gratitude and desire to follow your will. Bless us and be there for us in our time of need." She lowered the pitcher and slowly poured the mixture of seeds, milk, and honey into the earth's opening. She handed the pitcher to her followers and watched as each one reverently poured a little of the libation into the earth.

She received the empty pitcher from the last to offer the blessing and handed the pitcher back to Gabe. He then handed her another pitcher full of sweet, honeyed mead.

Cybele turned to her followers. "Hold out your hands and receive the final blessing from the Goddess." She began to pour the mead into their cupped hands. "As you lap this sweet potage of the Goddess from your palms, know that you are Her beloved children." Cybele smiled as she saw the bliss upon the faces of her flock. "The formal ritual is over for this evening. However, you may stay here and bask in the glory of the Goddess for as long as you wish. When you feel ready to leave, know that you leave with the Goddess. Her blessings will be with you wherever now you go."

Cybele walked away from her followers towards Gabe. They stood silently and watched as the flock slowly began to dissipate and move down the driveway to their waiting cars.

When the last one had left, Gabe turned to Cybele and shook his head amazedly. "That was quite a performance. I almost believe that you are a vessel for the Goddess."

Cybele paused wistfully. "Sometimes I almost believe it myself. Like I can feel the Goddess within me. Her power is..." She abruptly stopped and forced herself to speak more lightly. "Of course, I think that might be the first step to bedlam, so I just try to suppress that thought."

Gabe sighed in relief. "Good plan. I'm sure insanity is just a short journey away from godhead."

Cybele reached out and took Gabe's hand. "Don't worry. I don't suffer from delusions of grandeur." At least I don't think so. She squeezed his hand gently before letting go. "I want to talk to Janus about what happened at the police station today. Can you take care of the bonfire for me?"

Gabe looked down anxiously at her. "Do you want me to come with you?"

"No." Cybele shook her head. "It would probably be more productive if you weren't there." She reached up and tenderly stroked the side of his face. "Good-night, Gabe."

Gabe reached out to draw her closer but she gently pulled away. He watched her until she reached Janus's house. Then he turned his attention back to putting out the fires she had left.

With a small yawn, Cybele moved past Janus and into his living room. He carefully closed the door behind him and followed her into his house.

Cybele sat down on his couch and looked up at him. “I see you and your lawyer managed to spring the quartet from the big house.”

Janus sat down beside her. “We did. The police were just on a fishing expedition, hoping they could link us to the car bombing.”

“They are good crumb gatherers. But we don’t have a trail that links us to that, so let them gather their crumbs where they may.”

“Yes. Innocence is a wonderful state to exist in.” Janus got up. “Why don’t we have some wine? Celebrate the end of another successful week and the profit that comes with it.”

“Why not?” Cybele stood up and followed him into the kitchen.

Janus poured out two glasses and handed her one. “It doesn’t have the official blessing of the Goddess upon it, but it should still be pretty good.”

Cybele smiled wryly. “I’m glad you and your quartet made it to the rituals this evening. Everyone can benefit from a little spirituality, especially in these trying times.”

Janus looked searchingly at her. “Interesting invocation to the Goddess you made tonight. Came on a bit strong about the importance of respecting the natural balance of the world.”

Cybele looked uncomfortably back at him. “Well. The natural instinct of most human beings is to retaliate against those whom they feel have wronged them. I just want to ensure that our followers understand that we do not advocate lashing out against evildoers."

Janus shook his head contemptuously. "Love the sinner if not the sin, eh?"

"Precisely." Cybele looked sharply at him. "Something that protects us both philosophically and legally from any actions misguided converts might make in our name or in the name of the Goddess. You should be in favour of that."

"Legally, of course, I am." Janus took a slow sip of his wine. "The predicament the Friends of Gaea find themselves in could probably have been avoided if they had censored themselves more fully." He sighed deeply. "However, don't you ever get tired of political correctness? Wouldn't it be nice to be able to preach exactly what we wanted without worrying about legal ramifications?"

Cybele frowned in surprise. "I do preach what I believe, Janus. Even without the spectre of legal action hanging over my head, I would never advocate violence as a means to solving problems we may have with the less enlightened members of this world." She absently swirled the wine in her glass. "I don't believe the Friends of Gaea would either. But they are a good reminder of a fate we want to avoid." She tapped the side of her glass thoughtfully. "The more they are tarnished with the brush of eco-terrorism, the less chance they have for making a lasting difference in the world." She raised her glass and drank down deeply. "Violence only attracts violent people and solves nothing. It's a destroyer not a creator."

"No Shivas need apply for membership to the Mysteries of Cybele, eh?"

"Only Vishnus and Brahmas." Cybele looked firmly at Janus. "This cult is making us a lot of money and I like to think that we are doing some real good with it. But if the police ever leak their suspicions about us to the ravening media, none of that will matter. We will be tarred as eco-terrorists and potential customers, whether of our spiritual or more mundane products, will flock away from us in droves. The profit loss potential will be enormous."

Janus moved back towards the couch and sat down. "Well. We can't have that, can we?"

"No." Cybele moved to sit at the far end in opposition to him. "That's why I'm trying to make sure that nothing I say can be used against us later."

Janus snorted. "Good-bye, free speech. It was overrated anyway."

Cybele frowned at him. "We have a right to say what we believe and I do. But I also know that we are responsible for our words and any actions that might directly result from them."

Janus half-bowed towards her. "The prudent pagan."

She waved dismissively at him. "Prudence is a quality you should aspire to, Janus." She paused meaningfully. "Unless you enjoy having to pay lawyers to spring our employees from police custody?"

"Of course not." Janus straightened up and looked more seriously at her. "But don't you ever desire to break the shackles of social conditioning?"

Cybele looked at him uncertainly. “In what way?”

“Aren’t you ever the slightest bit curious?” Janus leaned forward towards her. “If only intellectually?” He leaned back again. “About the direction our members would go, if left to their own devices?” He carefully scrutinized her face. “Without you there to interpret the word of the Goddess to them, how do you think they would interpret it?”

Drawn in almost against her will, Cybele unconsciously nodded in understanding. “In controlled circumstances, that would be a fascinating social experiment.” She chuckled self-consciously. “Remember on the *Simpsons*, when Lisa created a world from her fallen tooth?”

Janus reached over and swatted her affectionately on her shoulder. “Right. Her civilization evolved from hunters and gatherers to space travel within a few days.”

“Yeah.” Cybele slowly became more serious as she remembered the episode more fully. “But they also fought a war with the evil Bart and there was a lot of violence and death.”

Janus shrugged nonchalantly. “A natural part of the evolution of a society.”

“Which is fine in cartoons.” Cybele began to gnaw on her bottom lip. “But blood and violence should not be so lightly dismissed in real life. Life should not be a social experiment.” She shook her head unconsciously. “If we left it up to our followers to interpret the will of the Goddess, She might end up echoing their desires for vengeance and the consequences could be far more damaging for all of us."

Janus snorted. "You do know that there is no Goddess, right? You made her up and Her will is really your own will."

Cybele snapped back. "I know that. I'm not delusional." She paused more thoughtfully. "But She is my creation, an alter ego, a shadow self. And as the Goddess, She will send the message of peace and tolerance to the world that I wish Her to send." Cybele raised her glass of wine in homage to the Goddess within her and drank deeply. "You know, Janus, just because the Goddess is my creation doesn't mean she's not real to me or to our followers. She represents the potential within us all for spiritual harmony with others and with our environment."

Janus shook his head scornfully at her. "So, you're not going to take the bracelets off your followers, eh?"

"No." Cybele glowed from within. "But when they have achieved true spiritual enlightenment, they will take off their own chains and walk freely from the caves. And for those incapable of such apotheosis, they can remain mesmerised by my smoke and shadows. They won't be harmed by the illusion and it will ensure that they go forth and do no harm."

Janus grimaced as he fought the urge to shake her serene smile off her face. "Isn't it a bit hypocritical to give freedom to some and deny it to others?"

"I am neither giving nor denying freedom, Janus." Cybele looked at him in puzzlement. "I am just making available the opportunity for spiritual growth. The truth is that not everyone desires the awesome responsibility that comes with free will. They would rather be told what to do than be forced to decide for themselves."

"People are sheep," said Janus in disgust.

"For the most part they are." Cybele nodded in acknowledgement. "That's why it is so important that their spiritual advisors be good shepherds."

"Keep the wolves away from the flock, eh?"

"Precisely." Cybele forced herself to laugh light-heartedly. "Especially those garbed in sheep's clothing."

Janus sighed dramatically and then forced himself to laugh as well. "Only proles and animals are free. Pity." He shook his head slowly regretfully. "It's just that damn intellectual curiosity. Guess I've always had a yen to see how people would remake the world if left loose to their own primal impulses."

Cybele narrowed her eyes as she tried to gauge Janus's true intentions from the expression on his face. "Then I suggest you watch post-apocalyptic movies." She paused for emphasis. "But don't be a wolf in sheep's clothing."

"Perish the thought," said Janus as he looked measuringly back at her.

Cybele nodded warningly. "Perish the thought." She placed her empty glass down on the kitchen counter. "I think it's time for me to call it a night."

Janus walked her to the door. "I have some more accounting to do before I can finish off my day. No rest for the wicked."

Cybele smiled good-bye. "Only the good die young."

Janus watched her leave and then walked back into the kitchen. He raised his glass in tribute to her. "Only the good die young." He drained his glass and then walked off to tally up his profit and loss statements for the week.

Chapter 21

Gabe closed the back door of the Mysteries of Cybele and walked towards the greenhouse. Good thing Cybele decided to sleep in this morning. He smiled. She really hates Mondays. Oh well. Gives me some time to do a little investigating without her wondering what I'm up to. Now I just have to hope that Janus's four close personal friends have decided to show up for work today. He peered through the greenhouse windows. There they are. Tan, Ixion, Ajax, and Ardiaeus. Hard at work. Standing around and drinking coffee. Can't believe Janus keeps them on the payroll. He shook his head. Has to be for something other than their dedication to work. Just hope they're in a talkative mood today.

Gabe opened the door to the greenhouse and sauntered in. The wind slammed the door shut behind him. The resulting bang startled Tan, Ajax, Ixion, and Ardiaeus. They jumped and turned to see who had entered. They relaxed slightly upon seeing it was only Gabe.

"Sorry," said Gabe as he smiled disarmingly. "Didn't mean to startle you."

"No problem." Tan nodded. "We thought you might be Cybele checking up on us."

"Yeah." Ardiaeus grunted. "She's always double-checking our work."

Unable to keep quiet, Ixion chimed in. "It's like she thinks we're too stupid to know how to do our job."

“I’m sure she doesn’t think you’re stupid,” Gabe said reassuringly. “But her name is on the business, so she’s responsible for what we do when we’re here.” He leaned casually against one of the work tables and picked up a container of incense. “She takes this stuff seriously. She’s just making sure the customers get their money’s worth.” He placed the container back down and turned to Tan. “I was surprised to see you guys at the rituals Friday evening.”

Ajax jumped in defensively. “Hey. Janus said we could come to whatever rituals we wanted.”

Ixion shook his head worriedly. “Yeah. Just as long as we respected the fact that Cybele was in charge of them…”

Ardiaeus broke in. “And we didn’t disrupt them or do anything to break the spell she was casting on the people.”

Tan smirked. “She’s a pretty good witch for such a bitch. Looked pretty hot in that costume of hers. Was almost tempted to make my move but decided against it.”

Ajax laughed as he elbowed Tan in the ribs. “Yeah. She’s too bossy to be any fun to be around.”

Gabe gritted his teeth. “Right.” Don’t get defensive. You need to know what they know. But still…” He tried but was unable to stop himself from defending her. “You know if she ever hears you calling her a bitch, she’ll fire you on the spot. And considering how much money she makes for the business, I doubt Janus would choose to re-hire you and chance pissing her off enough to quit.”

Ajax smirked. “Oh. I don’t think we have to worry about Janus firing us.”

Gabe looked sharply at Ajax. "Oh really?" He took a step closer to Ajax in an attempt to rattle him. "Why?"

Tan smoothly stepped between Ajax and Gabe as he threw Ajax an angry glare. "He means that we're cool, man. We're not stupid enough to call her a bitch to her face and it's not like you're going to run and tell her what you said, right?"

Gabe nodded. "Right." He forced himself to smile. I'm just one of the guys. No problem.

Ardiaeus laughed unconcernedly. "It's not like we're worried. You're stuck working with her all day. Her nagging must drive you insane."

Gabe smiled through his teeth. They're idiots. Just play along. "Or out to the greenhouse to get away from her and talk to people tall enough to ride a rollercoaster at the Red River Ex."

Ixion laughed excitedly. "I love the Ex. I go there every summer." He shook his head sadly. "But I never can seem to win the fairway games."

Gabe rolled his eyes. "That's a shame, Ixion. Better luck this year."

Ixion smiled broadly. "Thanks, Gabe."

Gabe resolutely tried to continue with his questioning. "I was surprised to see you at the ritual Friday because I had heard the police had been harassing you. I just thought the last place you would want to be after that is at work."

Ajax shrugged nonchalantly. "The ritual was pretty fun."

Ixion nodded happily. “And it’s not like we had to do any work. It was just like going to a party.”

“Right.” Gabe paused momentarily at a loss. Subtlety doesn’t seem to work with these guys. Unless...They’re really very smart and they’re just jerking me around. He looked over at them and shook his head. No. They’re not that clever. What you see is what you get. “So, what were the police bugging you about, anyway?”

Tan looked at Gabe blankly. “No big deal. Just wanted to know if we had heard anything on the streets about anyone who might have been involved in some car bombing.”

“Just on the streets?” Gabe asked.

Eager to show off his own knowledge, Ixion broke in. “Or at the Mysteries of Cybele. They wanted to know if Cybele had ever talked about some eco-terrorists, Friends of Guys, or something.”

Ajax laughed meaningfully. “Yeah. We told them Cybele is definitely not a Friends of Guys.” He winked at Gabe. “Definitely plays for the other team, if you get me.”

Gabe nodded back. “I get you.” Like to get you with a baseball bat but that won’t get me any more information. God. I can’t believe the police are stupid enough to think that Cybele is somehow connected to terrorists. She’s right. They are idiots. “I’m surprised they didn’t ask you about Janus. He is the ex-boyfriend, right?”

Tan frowned confusedly. “What do you mean ex-boyfriend? I thought the lawyer was a guy.”

Gabe winced. Shit. Cybele is going to be pissed if she finds out that I accidentally outed Janus.

Ixion looked at Gabe for confirmation. "Janus is gay?"

Ardiaeus wrinkled his forehead as he thought hard. "I thought it was strange he liked watching all those foreign films at the Globe. That explains everything."

Ixion nodded at Ardiaeus. "And he speaks French and likes to match his shirt colour with his socks."

Ardiaeus snorted. "What are you doing noticing what colour his socks and shirts are? Maybe you're gay too."

Ajax shoved Ardiaeus hard. "There's nothing wrong with being gay, if that's what floats your boat. My cousin Alex is gay. He's a great guy. A soldier." Ajax lit up. "Hey, I should ask Janus if he knows Alex. Maybe try to fix them up."

Tan growled and waved dismissively at them. "Would all of you just shut up a minute?" He turned towards Gabe. "What makes you think Janus is gay?"

Don't mention Cybele's name. Gabe forced himself to shrug nonchalantly. "I thought everybody knew. I mean why else would the police ask you about him unless he had some sort of connection to the victim?"

Ixion looked more thoughtful. "They did ask us about Janus, if he talked about the Friends of the Guys."

Ardiaeus smirked. "He's probably a member."

Gabe groaned. Idiots. "It's the Friends of Gaea, not the Friends of the Guys, and I don't think Janus is a member."

Tan waved Gabe off. "Whatever. They were more interested in what we knew about Cybele, not about what we knew about Janus."

Ajax agreed. "They definitely had a bug up their ass about her. She must have really pissed them off."

Ixion nodded. "Yeah. It's never a good idea to piss off the cops. They hold grudges forever."

Ardiaeus laughed roughly. "I guess she'd better watch her back if the cops think she's the terrorist. Maybe she'll have less time to boss us around if she's being bullied by the cops."

Gabe frowned at Ardiaeus. "The more time she spends at the police station, the less time she spends here..."

Ajax muttered under his breath. "That would be a very good thing."

Gabe glared at Ajax. "That would be a very bad thing. Without her, there is no business, which means no jobs and no money for you. Plus, even if the police think she's a terrorist, she wouldn't have been able to do it all by herself."

Tan nodded thoughtfully. "Which means they'll start looking around here for likely people she used to help her."

Gabe smiled meaningfully. "That's right. I wonder which guys they'll look at first." He looked over at them. "Hope none of you guys have police records. They always look at those guys first."

Ixion looked worried again. "Only as young offenders and those records are supposed to be destroyed once we become adults."

Gabe looked over at Ixion. "Oh. I'm sure the police have their own private records." He looked back over at Tan. "So, anyone who might think it was a good joke to blame Cybele for the bomb had better not be that stupid. Because they'll just draw the attention back to themselves. But that shouldn't be a problem, because no one has anything to hide, right?"

Tan nodded slowly. "Right." He turned towards Ardiaeus, Ixion, and Ajax. "Coffee break is over. We have a lot of work to get done today." He looked back at Gabe dismissively. "Do you have any special orders for us to fill because we have to get back to work now?"

Gabe shook his head. "No. Just wanted to drop by and make sure the police hadn't given you too hard a time Friday."

Ixion smiled. "No. Thanks. We're okay."

Tan snorted. "We're fine, Gabe." He then deliberately turned his back on Gabe and walked over to the work table to begin preparing orders for shipment. The others quickly followed his lead.

Gabe shook his head. Damn. I guess the well has dried up for now. Oh well. Better get back to the office. Cybele is sure to be wondering where I am. He turned and left without another word to them.

Once he was sure Gabe had left, Tan looked over at the others. "You guys stay here and get this work done. I want to go talk to Janus."

Ardiaeus nodded. "Okay. I think he's at home today."

"Good. I'll be right back." Tan left and walked over to Janus's house. He rang the doorbell.

Janus came to the door. "Tan? What are you doing here? Is something wrong?" He looked behind Tan. No police. Good. "So, what can I do for you?"

Tan looked uneasily at Janus as he spoke. "Are you gay?"

"What?" Janus took a step back in surprise. "What makes you ask me that?"

Tan shuffled his feet as he looked away from Janus. "Gabe said you were gay."

"That bastard." Janus looked over at Tan and hesitated. Should I tell him the truth? The boat's already sailed. Need to start rebuilding trust and loyalty. "Would it matter to you if I was gay?"

Tan shrugged uncertainly. "Just as long as you know I'm not, I guess not."

Janus sighed. "That's great. I'm not interested in you or any of the others in your posse, okay?" He paused. "I just consider you to be my friends. NOT my boyfriends, okay?"

Tan shrugged less uncomfortably. "Okay. I guess it's okay. I mean, it's not that big a deal, really." He kicked the door jamb nervously. "Isn't the mayor gay?"

"Yeah." Janus bit his bottom lip. "He is."

"Yeah. I thought so." Tan straightened up and began to look Janus in the eyes. "And Ajax's cousin is gay, so like, no big deal."

"Right." Janus looked consideringly at Tan. "So, you just came over to ask if I was gay?" Damn. He still seems a little uncomfortable.

Don't want him to see me as a threat. Especially with everything that's going on right now.

"Oh. No." Tan cleared his throat. "Actually, you know how you told us that we shouldn't talk to the other employees about what happened at the police station?"

"Yes. The less you say, the better. That way you're less likely to show more knowledge of what happened than you should have." Janus frowned. "Why? Has Cybele been asking you questions?"

"Not her. Gabe. He came by to see how we were after being harassed by the police on Friday. Seemed to ask us a lot of questions." Tan shrugged. "We didn't really say anything to him. He's just nosy. But I thought you should know that he's still sneaking around."

"Thanks, Tan. It's good to know who your friends are." Janus paused for emphasis. "And who your friends aren't." I need to cement their loyalty again. Or it might be dangerous to have them hanging around. The alienated youth. Damn. More trouble than they're worth. "Why don't you guys come back here for lunch? We can eat on the deck and since Cybele won't be able to see us, it won't matter if you guys have a few beers."

"Cool." Tan turned to leave and then paused. "So, what do you think is up with Gabe? Think he's some kind of police kiss-ass?"

Janus shook his head slowly. "I don't know. He's so nosy, maybe. Or maybe he wants to push you guys out of the business and move himself up in the world." Good. Need to make them see he's the enemy not me. Hmmm. Maybe Gabe is trying to find a way to push me out of the business so he can be partners with Cybele instead. Does she know what he's up to? What if she's conspiring with him against me? No. She would never choose him over me.

Janus looked carefully at Tan. "But you guys have nothing to worry about. I would never let Gabe and Cybele try to convince me to fire you. Just be careful about what you say in front of them."

"We will."

"Good. See you guys at lunch."

Tan turned and walked back to the greenhouse.

Janus slammed his front door and walked into his kitchen. He grabbed a beer from his fridge and began to drink it. Damn them all. Too many loose threads running around. Going to need a good pair of scissors to cut myself loose. He paused. How the hell did Gabe know I was gay? Maybe Cybele? He shook his head. No. She wouldn't have betrayed me. It had to be the police. They must have told him. Probably hoping to drive a wedge between possible co-conspirators. Achates did tell the police I was an ex-boyfriend. He nodded. I'm surprised the police didn't tell Tan and the others when they were brought in for questioning. I guess those guys can follow orders. I told them to ask for a lawyer the moment they were pulled in. I guess they did. At least I'm not forced to rely on total incompetents. He chuckled. That's what comes from using guys who know the system. They may not be Einsteins, but they do have a certain shrewdness about them.

He began to tap his fingers on the counter. What to do? Think. Regain trust of idiots. Can't be too hard. The rituals. Can't go wrong when you mix the feeble-minded with drugs and alcohol. Need to bind them back to me. Need to make sure that even if they do betray me, the police can't tie me to anything. He smiled. That won't be a problem. No one would take their word over mine. Besides, I've got the money. The rich don't do time. Money buys justice. He drained his beer. Nothing to worry about. Better get back to work myself.

Janus walked from his house to The Mysteries of Cybele.

He opened the door and walked inside. Gabe was in the kitchen making a cup of coffee.

Janus walked past him without a word towards Cybele's office. It was empty. He returned to the kitchen.

"Where the hell is Cybele?"

Gabe calmly took a sip of his coffee. "She had to run a few errands. Said she would be in late."

"Well." Janus tapped his foot angrily as he glared at Gabe. "She should have told me."

"Well. She told me." Gabe took another sip of his coffee. "I guess she felt that everyone who had to be notified was."

Janus walked up to Gabe and spoke very precisely. "What is that supposed to mean?"

Arrogant bastard. "Why nothing other than the fact that I'm her office assistant. I work more closely with her than you."

Janus looked searchingly at Gabe. Jackass. "Right. Just as long as you remember that working for her means you also work for me." He turned to walk to his office and then stopped. "So, what have you been up to this morning, here without any supervision?"

"Just doing my job. Making sure orders are filled correctly and go out without delay."

"You're right." Janus nodded. "That's your job. Doing the white collar grunt work that makes business possible." He leaned back against the kitchen wall. "But you seem to be doing more than your job today."

Gabe put his cup of coffee down. "Meaning?"

"Meaning your job is paperwork. You have no business interrogating other employees about things which are none of your concern."

"I'm sorry. Janus. You're going to have to be more specific. You're speaking in riddles." Gabe smirked. "Or maybe I should say tongues. Considering the type of business we're running here."

"Oh. We're not running a business, Gabriel. I am. You're a peon who happens to amuse my partner. But once she's over you, you're out of here."

"Wouldn't that be sexual harassment?" Gabe laughed. "You know. Being seduced by a partner and then discarded like a dirty tissue." He moved closer to Janus. "I'm sure that I could sue."

Janus growled. "Not when the EEOC hears about all the trouble you've caused."

Gabe looked innocently at Janus. "What trouble?"

"Tan came to see me this morning." Janus shook his head sadly. "He was very upset. Said he and the others were hard at work in the greenhouse when you came in and started harassing them." Janus smirked. "Said you were asking them a lot of questions about their personal lives." He moved closer to Gabe deliberately crowding him. "That's not part of your job. Disrupting the work of valued employees. Wasting their time. Creating a hostile work environment by telling homophobic jokes. Those seem to be good grounds for getting rid of you."

Gabe exploded. "That's a damn lie. I never said anything like that."

"Are you sure? Poor Ajax felt personally attacked. His dear cousin is gay, you know." Janus chuckled angrily. "Why, I might be the one able to sue you for sexual harassment, on poor Ajax's behalf, of course."

Gabe glared at Janus. "I don't know what the hell you're trying to do, Janus, but I'm no homophobe and I don't intend to let you brand me as one."

"Oh. It's not me, Gabriel. It's poor Ajax and the others." He smirked. "I do believe they heard you say things like that about me. You did make such a point of telling them that I was gay, didn't you?"

"You've lost it, Janus." Gabe shook his head contemptuously. "I have better ways to spend my day than listening to your paranoid ranting." He roughly brushed past Janus on his way to Cybele's office.

Furious, Janus pushed Gabe back hard against the hallway wall.

Now equally furious, Gabe pushed Janus back harder.

The two men squared off, each daring the other to throw the first punch.

"What the hell is going on here?" Cybele slammed the front door behind her. "Have you two totally lost it? This is a place of business not a schoolyard. What kind of example are you setting for the other employees?"

Janus snapped. "Tell that to your boyfriend. He started it."

"I did not." Gabe turned towards Cybele. "He..."

"Stop it, both of you." Cybele shook her head in disgust. "You even sound like children." She took a deep breath. "Can one of you, without blaming the other, try to tell me what's going on here?"

Both men began to speak at once. Each tried to speak more loudly than the other.

"Stop." Cybele turned to Gabe. "Would you please wait in our office? I'll talk to you later."

Gabe frowned but went into their office.

Janus smirked.

Cybele frowned. "Why don't we talk in your office?"

Janus gestured for her to enter. She did. He then carefully closed the door and walked over to his desk.

Cybele tiredly sat down in front of his desk. "So, Janus, what's going on?"

"Your boyfriend has been making trouble here all morning. You should keep him on a tighter leash."

Cybele's nostrils flared slightly. "Don't be offensive, Janus." She forced herself to speak calmly. "Just tell me what happened."

Janus shook his head angrily. “Loverboy decided to snoop around the greenhouse this morning. Asking Tan and the others lots of questions about their Friday encounter with the police.”

“He was probably just curious about what happened. I’m sure everyone is gossiping about it.” Cybele sighed. “We seem to be of more interest to the police than I hoped we would be.” She looked over at Janus. “The tension between you two seemed pretty high for it to be only about office gossip. I could smell the testosterone in the air when I walked in.”

“It’s not his job to gossip with the staff,” said Janus as he waved his hand dismissively at her.

Cybele rolled her eyes. Oh for the love of the Goddess. “Give it a rest. You can’t control gossip. And you shouldn’t try. You’ll just send it underground and make it worse.” She stood up. “So, if that’s all…”

“It’s not all.” Janus snapped. “He made a point of telling some of the employees that I was gay.”

“What?” Cybele sat back down. She rubbed her forehead. Damnit. She stood up again and began to pace.

“That’s right. He outed me. And the only reason he would have done that was if he wanted to cause trouble.”

Cybele reached out her hand to Janus. “Maybe it was an accident. Maybe it slipped out.”

“He did it on purpose.” Janus pushed her hand away angrily. “I told you the first time you met him that he was a troublemaker. You just keep refusing to believe me.”

She looked guiltily at Janus. “Sometimes things slip out.”

Janus’s eyes narrowed furiously as understanding dawned. “Oh. My. God. You did it. You’re the one who told him I was gay.”

“By accident.” Cybele looked beseechingly at him. “Not on purpose.” She shook her head. “It’s moot anyway. With the car bombing and all those police visits, it would have come out sooner or later.”

Janus slammed his hand down on his desk. “It was not his decision to make.”

“No. It wasn’t.” Cybele reached over and held Janus’s hand. “That explains why you were so angry. I’m sorry.”

Janus pulled his hand slowly away. “He’s trouble, Cybele.”

“He made a mistake,” said Cybele soothingly.

Janus smiled vindictively at her. “He made a point of mentioning that he could sue us for sexual harassment if we fired him because you’re a partner and he’s an employee.”

Cybele threw up her hands in frustration. “He what?”

“Said he would sue us.” Janus shook his head gloatingly. “I said he was trouble.”

“That’s just peachy.” She shook her head. “Don’t worry, Janus. He won’t sue us. I’m not going to fire him. I’m going to kill him.” She walked to the door and opened it. She turned and sighed. “I’ll tell him to try and stay out of your way, okay?”

“Okay.”

She nodded warningly. “But remember, you’re both adults. No more flaring nostrils and charging each other in the hallway, okay.”

"Fine." Janus turned back to his desk. I can't believe she betrayed me. Judas.

Cybele walked reluctantly into her office. She closed the door quietly and sank down in her chair behind her desk. She looked over at Gabe to find him watching her worriedly.

"Cyb, are you okay? You look..." Gabe paused. I've never seen her looking sad before.

"Disillusioned?" Cybele finished his sentence.

"About?" Gabe asked cautiously.

"You." She bit her lower lip. "Janus said you deliberately outed him today."

"I didn't. Not deliberately. It was an accident. I was talking to Tan and his friends about their experiences with the police on Friday. Just to find out if the police were focusing on you or Janus."

"Why? What does it matter?" Cybele threw her hands up in exasperation. "The police will soon find someone else to investigate. We had nothing to do with it."

"I know you had nothing to do with it." Gabe reached over and took her hand. "But I knew that you were worried and I wanted to reassure you that you were okay." I can't tell her that the police really do seem to be focusing on her. Not when she's this upset already.

Cybele pulled her hand away from his. "Janus said that you threatened to sue me for sexual harassment if he fired you. Is that true?"

Gabe groaned. Damn him. "I didn't mean it. I was angry. He was threatening to fire me just because I had been talking to other employees." He reached for her hand again. "I was angry but I didn't mean what I said."

Cybele pulled her hand away again. "You kissed me, you know. I didn't kiss you." She frowned. "In fact, that day in my apartment, you hugged me first. I didn't hug you."

"I know." Gabe smiled. "If you weren't the boss, you could probably accuse me of sexually harassing you."

"That's not funny." Cybele stood up and began to pace. "Some things, once said, can't be taken back."

"Outing Janus can't be taken back, I know." He paused ruefully. "I know that I betrayed your trust and I am very sorry about that. It was an accident."

She nodded reluctantly. "I believe you." She groaned. "I didn't really mean to let it slip to you either that time. Shit just happens." She sighed. "Just try to stay out of his way for a while. If you see him, walk away. I don't need any more things to go wrong right now."

"Nothing else will." Gabe reached out again for Cybele's hand. "We're okay, right?"

She shook her head and moved away from him.

"Cyb?"

She gestured between the two of them. "I don't think this is a good idea. The last problem I need right now is to be sued for sexual harassment." She turned her back to him. "It would be a mistake for us to get involved. Not while you work for me. I should have thought about how it might look to the other employees if we got together."

Gabe groaned. "It's not sexual harassment if I want to be involved with you."

"You say that now, but things could change. It's just too much of a risk. I'm sorry." She walked over to her door and opened it wide. She returned back to her desk and sat down. She pulled a stack of order forms towards her. "We should get back to work."

Gabe sat down at his desk. "Right. Back to work." I'll talk to her later when she's not so upset. If I push her now, she'll just get more defensive. He shook his head. And next thing I know, I'll be working in the basement. He smiled fondly at her. I'll just have to find a way to change her mind about us. After all, good things come to those who wait.

Chapter 22

Three hours later, Cybele finished the last of her filing and sighed. Thank the gods! She shook her head. The world will end not in a storm of fire and ice but a blizzard of paperwork. She stood up and stretched. My head is killing me. I must be getting a cold. Too bad I already sent Gabe out on his lunch break. I could have asked him to pick up some echinacea and vitamin C for me. Wonder if Janus has any left from the last batch I gave him. Janus. I really should apologize to him. He must be feeling so betrayed right now. He has to know I would never have done anything to deliberately hurt him. If only I hadn't let it slip while I was talking to Gabe. If only Gabe hadn't let it slip when he was talking to the other employees. I guess a secret doesn't stay secret long when more than one person knows it. She shook her head. Ohhh. I feel a bit light-headed. And not in a good way. I should try to apologize again. Make him see how sorry I am. Maybe try to get him to see that Gabe really didn't mean to. Maybe not. Mentioning Gabe's name might be like waving a red flag in front of him. Those two get along as well as Janus and Hector did. If the police truly knew how much Hector and Janus disliked each other, they never would think there was any way we could all be one happy family of conspirators.

Cybele walked out of her office to Janus's office. She knocked on the door. There was no answer.

Damn. I didn't hear him leave. He better not be inside sulking and deliberately ignoring me. She turned to go back to her office and then paused. I should leave him a note. Clear the air. She turned the doorknob. Locked. Wonderful. She returned back to her office and picked up her purse. She pulled out her key chain and returned to unlock Janus's door.

Cybele smiled as she walked into Janus's office. Lucky for me, Janus is always forgetting his keys. She sat down behind his desk and pulled a sheet of paper from his printer. Better make the apology heartfelt. He's probably pretty mad at me right now. She wrote out a short, simple apology and signed it. *Your most truly repentant friend, Cybele.*

Cybele looked around the room with a satisfied sigh. Good. The process of mending fences has begun. She frowned. Gods. Doesn't he ever dust in here? The light from the windows is so hazy. She grabbed a few tissues from the box and walked over to wipe off the windows. She walked back to his desk. Where's the garbage? She looked under the desk. No wastepaper basket. Just a stack of books. She peered at them more closely. That's a lot of books. I wonder if he's still managing to find the time to work on his thesis. He always had more discipline than I. I've pretty much given up on mine. Wonder if he's finally chosen a psychological perspective. She sat down cross-legged on the floor and pulled a few of the books towards her. She placed the crumpled, dirty tissues on the floor beside her and started to look through the books.

The True Story of David Koresh: A Descent into the Madness of Prophetic Delusions. Jim Jones: The Kool-Aid Killer. The Moonies: What Really Happened? Heaven's Gate: The Spaceship of Death. The

Cult in Modern-Day America. Visions of Mob Rule and Madness. Hmmm. That's odd. These must be books he's reading for fun. I don't see how he can use these for his thesis on street kids. Unless he's trying to understand the psychological implications of starting a cult. Trying to ensure that what happened with those cults doesn't happen with ours. She shook her head puzzledly. But those leaders were all delusional. They truly believed they were either gods or the mouthpieces for gods. They were hungry for power and they took advantage of the weaknesses of their followers in order to feed their own desires for control. I'm nothing like that. I try to help my members achieve spiritual enlightenment. I don't want to control their lives or have the power of life and death over them. I just want to give them a good show. Some pageantry and drama. Something to brighten up their lives and give them something to look forward to every week. I'm no more or less than any other religion. I'm nothing like those nuts.

Cybele looked at the last two books on her lap. The Stanley Milgram Paradox: Why Good People Do Evil Things. The Stanford Prison Experiment: An Exercise in Shifting Identities and Moral Codes. She frowned thoughtfully. I seem to remember Janus talking about these two ad nauseam a few months ago. He went on and on about them for so long that I just began to tune him out. She began to flip through the first one. Right. This is the one where average people were told to press buttons that delivered electric shocks to strangers. They followed the orders of the white-coated researcher. Two-thirds of them gave the most dangerous, deadly levels of shocks. They sublimated their moral conscience and justified it by saying they were just following orders. She looked at the notes Janus had written in the margins. Conscience is just a societal construction. It is a myth we use to avoid killing one another at the slightest provocation. It does not exist. A tree that falls in the forest with no one around to hear. Give the brutes a chance. They will exterminate us all. What the hell is Janus talking about? He can't possibly believe what he's written. It's just intellectual abstractions. Detached philosophizing. Cybele frowned as she continued to read the text. They never knew until much later that they hadn't actually hurt their subject. Cybele shook her head. Just following orders. That didn't go over too well as a defense at the Nuremberg trials.

She began to flip through the second book. As she did, a sheaf of papers fell from it. She distractedly placed them to one side as she began to read about the Stanford Prison experiment. Right. This is the one where volunteers were arbitrarily given the roles of prisoners or guards and placed in a specially built jail at the Stanford Psychology Department. She gnawed her lip as she tried to remember the significance of the experiment. It showed how when given complete control over another human being anyone can turn into a monster. Power and lack of power completely warped the subjects' personalities. She paused at the handwritten notes on some of the pages. *They started out as peaceniks and ended up as Nazis. Easy for so-called good people to descend into brutality and evil. Morality is flexible – determined by circumstance.* Cybele unconsciously shook her head. NO. Morality must not be flexible. It must be concrete for without structure we fall prey to the worst of our primal passions. She continued to read. *The researchers themselves became caught up in the experiment. They allowed horrific acts of brutality to continue unchecked out of an intellectual curiosity to see just how far the situation would go. Zimbardo's experiment was finally stopped when an outside observer, his girlfriend and fellow colleague, Christina Maslach walked into the prison on the fifth day of the experiment. Her horror at what she saw enabled Zimbardo to break free from the madness he had created and been implicated in himself and stop the experiment.* Cybele swallowed hard. What's going on? Why had Janus been so fascinated by something as horrible as this? It couldn't have just been as a cautionary tale. Not when he keeps talking about the cult as a social experiment. She looked at the notes Janus had written in the margin. *Ground-breaking research into power roles. Corruption of human morality. John Wayne. Nickname given to most sadistic of the guards. Adopted a fake Southern accent and different persona when he interacted with prisoners. People engage in anti-social acts when they feel anonymous or think they can get away with them. Morality is an illusion. Morality is dead.* Cybele slowly closed the book feeling sick to her stomach. She reluctantly reached down for the loose papers she had placed beside her. She squinted as she tried to decipher Janus's scrawl. *Human ethics bullshit. The 1965 Experiment could never take place today. Too much concern over subjects' rights prevents loss of true knowledge. Modern research is a joke. Any reputable psychologist who tried something like this would be blackballed in his profession. The trick is to be an objective, uncompromised observer, neither a participant nor a creator. Observational research is the key for the pendulum of political correctness has swung too far in the other direction. Zimbardo. Unforgettable psychologist. Unforgettable experiment. Cybele's cult as social experiment? Provocative research thesis? Or non-fictional bestseller?* She swallowed uncomfortably. Damn it. Janus, what are you up to? She looked at the last loose paper in her hand. *Dissection of Cybele. Powerful/Mesmerizing Speaker. Face of Modern Cult? Feminism? Mother Goddess bullshit. Becoming caught up in her own illusion? Where will she end up? Will she sublimate her moral code in her quest for power and control? Delusional? Fascinating social experiment. I am the social control. The outside, impartial observer. Maslach.*

Cybele's eyes narrowed in cold rage. You bastard. I'm your friend not one of your subjects. She carefully gathered the loose papers back together and shoved them back into the book. She placed the books back in a stack under his desk. She picked up the crumpled tissues as she stood. She looked at the note of apology she had left for him on his desk. Her face flushed angrily as she picked it up. What in Hades should I do now? He still deserves an apology but...so do I... She determinedly crumpled up the note in her hands and took it and the dirty tissues with her as she left his office. She paused on the threshold to take one last look to ensure she had left no sign of her presence. She carefully locked his door behind her. She slowly walked back to her office. She threw her garbage away as she sighed. I need to talk to Cassie. She grabbed her purse and paused.

I should leave a note for Gabe. She grabbed a scrap of paper. *Running errands. See you tomorrow.* She paused. Yes. I saw him take his keys. She locked the front door behind her and left. As she moved towards her car, Cybele sung softly under her breath. "I will be the one left standing…."

Cybele slowly walked into A Taste of Indulgence and heavily shut the door behind her. She looked over at Cassie who was behind the counter putting the finishing touches on a three tier wedding cake. Cybele smiled weakly at her.

"Cyb? What's wrong? You look like someone just died."

"It feels like everything that could possibly go wrong today has gone wrong." Cybele walked over to a chair in the counter. She slumped into it and sighed heavily. "Ever feel like you've stumbled into a parallel universe? You have to decide if either everyone around you has gone crazy or else you have."

"Sounds like you're having a *Star Trek*, through the looking-glass moment." Cassie quickly poured out a cup of coffee and brought it over to Cybele.

Cybele tried to relax as she inhaled the aroma of the coffee. "Do you remember when Kirk goes back in time through the Guardian of Forever and ends up having to let the woman he loves die because that was what was meant to happen. If he saves her life, then millions of other people will die." She took a tentative sip of her coffee. "I feel like I'm having one of those days."

Cassie smiled a bit patronizingly. That Cyb. Always up or down. "Are you sure that maybe you're not over-dramatizing it just a little?"

Cybele frowned. "No. I'm not." She took a long sip of her coffee. "Well. Okay. Millions of people's lives are not on the line but that doesn't mean life doesn't suck big time."

"Okay." Cassie patted Cybele's hand reassuringly. "Then tell me what sucks big time."

"I feel like I don't know who people are anymore. I always prided myself on being a good judge of character and now I feel like I'm the worst judge of character in the world." She looked over thoughtfully at Cassie. "Why do you think Janus became involved with the cult?"

"I'm not sure." Cassie looked at Cybele puzzledly. "Because you asked him to?"

Cybele shook her head slightly. "I just wonder if he had other, less altruistic reasons for saying yes."

Cassie leaned forward to look more closely at Cybele. "Such as?"

"Not just to make money." Cybele stared gloomily into her cup. "Have you ever heard of the Stanford Prison Experiment?"

"Vaguely." Still unaware of how upset Cybele was, Cassie joked lightly. "I think Janus was babbling about it a few months ago. Eventually, I just started to think about icing cakes whenever he got started." She chuckled. "My version of having glazed over eyes."

"Funny." Cybele began to explain the seriousness of the experiment to Cassie. "It was an insane experiment in the 1960s. Ordinary people were paid to act as prisoners and guards and to immerse themselves in their roles as fully as possible. There were really no safeguards. Horrible things happened or were done in the name of scientific research." She looked over at Cassie to gauge her reaction. "They gained invaluable knowledge about human behaviour but ethically..."

"Sounds like ethically, they broke all the rules," said Cassie uncomfortably.

"Yeah." Cybele rubbed her forehead anxiously. "So, I'm a little worried by how obsessed Janus seems to be about it."

Cassie tapped the side of her cup impatiently. "I don't quite know what you're getting at, Cyb." Spit it out. I don't have all day to hold your hand.

Cybele sighed worriedly. "What if Janus is using my cult to run his own personal Stanford Prison Experiment?"

"What?" Cassie snorted. "Why would you think Janus would do that?"

Cybele ran her finger over the rim of her cup. "For intellectual curiosity." She shrugged unable to look Cassie in the eyes. "To get an insider's analysis of the birth of a cult mentality."

"Okay. Say he is," said Cassie in disbelief but determined to try and humour Cybele.

Cybele looked up and met Cassie's gaze. "He is."

“Okay.” A bit uncomfortable now, Cassie squirmed in her chair. “So what?”

“What do you mean, so what?” Cybele jumped up and began to pace back and forth. “Didn’t you listen to anything I said about how horrible that experiment was?”

Cassie sighed in exasperation. “He didn’t create the cult. You did.” She shrugged. “He’s a psychologist. It seems only natural to me that he would see it as a fascinating social experiment. Something that he can study because since he didn’t create it, he doesn’t have to worry about the ethics of studying cult members.” She paused to look meaningfully at Cybele. “I mean, it’s not like he has direct control over the rituals of the cult. You do. You’re the one who runs the ceremonies and the Contemplative Motion classes. His only participation is with the phone sex operation and doing the overall bookkeeping. Seems only natural that he might wish to study the reactions of your members to your influence.”

Cybele’s mouth opened and closed without speaking.

Unable to stop herself, Cassie laughed. “Cyb. Don’t do that. You look like a guppy.”

Cybele threw her hands up in the air. “Gods. I can’t believe you would take his side over mine. What kind of friend are you?”

“Cyb…” said Cassie in a placating tone.

“NO.” Cybele stamped her foot angrily into the floor. “He. Is. Analyzing. Me.” She thumped her finger into her chest with each word for emphasis. “He. Betrayed. Me.” She sunk back into the chair. “He dissected me. He wrote horrible things about me.”

"I'm sure he didn't mean to hurt your feelings." Cassie reached out to pat Cybele's hand reassuringly. "He's probably feeling pretty badly right now if you reacted this way when he told you."

Cybele pulled her hand away. "He doesn't know."

"Really?" Cassie shook her head in surprise. "It's not like you to bottle things up. You should go back and talk to him."

Cybele looked away. "He doesn't know I know." She smiled bitterly. "Probably thinks it might corrupt the authenticity of the study if the subjects know their every move is being analyzed."

"If he didn't tell you, then how did you..."

"I happened to be in his office looking for a wastepaper basket. I just happened to see some notes he had made about me." She frowned. "That bastard wrote that I might be delusional." She growled. "I am not delusional."

Cassie looked sharply at Cybele. "You just happened to be in his office looking for a garbage can? Don't you have any in your own office?"

"That's not important." She frowned defensively. "I wasn't snooping. Friends don't have secrets from each other."

Cassie rolled her eyes. "Seems like some friends do."

Cybele began to gnaw on her lower lip. "It's not just that it bothers me that he's treating the cult as his own personal case study. You're right. He's a psychologist. That's what they do. But he did it behind my back. He thinks horrible things about me and I never knew he felt that way about me."

"He's closer to you than anyone else in the world." Cassie sighed wearily. "He might think horrible things about you in the abstraction but, in the real world, you're his best friend."

"That doesn't really make me feel better."

"I know. I'm sorry."

"It's also…"

"Also?"

Cybele shook her head uncomfortably. "He has a lot of books on cults. The kinds of cults that have apocalyptic endings."

Cassie waved her hands dismissively. "He's probably just doing research. And, I hate to break it to you, Cyb, but most cults seem to have doomsday scenarios," she said mockingly.

Cybele growled in protest. "They do not. All ESTABLISHED religions started out as cults. They didn't have mass suicides." Cybele paused reflectively. "Well, there was that unfortunate incident at Masada. But that was more a statement of social and political protest. Better to die free than live as slaves. And not in the philosophical sense but in the literal sense." She sighed heavily. "It was an unfortunate act but slavery would have been a never-ending genocide. Sometimes the best choice is still a pretty horrendous one."

Cassie patted Cybele on her arm. "Sometimes life just sucks."

Cybele pulled away. "I'm worried that Janus might have taken the wrong fork in the road. Ever since he and Achates broke up, he's been so angry. So hurt. He tries to hide it but he seems different. More detached from everything."

Cassie nodded sadly. "I've noticed it too. But, he'll get over it. He just needs time to heal."

Cybele rubbed the back of her neck anxiously. "He might do some things before then that he might not be able to take back."

Cassie shook her head in disagreement. "Cyb..."

"He wrote some things that make me wonder if he's as impartial an observer in the cult as..." She pumped Cassie's hand forcefully. "What if he's been instigating certain things? Setting up certain scenarios and seeing how events unfold from that point. He keeps telling me that he would love to see how the followers would react if I didn't try to moderate and channel their impulses." She loosened her grip on Cassie's hand and slowly pulled away. "I almost felt that he wanted to see if the cult would self-destruct just out of an intellectual curiosity to see how it would happen."

"Cybele." Cassie stood up and looked down at Cybele. She crossed her arms firmly across her chest. "Are you sure you're not just being overly dramatic again?"

"NO." Cybele jumped back up and began to pace.

"Stop doing that." Cassie rolled her eyes. "You look like a Jack-in-the-Box."

Cybele glared at her. "I'm not imagining the police who keep investigating us and our employees. No smoke without fire, right?" She pointed dramatically at Cassie. "Don't you think it's a might too convenient that Achates' new boyfriend's car blows up and my ex-boyfriend's organization is implicated in it." She tapped her foot on the floor. "Mighty coincidental that two people Janus doesn't like seem to have a lot of troubles on their plate."

"Don't you think you might be a little paranoid?" asked Cassie as she threw her arms up in the air.

Cybele froze. She threw Cassie a hurt look. "Paranoid DELUSIONAL?"

"No." Cassie tried to take back her words. "I know you're not delusional." Just too damn jittery today. Too much damn caffeine.

Cybele hugged herself and sighed. "Something about Janus has been bothering me for a while. He just seems so emotionally off-balance. I don't know what to think anymore."

Cassie patted her comfortingly on her back. "Cyb. I think you're hurt because of what he said about you. I think it might make you misinterpret what's going on at the cult." She paused. "Are Janus and Gabe still flaring nostrils at each other?"

"Yes." Cybele groaned. "I nearly walked into a fist fight between them this morning." She glared over at Cassie. "And that's not an exaggeration."

Cassie smiled back reassuringly. "Then maybe you're picking up on the tension between the two of them. Janus is probably angry with you for choosing Gabe over him."

"I didn't really..."

Determined to have her say, Cassie waved off Cybele's weak protests. "You hired Gabe and kept him even though Janus clearly hates him. What's worse is you're dating Gabe too. Janus probably thinks you're leaving him for Gabe. He might just see it as another loss. First Achates, and then you."

Cybele looked at her sceptically. "You might be right. I don't know."

"Well, before you paint Janus as some ruthless egomaniac, you should probably talk to him. Find out what's really going on at the cult." She shook her head patronizingly. "I hate to say this. But I just had a bad feeling about this cult. It just seemed like a mess of trouble."

Gods. I hate when people say I told you so. Cassie seems to think I'm just overreacting. I don't think I am but, the more I try to convince her, the less she seems to believe me. I feel like I'm locked in an asylum trying to convince the doctor I'm really sane. Doesn't seem to be working too well. I need proof. Either Cassie's right or I'm right. I have to trust my instincts. Take the blinders off and find out what's really going on. She shook her head doubtfully. Gods. I hope Cassie's right and I'm wrong. I can't believe I hope I'm actually delusional. How the mighty have fallen. She looked up to see Cassie watching her worriedly.

Cybele smiled at her falsely. "You've made some very good points, Cassie. You've given me a lot to think about." She laughed awkwardly. "Please don't tell Janus what I actually thought. He might be a little pissed."

"No. Don't worry." Cassie smiled back a little uncertainly. "I'm just glad I could help you come to your senses."

"Thanks." Gods. I hate when people say that. It's so condescending. She looked at her watch. "Gods. I'm running so late. Better go." She quickly walked through the door before Cassie could say another word.

Cassie groaned. That was a little abrupt. Why do I get the feeling that somewhere along the way she stopped listening to me and started placating me? She shook her head. *Que sera, sera*.

Cybele got into her car and began to drive away. She began to sing angrily under her breath. "Nobody listens or wants to see but me..."

Chapter 23

Cybele sat on the front steps that led up to Gabe's house. She stirred her melting slurpee. I don't even know what I'm doing here. Am I so desperate to be believed that I'm going to talk to someone I know dislikes Janus just to get someone on my side who can tell me I'm right. Tell me I'm not crazy. She looked up as she heard footsteps and saw a shadow move across her.

"Hi Gabe."

"Hi Cyb." Gabe sat down beside her and turned slightly towards her.

Cybele smiled faintly. "Some day, eh? Life seems to be turning into quite a soap opera at work. Who would have thought that creating and running a cult wouldn't be a walk in the park?"

Gabe moved slightly closer towards her. He smiled down at her. "Have to admit, it's a shocker for me." He gently put his arm around her. "I'm sorry about today. I didn't mean to start off your day with such a tense drama. I know how all those negative emotions bother you. Bad karma and all that."

Cybele smiled more genuinely. I knew I could count on Gabe to cheer me up. "That's okay. Sometimes shit just gets in the way of life's best intentions." She edged a bit closer to him. She leaned back against him.

Gabe tightened his grip on her. "You know, something occurred to me today. A possible solution to the problem of you and me seeing each other."

"Really?" Cybele looked up at him. "What?"

"The only reason you don't want us to date is because I work for you and that stupid comment I made to Janus about sexual harassment has made you wary about what might happen if our relationship ends badly, right?"

"That's pretty much it in a nutshell." Cybele sighed. "It's not that I don't trust you." She shook her head. "It's just that people don't always react well if a relationship ends. Hurt feelings and all that."

Gabe nodded solemnly. "A very good point. The last thing you would want is to worry about being sued on top of all that." He hugged her more closely. "So, here's my idea. I go to a lawyer friend of mine and get him to write out a declaration that I'm not being sexually harassed and choose to date you of my own free will. I give you a notarized copy of the letter and presto, no more fears about being sued."

Cybele shook her head in disbelief. "I can't believe relationships have come to this." She looked up at him and laughed. "But it's an excellent idea. Bring me that note from your lawyer friend and let the games once again begin."

"Consider it done."

Cybele moved slightly away from him and winked. "When it's done."

Gabe winked back. Nice to see that the games have begun again.

Cybele sobered up slightly. “So, tell me today passed without a visit from the police.”

“No police.” Gabe looked curiously at her. “Why? Do you expect more visits?”

Cybele shook her head slowly. “Dread not expect.” She looked more closely at Gabe. “Do you ever regret coming to work for me? Being involved with people suspected of a car bombing is not something you would ever want to put on your résumé.” She rubbed her forehead pensively. “Not to mention how most people have this horrible perception that all cult leaders are power-hungry, delusional, monsters. You might not want to admit to anyone that you even know me much less are seeing me.”

Gabe chuckled. “I don’t think you’re not a power-hungry, delusional, monster.” He nudged her playfully. “Now, Janus, on the other hand…”

Cybele looked sharply up at him. “You think that Janus…”

Gabe quickly shook his head. Oops. “I know he’s your friend. I was just kidding.”

Cybele sunk her head into her hands. “I used to pride myself on being such a good judge of character. I guess pride does goeth before the fall.”

“I’m not quite sure what you mean.”

Cybele spoke without looking up. “After you left for lunch today, I went to Janus’s office to apologize for being part of outing him.”

“I’m sorry…”

Cybele waved her hand in his direction. "He wasn't there but he had left some handwritten notes in one of his books." She looked up a bit guiltily. "I wasn't snooping maliciously, you know. I was just curious about what he was reading and writing about."

Gabe patted her back reassuringly. "Perfectly understandable. I'm often curious about the books people are reading. Gives a good insight into their mindset."

Cybele smiled in relief. "Precisely." She continued. "He had made notes on me. Analyzing me from a psychological perspective on my role as a cult leader." She bit her lip. "I had no idea he was spying on me. Using information he gained to write some kind of case study. I felt so angry. So betrayed."

Now Gabe looked guilty himself. "I'm sorry."

Cybele sighed regretfully. "He had written some other things too. Stuff about conscience being... a fictional construct... and morality being an illusion. I can't remember exactly how he phrased it but it bothered me. I felt as if he saw people as pawns to be used in some chess game with him playing against some unknown enemy." She frowned in discomfort. "I almost felt as if he saw me as some enemy. Or my conscience. Something he could manipulate and ultimately defeat."

Gabe pulled back and looked down at her thoughtfully. "Pretty heavy stuff. No wonder you looked so upset when I first saw you."

"At least you understand. Cassie seemed to think I was over-dramatizing what I found." Cybele shook her head uncomfortably.

"But with everything that's been happening lately, I just don't know what's real and what's an illusion anymore." She looked sharply at him. "That doesn't mean I'm delusional. I know things. I just don't know people."

"You're not delusional. Your spider senses are tingling. Just because you can't put your finger precisely on what's wrong doesn't mean that something isn't wrong."

Cybele beamed up at him. "Yes. You understand me perfectly." She shrugged. "I don't want to be overly dramatic but I'm worried that Janus may be running some sort of psychological experiment with the cult that I'm not aware of. Something that he might eventually want me to find out about and see if I will go along with it. See if I will sublimate my moral code as he put it." She looked up at Gabe to gauge his response to her worries. "Sometimes I feel like he's testing me. Seeing how close he can get me to some sort of moral abyss." She bit her lip. "It doesn't matter how far over it I go in comparison to how far he goes. Once I've taken the first step over, I've fallen anyway."

Gabe looked uncertainly at her. "He might be trying to set some sort of moral trap for you. I don't know." He rubbed up and down her arm as he spoke. "I did read somewhere once that sometimes the people we love the most in the world are the ones we seem to try the hardest to destroy. It's like if we can destroy what makes them special, then they'll have no choice but to stay with us, because no one else will have them."

Cybele leaned further into him. "I would never try to destroy someone I loved just so that they would stay with me forever." She grabbed his hand and held it to her. "That's not love. That's possession. It's like that saying, 'If you love something, set it free. If it comes back, it's yours forever..."

Gabe nodded in agreement. "If it doesn't, it never was." He cleared his throat nervously. "Cyb, I need to be honest with you. There's something about me that I think you should know."

She looked up at him suspiciously. "You're not seeing someone else are you?"

He laughed uncomfortably. "No. That's not it."

"Good." Cybele moved more closely towards him.

"It's just that...remember how you once asked me if I was an undercover cop?"

She glared at him. "Yes. And you told me that you weren't."

"I'm not. Not a cop." He gulped. "But I am a reporter."

"A reporter." Cybele nodded. "I see."

Gabe ran a finger around the back of his collar as he tried to explain. "I...I started out at the Loaves and Fishes to do a story on the street kids, you know, A Day in the Life, kind of thing."

"Okay. And now?" She frowned uncertainly. "What kind of story are you doing now?"

Gabe took a deep breath and forced himself to sound nonchalant. "I...I thought it would be an interesting article to talk about the life of a cult. You know, from genesis to..."

"To APOCALYPSE?" Cybele jumped up. "Because that must be the logical conclusion of any cult, right? Because cult leaders are so egomaniacal that they destroy their followers if they think they might be losing control over them. Because no one could possibly be part of some alternative form of religion without having lost their moral centre, right?" She threw her hands up in the air. "Because the only religions that have any sense of moral authority are the ones that have been around for thousands of years. That are so obsessed by rules and orders that horrible things are done in their name and everyone justifies it as a fact of life. Too Bad. So Sad." She began to tap her foot furiously. "Tell me, you don't know what I'm talking about. Those patriarchal institutions that help support the political and social systems that oppress others in the name of some *Father Knows Best, Touched by An Angel* bullshit."

Gabe shook his head weakly. "Cyb. That's not the kind of article I was going to write. I was going to slant it as an example of female empowerment. The return of the Mother Goddess." God. Please let her believe me. This honesty thing sucks big time. I'm not really lying to her. I'm sure that type of story would have eventually occurred to me. He paused. Hmmm. It would actually be a pretty topical story. Popular idea. Charismatic leader. Could actually work out quite well.

Cybele snorted. "Nice try. But if that's true, why didn't you tell me that from the very beginning?"

"I thought it would be more realistic if you didn't know..."

"That you were spying on me. Getting close to me so I would tell you things that I would have never told a reporter. Things I would never have told someone that I couldn't trust." She wrapped her arms tightly around her chest. "You used me." She shook her head. "Did you deliberately betray my confidences to you so you could see what effect that might have on my relationship with Janus?"

"NO." Gabe began to get angry. "Of course not. I can't believe you would think that I would do something like that."

"Why not? It's not as if I know who you are." She laughed angrily. "You're exactly like Janus. Both lying to me. Playing your little games. Not caring who gets hurt." She shook her head. "Can't tell the truth. Oh no. That would compromise the AUTHENTICITY of your little investigation." She waved her hand in dismissal. "I can't believe I let you kiss me. You used me."

"Cyb." Gabe walked over to her and tried to take her hand.

She angrily pulled away.

He sighed regretfully. "I did not intend for this to happen. I was just doing my job. Trying to find out what was going on at this new cult that had just sprung up in Winnipeg."

"Trying to get an exclusive?"

"Yes." He paused. "Everything got out of control. But… I didn't intend to hurt you. And my feelings for you have nothing to do with trying to get information out of you. They were totally separate from the story."

"Oh." Cybele rolled her eyes. "Well. That makes everything just peachy keen then." She growled. "Unlike you, I don't keep my feelings in my pocket. Keep them separate from the rest of my life." She pointed at him dramatically. "You betrayed me....Get bent." She turned and stalked away. The heel of her shoe caught on a crack in the sidewalk and she went down hard on her hands and knees. "Damnit."

Gabe rushed over to help her up. "Cyb? Are you okay?"

She waved him off. She slowly pulled herself up to a standing position.

"You're bleeding." Gabe reached out and gently pulled her wrists towards him

Cybele flexed her hands painfully. "It's just a few scratches. I'll be fine." She looked down at her knees. "Just a few spots of blood. No big deal." She smiled with difficulty. "So much for the dramatic exit, eh? I never could quite pull those off."

"Come inside." He gently touched her bloody palms. "I can get you some bandages for these cuts. Get out the little pebbles." He tried to turn her back towards his house.

She shook her head. "I'll be fine. I have to go." She turned to leave.

Feeling helpless and guilty, Gabe snapped. "Damn it, Cyb. You're not fine. I have your blood all over my hands."

She snorted. "Better get used to that feeling, Gabe." She limped away. Damn it. I think I twisted my ankle too. I knew getting out of bed this morning was a mistake. Nothing good ever happens on Mondays.

Gabe growled. Damn it. I am so screwed. He sighed. Getting out of this hole is not going to be easy. He looked down at the streaks of blood on his hands. Not bad for an exit line, after all, Cyb.

Cybele nervously shifted the bag of take-out in her arms as she waited for Janus to answer his door. Gods. I don't even know what I'm doing here. Nancy Druid, here I come. Take a deep breath. Centre yourself. Good. Just be casual and find out what's really going on in Janus's warped little mind. Make sure there are no visions of dancing apocalypses in there.

Janus opened the door. "Cyb, what are you doing here?"

Cybele slightly thrust the paper bag towards him. "I come bearing apologies and shrimp in black bean and garlic sauce."

Janus smiled and took the bag from her. "My favourite." He peered inside. "Looks like you got enough for an army." He stepped back inside. "Come in."

Cybele brushed past him. "Wine in the fridge?"

"Of course."

She poured two glasses of wine. Janus set out plates and cutlery on the counter. They filled their plates and sat down in front of the television in the living room.

"What's on?" asked Cybele.

"I was just watching *Terminator*."

"Great. I love the first one." Cybele tore into her egg roll with her fingers. "It's such a powerful fable about the dangers of taking the human element out of the most important decisions of our lives.

Emotions may be messy, but they're what make us human. A world run by an artificial intelligence." She shook her head in consternation. "Look at that nightmare Skynet creates. A world of logic untempered by love."

Janus stuck his egg roll into the plum sauce and bit off a large piece. "An apocalypse." He waved the rest of his egg roll at her as he spoke. "The image of those huge wheels uncaringly rolling over and crushing all those brittle human skulls gave me nightmares the first time I saw it."

"Me too. The world was one big graveyard. Auschwitz revisited on a global scale." She reached over for another egg roll as she spoke. "Human beings may often make the wrong choices, hurt people who don't deserve to be hurt, but that doesn't mean we should be wiped out and replaced by another form of life."

Janus sprayed out bits of filling as he spoke. "We're not just talking about the movie, are we?"

Yuck. Cybele grabbed a napkin and gingerly wiped up Janus's mess. She pushed the crumpled napkin next to his plate. "Maybe not." She dipped her own egg roll into the plum sauce. "I really am sorry for what happened today. Sometimes events just seem to spin out of control." She licked off the excess plum sauce and sighed in pleasure. "But I would never have done anything deliberately to hurt you."

Janus aimlessly moved food around his plate. He spoke without looking at her. "I just can't believe you told Gabe I was gay."

"I know. I'm sorry." She laughed awkwardly. "If it makes you feel better, it'll never happen again."

Janus scowled and then laughed reluctantly. "Funny."

She reached over and held his hand. "Friends again?"

Janus looked up and sighed. "Friends again."

Good. He seems to be more relaxed around me now. Time to try and pump him for information. "I guess I've been on edge for the last few days, ever since the police have started coming around. I just don't want anything to go wrong with our cult. Not when it seems to be doing so well." She paused to gauge his reaction. "I just want to make a relatively ethical profit by giving people spirituality in return for a little monetary compensation."

Janus smiled broadly. "Yeah. Our profits are extremely high in both the web business and the phone sex business."

Cybele began to munch on her stir-fried broccoli. "That's why the idea of further police involvement in our business bothers me. It could really damage our reputation."

"You're right." Janus wiped his hand across his mouth. "The more police involvement, the greater the potential for problems with our bottom line."

"Absolutely." Cybele began to chase a mushroom around her plate. She finally caught it by stabbing it. Holding it up in triumph, she spoke distractedly. "Have the police come by to interrogate any more of our employees?"

Janus nodded thoughtfully. "No. I think our having a lawyer on retainer might have caused them to be more restrained in their questioning of potential persons of interest." He popped a shrimp in his mouth and began to chew. "We haven't quite reached the post-democratic era of some of our dearest friends and neighbours. Until that sorry day happens and we wake up to find our rights have been chiselled away and we're in nothing more than an Orwellian state, the police still have to respect the rights of the accused or fear the wrath of the defense attorneys and the power of lawsuits."

Cybele looked warningly at Janus as she paused with a forkful of fried rice. "But even so, we still should make sure that whatever we do we try to stay below the police's radar."

"Always a good plan."

She swallowed her rice and reached for a shrimp. Picking it up, she licked off the black bean sauce as she spoke. "We have to make sure there is absolutely nothing we have done that can come back and bite us on our ass. And we have to make sure that our future actions all are within the parameters of the law."

Hmmm. I'm not quite sure what's she's getting at. Is she trying to give me a veiled hint that she knows what I've done and wants me to clean up my own shit once and for all? Is she trying to maintain a state of plausible deniability? It's certainly something I do when I speak to Tan and the others. He popped another shrimp in his mouth and began to chew. I had no idea Cybele was capable of such Machiavellian subtlety. Usually, her warnings are a bit more heavy-handed. He reached down unconsciously to rub his knee. Or heavy-footed. Warning received and understood, dear friend. "So, I guess that means no more smoking pot, eh?"

Gods. I hope I haven't been too subtle about the need to walk the fine line between personal civil disobedience and acts of violence against others. Cybele laughed uneasily. "Well, not as part of the official functioning of our cult. But, that doesn't mean I've become a born-again in my personal life. The police pretty much practice de-facto decriminalization. They go after the big sharks to get publicity but they pretty much leave the little fishes swimming in the little ponds alone." She shook her head. "Possession will only become a problem if we come to their attention in a larger criminal matter. Then pot use will be just an extra charge tacked on to show the extent of our alleged depravity." She bit her lip. "But since we're as pure as the driven snow..."

Janus laughed. "Whatever the hell that means."

"It means that since we don't piss in our own neighbourhood, we don't have to worry about personal pot use." Cybele narrowed her eyes. "And, it's not like you're stupid enough to grow your own personal pot on your own property, especially since we've come under such heightened police scrutiny..."

Janus waved his finger at her in rebuke. "I'm not an idiot."

She grabbed his finger and shook it gently. "Then we're basically free and clear. No harm, no foul." She sighed regretfully. "It's just a pity the pot laws are still so archaic. I hate having to break the law just to live free and do something that hurts nobody, not even myself."

"Cheer up. I'm sure we're just a hop, skip, and a jump away from decriminalizing it. Then you can smoke it to your heart's content without worrying about breaking those pesky morality laws."

Cybele rolled her eyes. "If pot was ever legal here, I'm sure King George the Second would declare marijuana a weapon of mass destruction and start dropping smart bombs on the growers' houses. I mean if it's a good enough Made in America solution for those pesky third world countries, it's a good enough solution for the problem of Canada too."

Janus laughed condescendingly. "Might make some Canadians really consider what fog of war and collateral damage really mean. I'm betting their perspective varies a hell of a lot from when they're the one dropping the bombs to when they're the ones the bombs are being dropped on."

"Would present an interesting quandary to those knee-jerk reactionaries who believe it is Canada's moral responsibility to support our friends and neighbours to the South whatever they do." Cybele laughed bitterly. "Do you rally around the Stars and Stripes, even though they're the ones bombing you because, after all, they're just trying to liberate you from the evils of weed or do you stand up for the Maple Leaf?"

"An interesting moral dilemma. Purely from a psychological point of view, I'd be curious to see how people would react in that situation." He paused thoughtfully. "Do you become a collaborator and spy on your friends and neighbours, pointing out the probable growers as potential targets to the invading force, or do you become a member of the resistance and fight against the occupiers whatever your personal beliefs about the legalization of pot?" Janus began to get more excited. "And how do you react as a member of the resistance, if you find out someone is a collaborator? What sort of vengeance do you visit upon him or her? And, how do the collaborators convince themselves that what they are doing is morally justifiable? Do they figure they're outgunned and would rather be on the winning side rather than the losing side? Or do they take the long view and convince themselves that what they are doing will save their nation? Can they really convince themselves the resistance is the enemy and the occupier is the friend?"

Cybele looked at him thoughtfully. "It is a fascinating situation. There are no real winners for the occupied people. It's the Nazi occupation of France and the Cardassian occupation of Bajor on *Deep Space Nine*, all over again."

"Yes." Janus nodded. "It's no accident that we're told over six million Bajorans were killed under Cardassian occupation. We're meant to remember the Holocaust."

"And when the writers make us start to feel sympathetic towards some of the Cardassians responsible for those atrocities, we're always reminded of how genial evil can be, until the velvet glove comes off the iron fist." Cybele thumped her own fist on the arm of the couch. No. "We can feel sympathetic to fictional characters, despite what atrocities they may have committed, but, in real life, we must never forget the suffering of real people. It's too easy to detach ourselves from reality and just see it as a fascinating social experiment." She looked at Janus meaningfully. "But if we ignore the suffering of others to gain knowledge, aren't we just watered down versions of Mengele?"

Janus looked back at her uncomfortably. "That's a pretty extreme comparison, Cyb. Research often demands objectivity and dispassionate observation."

"I know." She tapped her fork against the rim of her plate. "But researchers have to remember that they don't operate in a vacuum. Their actions have consequences in the real world. Ultimately, we are all responsible for what we do, despite what our intentions may have been."

Damn it. Does she know about the car bomb or this is just another of her pagan way speeches? I wish I could ask but I don't want her to know if she doesn't already. Janus grabbed the fork away from her and began to stack up their dishes. "Well. You've certainly given me a lot to think about. But I think it's time to call it a night."

"Yeah." Cybele got up and walked to the door. "See you tomorrow." She walked down the driveway towards her car and sighed. I hope he got the message. Don't do anything in the cult that could come back and bite us on the ass. Maybe the idea of profit will overshadow any intellectual interest he might have in recreating that damned prison experiment in our cult. She shook her head. Maybe Cassie's right. Maybe I'm over-dramatizing what I read. Although he did seem a little defensive when I mentioned Mengele. I just don't know.

Chapter 24

Cybele awoke with a gasp. Gods. What a horrible dream. Seeing all those glistening white skulls being ground up under those bulldozers. I wanted to scream but I couldn't. I was just too scared. She grimaced as she stiffly got out of bed. Sleep certainly didn't knit this ravelled sleeve of care. I feel worse than I did before. Maybe a hot shower and some coffee will help me feel more alive.

Cybele showered quickly and got dressed for work. After a quick cup of coffee, she forced herself to leave. She walked out of her building and stopped in surprise.

"Gabe." She crossed her arms warily. "What are you doing here? Still trying to get the personal angle for that story of yours?"

Gabe walked tentatively towards her. "Cyb." His voice trailed off. He handed her an envelope.

Cybele took it. "Please tell me this isn't a subpoena." She opened it up and took out two folded letters. She sat back against her car as she read the first one. *To Any And All Who Might Be Interested. I, Gabriel Anderson, am interested in having a romantic relationship with my employer, Cybele Moondragon. If our relationship ends badly, I will not sue her for sexual harassment since the relationship will have been of my own desire.* Cybele smiled slightly. She began to read the second letter. *I, Gabriel Anderson, would like to make it clear that I have no intention of writing a story about The Mysteries of Cybele that would hurt or cause legal problems for Cybele Moondragon.* Cybele rolled her eyes. "I can't believe you really had these notarized."

Gabe smiled in relief. "Luckily, I have friends in many walks of life. Lawyers, notaries, and spiritual avatars for Mother Goddesses." He paused. "I know the second one isn't really legally binding but I just wanted to convince you of my sincerity."

Cybele carefully tucked both letters safely into her purse. "You've made a good start."

"Good." Gabe moved closer towards her. "I don't want there to be any more misunderstandings between us."

Cybele straightened up from against her car. She carefully brushed nonexistent dust off the front of her skirt. "I don't want to feel that there are any more secrets between us either. I need to be able to trust the people in my life."

"You can trust me."

Cybele slowly looked up at him. "Yes. I believe I can."

Gabe carefully placed his arms around her. "Speaking of misunderstandings, what exactly does it mean to 'get bent'?"

Cybele smiled a bit embarrassedly. "Think of why you would never want to drop a bar of soap and have to bend over to pick it up, if you were taking a shower in prison."

Gabe thought through the scenario and then laughed. "A more metaphorical way of telling someone to fuck off."

Cybele leaned more closely into his hug. "I'm glad you approve." She sighed dramatically. "Commonplace vulgarity is so beneath me." She shook her head. "If I'm going to spend the time and effort to cause a scene and tell someone off, then by the goddess, my insults are going to be memorable."

"Oh, they were."

"Good."

"Hey, you two, get a room."

Gabe and Cybele moved apart and looked around to see who had shouted.

Cassie walked towards them smiling. She was carrying several bags of groceries.

Cybele waved in greeting. "I didn't know that you had today off." She reached out and took several of the bags from her.

Gabe casually reached out and took the bags from Cybele. She smiled approvingly at him. All of them began to walk back into the building.

"Oh, Marie occasionally lets me out of the salt mines." Cassie whacked Cybele playfully on the arm. "Especially, when she knows she'll have to pay overtime if she doesn't."

Cybele whacked her lightly back. "Does nothing from the goodness of her heart, eh?"

Cassie sobered up and shook her head. "Trust me, she doesn't have a heart."

They walked into their kitchen and began to unpack the groceries.

Cassie looked over at Cybele and Gabe. "Aren't you two running late this morning?"

"It's a long story," said Cybele hesitantly. "I sort of want to avoid Janus this morning." She looked a bit uncomfortable as she continued on. “If I go in late, he’ll already have left for his counselling sessions at the Loaves and Fishes today.”

Cassie shook her head in annoyance. “Cyb. You and Janus should really clear the air. I can’t believe you still suspect him of being some sort of Machiavellian scientist who’s running his own private experiments within your cult.”

Cybele frowned. “I know it sounds pretty far-fetched but that doesn’t mean it’s not true. You know the old saying, ‘The greatest trick the devil ever pulled was convincing the world that he did not exist.”

Cassie snorted. “Please tell me that you’re not equating Janus with the devil. Isn’t that a little too established, patriarchal religion for you?”

Stay calm. Don’t get side-tracked. Cybele poured herself a cup of cold coffee from her percolator and took a long sip. Yuck. “I’m not saying that Janus is a devil or even that he is evil. I’m just saying that our close friendship with him might make us not want to see what his real agenda with the cult could be. It might be a dangerous mistake to continue to give him the benefit of the doubt.”

“What do you think his agenda might be?” asked Gabe curiously.

Cybele shrugged uneasily. “He keeps sending me such mixed messages that I’m not sure what he’s thinking. I am definitely worried that he might have too much influence over some of our employees especially the ones from the Loaves and Fishes whom he’s been counselling. He seems unusually close to them. Far closer than most bosses are to their employees. "

Cassie looked meaningfully from Cybele to Gabe. "Isn't that a little like the pot calling the kettle black? You and Gabe are closer than normal too."

Cybele acknowledged Cassie's hit with a salute of her cup. "Touché." She continued on to explain the difference between Janus and herself. "But I see Gabe as a human being not a research subject that I can manipulate in order to see what he will do in different situations."

Gabe smiled fondly at Cybele and then frowned. "Do you think that might be what Janus is doing with some of our employees like Tan and the others?"

"Yes." Cybele sighed. "I keep thinking about how everyone believes the natural evolution of a cult is to end with an apocalypse. What if Janus feels that way too? He might be tempted to give evolution a helping hand." She thoughtfully drummed her fingers on the side of her cup. "I know he's definitely curious about what would happen if I wasn't there to moderate the religious fervour of some of our members."

"But you are," said Cassie, "So, I don't see what the problem is." She looked over at Gabe to judge his reaction to Cybele's vague suspicions. She was relieved to see that Gabe appeared interested but not overly concerned by Janus's behaviour. With an effort, Cassie forced her attention back to Cybele who was still talking.

"Not all the time. I don't have any control over what happens when I'm not there." Cybele looked worried. "And Janus is closer to many of the employees from the Loaves and Fishes than I am. They participate in the rituals as much as any of the paying members and they're as vulnerable to manipulation as everyone else."

"Maybe more since Janus already has such an influence over them because of his earlier relationship with them as their counsellor," said Gabe.

Cassie shook her head at the two of them. "Or maybe less, because they at least work for the cult for money." She looked meaningfully at Cybele. "They aren't using the cult to fill some void in their lives by finding a highly, constructed experience of spiritual fulfillment."

Cybele glared at Cassie. "I never would abuse the power I hold over my members by leading them to some sort of apocalypse. There's no certainty that there is a life after this one. To abandon this life out of curiosity about a possible afterlife seems the epitome of stupidity to me." Cybele turned to Gabe. "But I don't believe Janus is as scrupulous as me. If he does want to bind some of our employees more strongly to him, he could do that by holding his own private rituals." She gnawed her bottom lip worriedly. "I had noticed that we seemed to be using up some of our incenses and the wormwood we use in the wine faster than seemed normal. But since I'm not there all the time, I just thought it was due to spillage or mistakes made in the preparation process that required new batches to be made up. I figured once people became more experienced, they would become less wasteful."

Gabe's spider senses began to tingle. "But, now you think the decreasing stocks could also be the result of Janus holding private rituals?"

"Maybe," said Cybele reluctant to commit herself fully.

"Cybele, you can't condemn Janus without evidence." Cassie grabbed Cybele's arm and pulled her into the living room. "Have you even considered the fact that Janus might be doing nothing sinister at all? You might be overreacting, egged on by your new boyfriend, especially considering that he and Janus seem to be such enemies?"

"I'm not overreacting." Cybele pulled roughly away from Cassie. "And Gabe has nothing to do with my feelings about Janus. Hard as it seems for you to believe, I am capable of evaluating a situation and coming to my own conclusions about what to do."

"So, you actually believe Janus is running a version of the Stanford Prison Experiment within your cult?" Cassie threw her hands up in the air in disbelief. "You believe your best friend since Kindergarten is that evil and manipulative a person?"

"Cassie." Cybele shook her head sadly at Cassie's naiveté. "Do you think that experiment was some blip on the radar scale of human morality? Do you know that more than fifty people, outside, supposedly impartial observers, presumably no more immoral than you and I, saw what was going on and did nothing to stop the experiment. Only one person had the courage to resist the peer pressure and speak out against it." Cybele slumped heavily against the television. "I don't think Janus is evil. I just wonder if he's part of the fifty collaborators or the one who did not allow herself to be distanced from the suffering she saw by putting the pursuit of knowledge over the most important rule of all. First. Do. No. Harm."

Cassie sat down on the couch and covered her face with her hands. "I just don't want to believe Janus could be like that."

Cybele sat down beside her and placed her arm around her. "I don't want to believe it either. But, I have a responsibility to find out. I can forgive Janus for not telling me he was observing the cult and my role in it, in order to write some breakthrough psychological paper. You were right. It was a golden opportunity for him that he would have been foolish to pass up." She sighed. "But being an observer is very different from being a catalyst." She bit her lip determinedly. "I cannot allow Janus whether consciously or unconsciously to manipulate more vulnerable members of the cult into performing some sort of group suicide to satisfy his intellectual curiosity about the thinking process that goes on within those minds."

Good. Cassie seems to have calmed down. At least she's stopped shouting. Gabe walked into the living room and sat down on the coffee table to face both Cybele and Cassie. "Cassie, I think Cybele might be right about Janus. I don't think he's an evil person, but I think he might feel emotionally distant from most people and that might make it easier for him to see people as experimental subjects than as living, breathing human beings who matter in the real world."

Cassie looked up and glared. “What could you possibly know about Janus? You just met him. We’ve all been friends forever. Everything was fine until you came along.”

“Cassie, don’t blame Gabe for this mess. Maybe we needed an impartial observer to give us some insight into what was going on with Janus.”

“Hardly impartial. Naturally, your boyfriend would be on your side.”

Gabe sighed impatiently. “Cassie, I started out as an impartial observer. I was always uneasy with how Janus acted at the Loaves and Fishes. He always seemed so distant from the kids there. Always seemed slightly contemptuous of them as if he really didn’t think there was any use in helping them because they were incapable of changing their lives for the better.”

Cassie shook her head. “You’re exaggerating now. Janus may be slightly elitist but he’s not a monster.”

“No. He’s not a monster.” Gabe agreed. “But I was disturbed by how callous many of the comments he made in his files about some of his clients like Tan and the others were.”

Cassie and Cybele looked up at him quickly.

Cassie frowned. “How would you know the types of comments Janus had made in his patients’ files unless...?” She stood up angrily. “You broke into his office.” She turned to glare at Cybele. “See. Janus wasn’t being paranoid in his dislike of Gabe. Clearly, he had a good reason to mistrust him.”

Gabe looked over at Cybele. “You didn’t tell her about...?”

"Tell. Me. What." Cassie interjected angrily.

Cybele looked uncomfortably over at Cassie. "Surprise. Gabe's a reporter." She spoke rapidly hoping to get all the bad news out as fast as possible. "Turns out he was working undercover writing a story about street kids when he stumbled onto the mother of all stories." She threw Gabe a slightly annoyed look. "The birth of the Mysteries of Cybele cult in Winnipeg."

"I see." Cassie sat back down and crossed her arms. "And how long have you kept this little secret from me?"

"I just found out yesterday," said Cybele defensively. "Gabe told me because he didn't want there to be any more lies between us."

"Yesterday?" Cassie's voice rose to a shrill shriek. "And you still feel he can be trusted over Janus?"

Aargh! Cybele forced herself to be patient. "It's not a question of trusting Gabe over Janus. It's a question of being able to trust both Gabe and Janus and whatever agendas they may have. At least, Gabe told me the truth about who he was." Cybele massaged the back of her neck. "Whereas, I know Janus has lied to me several times over the last few weeks and he's still denying those lies. I need to find out the truth about Janus since I cannot trust him to tell me it."

Cassie shook her head in disbelief. "What if you find out the truth and you realize how wrong you were about Janus? How can you continue to be friends after suspecting him of such horrible things?"

"Cassie," said Cybele regretfully. "The fact that I do suspect him of such horrible things already means that our friendship needs a lot of repair work. I'll apologize sincerely to him if I'm wrong, and we'll try to pick up the pieces of our friendship..."

"And what will you do if you're right?"

"I don't know. I'll cross that bridge when I come to it."

Cassie shook her head bitterly. "Don't you mean burn that bridge?"

Cybele sighed. "I guess. We'll see."

Gabe patted Cybele reassuringly on her shoulder. "So, what's the plan of attack?"

Cybele shrugged. "When in doubt, keep it simple."

Cassie raised an eyebrow. "You mean, ask him?"

Cybele looked back at her uncomfortably. "I don't believe Janus would tell me the truth. He hasn't done such a good job of that lately. I think the best bet is to search his office at the cult house and also his home to see if he's left any evidence of his ultimate intentions towards the cult."

Gabe nodded approvingly. "That's a good plan. But, he's more likely to have evidence in his home than in his office."

Cassie broke in sarcastically. "Especially, since he thinks Gabe broke into his office at the Loaves and Fishes, which, of course, he did. He's hardly likely to leave anything incriminating at The Mysteries of Cybele, with the same potential office-burglar across the hall from him." She sniffed. "Supposing there is anything incriminating to find, of course."

"Of course." Cybele looked over at Cassie. "I don't want to be right about this, but I will not close my eyes to the possibility. I seem to have made a bad habit of that lately. But, there's too much at stake, to do that now."

"When should we do this?" asked Gabe.

Cassie smiled bitterly. "If it were done, when 'tis done, then 'twere well it were done quickly. Since Janus is going to be at the Loaves and Fishes this afternoon, we can do it them."

"We?" asked Cybele sceptically.

"Janus is my friend too. If there's something's wrong with him, I need to know it too."

Gabe stood up. "Okay. We'll do it together."

"We should leave now. Gabe and I are pretty late for work," said Cybele. She turned to Cassie. "Come by around noon. Janus will be gone then."

Cassie nodded.

Cybele and Gabe left for work.

Cassie shook her head. I really hope Cybele is wrong about Janus. The Janus she describes just doesn't seem to be the Janus I know. She sighed. Maybe no one can really know anyone else. All is illusion. Castles in the air.

Chapter 25

Gods. Is Janus ever going to leave? He had to pick today to go even later than usual to the Loaves and Fishes. Cybele tensed as she heard Janus close his office door and then heard the front door of the cult house close as well. She walked into the kitchen and looked out the window. Janus's car was pulling out of the driveway.

She turned to Gabe who had silently followed her into the kitchen. "I guess it's time to get started."

"Do you think we should wait for Cassie?"

"No. She'll come soon enough." Cybele crossed her fingers. "Maybe we'll even be done by then."

Gabe peered past her. "Looks like she's already here."

Cybele turned back to the kitchen window and sighed. Cassie's car was pulling into the driveway. "Wonderful."

They hurried out to meet Cassie.

Cassie looked up at them. "Well, looks like the gang's all here. What's the plan?"

Cybele handed Cassie a set of keys. "These are the keys for the front door of the cult house and Janus's office. Search his office and see if anything turns up that seems out of place."

"Other than me?" asked Cassie.

"Other than you." Cybele bit her lower lip as she looked at Cassie's distraught face. "You might find it pretty informative to look at some of the notes he has written in some of his books. There were a stack of them under his desk the last time I checked. Then search the kitchen and the basement supplies to make sure the only herbs there are the ones we use for the potions and incenses we make. You're familiar enough with the ingredients to spot any ones that should not be there."

"And then what?" asked Cassie a bit aggressively.

Cybele forced herself not to bristle at Cassie's tone. "Then come to Janus's house. You can help Gabe and me, if we're not done searching it by then."

"Fine." Cassie fiddled with the keys as she walked away from Cybele and Gabe.

Cybele turned to Gabe. "I guess we better get started on our search too."

They walked quickly up to Janus's front door. Cybele pulled a set of keys from her pocket. "Good thing Janus always asks me to housesit when he goes away on vacation." She shook her head sadly. "I never thought I'd be using them to break into his house. Life's funny that way, I guess."

Gabe squeezed her reassuringly on the shoulder. "Life doesn't always work out the way we planned."

They walked inside and Gabe carefully closed the door behind them.

Cybele turned to Gabe. "Start searching his living room and study. Then go through his basement. I'll go through the kitchen and the upstairs rooms. Whoever finishes first should also check the bathrooms."

Gabe nodded. He walked off into the living room.

Cybele quickly went into the kitchen and began to open cupboards and look through them. Nothing. Everything looks normal. She pulled out a chair and stood on it. She ran her hands over the top of the cupboards. No hidden envelopes of doomsday messages or confessions to having been involved in a car bombing. She grimaced. I can't believe I'm in Janus's house looking for stuff like that. She jumped down from the chair and placed it back under the table. She opened the dishwasher. Yep. Full of dirty dishes. She closed it. Unconsciously, she found herself reaching for the soap to put into the dishwasher to run the load. She stopped and looked at the box she was holding. Hmm. Maybe I'm going about this search wrong. She placed the box back into the cupboard and stood up. Cassie and I spend a lot of our time in the kitchen. It's one of our favourite places. I make my potions and incenses there and Cassie does her cooking and baking there. But, to the king of take-out, it's just a room. Janus would hide his secrets in a room he felt comfortable in. A room he spent a lot of time in. She looked out towards the deck. Maybe. She shook her head. Too open to the elements. And anyone could have access to it. The police could do that whole plain sight so no warrant necessary bullshit. Janus is too smart to leave himself open to that possibility. He would pick somewhere more personal and intimate. She nodded. His bedroom or the guest room he redid to showcase his comic book collection and his other collectibles. She walked over to the living room.

"Find anything?"

Gabe held up his hands which were covered in grey fluff. "Just dust bunnies."

Cybele laughed. "Me neither. Just keep searching and try not to sneeze." She wrinkled her nose thoughtfully. "Do the basement next, and then meet me upstairs." She turned and quickly ran up the stairs.

Cybele paused as she crossed the threshold into his bedroom. Goddess. Why do I feel like such a Judas? She shook her head. I'm doing the right thing. What must be done.

Cassie sighed uncomfortably as she walked into Janus's office. I can't believe I let Cybele talk me into doing this. I must be delusional. She walked over to his filing cabinet. Please let it be locked. She pulled the drawer door and it opened. Damn. She bent down and began to flip through his files. Wow. That phone sex line is really pulling in the money. Janus must be over the moon with delight. She closed the drawer and looked around. She walked over to the closet and opened it. Hmm. Just some office supplies and a box of incenses. She bent down and rifled through the box. That's a lot of wormwood. But, as long as it's used in moderation, there's nothing wrong with that. She stood up and cracked her back. Maybe Cybele was right. Janus might be holding his own private rituals for some of the employees. But, there's nothing really sinister about that. Why shouldn't he have some fun too? Be the star of his own show and not just an extension of Cybele's. Maybe Cybele's just worried that his rituals will eventually eclipse hers in importance. Cassie groaned. I love them both but short of ego and a certain arrogance they are not.

Cassie walked over to Janus's desk and quickly looked through his drawers. Nothing seems incriminating to me. She sat down on the floor and looked at the pile of books beneath it. Aha. The smoking gun that so upset Cybele. She sighed. Better take a look. Cybele will be seriously pissed with me if I don't. Cassie pulled the pile towards her and began to skim through them. Cults and apocalyptic endings. She shook her head. Go together like vanilla ice cream on warm apple pie. Mmmm. I'd rather be eating that than doing this. Hmmm. The infamous Stanford Prison Experiment. She began to read through the book. Disturbing premise but hardly evidence that Janus is instigating an apocalypse within the cult. *People engage in anti-social acts when they feel anonymous or think they can get away with them. Morality is an illusion. Morality is dead.* She frowned. I don't like the sound of that. She began to look through the sheaf of handwritten notes at the back. Aha. Janus's dissection of Cybele. *Powerful/Mesmerizing Speaker. Face of Modern Cult? Feminism? Mother Goddess bullshit. Becoming caught up in her own illusion? Where will she end up? Will she sublimate her moral code in her quest for power and control? Delusional?* A bit harsh. No wonder she was so pissed at him. People definitely do not like to see their faults written out so clearly and analytically for all to see. She turned the paper over and looked at the comments on the back. *Cybele clearly getting off on the control she has over her followers. The Power is seductive. Addictive? What would she do to maintain control of her power base? Would she commit criminal acts? Would she cover them up? How different is she/will she be from the other cult leaders who have become before her? What will she justify/rationalize? Can morality survive in the real world or does experience force us to discard it? Survival of the fittest? Will she continue to impose her artificial code of morality on others or will she allow them free will? Share the apple or keep it for herself? Possible catalysts? Crucible? Trial by Fire?* Damn. Maybe Cybele is right. Janus is definitely sounding more like a catalyst than an impartial observer. She carefully placed the papers back into the book and shoved the pile under the desk into the same position they had been in before. Cassie stood up and walked out of the office. She pulled the door shut behind her and locked it. Time to do some more reconnaissance.

Cybele began to search through Janus's belongings. Nothing seems out of the ordinary. No diary with apocalyptic entries. She rummaged through his bedside table and the bookcase beside it. Just books and a stack of *Playgirls*. Reads them for the articles I'm sure. She rolled her eyes. And enough leftover Halloween candy to choke a horse. Did he even give any out last year or just keep it all for himself? What a sweet tooth. Maybe he's planning to use the stale Twinkie defense if he gets caught. She walked over to the closet and began to search through it. Nothing enlightening. Damn. She turned away in frustration and then stopped. Why does Janus have an open box of latex gloves in his closet? Is he trying to avoid leaving fingerprints? She pulled the box towards her and looked through it. She pulled out a baggie full of leaves. That's not pot. She took the baggie and walked over to the window to see it in natural light. That looks like Yerba del Diablo. She opened the baggie and took a sniff. Oh yeah. That's Yerba del Diablo all right. She reached in to touch it but quickly pulled her finger back before she did. Gods. I forgot that just touching it gives me a rash. It's so poisonous. She closed the baggie. I hope this isn't the smoking gun I didn't really want to find. She bit her lower lip. Maybe not. It does have use in rituals of protection. It's so dangerous that I would never use it, but that doesn't mean others don't. Janus could have bought it from lots of reputable dealers or he could have even grown it himself. She sighed. It's just ...Why the hell does Janus have this much of it? There are far safer ways to banish evil spirits than using this. She carefully placed the baggie back in the box and put everything back exactly where she had found it. She left Janus's bedroom and walked towards his spare room. She shook her head. Hope the only things I find in here are evidence of a Peter Pan who never wants to grow up and put away childish things.

Gabe frantically rushed up the stairs. "Cybele," he shouted.

"What?" She turned towards him. "Did you find anything in the basement?"

"Oh yeah." Gabe shook his head distractedly. "But we don't have time to talk about it. I just saw Janus's car pull up. We have to get out of here."

"Damnit. Cassie was supposed to keep watch and call me on my cell if she saw him." Cybele raced down the stairs.

Gabe followed behind her closely.

She paused and looked through the window at the front door. "He's getting out of his car. If we try to leave, he'll see us." She turned. She hastily looked around the main floor. "We'll leave through the deck doors and sneak around back to the greenhouse. If we're careful, he won't see us."

"We won't be able to lock the deck doors behind us," said Gabe doubtfully.

"I know." Cybele was already moving towards the deck doors. "But he might just think he forgot to do that. He is a bit absent-minded at times." She motioned at Gabe to hurry up. "We can't be caught in here."

They quickly left Janus's house and snuck around the side. They stopped as they heard the unmistakeable murmur of Janus and Cassie's voices. The voices trailed off into the distance. Gabe peeked around the corner. He could see the backs of Janus and Cassie walking towards The Mysteries of Cybele. He turned to Cybele and silently motioned for her to follow him. They quickly walked past the greenhouse and casually into the back door of the cult house.

"There you two are." Cassie turned towards them and smiled nervously. "Janus and I were wondering if you were in the greenhouse or taking advantage of such a beautiful day and taking a break outside."

Cybele and Gabe walked towards Cassie and Janus.

Cybele forced herself to sound nonchalant. "Oh, we're still hard at work."

Eager to keep the pretense going, Cassie chimed in. "I just stopped by to see if you and Janus wanted to go out for an early dinner at Nirvana's and then a movie. We haven't done that in a long time."

Janus shook his head. "That sounds like fun, but I have a lot of work to catch up on tonight."

Cassie nodded at him. "Too bad." She then turned to Cybele. "What about you, Cyb?"

Cybele nodded meaningfully at Cassie. "I have to finish some work up here and then I'll meet you at Nirvana's for five."

Cassie left.

Janus and Cybele looked awkwardly at each other. Then Janus walked into his office and closed the door.

Cybele and Gabe looked at each other and then quietly walked into their office.

Cybele shook her head when he would have begun speaking. She whispered, "We can't talk here. Let's just get our stuff and meet Cassie at the restaurant."

Gabe whispered back. "Won't it look suspicious if he doesn't hear us talking and then we just leave?"

She shook her head and spoke in a slightly below normal voice. "He'll think I just didn't want him to know you were going with me."

"Makes sense," said Gabe in a slightly more normal voice.

They gathered their stuff and left the cult house. They quickly got into their cars and drove away to Nirvana.

Cybele gently withdrew her hand from Gabe's and gave a tentative half-wave to Cassie as she walked across the restaurant towards their table.

Cassie sat down beside Gabe. She frowned slightly and looked over at Cybele. "I hate to admit it, but you might be on to something. Janus might be using the cult to play out his own inner demons." She stopped talking as the waiter came up to take their orders.

After he had gone, Cybele leaned forward. "Did you read what he had written about me in his notes?"

"Yeah. His critique did seem to be a bit harsh." Cassie smiled inwardly. If a bit true. "But I was more disturbed by what he said about the artificial nature of morality and the idea that he might be running an experiment on you – trying to test the limits of your own conscience."

Cybele drummed her fingers on the table. "I know. I just can't figure out what he's thinking. What's motivating him to do what he's doing?" Cybele looked over at Gabe. "Why don't you tell Cassie what you found out in your search?"

Gabe looked over at Cassie who was playing with a loose thread from the table cloth. He waited for her to look up but continued when he realized she was deliberately choosing not to meet his gaze. "In his basement library, I found some rough notes he had jotted down about specific rituals followed by cults that had committed suicide, everything from Jim Jones to Heaven's Gate. They were stuffed in a book on brainwashing and LSD experiments performed by the CIA in the 1960s." He smiled grimly. "I even found a psychological dissection of the botched mass suicide on *Deep Space Nine* that he had done. You know, when the Pah-Wraith followers of

Dukat were thwarted in their attempts by the intervention of Major Kira."

Cybele looked over at Cassie who was also refusing to look at her. "He could just have wanted to explore what could go wrong. The best laid plans...but somehow..."

Cassie bit the inside of her cheek as she spoke. "The unexpected, unintended catalyst." She looked past Gabe and Cybele as she tried to make sense of these disturbing revelations. "Maybe Janus is playing with your mind. This could be one big, practical joke. He knows how much you love conspiracies. He could be setting up these clues for you to find just so he can yell 'gotcha' when you confront him with them."

Cybele reached out to touch Cassie's hand. "I wish I could believe that, but that doesn't fit with everything else that's going on."

Cassie looked unconvinced. "Such as?"

"It's not just the cult or have you forgotten the so-called terrorist bombing of Achates' new boyfriend's car? I'm still convinced that Janus knew more about that than he's admitted." Cybele tightened her grip on Cassie's hand as she tried to break through her wall of denial. "Why else would he have a lawyer on retainer and why did those two cops come to interrogate us?"

Cassie shrugged uneasily. "Prudence. Coincidence? I mean, did we really find anything specific in our search that would prove Janus was trying to instigate a ritual suicide within your cult?" She pulled her hand away from Cybele. "Have YOU really manipulated your followers to such an extent that you think they would somehow prove vulnerable to Janus's influence? I mean, he doesn't really participate in your rituals." She looked pointedly over at Gabe. "Gabe's more your Attis than Janus ever was."

Cybele looked stunned. "Do you blame me for what's happening now?"

"No...but... Damnit, Cyb. I told you that starting a cult was a dangerous idea. You can't play with people's visceral beliefs and not be surprised when it comes back to bite you on the ass. It's all fun and games until there's an apocalypse." Cassie started to yank more forcefully on the loose thread. "You're the messianic figure. How could Janus influence your faithful unless it's through you? Maybe that's what he's testing – if power will corrupt you – and what you might do to hold on to that power." She leaned back and looked steadily at Cybele. "You're a mesmerizing, charismatic speaker. Have you considered that maybe you've fallen under the spell of your own illusions? Maybe in the play you've created, you're unconsciously expecting to be betrayed by your best friend. Every Jesus needs a Judas."

Then who's Gabe? My Mary Magdalene? Cybele took a deep breath. Do not explode. Speak calmly. "Maybe... Janus... isn't my Judas."

"And what's that supposed to mean?" Cassie almost spit her words at Cybele.

Cybele bristled. You are. "I didn't create a patriarchal religion that involved betrayal," she said angrily. "I resurrected a Mother

Goddess religion that brought people together in a communion with nature." So there.

Gabe broke in trying to defuse the situation. "I don't think we gain anything if we proceed under the assumption that Cyb is delusional." He looked over at Cassie. "You know she's not and, at some point, coincidences stop being coincidences."

"No smoke without fire," mocked Cassie angrily.

Gabe mimed the playing of a violin. "All roads do seem to lead back to the cult house and back to Janus and Cyb." He turned towards Cassie. "Who do you really think is more likely to be involved, Janus or Cyb?"

"Why. Not. Neither?"

"Because I have faith in Cyb and trust that her unease with Janus's behaviour is justified. Why don't you?"

Cassie threw up her hands in exasperation. "Because Janus and Cyb both seem to live more in their minds than in the real world. I just don't believe Janus would ever do anything that would hurt real people. Fantasy is not a crime. We're not ruled by the Thought Police, at least not yet."

Determined to get Cassie on her side, Cybele chimed in. "Cassie, my spidey senses are tingling. Something about Janus's behaviour and his relationship with some of the workers is bothering me. I think he's crossing the line from observer to manipulator."

Cassie smiled ruefully at Cybele. "The problem is that you don't have spidey senses, Cyb."

Cybele snorted. “You’re right, Cassie. Maybe it’s just a delayed reaction from my exposure to Yerba del Diablo.”

Cassie jumped slightly in her chair. “What! I can’t believe you were fooling around with that stuff. You know how dangerous it is. There are far safer alternatives to use than…”

“Oh, it wasn’t my Yerba del Diablo, Cassie.” Cybele smiled smugly. “It was Janus’s.”

Cassie looked searchingly at Cybele. “Why does Janus have?...”

“I. Don’t. Know.” Cybele lightly thumped her hand on the table. “But don’t you worry that it might somehow be connected to all this information Janus has about ritual suicides?”

Cassie shook her head. “I still don’t see how…”

“What’s Yerba del Diablo?” asked Gabe impatiently.

Cybele turned to him. “It’s a plant that’s used in some pagan rituals, but it’s quite poisonous. You might know it by its other name, datura.”

Cassie frowned. “I still don’t see how Janus could use it in one of your rituals. You would notice it for sure.”

Cybele arched an eyebrow. “What if it’s not intended for MY rituals?”

“What do you mean?” asked Cassie.

“You’re right that Janus doesn’t have much of an influence over MY worshippers, but he might be collecting a few of his own. Some of those employees who keep goofing off and yet he seems unable to fire.”

Cassie looked hard first at Gabe and then at Cybele. "If you really think Janus might be involved with a mass suicide, why don't you go to the police?"

Gabe shook his head. "What could the police do if we told them? It's not a crime to make notes about ritual suicides."

Cybele shrugged helplessly. "I insisted that everyone who works for us be an adult. Janus's followers may be young and misguided, but technically, they're adults too. I don't think the police could do anything."

Gabe agreed. "The police are great for cleaning up messes, but not good at preventing them in the first place."

Cybele groaned. "Besides, that's assuming they believe me and judging from past experience, I get the feeling they think I'm the Lex Luthor of this piece." She rubbed her forehead wearily. "And if Janus has managed to talk some of his followers into a ritual suicide, it's not enough just to stop them from this one. Not if they end up glomming on to someone else who convinces them to do it again."

"So, what's the plan, then?" asked Cassie.

Gabe looked over to Cybele. "We need more precise information on what Janus is planning and we need to find a way to convince his followers that committing suicide is not a good idea."

Cybele nodded. "I'll go talk to Janus tomorrow and try to find out what's going on. Maybe try to convince him that I'm as seduced by the power as he is. Shouldn't be hard. He seems to think I'm ripe for corruption."

Cassie yanked too hard on the loose thread and a hole appeared in the table cloth. She looked down guiltily. Oops. She looked up and firmly met Cybele's gaze. "I hope you're wrong about Janus, but we need to put this to rest, one way or another."

They stopped talking as the waiter returned with their food. Silently, they began to eat.

Cybele looked back over at Cassie. I can't believe she doesn't believe me. Some friend.

Cassie looked away from Cybele. I can't believe Cyb would believe Gabriel over Janus. That's loyalty for you.

Gabe looked over at Cybele and then at Cassie. Silent night. He took a bite of his veal and mechanically began to chew it. Better not rock the boat.

Chapter 26

Janus looked up through the greenhouse windows at the night sky. He smiled half-heartedly. "What rough beast...slouches towards Bethlehem to be born?" He gently fondled the tendrils of his fern as he carefully placed it into a larger pot. My faithful friends. He shook his head. I wish I may, I wish I might, have this wish I wish tonight.

Cybele peered through the greenhouse door. There he is. Gods. How do I go about asking someone if he's deciding to Jim Jones some of his faithful flock? She shook her head. Shit. She opened the door and walked half-way through. She forced a jovial tone into her voice as she spoke. "Beware, Janus, something wicked this way comes."

Janus snorted. "Tired of your new boyfriend, already?" He grimly wiped the soil off his hands as he looked up at Cybele.

Cybele leaned up against the door and frowned. "Have you ever thought you'd have more friends if you weren't always such a jackass?"

Bitch. Janus determinedly turned his attention back to the tendrils of the fern and proceeded to ignore Cybele.

Cybele groaned. Why is nothing ever easy? She took a deep breath and slowly released it. Remember. You're not here to fight. You're here to find out what he's up to. "Come on, Janus, don't be such a grouch." She moved more fully into the darkness of the greenhouse. "How about we try that again?" Cybele forced herself to sound light and friendly. "Hey Janus, want to have a drink with your best friend in the whole wide world? Maybe we could even have two or three. It'll be like old times." Cybele rolled her eyes. "You know, like when we were young and carefree. You know, like yesterday."

Janus sighed. "Fine. We can sit on the deck and meditate on the good old days. You know, when the earth was new and life seemed full of promise. "

Cybele gently laced her arm through his and began to pull him out of the greenhouse. "Life is still full of promise, Janus. You just have to dig past everyone else's manure to reach your goals."

Janus looked down at her. He hesitated. What is she up to now? He slowly began to disengage his arm from hers and then stopped.

Cybele looked up at him and smiled half-sadly. "Come on, Janus. We've been friends are entire lives. Can't we kiss, drink, and make-up?"

Janus reached down and hugged her. Friend or enemy? Whatever. She's still my Cyb. "Too bad we don't have any grape Kool-Aid."

"Too bad. But we're adults now, Janus. We can drink of the grape instead." Cybele reached into her purse and pulled out a small paper bag. "But I did manage to score some of the good stuff."

Janus spoke in a exaggeratedly shocked voice. "Not pot?"

"Better." Cybele began to lead him slowly through the doorway. "Peanut butter cookies. Freshly made as only Subway can make them."

Janus paused on the threshold. Are we making up or setting each other up for the fall? Friend or foe? I guess time ...He paused thoughtfully. And maybe wine reveals all. He went through the doorway by himself following a step behind Cybele.

Two bottles of wine later, Cybele leaned slightly unsteadily back against the deck chair and looked blurrily up at the night sky. So many points of light. So much beauty in this universe. She blinked away tears. She drank some of her wine and then looked over at Janus. She could barely see him in the shadows. Raising her arm in the air, she proclaimed, "And the Goddess said, Let there be Light and then there was."

Janus snorted. He lifted his wine glass up half-heartedly in the air. "And the God said, 'Let there be mosquitoes. And then there were." He leaned unsteadily towards Cybele. "If you want light, it'll have to be the light from my bug-zapper. Anything else would be just asking for an attack."

Cybele shook her head fiercely as the world spun around her. "I prefer my light unaccompanied by the sizzle of death." She sighed into her wine glass. "How about you?"

Janus began to munch nonchalantly on his cookie. "You've never had a strong stomach, Cyb. Nothing is ever gained without something being lost. It's a law of nature." He leaned forward towards her and thumped her a little too hard on her shoulder. "Remember, Gaea is a heartless bitch."

Cybele smiled sadly. "Ah, yes. I haven't forgotten. Of course. We're not really Gaea."

Janus pulled his legs up to his chest and hugged himself. "Aren't we the shepherds not the sheep?"

Cybele looked over at him sharply. "Shepherds don't kill their sheep. They protect them from predators."

Janus put his head down wearily upon his knees. "Enough, Cyb. It's too late to play fortune cookies with you." He brushed crumbs off his knees. "Or maybe I should say peanut butter cookies, eh?"

Cybele placed her wine glass down and slid over on her hands and knees towards Janus. "What are we doing?"

Janus reached down and drunkenly hugged her to him. "Don't you know? Under the swinging chestnut tree, I sold you and you sold me."

Cybele looked up at him. "Never, Janus. I would never betray you. You're my best friend. Forever." She sighed mournfully. "But you have to trust me. I can't help you if you don't trust me."

Janus looked down at her questioningly. "Why should I trust you, Cyb?"

Cybele reached up and cupped the side of his face. "Because I know what you're planning to do and I just want to help you get out of this mess without anyone getting hurt."

Janus shoved Cybele roughly away from him. "How the hell could you possibly know what I'm planning?"

Cybele pulled her knees into her chest and placed her head tiredly upon her knees. "Because I'm not an idiot, Janus. I know you're planning some Jim Jones type apocalypse. I just don't know why."

Janus glared at her. "You don't know a goddamn thing, Cybele."

"What's the big fucking secret, Janus? Why not let me in on it? What's wrong?" She shouted unsteadily. "Am I not drunk enough on my own power? Not delusional enough yet to be your own little puppet who kills?"

Janus slammed his hand down on the floor of the deck. "You're not my damn puppet, Cyb. You're society's little token rebel. Hypocrisy's puppet."

Cybele shook her head confusedly. "What in the name of the Goddess are you talking about?"

Janus snorted. "You and your fake freedoms." He violently rolled back on his heels almost falling over. "You're a hypocrite. You believe in personal freedoms but not for anyone else but you."

"What are you saying?" Cybele bit the bottom of her lip. "Of course, I believe in personal freedom for everyone."

"No. You don't." Janus pushed himself further away from her. "Either people have free will and can choose to live or die as they please or you're their master controller and you get to impose your will on them." He smirked. "After all, aren't you the new Goddess come to save us all – prevent all your mindless sheep from having to make any of their own decisions." He chuckled. "If I'm doing anything, it's just showing them the way to true personal freedom – free of the chains of religion you have enslaved them with." He mockingly raised his wine glass to her. "It's not hemlock, but oh well. We who are about to live free salute you."

"By the Goddess." Cybele pushed herself closer towards Janus. "You can't live free if you're dead." She reached out and grabbed his hand and gently lowered the wine glass to the ground. "Please tell me why? Is any of this shit connected to Achates?" She squeezed his hand hard. "You're better off without him, Janus. Just tell me. Why are you doing this?" She pulled him to her. "Damnit. You're not a killer, Janus."

Janus pulled away indignantly. "Of course, I'm not a killer, Cyb. I'm not DOING anything. I'm just a watcher – like the ones on *Highlander*." He hugged himself as he began to rock back and forth. "I watch the madness of others and document it for the benefit of future generations. I'm just the observer. You and the others are the ones playing all your mindless games of sound and fury signifying nothing."

Cybele slowly released her breath. "I'm not one of those, Janus. I'm a watcher like you." She slowly poured some of her wine into his glass. She put his glass back into his hand. She gently clinked her glass against his. *"In vino veritas."*

Janus looked at her suspiciously. "How do I know I can trust you?"

"Because you and I are the same, Janus. You were right. I was being a hypocrite. Either all people have free will or they don't." She laughed bitterly. "I fell under my own spell but now I've woken up." She took another sip of wine. "I feel like the lioness who spent her life being raised by sheep. She never knows what she is until when her flock is attacked by a hungry lion."

Janus began to smirk. “And then she knows what she is.”

Cybele smiled back falsely. “And then she remembers what she is.” You bastard. I hope you’re too drunk to remember that in the story the lioness defends her flock and drives off the lion. Cybele raised her glass once more to her lips. “So, what’s the plan, Janus? How are we going to keep making money off our cult if our members are allowed to kill themselves?”

Janus patted her hand. “Just the throwaway members, Cyb.” Yep. Just the ones who could possibly tie me to a car bomb.

Cybele looked at him curiously. What’s gone wrong with you? How can you be saying these things? “Even throwaways have families. What happens to our business if we get sued or the police think we facilitated their suicides? The point of starting our own religion was to make money not to go to jail.”

“Don’t be such a killjoy, Cyb.” He chuckled smugly. “We can’t be held responsible for the actions of a few followers who broke away from our religion to follow their own practices.”

Cybele took a slow sip of her wine. “You’re right. After all, that’s how we know our religion has finally made it – when we have our own fanatics.” She yanked on his arm. “But how will you make sure they really do kill themselves? Survivors could point their fingers back at us.”

Janus frowned. Damnit. She’s right. It’s not like I can trust those idiots to do anything right on their own. I’m going to have to be there to make sure everything goes according to plan.

Cybele leaned closer. "And how are you going to get rid of the bodies? Their rituals will have to take place far enough out of Winnipeg that their deaths can't be connected back to us."

Janus patted her on the shoulder. "Don't worry, Cyb. I have the perfect place in mind." The land opposite Circean Dreams. Why not tie everything up in a bow for those idiot police? Eco-terrorists decide to martyr themselves at the very place whose politics they're protesting. It's the Canadian version of those monks who are always setting themselves on fire protesting some fucking injustice or another.

"Of course, you do." Cybele said. "After all, you are the master."

Janus frowned and looked away. He was slightly uncomfortable with the way she had acknowledged the greatness of his plan. He tapped his fingers on the deck floor. Cyb can't be a loose end. She must be a part of the plan. It's too dangerous to me for her just know about it.

Cybele became slightly uncomfortable at his silence. Goddess. What is he thinking? Is he having second thoughts about telling me of his plan? She took a quick breath. "We should perform the rituals for them together, Janus."

His head snapped towards her. "What?"

"The *hieros gamos*, Janus." She scooted closer to him. "You be the Attis to my Cybele. It was meant to be this way."

"Yes." Janus nodded. The sacred marriage. I was supposed to be your Attis. Not Gabriel. Not Achates. Me. He looked down into her upturned face. "They will be more eager to participate if the Great Goddess Cybele herself is there." And if you betray me, Cyb, well, patriarchy usurped matriarchy once before.

"So, tell me." Cybele took a quick gulp of wine to mask her discomfort. "How are you planning to survive your own private little apocalypse?"

Janus chuckled sarcastically. "Don't you mean we, *kemo sabe*? Not turning into a shrinking violet on me, are you?"

Cybele forced herself to take a leisurely sip of her wine. "Not at all." She raised her glass in a mocking salute. "I just thought that since everyone knows that real men are swallowers not spitters, you might have a little problem with the passing of the sacred gourd."

Janus glared at her. "Well, I guess we'll have to make two very special brews, one for them and one for us." He reached over and patted her condescendingly on her shoulder. "Try not to mix them up, eh? I know how good you are at dealing with those pesky details."

Cybele patted him back harder. "Don't worry. When it comes to life and death, I tend to pay a little more attention."

Janus leaned back satisfied. "See that you do. I have no desire to see the light at the end of the tunnel."

Cybele snorted. She quickly coughed to cover her involuntary sound of disbelief. No worries there, *kemo sabe*. If you do see a light, it'll probably from the fires at the end of the funnel. She quickly squeezed his hand. "You can count on me, Janus." She got up and began to walk away. "Best friends forever but now it's off to sleep I go."

Janus watched her walk away. Best friends forever. He looked up at the stars. Too bad you can only see them at night. He sighed and went off to bed.

I'm drowning. I'm drowning. Why can't anyone save me? Gasping for breath, Janus awoke. I'm alone. He shuddered. I'm alone. He quickly wiped the wetness from his eyes. Damn dreams. Must have drunk too much last night. He dragged himself out of bed. I know what I have to do. No second thoughts. It's me or them and it's NOT going to be me. Janus showered, dressed quickly, and made his way across the lawn to the greenhouse.

Seeing Janus, Ardiaeus quickly ground his cigarette on the ground. "Hey, Janus. Man is it good to see you. That Cybele has been making us work like dogs all morning." He snorted contemptuously. "Good thing she left to get some stupid supplies for her witch's brew."

Janus looked pointedly at his watch. "It's only ten o'clock. I think you have a few good hours of work left in you."

Tan looked at Ardiaeus warningly. "He's just kidding, Janus. We know you told us to do what she says and we are."

Ajax nodded. "We're doing everything you tell us to."

"Yep," chimed in Ixion.

Janus rubbed his forehead. Great. If that were only true, my problems would be over. How am I going to convince these morons to kill themselves tomorrow evening? Think, Janus. Think.

Ixion sidled up to Janus and stood motionless directly in front of Janus.

Janus looked around perplexed. Tan, Ardiaeus, and Ajax were giving Ixion encouraging looks.

Janus frowned down at Ixion. "What?"

Ixion cracked his knuckles nervously. "Say. Do you think we could have some more of those free phone sex cards?" He gulped. "We've been working real hard."

Janus paused. Sex. That's it. The best instrument of social control there is. Now I just have to figure out how to use sex to get them to kill themselves. I need to think. Janus walked away from Ixion without answering him.

Tan quickly pushed Ixion out of his way and strode off Janus. "Wait. He was just kidding. We're still on for the private Friday rituals, right?"

Janus turned slowly and put a false expression of concern upon his face. "There might be a slight problem with the Friday rituals. It might not be as private and as fun as before." He sighed. "Cybele's feeling a little left out and wants to join us." He shrugged. "I tried to convince her it was better if it was just us guys, but, she's the boss."

Ajax pouted. "But it won't be as much fun if she's there."

Ardiaeus scowled. "Isn't it bad enough we have to work for her? Why do we have to party with her too?"

Afraid of pissing Janus off further, Tan broke in. "Cool it, guys. I'm sure Janus did his best to get her not to come but she's the boss."

Janus looked approvingly at Tan. "Yes. She is." He frowned. "If only there was something we could do to let her know that our private rituals are for men only. Maybe. We could. No." Janus turned away. "No. We couldn't do that. That would be too mean." He began to walk away slowly.

"Wait." Ardiaeus yelled. "What did you think we could do?"

Janus turned back fighting to keep the smile off his face. Ahh. Always count on the bully to be easily manipulated. "I thought we could play a little bit of a practical joke on her. You know. Just to let her know that we guys really prefer to perform our rituals without women around."

Tan smirked. "Yeah. I wouldn't mind teaching her a lesson."

Ixion and Ajax quickly nodded their agreement.

Janus smirked. You can never go wrong appealing to misogyny. He gestured for them to come closer and began to whisper his plan to them. "What if we scare Cybele by convincing her that we are all going to kill ourselves Friday night? We can pretend we're drinking poisoned wine. We'll wait a few minutes after we've drunk the wine and then pretend we're dying. It'll freak her out so badly that she'll never want to gatecrash our private parties again."

The boys started to laugh but Ixion looked a little worried. "Won't she be mad when she realizes we tricked her? She might fire us."

Janus shook his head reassuringly. "She won't know it's a joke until the next day and by then she'll be so upset that she won't even think of firing you. In fact." He dramatically rubbed his chin. "To make her even more upset, we should all write suicide notes and leave them on us. We can blame our killing ourselves on her making us firebomb her enemies' cars." He laughed unpleasantly. "Trust me. Cybele will want nothing to do with us after that."

Tan smirked. "That's an awesome plan, Janus. That'll show her who's really boss."

Ardiaeus and Ajax nodded their agreement. Ixion still looked a little worried. "But, I'm not good at writing. I don't know if I can write a good suicide note."

Janus reached over and patted Ixion on his shoulder. "Don't worry. I'll help all of you come up with the perfect notes. Let's go to my office and get them written now before Cybele comes back."

They quickly followed him into his office and sprawled messily in varying positions on Janus's floor.

Taking the pen and paper Janus gave out, Tan wrote quickly and with little hesitation. Dear family, I always want what's right in front of me, but I can never reach it. I'm tired of trying.

Flicking his pen back and forth between his fingers, Ardiaeus paused uncertainly. "I'm not sure..."

Janus broke in reassuringly. "Just say whatever's in your heart. Remember." He paused dramatically. "No one but Cybele is ever going to see those notes so you can say whatever you want." He looked around at the others still struggling to write their own notes. "That goes for all of you."

Ardiaeus sighed heavily and then laboriously began to write out his suicide note. If I could, I've always wanted to set the whole world on fire and watch it burn. It's better this way.

Also slightly uncomfortable at putting his true feelings down on paper, Ixion wrote slowly. *I don't want to be left behind. I just want to be free like the clouds in the sky.*

Ajax smirked vindictively. A chance to say what I always wanted. Perfect. *This is all your fault. You never wanted me and now I don't want you.*

After they had all finished writing, Janus rewarded them with free phone sex cards. "Don't have too much fun with these tonight." He smirked. "Save something for Friday."

They nodded eagerly.

Janus pointed dramatically to the doorway. "Now, get back to work before Cybele returns from shopping." He watched them file out and then leaned slowly back in his chair. Like lambs to the slaughter. Janus sighed thoughtfully. Maybe I should feel guilty at what I'm doing but I just don't. Maybe I have absorbed too many of Cybele's pagan way lectures. Nature is full of predators and prey. If you can't do whatever it takes to survive, you don't deserve to survive. I'm just cleaning out the gene pool. He closed his eyes. *Conscience is just a societal construction. It is a myth we use to avoid killing one another at the slightest provocation. It does not exist.* Janus shook his head and opened his eyes. All right, Cyb. Time to choose your side. He snorted contemptuously. So much for your hero Sisko's 'these are the times that try men's souls.' Janus stood up and deliberately slammed his chair hard against the wall. Let the games begin.

Chapter 27

At that precise same moment in her apartment, Cybele was running her finger in a circle over the rim of her cup as Gabe and Cassie waited expectantly for her to speak. Cybele raised her cup in a mocking salute. “Well, it’s official. Janus has definitely lost his marbles. He’s going full steam ahead for his own private Kool-Aid party tomorrow night.”

Cassie shook her head in disbelief. “You know, Cyb, you and Janus had a lot to drink last night. Are you sure he wasn’t yanking your chain?”

Cybele reached across the kitchen table and patted Cassie’s hand gently. “I had a lot of time to think things through while I was waiting for Gabe to come by and pull my car out of that ditch.”

Gabe frowned. “I still can’t believe YOU would drive after drinking that much.”

Cybele dropped her gaze in chagrin. “You’re right. I knew better. I just had to get away...” She gnawed the bottom of her lip. “I just felt like I was drowning in Janus’s bitterness.” She brought her cup to her lips and then put it down again without taking a sip. “I just don’t know what to do.”

Gabe put down his coffee cup with a little thud. He leaned forward and looked Cybele directly in her eyes. “You know what you have to do. You have to tell the police about what Janus is planning so they can stop him.”

Still in a state of denial, Cassie shook her head from side to side. "How can the police stop something that might just be Cybele and Janus bullshitting each other?"

Gabe scowled down at Cassie. "Look, Mary Poppins, the time has come to take a stand. How much more evidence do you need that Janus is planning something deadly and dangerous?" He slammed his hand down on the table. "Will it take bodies for you to start believing Cybele?"

Cassie pushed herself away from the table with a hurt sniff. She walked over to the kettle and began to refill it with tap water.

Cybele stood up and began to pace back and forth thoughtfully. "Don't yell at Cassie, Gabe. She has a good point. The police can't do anything." Cybele snorted. "They're better at cleaning up aftermaths than preventing messes in the first place." She leaned up against the wall and began to stretch her back. "Besides, what's the point in getting the police involved, now?"

Gabe stood up. "What's the point?" He threw his hands up in the air. "How about NOT being an accomplice to a mass suicide? Do you know what the punishment for that is?"

Cassie turned away from plugging in the kettle. "No Gabe," she said sarcastically. "Why don't you tell us idiot women what the punishment is?"

Cybele shushed both of them. Damnit. These are the times that try our souls. "No sense fighting amongst ourselves." She turned to Gabe. "What I meant was if Janus's friends really want to die then the police won't be able to stop them from ultimately doing what they want to do."

Cassie forced herself to unclench her teeth and not yell. "Now, Cyb, this is no time for speeches about free will and the right to self-termination. You could be in a lot of trouble here."

Cybele laughed bitterly. "Janus was right when he called me a hypocrite. I only believe in free will for myself. I seem to have this uncontrollable impulse to control the actions of everyone else." She shook her head angrily. "Well, to Hades with them. I'm not allowing those idiots to kill themselves during one of MY religious rituals and allow them to blacken MY matriarchy. If they want to cross over, they're going to have to find another way to do it."

Cybele started to pace again. "I have to find a way to show them the error of their ways. I need to get them away from Janus's influence. If I hadn't started this religion, Janus never would have been able to use them as his test subjects." She leaned back against the wall and sighed. "I'm going to have to show them that Janus is unworthy of their devotion." Damnit. Why couldn't they have followed me and not him?

Cassie paused uncertainly as she tried to decipher the odd expression on Cybele's face. "You do have a moral obligation to set things right, Cyb."

"Yep." Cybele tapped her foot thoughtfully. "And I know just what I have to do."

Cassie snapped her fingers together. "I know." She smiled in relief. "You're going to switch chalices. The wine they drink won't be poisoned. That way when they don't die, they'll know suicide wasn't meant to be."

Cybele hugged herself in delight at her own brilliance. You've read my mind. "It'll be like those Y2K fears. Once the time passes and no apocalypse happens, his followers will be forced to go on with their lives."

Gabe scowled at both of them. "Aren't you taking an awfully big risk? What if ALL the wine is poisoned? What if Janus's real plan is to have everyone die in a blaze of glory?"

Cybele blinked sceptically at him. "Janus is too much the ultimate survivor ever to kill himself."

Cassie agreed. "Just make sure NONE of the wine is poisoned. Keep a close eye on Janus though. He can be tricky." She sighed worriedly. "Whatever happens though, you will have done your best. You can't do more than that, Cyb."

Gabe still looked unconvinced. "I don't think this is a good idea. Maybe I should come along to keep an eye on everything."

Cybele shook her head at his suggestion. "No, Gabe. If Janus sees you, he'll know something's up. He'll just find another time and place for his apocalypse." She rubbed her forehead. "No. This will be settled between Janus and I, once and for all, on Friday." She smiled wearily at Cassie and Gabe. "It's written in the stars. Superman and Lex Luthor always have to face each other down alone." She gnawed her lip as she tried to make them understand. "Think of *Highlander*. There can only be one."

Aargh! Cassie rolled her eyes. "This is a little more serious than the quickening."

Cybele gently caught Cassie's hand in her own. "I know." Cybele then turned to Gabe and took him also by the hand. "Know any good lawyers? I might need a good one when all this is over."

Gabe squeezed Cybele's hand gently. "Don't worry. When the shit stops flying, none of it will be stuck to you."

Cybele wrinkled up her nose. "Good to know. Fashion rules be damned. I've never been one for stripes." She slowly released Gabe and Cassie's hands. "Wish me luck." Heigh-ho, heigh-ho. Off to apocalypse I go.

Cassie looked helplessly at Gabe. "Don't worry. Cybele could fall into a pile of shit and come out smelling like a flower. She's just lucky that way."

Gabe shook his head. "Hope the same thing can't be said about Janus." He walked to the door. "I'd better start looking now for a good lawyer."

Cassie shut the door firmly behind him. She turned with eyes closed and leaned heavily against the door. What a fucking mess. Why does no one ever listen to me?

Sitting at her office desk late Friday afternoon, Cybele slowly massaged the back of her neck. Gods. I can't believe the quickening has come. She sniffed the fragrant air. Janus's cauldrons are bubbling away nicely. She snorted. He's so predictable. I knew he would use my recipe for sweet mead to disguise the Yerba del Diablo. Sweets before death. She turned her head slightly to look at her *Ecumenical Council* poster. The time of sacrifice has arrived, but the age of Pisces has run its course. Grabbing her knapsack from beneath her desk, Cybele stood up regretfully. She walked over to her mother goddess figurine. Slowly, she bent down and rested her forehead on the terracotta head. Matriarchies should not have to suffer for the crimes of those invested in patriarchy. She straightened up and marched determinedly to her doorway. I WILL succeed tonight. I will NOT allow Janus to destroy my resurrection. The world needs the Goddess too much.

Cybele placed her knapsack gently against the outside of the doorway as she paused in front of the kitchen. Fire burn and cauldron bubble. I see Janus is still hard at work. Well, apocalypse delayed is apocalypse denied. She crossed the threshold and forced a deliberately light tone to her voice. “Hey. Need some more help in here? The master of all things magical has arrived.” She walked towards Janus and removed the lid off one of his two slow cookers to inspect the concoctions he had brewed with her help. “Or should I say mistress? Must be politically correct, don’t you know.” She looked down at her Book of Shadows lying on the counter. Nice. He’s spilled crap all over it. Good going, Janus.

Janus gave her a strange look. “You’re in a good mood tonight.”

Cybele replaced the slow cooker lid and straightened up. She gave him a deliberately perplexed look. “Why wouldn’t I be?” She grabbed a tea towel to wipe the condensation from her hands. “I did say my cult would be a success when we had our first apocalypse and tonight's the night." She threw the towel pseudo-playfully at him. "As long as we don't get any bad press from tonight's work, our profits shouldn't suffer any."

Janus reached up and caught the towel. He unconsciously began to straighten it out and then fold it. Things are finally getting back to normal between us. She understands that everything is happening for the best. He smiled. First she makes a point of telling me we have to stay below the police's radar and make sure nothing can come back to bite us on the ass. Then she deliberately walks out of the kitchen when I pull out my Yerba del Diablo. Typical Cyb. Close your eyes. See no evil. All for plausible deniability.

Cybele ran her fingers lightly over the two empty bottles sitting on the counter beside the slow cookers. One red and one green. Interesting. Colour-coordinated death. She raised one eyebrow meaningfully at him. "I hope all the special ingredients have already been added to their mead." She chuckled. "And not to ours. After all, we're not the ones who want to cross over."

Janus snorted. "Don't worry. As long as we drink the mead from the red slow cooker and not the green slow cooker, we'll be fine."

Nice. Red for life and green for death. Trust Janus to do everything ass-backwards. Shit. I hope he's telling the truth. Tonight is definitely not a good day for me to die. Cybele reached down into the drawer and grabbed two funnels. She pulled them out and turned to face Janus. "Let's fill these suckers and get the show on the road."

She casually leaned back against the counter and looked Janus straight in the eye. "Not to get too crime scene investigator on you, but have you destroyed everything that could link their deaths back to us? The last thing we need is police getting a search warrant and ripping your house and this kitchen apart looking for evidence that we assisted in their suicides." She gestured at the dirty dishes in the sink. "We are going to have to wash everything with bleach to destroy any evidence of..." She paused meaningfully. "Whatever might have been added to the mead when I was out of the kitchen. The bleach should also destroy any trace of herbs in the drain."

Janus nodded approvingly. "I hadn't thought of bleach. Good catch, Cyb."

She gently slapped him on the shoulder. "We're partners. We have to cover each other's asses." She smiled thoughtfully. "Speaking of cover, are you absolutely sure those idiots aren't going to blame us for their suicide? That would leave us wide-open for lawsuits. Even throwaways have families who like money."

Janus shook his head playfully. "Cyb. When are you going to learn to trust me?"

Maybe when I don't have to buy bottles of bleach to destroy evidence of poison. Cybele forced herself to chuckle through waves of bitterness.

Janus chuckled back. "Don't worry. I personally supervised their writing of their suicide notes. We're never mentioned at all." Besides. All the evidence that will be found with them will link them back to the Friends of Gaea. They can be Hector's problem then. Of course, Cyb might have some explaining to do about her connection to Hector and dead eco-martyrs. But she's a survivor. She'll be fine. She'll keep quiet to keep her little religion going. He snorted loudly. Power IS the ultimate corruptor.

Cybele looked curiously at him. I wonder what's so funny. She forced herself to continue. "Good. I don't want to be Canada's poster child for apocalypse."

"Neither do I," said Janus forcefully. Why does everything have to be about her? What am I? Jimmy Olson?

"Great." Cybele touched the sides of the slow cookers. "The mead should be cool enough to pour out now. I'll do that and then I'll wash everything down with bleach. I'll take a bottle of bleach with us. We can wash out the green bottle out afterwards."

Janus nodded. "Good thinking. You do the dishes and I'll make sure there's nothing left in my house that could get us in trouble." I should definitely get rid of the extra Yerba del Diablo. I'll burn it and then flush it down the toilet with a shitload of bleach. He looked down at his watch. "An hour should be enough time to get everything cleaned up. Then we'll take my car to the ritual site."

Typical. His car. All about being in the driver's seat, eh Janus. "Sounds like a good plan." She turned away. So easily manipulated. Good thing for MY plan that I could never overestimate Janus's desire for self-preservation and for avoiding menial work. Or "womenial" work. Cybele busied herself with loudly moving dishes around in the sink until she heard the front door close. She waited for sixty seconds and then tiptoed to the door to make sure Janus had truly left. He had. She could see his shadowy figure moving away. She quickly removed two small round vials from her pocket. She dipped one in the red slow cooker and the other in the green slow cooker. She carefully labelled each vial. Red. Green. She then tightened the lids and placed the vials securely back in her pocket.

Good. Next she dumped the contents of both slow cookers down the kitchen drain. No use taking chances. Janus is just a little too comfortable with apocalypse for my comfort. She hurried over to her knapsack and pulled two plastic containers from it. She carefully poured the mead from her green plastic container into Janus's red bottle. Then she poured the mead from her red plastic container into Janus's green bottle. Damn Janus. Would have to make everything complicated. Everyone knows red is death and green is life. Well, in this case, green will have to stand for please Goddess give me the mercy of death. Too bad I couldn't spike the red bottle but I don't want to suffer too. She snickered. Better wash up all the evidence and get ready for the rituals for tonight is a night that will live forever in infamy. To the victor go the spoils.

Chapter 28

Cybele watched in the side mirror as the lights from the city receded further and further away until all she could see was one distant point of light. Journey into the heart of darkness. What better way to spend a Friday night. She looked over at Janus. He was tapping his fingers against the steering wheel and singing under his breath.

I will survive....Focus, Janus, focus. Janus forced himself to take a deep breath. Everything is falling into place. He reached over and lightly shook Cybele by the shoulder. “Not falling asleep, are you?”

Cybele pulled slightly away in order to dislodge Janus’s hand. “Just meditating. Putting myself in the mood to invoke the Goddess for tonight’s festivities.”

I’m going to enjoy this. Janus cleared his throat in fake discomfort. “Actually, these rituals are more for Attis than Cybele.” He looked over to gauge her reaction. Her face was hard to decipher in the shadows of the car. Janus continued. “Since this is a men’s empowerment session, I, as Attis, will lead the rituals.”

Of course. I’m just his humble acolyte tonight. Patriarchy trying to subvert matriarchy once again. Don’t hold your breath, Janus. Although that actually might be a good idea for the final act of tonight’s performance. Great Goddess. Cybele placed her hands protectively over her nose. “What in Hades is that stench?”

Janus laughed. “We’re nearly there.” Good. She doesn’t seem to be upset at playing second fiddle to me tonight. There’s hope for this partnership yet. He hit the brakes and turned the car down a barely visible rural road. The car jerked violently up and down. Gravel started to hit the windshield. Janus ignored the gravel and continued rapidly forward.

Cybele reached out and grabbed Janus's shoulder. "Slow down. You're going to get us killed." She peered into the darkness around them. "Where in Hades are we?"

Janus brought the car to a neck-wrenching halt. "We're right beside Circean Dreams. You're smelling pig shit. Don't worry. You'll get used to it." He smirked. "I thought it would be the perfect place for our noble followers to cross over." Not to mention that the location will tie them back to the Friends of Gaea. Eco-terrorists of the world unite!

Cybele shook her head in disbelief. Jackass. Who comes out here to party? She peered through the car window. "I think I see lights."

Janus got out of the car and looked off in the distance. "Yep. Looks like the gang's already here." He turned to Cybele. "Need help with your bag? We don't want any accidents along the way."

Cybele took a tighter grip on her bag. "I'm fine. Why don't you concentrate on leading the way, Attis? After all, you are the LEADER of tonight's little apocalypse."

Meow. Guess Cyb's a little jealous that I'm stealing the spotlight from her tonight. Too bad. Tonight she can be just another bleater. Janus turned sharply away from Cybele and began to hurry towards the light.

Cybele forced herself to keep up. She swatted angrily at the branches that were whipping across her body. Goddess. I feel like Prince Charming trying to cut his way through thorns to rescue Sleeping Beauty. She stopped at the edge of the path and looked at the scene below. She could just make out shadowy figures sprawled on the ground around a blazing barbeque fire. The smell of tomato sauce, burnt cheese, and pepperoni hung heavily in the air. She stepped forward and half-fell to her knees. Damnit. She reached down and picked up a half-crushed can. Warm, pungent beer spilt down over her thigh as she pulled herself painfully off the ground. Great. Now I smell like piss. She threw the can behind her and continued forward.

Janus approached the portable barbeque. The men sprang up to greet him.

Tan clapped Janus on the shoulder. "Hey. How's it hanging?" Tan turned to Ixion, Ajax, and Ardiaeus. "Now the fun can really begin."

Cybele slowly walked into the light cast by the barbeque. "Picturesque little spot. All we need is the sign giving directions to Crystal Lake and strange noises emanating from the woods."

Janus laughed at her. "Trust me. The sign would have to say Lac du Merde in honour of Circean Dreams." He looked around in exaggerated fear. "I don't see anyone with a hockey mask. I think you're safe from Jason." Besides. I don't see anyone here wanting to have sex with you.

Cybele snorted. Death stalks us all. She placed her knapsack on the ground and carefully began to pull out her supplies.

Janus grabbed her trowel off the ground and started to saw away at the circular trench already dug around the barbeque. He glared at Tan. "You know there can't be any grass in the hole when we set this shit on fire." He stood up and wiped his muddy hands on his pants. He looked over at Cybele who had prepared and filled two gourds. Hope she didn't fuck up which one was which. Oh well. Uncertainty is what makes life interesting.

Cybele stood up and handed one gourd to Janus. "For the *hieros gamos*. She nodded down at the second gourd still in her hand. "For the faithful flock."

Janus gestured for Cybele to place the second gourd down on the ground.

Cybele nodded and placed the gourd carefully between her feet.

Janus then turned to his flock. "Let the ceremonies begin and every man assume his position." They did so with the easy familiarity of long practice. Janus stood at the head of the circle, Tan on his right, Ajax on his left. Ixion and Ardiaeus were at the farthest points from him.

What am I? Chopped liver? Cybele picked up her gourd and moved to stand beside Janus, but he sharply pointed to the bottom of the circle.

Cybele moved towards the foot of the circle, forcing Ixion and Ardiaeus to make room between themselves for her.

Janus nodded approvingly at Cybele's positioning. Trying to steal my thunder. I don't think so. He raised his gourd high in the air. "Things fall apart. The centre is unstable."

Cybele nodded unconsciously. Anarchy has been loosened upon the world.

Janus paused to check that his flock's gaze was fixated upon him. They were motionless, waiting in anticipation for his next words. "Innocence is drowned by the sound of blood being spilt upon the earth."

Cybele wiped away a single tear trickling down her cheek. The worst are full of passionate intensity. Oh, Janus. We could have changed the world. It would have been reborn.

Janus peered intently through the dancing flames. He couldn't see Cybele's reaction but she appeared to be looking directly at him. A little self-consciously, Janus continued. "The Second Coming is at hand. *Spiritus Mundi* is on the prowl."

Cybele smirked. Not on your life. The time of Pisces is over, my friend. Goddess. What a performance. He has them right in the palm of his hands. Rosemary for remembrance. The more you tighten your grasp, the more will slip through your fingers.

Janus began to raise his voice, gradually building to a crescendo. "We are in darkness surrounded by enemies. All we need to know is that those who are not with us are against us."

Cybele groaned inwardly. This is a masterful performance. No wonder his flock is spell-bound. It's not just the pot and beer. Janus has the gift. Must think happy thoughts. Soon this show will be over and then the games will really begin. Ahh. Good. Janus is starting to wrap things up.

Janus lowered the gourd to his lips and quickly chugged all of the mead. He then gestured imperiously at Cybele. "Why don't we have the Goddess bless her special mead and then pass it around?"

Cybele looked over questioningly at Janus. What's going on? We're supposed to share one gourd. It's the *hieros gamos*, damnit.

Janus quietly held his gourd upside down and shook it out to show Cybele there was nothing left.

Furious, Cybele raised the second gourd high in the air. "By the light of the Goddess, I bring you this blessing. Let no one who drinks from this elixir remain unaffected by the compassion and wisdom of the Goddess." She lowered the gourd to her lips and pretended to take a long swallow. Fucking Janus. Nice move having me fake drinking from this damn gourd. Her eyes narrowed. Bastard's probably trying to get revenge for my crack Thursday about swallowers and spitters.

That a girl! Always knew Cyb could fake swallowing with the best of them. Janus sarcastically nodded approval at her technique. "Maybe the Goddess could now share her mead with her lowly supplicants." He quietly stepped out of the circle to avoid the gourd as it made its way around his flock. Ixion, Tan, Ajax, and Ardiaeus drank up eagerly. Janus carefully took the gourd away from them and tossed the remaining fluid into the fire. He then tossed the gourd into the fire.

Idiot. The fire will probably bake our fingerprints right on for all eternity. Cybele smirked. Good thing Janus can't see my black cotton gloves in this darkness. I'm footloose and fingerprint-free. She reached deep into her pocket to fondle her two round vials. Oh, the fun we'll have. The places we'll go.

Janus knelt down by the trench and sprinkled it with Cybele's special hallucinogenic potion. He then set the liquid on fire. Attracted by the sparkling lights, first Ardiaeus, then more slowly, Tan, Ixion, and Ajax drew closer.

Like moths to a flame. Cybele casually flicked the light on her watch to check the time. Should be any moment now.

Suddenly, Ixion began to groan loudly. "My stomach hurts." He began to make gagging noises. "I don't feel so good."

Ajax snapped. "You just had too much pizza. Don't be such a baby." Unless. He scratched his head puzzled. Is he pretending to be dying so we can fool her? I thought we were supposed to wait until Janus gave us the signal. He hasn't said the final rituals yet.

Ardiaeus's stomach began to make horrific rumbling noises. "I. I. I think I'm gonna be sick." He fell down on his knees. His body began to convulse.

What the hell is...? Tan fell down to the ground and curled up howling in the fetal position. The pain. The pain. "Heeelp me..."

Ajax started to sway back and forth. Jesus. What's happening? He fell to the ground and began vomiting all over himself.

A chain reaction of uncontrollable vomiting and screaming began.

Janus looked around stunned. Why are they vomiting? They should be dead. This is horrible. What the hell is going on?

Cybele used her right hand to squeeze her nostrils tightly closed. Oh my Goddess. I'm going to be sick. I don't know what's worse. The sounds they're making or the horrible smell. She looked around guiltily at the four men throwing up and screaming in agony. It is a far, far better thing I have done than I have ever done before. She fought the urge to gag. I just have to keep telling myself that. Especially since, any minute now, things are going to get worse.

Janus grabbed her roughly by the shoulders and shook her. "What the fuck is going on?" He lowered his voice. "Why aren't they dead?"

Cybele laughed angrily. "Don't bother whispering. Trust me, they're in no condition to listen."

The pain-filled screams changed to howls of rage and disbelief as their bowels released and they started having uncontrollable diarrhea.

"Oh my God! Have you gone crazy? What did you do to them?" Janus began to gag. "Why the hell are they shitting themselves now?"

The smell of vomit and diarrhea blanketed the small area. Cybele began to gag herself. She managed to reply through clenched teeth. "A little too much cassia, I think. Sorry, Janus. Looks like the apocalypse will have to be rescheduled. Your followers are too busy vomiting and shitting themselves to crawl towards the light." She began to back away from the nightmarish scene. She clamped down harder on her nose to prevent herself from throwing up as well. "I think, after this little misadventure, your flock won't be so willing to risk death by poison again."

Janus screamed impotently. "Bitch. You have no idea what you've done to me."

"I don't give a goddess-damn what I've done to you." Cybele spoke softly but forcefully as she continued to walk further away from the light and deeper into the woods. She whispered under her breath. "No Jim Jones on my watch." She flipped out her cell phone. Time to get medical help for these lost souls. She spoke into the phone. "Yes. I need to report an accidental poisoning in the woods near Circean Dreams. We need four ambulances at Olibanus and Rosemarinus." She shook her head. "Don't worry. I'll be your guide once you make the turnoff."

Janus stalked angrily towards her. "You're crazy. You're going to jail for poisoning these idiots."

Cybele quickly double-checked that she had accidentally on purpose disconnected the 911 operator. "Better cassia than Yerba del Diablo." She paused for dramatic effect. "At least, Cassie and I thought so."

Et tu, Cassie? Janus growled in impotent rage. "You have no proof that I was ever going to do anything like that." He looked around at his vomit and shit-soaked flock. "The only person they are going to blame for their misery is you. Good luck in trying to make this shit not stick."

Cybele shook her head chidingly. "Don't even sing that song, Janus. This little misadventure is going down as an accident and you have no choice but to back me up." She paused to savour her final triumph. "You're also cutting all ties with the Mysteries of Cybele. Your services as Attis will no longer be required."

Pure rage shone from behind Janus's eyes. He grabbed Cybele and shook her again. "Like hell. I'm not going anywhere." He shoved her roughly away from him. "I'm going to be the one in charge of this little cult and you're going to do what I say." He gestured at the hellish scene behind him. "Here's what we'll say..."

Furious at being manhandled, Cybele came forward and kicked him viciously in the balls. Janus went down with a tortured whimper. Cybele squatted down beside him and whispered her warning over his moans. "I have samples of the potions you were going to use tonight." She then lied without the slightest hesitation. "I taped you confessing what you've done and what you wanted to do." She patted him condescendingly on the shoulder. "Game over, Janus."

Janus snarled as he struggled to get up. He fell back down with a helpless groan. "How could you betray me so completely?"

Cybele straightened up and chuckled incredulously. "You're the Lex Luthor of this little piece tonight."

The distant sound of sirens began to filter through the trees. "The *deus ex machina*," she whispered. With a feeling of regret, Cybele turned and finally walked away from Janus.

A dark shadow quietly detached itself from the trees and followed her down the trail.

Cybele felt the presence behind her and turned warily. What now? Psycho-serial killer?

The shadowy figure came closer and called out. "Cyb. It's me. Gabe."

Cybele waited for him to draw nearer. "What are you doing here? Didn't you trust me to handle this on my own?" She frowned. "Or are you here as Gabe Anderson, ace investigative reporter?"

Gabe grimaced in exasperation. "Are you going to get mad at me because I didn't want you to be alone in the woods with a bunch of apocalyptic-seeking freaks?"

Cybele sighed. "Well. When you put it that way, I guess not."

Gabe cupped her face with his hands. "Although from what I saw, Cassie was right. You CAN fall into a pile of shit and come out smelling sweet."

Cybele took a quick whiff of the scent that hung around her. "Oh. I think some smells stick a little longer than others." She laughed. "Luckily, soap and water can wash away a multitude of sins." She leaned into Gabe and wrapped her arms around him.

Gabe leaned down and kissed her hard.

She kissed him back harder. Then with a sign of regret, Cybele pulled out of his arms. She took him by the hand and led him through the darkness. As they drew near to Janus's car, a parade of flashing red lights and blaring sirens screamed towards them. She tightened her grip on his hand. "I hope you got me a good lawyer. I have a funny feeling there are still some battles left to fight tonight."

Gabe squeezed her hand reassuringly. “Don’t worry. Keep quiet and everything will be all right.” He gently pulled her out of the path of the frantic paramedics and police officers. “After all, the Goddess is on your side.”

Cybele looked up at the luminous night sky and sighed in heartfelt satisfaction. “Yep. She certainly is.” After all, She’s a practical bitch. Blackmail will be Her instrument for justice and social change. Cybele pulled Gabriel closer to her. And as for me. She wrapped her arms around his shoulders and pulled him down towards her. I’m through with doubts. She began to kiss him deeply and forcefully. Get ready, world. Come what may. I’m not backing down.

Chapter 29

The stench of fear permeated the sulphurous air around Cybele. She gasped for breath, inhaling life-giving oxygen. Perspiration dripped from her face. She quickly wiped it away with the back of her hand. She could glimpse a faint light at the end of the corridor. Bile rose in her throat. Was that the sound of merciless laughter? No. She had not come so far only to be defeated now. She would not go down without a struggle. She was the Goddess incarnate. Scheherazade. She would challenge the Fates and create her own meaning. Cybele stiffened her back and walked without further fear down the hallway. She swerved to avoid the ashes littering the floor beneath her. Goddess. You'd think a television studio could afford to clean up after their nicotine addicted guests.

"You're on in two," hissed her companion.

Cybele nodded and took a deep breath. Her feet remained glued to the floor.

With an exasperated sigh, the talent wrangler for the *Vicki Gabereau* show shoved Cybele across the doorway and on-stage.

Cybele beamed as the audience began to applaud. Time to spread the word of the Goddess. Cybele walked over to the table where Vicki sat waiting for her. "It's such a pleasure to be on your show. Watching you every day is a definite inspiration for women everywhere."

Vicki smiled back at her. "I'm glad to have you. I thought your book *Resurrecting Cybele* was the most inspirational thing I've read in a very long time." She turned to look out at her audience. "For those of you who have been under a rock the last nine months, this is Cybele Moondragon, the Canadian poster child of a new age matriarchal religion called the Mysteries of Cybele." She turned back to Cybele. "So, tell me, what inspired you to start your own religion?"

Cybele chuckled. "Well, you only have to look at the world today to know that there is a definite need for a matriarchal resurrection." She leaned forward in her chair to look straight at Vicki. "The Goddess called on me to fill it."

Vicki looked surprised and a bit taken aback. "Do you really believe that?"

Cybele glowed as if filled with an inner light. "Absolutely." She casually leaned back in her chair. "You know, Vicki, there are many paths to enlightenment. The Goddess is just the best way for me and many others."

Vicki leaned forward to look directly at Cybele. "How do you respond to the allegations made about you by Janus Styx?"

Cybele frowned sadly. "Janus's claim that I tried to poison some of his friends deliberately because I was jealous of him is preposterous. That incident clearly involved Janus misreading one of my recipes and then blaming the mistake on me." She sighed. "But Janus has bigger problems than an accidental poisoning. He and those friends of his first have to find their way out of criminal charges relating to eco-terrorism before they can begin to look for salvation." She looked beseechingly at Vicki. "I can't save people from themselves, however much I might want to."

Vicki reached out to pat Cybele's hand comfortingly. "No one can." She continued reassuringly. "Well, you were certainly lucky that there was an undercover reporter on-scene who could support your version of events."

Cybele nodded serenely. "Truth always wins out in the end, Vicki."

Vicki nodded in agreement. "How about forgiveness? Do you think you can ever be friends with Janus again?"

Cybele shrugged uncertainly. "They say... time heals everything, but... I'm still hoping and praying to the Goddess for Her mercy."

"Tell me, Cybele, have you ever thought about disbanding your religion as many critics have urged you to do?" Vicki looked concernedly at Cybele. "They say you are playing with fire and the lives of impressionable people. That you're another Heaven's Gate waiting to happen."

Anger burned deep within Cybele's soul but she forced herself to respond with gentle incredulity. "Now, Vicki, there's nothing inherently apocalyptic in matriarchal religions. A better question might be where those critics are when followers of patriarchal religions commit mass suicide." She deliberately took a sip of water to help quench her indignation. "How many called for the disbandment of Christianity after Waco?" She shook her head. "I can't bring myself to do what these hypocritical others think I should. Sure...starting the Mysteries of Cybele turned my whole world upside down. But, you know what..." Cybele turned to look directly into the camera. "I kind of like it."

Vicki turned to look into the camera as well. "Any final words before we go for commercial?"

Cybele chuckled. "Absolutely." She paused for emphasis. "Medean Productions is turning my book into a movie that will be in theatres next summer. Everyone should go out and experience it for themselves. Don't let others scare you from the light of the Goddess."

Vicki held up *Resurrecting Cybele* to the camera. "So, I guess we haven't heard the last about the Mysteries of Cybele, then."

"Oh no." Cybele leaned forward to look into the faces of those in the audience. "We've only just begun."

Vicki turned to her audience. "After the commercial, it's Dog of the Week."

The audience applauded enthusiastically.

Cybele groaned inwardly. Aargh! I opened for a French poodle. She stood up and waved at the audience. Oh well. Maybe I've opened SOME eyes to the gift of matriarchy. She turned and walked off-stage and out of the building. Outside the rain was coming down in a gentle drizzle.

A familiar voice called out her name. "Cyb."

She turned and looked. Gabe stood expectantly behind her. She smiled. "Couldn't wait until I got back to Winnipeg, eh?"

He laughed and kissed her. "Nope. I had to be here in Vancouver for the beginning of your press junket." He held her in his arms and smiled teasingly down at her. "So you opened for a dog?"

Cybele rolled her eyes at him. She grasped his hand and began to pull him down the street. "You know what they say. Any publicity is good publicity." She paused and smiled affectionately up at him. "I'm so glad you're here with me today."

Gabe chuckled. "Ah. Cyb. You're making me blush."

Cybele casually swatted him across his chest. "You know the only thing that could make this moment more perfect would be if the clouds parted right now and the sun came out to shine down upon us."

They both looked up at the sky expectantly. Nothing happened. The rain continued to fall steadily.

Gabe laughed. "Oh well. I guess the Goddess still needs to gain dominion over the earth before she can control the heavens."

Continuing to look up at the clouds, Cybele smiled mysteriously. "Give Her a few thousand years. She'll change the world." She turned to Gabe and gently caressed his face. And as her avatar, so will I.